Velvet Claws

Velvet Claws

CLEO CORDELL

BLACK
lace

Black Lace novels are sexual fantasies.
In real life, make sure you practise safe sex.

First published in 1994 by
Black Lace
332 Ladbroke Grove
London
W10 5AH

Typeset by CentraCet Limited, Cambridge
Printed and bound by Cox & Wyman Ltd, Reading,
Berks

ISBN 0 352 32926 2

Chapter One

*I*n the conservatory, where Chinese lanterns glowed amongst the lush foliage, Gwendoline overheard her brother talking to one of the party guests.

She knew she should not eavesdrop. Apart from it being very bad manners, the men were talking business and she had been told often enough that a young lady should not concern herself with such things. Still, the conversation was fascinating and Gwendoline. was no stranger to subterfuge when necessary. She stood in the shadow of a large palm and gave her whole attention to the conversation between Edward and his old college friend.

'Think of the prestige, my dear fellow,' Jonathan Kimberton was saying. 'A collection like that would do your reputation a deal of good. The Natural History Museum has put up some money, but we're well short of the full amount needed. What d'you say? Shall we do it? Your money and my expertise. A capital combination.'

Gwendoline heard her brother laugh. 'Back in the country for only months and you're fretting to be off on your explorations again, eh? I must say that country's like a drug to you. Still the prospect's a pleasing one. I've a fancy to see Africa myself. Let me think about it for a while longer. I'll give you my decision before the weekend's over. Now, no more talk of trips or finance, it's Gwendoline's birthday. She won't thank me if I monopolise you. Let's enjoy the party.'

The strains of the quartet, hired especially for the occasion, floated in through the iron and glass doors. The peppery scent of orchids was strong in the warm air. Gwendoline bent closer to hear Jonathan's reply.

'Ah, yes. Gwendoline. I admire your sister, Edward. If you don't mind me saying so. She's a remarkably accomplished young woman. So many women of our class are vapid and colourless. Gwendoline's intelligent, if a little opinionated, and talented. Those paintings of hers are really good.'

'They're well enough,' Edward said in a grudging tone. 'Don't tell *her* you think she's talented. And you make her stubborness sound like a virtue. She does have a tendency to get over-excited you know. Father worries that she will damage her health.'

As the men made to move away, Gwendoline paused for a moment. She was surprised that Jonathan had expressed any opinion concerning her. He had always been aloof and rather remote on his few visits to Halton Hall. Though she was aware of his formidable reputation as an explorer and anthropologist, she did not think he had even noticed her.

She parted the strands of the palm and leaned closer, studying the face of the tall, well-built young man. For a moment Jonathan's profile was gilded by the light of a lantern. The deep tan, severe – almost harsh features, and the scar on his neck gave him an exotic, dangerous look.

Gwendoline was not at all sure that she liked her brother's friend. He was unconventional and a little alarming, but there was no denying the fact that he was the most interesting man she had ever met. He wore his hair longer than was fashionable and tied it at the nape like any common seaman. The frock coats he wore were of black broadcloth with satin lapels, of excellent quality and cut. His one touch of vanity was his waistcoats; the pockets of which were often embroidered or trimmed with gold thread.

An air of unpredictability hung around her brother's friend. He had an unusual way of moving. There was a compelling, almost animal grace about him. On more than one occasion Jonathan had startled her by appearing at her side, silently, as if by magic, only the scent of the spicy cologne he wore giving away his presence.

When she challenged him about it, he grinned.

'I apologise for my presumption,' he said, sounding not sorry at all but vastly amused. 'One loses the knack of observing the niceties when in female company. I'm afraid I've spent too much time in Africa. The way of life is very different there.'

Gwendoline felt a quickening in her blood as she recalled that conversation. The thought of Africa, with its wild, untamed beauty, and tribes of natives, seemed to her to be the last word in excitement.

As she walked quickly out of the conservatory, a murmur of aristocratic voices rose on the air. Long, linen-draped tables had been placed on the lawn. They were piled high with roast meats, savoury dishes – both hot and cold, fruit compotes and towering confections made of sugar.

Women in silk gowns with graceful, bell-shaped skirts and men in evening wear, sat around on the terrace sipping wine from goblets of Venetian glass.

Many of the women wore elaborate decorations of ostrich feathers and jewels in their upswept hair.

'Well here's the guest of honour,' smiled a business friend of her father's as she drew near. 'How does it feel to be nineteen years old, m' dear?'

'Wonderful. Thank you. It is so good of you all to come to my party,' Gwendoline smiled, bobbing a polite curtsey and moving on.

She passed by the other guests, nodding and smiling as they too offered congratulations. The tempo of the music changed and people took partners and began dancing a waltz on the terrace. Light streamed out from the open French doors of the main house, reflecting off the pastel silks and sending flashes from diamond and emerald jewellery.

The party was going on around her, all of it designed to make this day special for her, but Gwendoline hardly noticed it.

There was a strange feeling building in her chest, half excitement and half fear.

She knew, from Edward's self-satisfied tone, that he would agree to help finance Jonathan Kimberton's trip to Africa. Edward greatly admired his scandalous friend, whose reputation had been enhanced rather than wrecked by his translation into English of some tracts of erotic Indian poetry.

Secretly Edward hungered for something of interest to spur him out of his mundane existence. Gwendoline could sympathise with that view. The family business, well-founded in the cloth trade, while lucrative, could by no means be stimulating for a young man like Edward.

Gwendoline felt that she understood her brother perfectly; they were more alike than he realised. Indeed she knew a great deal about Edward's private affairs, monetary and otherwise. A fact which would have caused him great discomfort if he knew about it. She took pains to see that he did not.

Oh, yes, Edward would be leaving for Africa along with Jonathan Kimberton. And Gwendoline had just made the decision which would change her life forever.

She was going to go with them.

Throughout the long evening and into the small hours, when the last guests wandered away unsteadily to their rooms in the main house, Gwendoline nursed her secret knowledge.

The fact that it was impossible because of her sex and social standing, did not deter her. She had never wanted anything quite so badly as this. It was the chance she had been waiting for. The chance to make her mark on the world.

She didn't know how she was going to persuade Edward to agree to take her, nor how she was going to get her parents to agree.

But somehow she'd find a way.

It was early when she rose. Before six. No one was about except cook and the housemaids.

Gwendoline dressed quickly, thrusting her red-brown curls under a frilled cap and wrestling with the hooks and eyes that fastened her dress. She couldn't reach to do up the hooks between her shoulder blades but was loath to call Agnes to help her dress. Impatiently she threw a silk shawl around her shoulders and crossed it over the bodice of the dress.

There, that would do. Gathering the wide skirt of the striped muslin morning-gown in two hands and, chancing a quick look to make sure she was unobserved, she ran lightly along the corridor and down the back staircase.

The sound of pots and pans clattering came from the kitchen, but the house itself was silent. Opening the door of the parlour she peered in. Ah, Hetty was there as she had known she would be.

Hetty looked up from laying the fire as Gwendoline came into the room. She stood up, wiping her hands on her apron, and bobbed a curtsy. Her full mouth curved in a knowing smile.

'Mornin' Miss. You're an early bird. Are you lookin' for somebody?'

Gwendoline grinned. 'You can stop play-acting. It's you I want to talk to and you know it.'

Hetty's big brown eyes opened wide in mock innocence. Her flaxen curls poked out from the frill of her linen cap.

'How can I help you Miss?'

'I want you to tell me whether Edward came to your room again last night.'

Hetty's eyes slid sideways. She had a fresh-faced country prettiness. A flush crept into her cheeks.

'Oh, Miss. You didn't ought to keep asking me these things.'

Gwendoline straightened her back. 'Would you rather speak about them to my stepmother?' she asked softly.

'You wouldn't, would you? I'd be dismissed at once, sent off back to the farm without no reference!'

'Precisely.'

Hetty clasped her hands together and looked up at Gwendoline through lowered lashes. She nodded shortly.

'He did come to me, Miss.'

'I thought so. Now. You are to meet me in the summerhouse after breakfast.'

Hetty's chin rose. 'Miss?'

'And be prepared Hetty. I want to know every-thing, do you hear me? I want you to tell me *exactly* what you and Edward did together.'

While Hetty was still smiling and affecting innocence, Gwendoline swept from the parlour.

Jonathan Kimberton strolled around the rose garden.

The morning air was fresh and a hint of mist masked the wide, grass paths. Violas and pinks grew around the stems of rose bushes, wreathing them with pale purples and mauves. He breathed deeply. English air tasted of cool greenness and the breath of flowers, he decided.

A pleasant enough aroma, but somewhat lacking when you had experienced the compound, dusty richness of Africa.

He should have been born a native of that land. It had wormed its way into him, colouring his very soul with its blood-red sunsets. Edward had to help with finance for this new trip. He just had to. Jonathan didn't want to spend a day more in England than was necessary to arrange the details of transportation.

Though admittedly, there were compensations.

He smiled, remembering the way that Gwendoline had eavesdropped on his conversation with Edward in the conservatory. Edward would have been scandalised if he'd realised that she was there, screened by the palms and tree ferns.

Gwendoline was an enigma. She was rich, spoiled, undoubtedly talented, and with a propensity for acquiring the morals of a common trull. Oh, he doubted whether Edward or his parents had realised this, but Jonathan was a worldly man and he trusted his instincts in such matters. He laughed aloud. What a worry she was going to be for the Farnshawes.

He was surprised that they hadn't tried to marry her off already to some respectable, dour businessman. Or perhaps they were aiming higher, a baronet perhaps or an earl.

If there had been time to linger, Jonathan would have liked to get to know Gwendoline better. Intimately in fact. She might not know it, but she was a fruit ripe for the picking. The fact that she was spirited and intelligent as well as beautiful made the idea of seducing her all the more attractive.

Jonathan relished a challenge. He couldn't imagine that Gwendoline would allow herself to become any man's plaything. And he was suddenly sure that he would want more than that from her. She was the sort of woman who could get into a man's blood and stir up feelings of obsession.

It was a disquieting thought for the sexually-experienced adventurer. So far he had never found everything he wanted in one woman. A number of different women had served his needs throughout his journeys through Africa. The custom of some tribes of lending out their wives to a guest for the night, was a welcome one.

There had also been various European women; wives of soldiers and diplomats and once a lapsed missionary. He'd have loved to tell that tale to Gwendoline. Somehow he knew that she'd find it amusing, if a little shocking.

As he walked under a pergola, festooned with fragrant blooms, Jonathan smiled to himself. How many times had he visited the Farnshawe's home over the last few years? Maybe half a dozen times. He'd watched Gwendoline turn from a wilful young girl into a poised and self-assured young woman. Yet he doubted if she acknowledged his existence.

At thirty years of age, he must seem like an old man to her.

His stomach rumbled; reminding him that he had not yet eaten. He was looking forward to a meal. English country house breakfasts were vast affairs with their covered dishes of braised kidneys, bacon, kedgeree, coddled eggs and so on.

The Farnshawes certainly saw to their comforts and those of their house guests. It had been pleasant to be woken that morning by a maid bringing him a tray with a pot of coffee and cream.

He made a move towards returning to the house. It was time that he put the delectable Mistress Farnshawe out of his mind entirely. The planned trip would claim all his energies for weeks to come. There were provisions to order and the ship to fit out, although he saw no problem there as the Farnshawes owned their own brig. There were also letters to write to the governors of the various regions they planned to visit. And then he would be away for fully six months.

He truly meant to stop thinking about Gwendoline. And perhaps he would have achieved his aim, if he hadn't, at that precise moment, seen the slim figure in the striped morning gown hurrying towards the lower end of the garden.

Gwendoline? He was sure it was she. And by the look of her she was hurrying to an assignation.

Without a second thought he quickened his step and followed her.

Gwendoline was waiting as Hetty walked down the path leading to the summerhouse, which was screened by a tall hedge. It took her a moment or two to regain her breath.

Hetty slipped inside the door. She had taken off her apron and wore a high-necked blouse over a dark-blue skirt. A straw bonnet topped the frilled cap covering her hair. Strands of her frizzy, corn-coloured hair escaped from the cap and fell forward onto her forehead.

Gwendoline smiled to herself. Hetty's hair had a will of its own.

'Did anyone see you leave the house?' she asked.

'No, Miss. But I'll check and see, just to be sure.' Hetty ran to the door and peered outside. Looking over her shoulder and closing the door, she said, 'Oh, Miss I shouldn't have come. This ain't right!'

Gwendoline laughed and clapped her hands together softly.

'You would make a wonderful actress, Hetty! Anyone would be convinced by your air of outrage. But I know how much you enjoy these sessions of ours.'

For the first time Hetty caught sight of the riding crop that Gwendoline held. It had been half-hidden by her striped skirts. Hetty smiled archly and caught her full underlip between her teeth.

'Ain't that the truth,' she whispered under her breath. 'Miss, you're a real caution. No one would think it to look at you.'

Gwendoline took a step forward. She drew the crop partway through her palm, then tapped the notched end menacingly.

'I don't expect I'll need to use this,' she said. 'But I will have all the details.'

'Yes, Miss,' Hetty said obligingly. 'Where shall I start?'

'Tell me what you were doing when Edward came to your room?'

Hetty hesitated.

'Come along. You can tell me anything. You always do in the end, remember?'

'I . . . I was using the chamber pot.' Hetty paused and looked down uncertainly.

'Yes. Go on.'

'I don't like to speak of it. It's indelicate.'

'Come along now!' Gwendoline said shortly. 'You know what I want. Let me hear it all. I want every sordid little detail. What did Edward do? Did he just walk in and catch you?'

'Yes, Miss. Exactly that. I was squatting down, with . . . with my chemise lifted up above my waist. And Master Edward just walks in and he says, "Don't stop on my account, Hetty. I'll wait." And he just stood there and watched me. His face was all red and he kept touching the front of his trousers. He made me lift up a bit, in a half-squat like, so's he could see me doing it.'

'And you did as he asked?'

'I daren't disobey him. He's the very devil when he's crossed, as you know.'

'Did he say anything?'

'Yes . . .' Hetty paused again.

'Well. Tell me then. You needn't think that I'll be shocked by your rough language.'

Hetty went on in a rush. 'He . . . he said as how I had a lovely big bum. And that the sight of my water pouring out from the hairs on . . . on my juicy little quim, had made him feel as randy as a stallion. Oh, Miss that's enough now, ain't it? I never ought to be telling you this. You being a gentlewoman an all – '

'Don't worry that you'll upset my sensibilities, Hetty,' Gwendoline said lightly. 'I really don't understand why ladies are supposed to be physically delicate, retiring in their manners, and ignorant about certain bodily acts. Edward says I'll damage my health if I insist on taking so much exercise and asking so many questions. Fiddlesticks to that! I'm as strong as a horse.'

Hetty grinned. 'That you are, Miss.'

Gwendoline, her breast heaving with emotion rushed on. 'Why, country lasses like yourself work all day without threatening their constitutions and are well informed about all manner of fornications! Why should things be different for you? You *must* share your knowledge with me. Who else is there to tell me these things?'

'No one, Miss. Just your friend Hetty.'

'Quite. So do stop protesting. Tell me what happened next.'

Hetty's brown eyes gleamed as she told Gwendoline how Edward had thrown her across her narrow bed, pushed the chemise up to lie in folds around her neck, and proceeded to kiss and stroke her breasts.

'He sucked on my nipples, too. Just like a calf at the teat.'

Gwendoline's breath was coming a little faster. She felt hot and pleasantly weak. 'How did that feel? Did you like it?' she said.

'Oh, yes. I felt sort of warm and tingly. His mouth was hot and wet and his tongue tickled my skin.'

Gwendoline coughed, her mouth was unaccountably dry. 'And then?'

'Well you know, Miss. I told you before.'

'Tell me again. Did . . . did he spread your thighs?'

'Not straight away. He kissed my stomach and sort of nuzzled at the hair on my . . . you know what. I giggled. It made me feel all sort of soft and lazy. He pinched my thighs gently and called me his naughty wanton. Then he unbuttoned the flap on his trousers and took his thing out.'

Gwendoline's face flushed a deep rose-red. She never tired of quizzing Hetty about her assignations with Edward. She wished sometimes that she was like Hetty, farm-born, earthy and sensual, able to take her pleasure as she wished. But it was unthinkable for a woman of her own status to express even the slightest interest in such things, let alone seek to gratify her secret desire for knowledge. Hetty was her only possible source of illicit information.

For a moment she felt guilty and afraid. Would she be damned for what she was doing? Sometimes she felt like an unnatural monster. Everyone knew that women did not feel the same base urges as men did. Then why was there a throbbing between her thighs, a sweet feeling of dampness inside her secret place?

It was confusing, but totally fascinating to her.

'What does Edward's "thing" look like?' she asked shakily. 'Describe it to me. And call it by that crude name you usually use.'

'Very well, Miss,' Hetty said, smiling with pride at her superior knowledge. 'His cock, is what I calls it, Miss. His cock. It's very fine and stout. It has a great red crest on the end, like a sort of plum. There's a lot of curly brown hair where the stem joins his belly. His balls are heavy . . . Shall I go on Miss?' She smirked. 'You look a little faint.'

Gwendoline waved her hand dismissively, but her heart was beating wildly. She was sure that her palpitations were the result of her tightly-laced stays. She'd been in such a hurry to dress herself that morning that she'd fastened them wrongly.

Drawing in a ragged breath, she smoothed her hands over the silk shawl which was crossed over her breasts.

'I'm perfectly well, Hetty. Do go on.'

'Well then he threw himself onto my belly and pushed his thing – begging your pardon, his cock – right inside me,' Hetty said with relish. 'He gasped and panted while he thrust it in and out, then in a while, he gave a great groan and drew it out of me. His seed spilled all over my belly. He always does that, Miss, so's I won't have no babies.'

This had been a particular revelation when Hetty first told Gwendoline about her sexual encounters. It was the first time she had found out how babies were made. She had never dreamed that men and women took steps to avoid pregnancy, indeed she had not realised that it was a possibility.

'But is it not a sinful practice?' she had asked.

Hetty had thrown back her head and laughed. 'Course not. Lord love ya' Miss. The sin would be in bringing all them unwanted babies into the world. How would we feed them all? Everyone does the same thing.'

Hetty had almost finished relating her latest story. She sat down on a rattan chair. 'There's nothing more to tell really. Edward tidied his clothes and I cleaned myself up and got into bed.'

Her pretty face brightened. 'Edward's promised to bring me a present from Africa.'

The last sentence penetrated Gwendoline's thoughts. She smoothed back her hair, surprised to find that her forehead was damp. So, it was as she had suspected. Edward had decided already to finance the trip. In a few months, he and Jonathan would be leaving for Africa – the Dark Continent.

Just the name of the place conjured up adventures and landscapes beyond her wildest imaginings. Ah, what paintings she would produce. She longed to splash her canvasses with great sweeps of hot colour, violet and orange and crimson. Instead of the pale greens and pastels of her present English landscapes.

She *must* go with them. She wanted the experience so badly she could taste it. There would never be another chance like this. And suddenly, she knew how she could persuade Edward to take her along.

'Hetty,' she said now, warming to the idea. 'I want you to do something for me . . .'

For a moment after Gwendoline had outlined her plan, Hetty sat in stunned silence.

'I can't, Miss. I just can't,' she said at length. 'It wouldn't be right. It's much worse than telling you about what me and Edward gets up to . . .'

Gwendoline smiled. Hetty always protested at first. She usually gave in to Gwendoline's demands in the end. All she needed was a firm talking to. She went through her plan again, making certain that Hetty understood what was required of her.

But this time Hetty resisted all her efforts at persuasion. Threats, promises of gifts, and appeals to her better nature didn't work.

'Very well,' Gwendoline said, growing hot with anger. 'You leave me no choice.'

Her mouth set in a thin line. She would not be swayed from her set course. The African trip beckoned and Hetty was going to help her to influence Edward, and through him her father and stepmother. No parlour maid was going to stop her getting what she wanted.

'You'll do as I say, Hetty. Whether you like the idea or not!'

Gwendoline folded back the frilled cuffs of her gown slowly and deliberately, all the while keeping her eyes on Hetty's stubborn face. There was more than one way to ensure a servant's obedience.

'Stand up!' she ordered Hetty, tapping the riding crop against her skirt-covered thigh. 'Bend over that table and lift your skirts!'

Hetty's stubborn expression dissolved. She threw Gwendoline a horrified glance. 'You wouldn't, Miss! Oh, please!'

Gwendoline acted before she could give way to second thoughts. Her pulses were hammering. She did not like resorting to physical punishment, but she would not tolerate Hetty's disobedience.

Taking Hetty by surprise she pushed her so that the parlour maid sprawled across the rattan table. Hetty struggled and would have righted herself.

'Don't you dare to move!' Gwendoline hissed. 'Now pull up your skirts. Do it!'

Hetty hesitated, then slowly she reached around and hitched her skirts and frilled petticoats up to her waist. Her plump behind and sturdy thighs, clothed in clean white cotton, came into view. She made little breathy sounds of denial, as if still not quite believing this was happening.

'I ain't done nothing wrong. Don't, Miss! Oh, please don't beat me!'

Gwendoline brought the crop down smartly, hitting her across both wriggling cheeks. Hetty gave a cry of pain and surprise as Gwendoline gave her three more blows in rapid succession.

'Muffle your cries,' Gwendoline ordered, pausing to hiss in Hetty's ear. 'If we're discovered there'll be a deal of explaining to do, and you'll be the loser, be quite certain of that.'

'Oh, Miss. Please don't . . .' Hetty pleaded.

'You'll do as I ask then?'

'I'd like to help. Truly I would. But I can't. It's not right . . .'

'Very well,' Gwendoline said, dragging down the cotton drawers to reveal Hetty's bare flesh and proceeding to swing the crop back for another smarting blow.

Hetty's buttocks twitched as each blow connected. The crop whistled as it cut through the air. The maid's hips worked back and forth as she tried to avoid the blows. Gwendoline pressed the palm of her free hand to the small of Hetty's back to hold her still.

She felt the perspiration trickle down the inside of her dress as she wielded the crop. With a start, Gwendoline realised that she was enjoying herself. The feeling of power seemed mixed with something else. It was a tantalising, unique sensation.

The sight of Hetty spread out helpless before her caused a warm feeling to spread through her belly. Hetty's round buttocks were a deep rose-red. The sound of each blow as it slapped the firm flesh gave her a little shock of pleasure. She liked Hetty's breathless moans, her muffled cries of pain, her pleas for mercy. And, when Hetty twisted her head to one side, displaying her flushed and tear-stained face, she liked that too.

Suddenly she felt a rush of shame. Whatever was she doing? She had no right to bend Hetty to her will in this way. She paused and lowered the crop, then flung it to the ground. She was about to ask for Hetty's forgiveness, when, in a small voice, Hetty said, 'Very well. I'll do it. I'll help you.'

The sweet taste of triumph washed away Gwendoline's feelings of guilt. Her plan would work. She was partway there already. Pulling up Hetty's drawers she covered her abused buttocks. Then she helped Hetty to her feet, pulling down her skirts and smoothing them back into place. Then she gathered Hetty into her arms and stroked her wet face.

'There now. That wasn't necessary was it? You silly goose. You only had to say yes. You know how I am if I don't get my own way, but I would never let any real harm come to you. I'm too fond of you, dear Hetty.'

On impulse Gwendoline kissed the maid's cheek. The feel of Hetty's damp flushed cheeks was like warm silk. The taste of her tears was salt-sweet on her lips. Hetty smelt of lemon soap and lavender polish.

Gwendoline felt confused by the riot of new emotions she had just experienced. The punishment and now the making up was unexpectedly pleasant.

She held onto Hetty for a moment longer than was necessary, feeling how the other woman swayed towards her. In some strange way the punishment seemed to have forged a new bond between them, as if they now shared a secret. Finally, she set Hetty at arm's length and smiled into her troubled brown eyes.

Hetty wiped her eyes and smiled shakily.

'It's all right, Miss. And it wasn't so bad really. It's not the first time I've been beaten.'

'Oh and now I've done the same thing. I've hurt you. I'm sorry Hetty, dear. I don't know what to say. Who beat you before? Was it your father?'

'No, Miss,' Hetty said slyly. 'One of the farm labourers used to spank me with the flat of his hand before he had me. I used to love the way the hay tickled my bare belly while he paddled my buttocks. It added a sort of specialness to things – like . . . like mustard on roast beef.'

Gwendoline's green eyes opened wide. 'You mean . . . you liked the spanking?'

Hetty laughed and nodded. 'In a way I did. It hurts at first, then there comes a warm feeling and a sort of itchy tingling.' She wriggled as if demonstrating how pleasant her abused buttocks felt.

Gwendoline watched in amazement as Hetty calmly shook out her creased skirts and then began to tuck her wayward frizzy hair into her cap.

Hetty chuckled. 'You do look shocked, Miss. If you don't mind me saying so, you've a lot to learn about men and women! What you need is a man of your own. There's only so much talking you can do. You needs to try this out for yourself. I can show you how to start . . .'

18

'That's enough, Hetty. You're being insolent now!' Gwendoline said sharply, back in control.

For a moment it had seemed that their roles were reversed. Hetty was so knowledgeable, so experienced. Gwendoline felt her status diminish as it became clear how green a virgin she truly was. It was an unpleasant sensation.

Hetty bowed her head. 'Sorry Miss.'

'Yes, well. Run along now. You must have duties to attend to.'

Hetty walked to the summerhouse door. Her movements seemed deliberately slow and sensuous. Gwendoline found Hetty's changes of mood most disturbing. Her enjoyment of life sometimes seemed childlike, almost innocent, but, conversely she was capable of exhibiting a flamboyant sensuality.

Gwendoline was pleased with the way things had gone. Their little talk had been more than usually stimulating. She watched the parlour maid walk down the screened path, remembering only as she reached a bend to call after her.

'And don't forget our bargain,' Gwendoline hissed.

Hetty turned and grinned. She tapped the side of her nose with her finger and mouthed. 'I won't forget. Tonight.'

Jonathan Kimberton waited until Gwendoline had slipped out of the summer house and gone on her way before he moved.

He had caught odd details of the plot they'd hatched together and his curiosity knew no bounds. If only Gwendoline had been facing him all the time he would have heard everything. What the devil was Gwendoline up to? Should he confide in Edward? It was clear now that Gwendoline had been running wild.

All of a sudden he was afraid for her. In the circles she moved in reputation was everything. A young woman with such strong, though as yet undiscovered, passions was bound to come to grief before too long. If only Gwendoline lived in a different culture.

She was more like he was. In Africa he had found the freedom to be himself. There was a different, more relaxed, moral code there. His present trip was to encompass Africa's west coast, but he had ideas about travelling as far as the east. He'd heard just recently that small colonies of wealthy Europeans were setting up home there, buying up land, employing the natives, and beginning to make a new life for themselves.

Jonathan admired their vision and tenacity. The interior, though beautiful, was wild and dangerous. There were few white people there as yet. He planned to visit the colony on this trip and if he found it to his liking, maybe he'd settle there with them when he'd done with exploring.

He considered that it was the English climate that forged the reticence and hypocrisy of a certain class of English person. The heat of Africa warmed a man's soul, brought out the sunlight inside him. Somehow it spurred one on to enjoy life. It was a pity that Gwendoline would never know that freedom.

As he returned to the house he considered what he should do. He could, of course, do nothing at all. And in the event that's what he decided on.

Let Gwendoline hatch her plots and go her own sweet way.

He chuckled. It would be interesting indeed to see where that led.

Chapter Two

*E*dward drained his glass of port and stretched.

'Well, I'm going to turn in. It's been a long day. I bid you good night father. Good night Jonathan.'

Edward left his father and friend playing cards and climbed the main staircase. On the first floor landing he looked at the grandfather clock. It was late, well past midnight, and quiet now that most of the other house guests had departed.

His stepmother and Gwendoline had retired an hour ago. The house staff would be abed too, except the butler who only retired after the master of the house indicated that he no longer required any attention.

Edward opened a side door and crept up the back stairs. Hetty's room was in the attic. He placed his foot carefully on each uncarpeted stair, wincing when one creaked. The hem of the full-skirted robe he wore brushed against the bare wood. His palms were damp with anticipation.

Hetty slept alone, since the other parlour maid, a

girl of sixteen, had left to visit her sick mother. He meant to make the most of the time before the younger girl returned. He thought of last night's bed-sport with relish.

How delightful Hetty had looked, poised over that chamber pot. And how willing she was to do anything he asked of her. The sight of her sturdy white thighs and big bottom, poking out of her chemise had given him an instant erection. She had grinned up at him as she raised herself higher and parted her thighs, so that he could see the stream of urine splashing into the chamber pot.

Her pubic hair had glistened wetly. He could just see the parting of her sex-lips and glimpse the red of her secret inner flesh. Lord, but he was hard again just thinking about her. She was a fine ride, all right. Bouncing under him and gasping with pleasure as he ploughed a fine furrow in her moist flesh.

Hetty's door was unlocked. He opened it and slipped inside. By the light of the single candle he could see that she was already in bed.

'Hetty,' he whispered, sinking down to kneel on the rag-rug beside her narrow bed. 'Hetty, it's me.'

She turned over and yawned sleepily. Her thick hair, twisted into a night plait, lay across one shoulder. Seeing his face close to hers she held out her arms and smiled. Edward undressed quickly, kicking off his shoes, loosening his cravat, and throwing his quilted robe to the floor. Dressed only in his loose shirt and drawers he threw back the covers and embraced Hetty.

The clean musky smell of her filled his nostrils. He pressed kisses to her neck and thrust his hands inside the loose neck of her chemise.

Hetty moaned as he stroked her plump breasts, pinching her nipples, rolling them between finger and thumb until they stood out in hard little peaks. Closing his lips on one nipple he sucked and teased it, drawing it right into his mouth and grazing it gently with his teeth.

'Pretty Hetty. You're fresh as a flower,' he murmured, loosing the nipple and beginning to pull up her chemise.

He stroked the pout of her belly, rubbing at the soft skin with his palm, then his fingers strayed lower. She thrust her hips towards him and opened her thighs wide. He loved her eagerness. There was no pretence, no coyness about Hetty. She wasn't cold and frosty like the women of his own class.

His searching fingers moved between her thighs. He parted the thick bush of dark-blonde hair and found her secret flesh. She was hot and wet already and she buried her head in his shoulder to muffle her groans as he stroked her. The slippery folds seemed to thicken under his fingers.

'What d'you want Hetty? Tell me?'

Hetty laughed huskily. This was part of their game. He'd taught her well.

'I want you to futter me with your big hard cock, Sir.'

Edward felt his passions rising. He loved Hetty to order his actions. The explicit terms, delivered in her soft country brogue, added an extra edge to his desire.

He rubbed her slit with two fingers, working the fleshy folds and pinching the hard little nub within them. Soon his fingers were rich with her juices. He slipped them inside her.

'Is that good, Hetty?' he said, as he felt the warmth of her body surround his thrusting digits.

'Oh, yes Sir. My quim is all wet and ready for you,'

she whispered, moving forward to rub herself wantonly on his knuckles.

He used his thumb to apply pressure to her hard little bud, feeling it flicking back and forth as she moved against him. Soft moans came from her open mouth.

Edward was breathing hard. His penis pushed against the opening of his drawers. Reaching down, he freed it and pushed the head of it against Hetty's ready sex.

'See what I've got for you? Shall it be now?'

'Yes. Oh, yes,' Hetty sighed. 'Futter me. Futter me.'

Edward had to wait a moment. If he entered her now he'd spend at once. He'd never known Hetty quite so eager, or so unrestrained in her language.

It was a little alarming, but very flattering. He felt like the king of the world. Damn it he couldn't wait any longer. Moving forward he gave a thrust of his hips and buried himself inside her. The liquid heat surrounded him. He began pushing in and out, while Hetty moaned and thrashed. Reaching down to her sturdy thighs he lifted them. Hetty wrapped her legs around his broad back obligingly.

'Oh, Lord,' Edward groaned as he plumbed the depths of her sex. He felt the soft neck of her womb rubbing against his cock-head.

Lost in sensation, surrounded by the rich scent of Hetty's female musk, Edward did not hear the door open. He drew out of Hetty a little way and worked into her with rapid jerking movements, rimming her entrance the way she liked it.

'Oh, Sir,' Hetty whispered, her mouth slack and her cheeks flushed a deep rose-pink. 'Oh yes, Sir. Just like that.'

The slick female flesh slid back and forth across his

cock-head. Edward was oblivious to everything but his approaching climax. Hetty dug her nails into his flesh as her pleasure overcame her. He drove deeply into her as she cried out.

As the first pulsings squeezed his shaft his own climax broke over him. Pulling out of Hetty with a loud groan, he spent himself on her soft white belly. His creamy emission clung to the surface of their warm flesh.

Collapsing onto her Edward laid his head on her bare breasts and sighed with contentment. He liked to lie on her, sated and replete, with the juices of their lovemaking drying on their bodies. Ah, if only he could meet someone of his own class who pleasured him the way that Hetty did. He'd marry her in an instant – as long as she was rich as well.

At that moment Hetty let out a strangled scream and squirmed under him.

'What . . .' he stuttered.

Edward raised himself and turned his head towards the door. Only then did he become aware of the figure standing there. Shock sent cold waves down his back. He rolled off Hetty and sat up.

'Good Lord! Gwendoline! What the devil . . .'

Gwendoline was silent. She looked at him calmly. In his panic it did not occur to him to wonder why she was fully dressed and composed. Hetty rolled onto her side with a little moan of distress and hid under the bedclothes.

Edward recovered fast. He pulled down his shirt and reached out a shaking hand to pick up his robe. He was too amazed to be angry. He stood on one leg, fighting to keep his balance, and began to fasten his drawers.

'I . . . I heard Hetty call out,' he stammered,

thinking fast. 'She felt ill. Faint. I was trying to revive her . . .'

'Shut up Edward,' Gwendoline said.

Edward's mouth fell open. She had never spoken to him in that tone before.

'Gwendoline? I know this looks bad . . .'

'I know what you were doing, Edward. Do you think I'm a ninny? The question is, what am I going to do about it?'

Edward thought quickly. He meant to make his tone imperious, but his voice sounded oddly pleading.

'You won't tell father?'

'That depends.'

'On what?'

'On whether you'll do something for me.'

Dressed in drawers and shirt, and covered by the voluminous robe, Edward had recovered his dignity. He straightened his back and looked down at his sister. In the voice he used to his hunting dogs, he said.

'Confound it woman! Are you telling me that you're going to blackmail me?'

'That's right,' Gwendoline said equably.

'Oh,' Edward said nonplussed.

He didn't seem to be able to think straight. Could this really be his mild little sister? He hardly knew her.

'Now look, Gwenie,' he began, in a more reasonable tone. 'Can't we forget this. It's all been a ghastly mistake. You're not yourself. It isn't like you to be creeping around the house like this, poking into things which don't concern you. Are you ill? You look flushed and only half-awake. Yes. That's it. You have a fever. You've been overdoing things. I'll get stepmother to send for the doctor in the morning.

He'll make you up a cordial. Go back to bed now, there's a dear.'

He laid a hand on the sleeve of her poplin dinner gown. It was going to be all right. He felt in control again. This was definitely the tone to take.

'Young ladies shouldn't meddle in the affairs of their menfolk,' he said soothingly. 'It's just not done. Come along, my dear. I'll walk you to your room. In the morning you'll only remember sleepwalking . . .'

Gwendoline shook his hand off.

'Do stop blustering, Edward. And stop making up silly excuses to divert me. It's no good. I know what I saw and you won't persuade me otherwise. You've been futtering Hetty for weeks now.'

Edward's mouth opened but no sound came out. Gwendoline suppressed the urge to laugh. Edward sank onto the bed and put his head in his hands.

'Oh God,' he moaned.

He'd be ruined if this got out. It was common enough for young men of breeding to form liaisons with housemaids, but he could not bear to commit the unforgiveable sin of being found out. He felt a cold fury settle in his stomach.

Damn their new stepmother. It was her influence, her modern views, that had fostered this new asperity in Gwendoline's behaviour. Gwendoline had always been spoiled and headstrong, but father had kept her in order. Now all father could think about was his pretty new wife.

Useless to comment on the fact that she was too indulgent with Gwendoline. The old boy wouldn't hear a word against the woman.

His shoulders slumped in defeat. 'What do you want?'

Gwendoline said, very slowly and firmly. 'I want to come to Africa with you and Jonathan Kimberton.'

27

Edward's head snapped up. 'You're not serious!'

'I've never been more serious about anything in my entire life.'

Edward's shoulders shook as he began to laugh. The idea was so outrageous. Wherever had she got that harebrained scheme from? He wiped his eyes and grinned in a superior brotherly sort of way.

'That's quite impossible, my dear. You must know that it's completely out of the question. We're not going on a picnic. The country is wild, unpredictable. There'll be dangers, disease. A woman like you, on a trip like that! Why it'd be the limit, the very limit!'

He chuckled confidently, sure that he'd heard the last of her ridiculous request.

'Get along to bed now Gwendoline, there's a dear. We'll talk in the morning.'

He picked up his shoes and ushered his sister out of the door. He was still chuckling as they parted on the landing.

'The very idea,' he muttered, wiping his eyes.

He took three steps down the corridor towards his own room before he was brought up short by Gwendoline's parting comment.

'Best get used to the idea, brother dear. And wipe that silly laugh of your face, because I *am* coming with you.'

She placed her hands on her hips and faced him, her expression as hard and calculating as any fishwife in the market place. 'And if you don't agree to take my side when we discuss it with father,' she went on. 'I'll be certain to tell him what you have been doing with Hetty for weeks now. In detail. Believe me. In great detail.'

And tossing back her red-brown curls she stalked down the corridor.

* * *

Hetty lay in her bed listening to the muffled voices on the landing.

She pressed her knuckles to her mouth to hide her laughter. Oh, Gawd, Edward's face when he saw Gwendoline standing there! She felt a bit sorry for him, but it served him right really. He was altogether too pompous and full of himself. Gwendoline had made mincemeat out of him.

Gwendoline was a real card. She could not help but admire the young mistress's spirit. The way she'd faced Edward down. Hetty hadn't thought Gwendoline had it in her. Well, well. Things were certainly changing at the Farnshawe's residence.

The angry whispers faded. She heard footsteps retreating, then all was quiet. Hetty plumped up her pillow and sighed contentedly. It had been a daring plan, but all would be well.

Gwendoline would get her own way and Edward would take her with him, albeit unwillingly.

It would certainly be quiet with both Edward and the young mistress gone. Whatever would she do for her pleasures? Her healthy young body was warm with the afterglow of Edward's attentions, but soon enough she'd feel the urge for a man's touch again.

She'd always been that way. Since the ploughman from the next village had seduced her one warm summer evening, she'd craved regular sexual release. She was a natural, he had told her, as he pushed her onto her back in the hay rick. He'd spread her thighs and sucked and licked her sex. The wonderful feelings had spread through her whole body and she was soon gasping and bucking against his mouth.

She hadn't known that men did that. Animals were more straightforward in their matings. Many a time she'd stood by while the ram was put to servicing the ewes, cheering him on with the rest of the girls. They giggled as the ram grunted and his great ballocks swayed back and forth.

'Go on there lad. Give us lots of spring lambs,' she'd called.

The ploughman was as lusty as a farm animal and a robust and generous lover. By harvest time he had coaxed her to many acts of pleasure, but it was the memory of that first deflowering, so hot and gentle, that always aroused her.

Hetty felt the familiar warmth spread to her groin. Lawks, but she was feeling randy again. She stretched her hands down the bed and stroked the thick curling hairs between her legs. The flesh was still damp and tingly. Gently she parted her sex-lips and ran her fingers lightly up the generous folds and over the still swollen bud.

The ploughman had told her that her sex was beautiful, big and red like an exotic blossom. The abundance of hair on her mound and around her sex, had delighted him. He'd loved to tweak and pull it until she squirmed out of his grasp. Then he'd wrestle with her and hold her down while he plunged his hardness into her willing body.

Edward found her hairiness attractive too. He loved to nuzzle her armpits. And once he'd woven silk flowers into the dark-blonde pubic curls. In fact all the men she'd taken pleasure with had loved that exuberant female place.

Her eyes closed to slits of pleasure as her fingers dipped inside and out, stroking and pressing until she felt the pleasure pooling in her belly. She circled the area just below her mons where her sex-lips pouted and then divided into that adorable little slit. The hard little nub began throbbing warmly, then came those pulsings that she loved, hot and deep and prolonged.

Hetty shuddered as the rich waves of pleasure swept through her. As they died away the familiar lassitude spread through all her limbs. All she wanted to do now was relax and allow herself to sleep. Tonight she'd dream of the ploughman and his lusty lovemaking.

Gentlemen were all right. As her mother used to tell her: 'You knows you've got yourself a gentleman when he don't wipe his cock on the bedcurtains.'

Hetty chuckled at the memory. Gentlemen brought you presents and called you pretty names, but there was nothing to beat a strong country lad for good, honest loving.

With a sigh of pure contentment, Hetty snuggled into the bedclothes. It was only as she was half-drifting into sleep that the thought came to her.

Mistress Gwendoline could not travel to Africa without a lady's maid to dress her and take care of her clothes. And Agnes, who occupied that post at present, was knocking on in years. She'd not be willing to accompany Gwendoline to the other side of the world.

Gwendoline was going to need someone to fill the post. And who better than herself? She smiled. She would have a few weeks to learn what was required. Agnes could teach her. Hetty knew that she was fully capable of looking after Gwendoline's beautiful clothes.

There were broadcloth riding outfits; morning gowns and afternoon dresses of muslin; evening wear of silks and satin; not to mention the scarves, sashes and bonnets. All of it needing washing, starching, and pressing. She'd seen how garments were packed for journeys, the sleeves and ruffles stuffed with tissue paper and powdered orris root sprinkled between the folds.

'Course she'd need new clothes herself and an allowance.

Hetty sat up, suddenly too excited to sleep. What had started out as a half-serious idea seemed suddenly possible. Why not? The other parlour maid would be back by then from nursing her sick mother. The family could spare Hetty. Besides there were plenty of girls on the estate who would be only too willing to work up at the big house.

Oh, yes. Gwendoline must take Hetty with her. What adventures they'd share. And who else could Gwendoline trust so completely?

'It's out of the question of course,' Edward said, expecting Jonathan to agree with him at once.

Jonathan gave a long slow smile. A smile that made Edward feel deuced uncomfortable, though he would have been at a loss to explain why.

'Well isn't it, old man?' he prompted. 'Gwendoline will listen to you. If you say she can't come, then that's final.'

'She's serious about coming with us?' Jonathan said.

'Well, yes. Deadly serious. But what's that got to do with it? She has to be taught that she can't have her own way in everything.'

'And you want me to explain why she's not allowed to accompany us?'

'Ah, yes. If you would, old man. I've . . . er . . . tried talking to her myself, but she won't pay me any heed. She's deuced headstrong, y'know. Says she'll run to father with some silly tale she's dreamt up about me if I don't co-operate – '

Edward broke off as Jonathan made a strangled

sound in his throat and then dissolved into a fit of coughing.

'I say. Are you all right. That sounds nasty. Must be our damp English air. The sooner we set off for Africa the better, eh?'

Jonathan wiped his eyes with a handkerchief. 'Quite,' he said, having trouble keeping a straight face.

'So you'll have a word with Gwendoline? Oh, that's a relief. Now might be a good time actually. She's out riding on Midnight. She'll be somewhere near the copse in South Field. It's a favourite place of hers.'

Jonathan nodded. 'I'll change and go along to the stables, right away.'

'That's capital, old boy. Ask the stable lad to saddle up my hunter for you. Redcoat's a spirited ride.'

Jonathan suppressed a grin. Just like your sister, I'd wager, he murmured under his breath. The more he heard about Gwendoline, the more he liked her. What a woman! She'd tied poor old Edward up in his own shirt tails, good and proper.

The thought of having her along on the African trip was beginning to seem more attractive with each passing moment.

Gwendoline leaned forward over Midnight's neck and moved with the rhythm of his body. The gelding's hooves thudded on the grass as he cantered towards the trees.

The farm workers stopped and waved as she passed them. She waved back, conscious that she cut a dash in her new riding habit of dark-green velvet with gold buttons. Under her black tricorn hat, her curls were tied back with a velvet ribbon.

Reaching the copse, Gwendoline reined Midnight in.

'Whoa, there my boy,' she said, patting his silky neck. 'I'm off for a stroll by the river and you can rest for a while.'

The gelding's ears twitched as she spoke to him. Lifting her right leg free of the side-saddle's pommel, she slid to the ground. Midnight turned his head to nudge her with his soft snout.

She laughed and petted him, feeling in the pocket of her waisted jacket for the chunks of sugar she had chipped off the cone-shaped loaf before setting out that day.

Cook had tutted at such waste. 'It's wicked to give it to an old 'orse, Miss. It's that expensive.'

Gwendoline only laughed.

'Midnight loves it,' she said. 'But I don't like sweets. He can have my share. We have lots more.'

The gelding's jaws rotated as he crunched on the sugar. Gwendoline secured him on a loose rein and began walking towards the river bank.

The afternoon was hot and the breeze near the river was pleasant. Sitting on the bank she pulled off her riding boots and rolled down her stockings. There was no one to see. The field workers were just dots in the distance.

Pulling her skirts above her knees she dunked her feet and ankles in the water. The cold made her gasp at first, then the delicious coolness spread through her.

She trailed her fingers in the water, watching moorhens scuttling in and out of the reeds on the far side of the river. Two swans sailed past, as stately as flagships. It was so peaceful, so English.

Would she miss this, she thought, when she was

in Africa? She laughed. How maudlin she seemed. It wasn't as if she'd never return.

Taking off her hat she laid it on the bank and shook out her chestnut curls, then she unbuttoned her jacket and loosened her white silk neck-stock. She lay back, watching the fluffy white clouds slip across the sky; it was so blue, like cornflowers.

The sun was warm on her face. Agnes would scold if her freckles came out and her skin turned golden, but she didn't care. Closing her eyes, she slipped into a light doze.

The shadow on her face, closing out the sun's warmth, woke her up. Startled she pushed herself into a sitting position.

'It's polite for a gentleman to announce himself!' she said tartly.

Jonathan smiled lazily. 'Forgive my rudeness, but for a moment I was not sure whether you were a river nymph. With that green outfit you're wearing and the way you were lying, with your feet trailing in the water . . . Well, you seemed more water sprite, than woman . . .'

Despite herself Gwendoline smiled. She could imagine how she had looked. Then her face clouded. What must he think of her, lying there with her jacket unbuttoned, the stock loose about her neck? Her legs were uncovered to the knee. What a wanton picture she had presented.

Her cheeks grew hot as she realised that the top of her breasts were visible above the low neckline of her chemise. She took hold of the two sides of her jacket and pulled them together.

'How . . . how did you know where to find me?' she asked.

'Edward told me you'd be here.'

'I see. So you've come to tell me that I cannot come

35

with you to Africa?' She didn't wait for his reply, but rushed on regardless. 'I must tell you, Mr Kimberton, that I have every intention of accompanying you. And neither anything you or my brother has to say will dissuade me from that course.'

Jonathan let her finish and paused before replying.

'I have no intention of forbidding you to do anything Mistress Farnshawe. Indeed I think it unlikely that anyone could influence you, once you have set your mind on something.'

She inclined her head slightly, surprised by his perception.

'Then what – '

'I want to discuss this venture with you.'

Gwendoline smiled dryly. 'To test my mettle, you mean,'

'I must congratulate you on your candour. May I speak as openly?'

Gwendoline inclined her head. Jonathan made himself comfortable before he answered, stretching his long, lean form beside her. The dark-brown frock coat and breeches fitted him like a glove and his white waistcoat, buttoned to the neck below a spotted silk cravat, showed off his tan.

For the first time Gwendoline thought how very attractive he was. Close to, his face did not look so harsh and his mouth was firm and well shaped. Even the scar on his neck looked rakish and exciting. She wondered how he had come by the injury. One day she would ask him.

Leaning on one elbow Jonathan regarded her from deep-set, dark eyes. In their depths she detected amusement and something else. Had he realised what she was thinking? She was glad when he began to speak.

'The women of a certain African tribe oil the lips of

their sex. Then they massage, pull, and stretch them. So that the lips elongate and give extra pleasure to their men when they thrust their members inside the women.'

Gwendoline stared at him in utter amazement. Heat flooded her cheeks. She had expected him to tell her about dangerous wild animals, the heat, the lack of sanitation, anything but what he'd just said.

She swallowed hard.

'If you are trying to shock and offend me, Mr Kimberton, you have succeeded,' she said levelly.

She thought she saw admiration in his expression.

'You are an unusual young woman,' he said. 'My own mother would have fainted or gone into a fit of the vapours if I had spoken those same words.'

'It was some sort of test, I presume? And have I passed?'

He grinned. 'Let us say that you've cleared the first jump. Please believe me when I say that I did not speak just to provoke a reaction. You will see many things in Africa that are new, alien to you. The customs there are not ours. You will have experiences which will frighten and enthrall you. Your senses will be awakened, torn in two, heightened until you think you might faint with pleasure . . . What is it? You look so strange. Have I at last succeeded in alarming you?'

'No . . .' Gwendoline felt breathless and a little light-headed. 'It's the way you're speaking, as if you've decided that I will be coming with you.'

'Well, you aren't you? I got the impression that it was a foregone conclusion.'

Gwendoline gaped at him. Only now did she really believe that she was going. Right up to this point it had still seemed like an impossible dream; no matter how strongly she had insisted that she was going.

She could have wept with gratitude. The last barrier had crumbled. Edward would not hold out against both Jonathan and herself. And father could have no objections if her brother and his friend were in agreement.

'Oh, Mr Kimberton . . .' she breathed, swaying towards him to kiss his cheek.

In one swift movement he turned into her and pressed his mouth to hers. No one had ever kissed her like that before. Even to call it a kiss, was to call a rose a weed.

His lips moved on hers, savouring her, easing her lips apart. His tongue slipped into her mouth, tasting and teasing. She felt his teeth as they nibbled at the tender insides of her lips.

She was acutely aware of everything about him; of the lock of his hair that tickled her cheek; his hand in the small of her back as he pressed her to him; the smell of him – clean hair, horse sweat, and that familiar spicy cologne.

She felt the moan begin somewhere in her belly and rise to lodge in her throat.

Her senses were swimming. A tight knot of desire had awoken in her belly. When his other hand moved inside her unbuttoned coat and slid across to her chemise, she did not pull away. And when he pushed aside the fabric to release her breasts, she did not move to stop him.

His fingers coaxed sensations like hot flames from her as he stroked and squeezed her nipples. He released her mouth for a moment, so that he could nuzzle her neck and trace a path of kisses to her ear.

'Please . . .' she whispered, not knowing what she was asking for.

He laughed huskily and closed his fingers hard on one nipple. The spiked pain of it sent shards of pleasure to her groin. Then he dipped his head and took the abused morsel into his mouth, soothing and polishing the glowing nub with his spittle.

Gwendoline felt giddy. The sensations were piling up in layers. A throbbing began between her legs. She felt heavy there and swollen. This is what Hetty had talked about. Hetty told her it felt like this. She was about to discover for herself how it felt to have a man thrust himself into her.

She was afraid and eager all at the same time. Her fingers clutched at his coat. Dare she look down to his trousers? She wanted to see if he was as excited as she was. She wanted to see his hard manhood. For the first time to actually see the male organ. To touch it . . .

Then suddenly the caresses stopped. Somehow she kept the cry of disappointment caged by her teeth.

Jonathan had let her go. He rose to his feet, a sardonic smile on his hard face.

'That's just to let you know what else you will have to face in Africa. I'm myself there. My true self. No longer the English gentleman restrained by notions of good taste, forced to behave in a way which society expects. You will find me as wild and untamed as the landscape.'

She stared at him unable to comprehend this sudden change of mood. Had he been playing with her? A cold fury banished the desire he had kindled.

'I have always pursued the things I wanted,' he went on in the same light tone. 'And I want you Gwendoline Farnshawe. Ah, but not the cool English lady. I have particular tastes and they don't include deflowering virgins. I want to meet you head on, when Africa has worked her magic on you and turned you into a complete woman. Can you – will you – meet that challenge?'

And Gwendoline, trembling and shocked to the core, managed to croak, 'Damn you for your insolence! I'll meet your challenge. And don't think I'll bend to your will like your native women. Neither will I crawl or beg to you for favours. I'll have you on my own terms!'

She lifted her chin and stared at him disdainfully. Her green eyes were chips of emerald.

'In fact, you'll be sick with wanting me before I look at you again. And I swear you'll have to get on your knees before I let you kiss the hem of my skirt!'

Scrambling to her feet, she scooped up her boots and stockings and stormed over to Midnight.

Behind her Jonathan remained where he was. He threw back his head and laughed, a deep rich belly laugh.

'By God, Gwendoline I look forward to that day. Indeed I do!'

Chapter Three

Gwendoline twisted and turned. The dream spread through her like warm honey.

'Jonathan . . . no . . .' she murmured.

Jonathan's dark eyebrows dipped in a frown as he looped the silk ropes around her wrists. She tried to resist him, but he was too strong. He overcame her struggles easily. His face was flushed under his tan. His well-shaped lips parted as he breathed heavily. She caught the glint of his white teeth.

In her sleep, Gwendoline cried out. In the next room Agnes slept on, breathing deeply and evenly like a baby. The soft snores rising from the maid's sleeping pallet were audible through the door.

In a moment Jonathan had secured Gwendoline's wrists, so that her arms were pulled to the sides. He grabbed her flailing ankles, wrapped the ribbons around them, and secured them likewise. A delicious terror spread through her as she lay looking up at him. Though fully dressed in an apricot silk gown she was spreadeagled on the bunk, helpless to stop him doing whatever he wished with her.

Curling his fingers inside the neck of her gown he tore the bodice open to the waist. Gwendoline's dream self, twisted her face into the pillow, avoiding the intense dark eyes of the man who loomed over her. Jonathan laughed and leaned forward to mouth her neck. As his hot lips travelled over her skin, his fingers went to work on her chemise, tearing and loosening the flimsy fabric. Soon the tops of her stays were exposed and the creamy mounds of her breasts. She felt the chill night air on her bare skin.

Jonathan pressed kisses along her jawline and took her earlobe between his teeth. He bit down on the flesh, not hard, just enough for Gwendoline to register a tiny moment of discomfort. She tried to give voice to her rage, but the only sound she made was a sigh of mingled fright and eagerness. Jonathan's tongue probed the inside of her ear. The tip running lightly around the delicate contours, then dipping into the tender channel.

'You taste bitter-sweet my darling,' he murmured. 'I'm going to taste every inch of you. And then you're going to ask me to make you a woman.'

'Never! I won't do it!'

She shivered as little shocks of sensation ran down her neck. Arching her back she strained away, or was it towards him? His hands covered her breasts, drawing them upwards and free of the boned stays, as if he was working them into points.

Now her nipples were exposed as the under-swell of flesh rested on the stiffened fabric, thrusting her breasts into startling prominence. It seemed as if the wanton globes were avid for his touch. The thought of the picture she presented filled Gwendoline with a delicious horror.

Jonathan was not gentle as he clutched her. He rubbed his palms across the swelling flesh, chafing and dragging her breasts together. Now and then he darted out his tongue and pushed it into the valley between them. She felt a dart of concentrated pleasure go straight to her belly. Jonathan pinched her nipples, hard. The pleasure-pain was intense.

Gwendoline tossed her head in shame at her help-less arousal. Her tortured nipples burned and throbbed so sweetly. He slapped the under-swell of her breasts, only lightly, just enough for the firm flesh to tremble. Then he turned his attention back to her nipples. They were hard beads now, shameless rose-pink cones. Casually he leaned forward and teased them with long tender licks, soothing the ache his wicked fingers had imparted.

'You fiend!' she blazed at him, her breath catching in her throat at the awful realisation that she felt disappointment at his gentleness . . .

Gwendoline sat upright in the bed with a start.

The dream faded gradually, leaving her trembling and cold. Confound the man. He was invading her sleep now, the images almost a mirror of what had happened beside the river. And I react to him the same way, whether awake or dreaming, she thought angrily.

Dear Lord, but the dream had seemed real. She pushed back the heavy mass of red-brown hair. Her forehead was damp. There was a sheen of sweat along her top lip. Her nightgown had ridden up and become twisted around her waist. She pulled it down to cover her bare legs, uncomfortably aware that the place between her legs felt very sensitive. It was swollen and heavy-feeling. As she moved she felt a slick of wetness and a pleasant pulsing sensation.

She was tempted briefly to investigate the fascinating area with her fingers, but from force of habit she pressed her hands tightly to her sides. She seemed to hear her governess's voice echoing across the years. It was possible, Miss Templeton had said, to be tempted to perform unclean acts. When Gwendoline asked what these acts were, she'd been beaten and sent to bed without any tea.

'It isn't something we'll speak of again,' Miss Templeton said, tight-lipped.

It had also been Miss Templeton who told her that men were beasts and women were altogether finer and more spiritual creatures because they were free from immoral needs. Gwendoline had wondered what 'immoral needs' were for years. Even her recent clandestine talks with Hetty, her growing knowledge of what men and women did together, had not entirely banished the influence of Miss Templeton and those early lessons in repression.

Her senses were awakening along with her imagination, but she had not yet touched herself – there. Though the temptation was strong, the censorious voice of Miss Templeton lingered on long into adulthood. Gwendoline bit her lip. Perhaps she ought to take a cold bath. Her thoughts and now her dreams were filled with colourful and lurid imaginings.

Shakily she swung her legs out of the bed and poured water into a glass on the dresser. She sipped slowly, feeling the coolness trickle into her stomach. Taking a linen handkerchief from a dresser she dampened it and dabbed the cool cloth to her neck and cheeks.

Back in bed, she pulled the covers up to her chin and lay looking into the darkness. It was a chastening experience to realise that she had enjoyed the dream, hadn't wanted it to stop. It was more chastening still to own to the fact that she wanted Jonathan to do those things in reality. She had relished the mixture of cruelty and gentleness that he displayed.

She remembered how she had felt when she used the crop on Hetty in the summer house. The feelings had been similar. Yes, she had gained pleasure from seeing the parlour maid's distress. Her shoulders shook as she began to cry. She was so confused. Was she twisted to long for such things? Normal people didn't have such dreams, such desires, did they?

Then she remembered how Hetty had told her that a former lover had spanked her and she had liked it. Perhaps she wasn't alone in feeling this way. Gwendoline dried her tears, sat up, and gulped down the last of the water.

She had thought of herself as spirited and independent. It had seemed a great victory to force Edward to take her on this trip. But in many ways she was a child. She did not know her real self at all. And what's more, the glimpses she had seen into her secret desires, terrified her as much as they excited her.

It was all so confusing. She was a well-bred lady, so how was it that she had these thoughts? Thank heaven that no one but Hetty knew anything about that side of her. She must always hide it from the family, from Edward too. For, however much they loved her, the family would pack her off to an institution if they ever guessed that she was morally flawed.

Gwendoline lay awake for a long time, agonising over her split nature.

Gradually the darkness thinned. Throwing aside the bedclothes she padded across the room, her frilled white nightgown sweeping the polished floor. A thin, dawn light was seeping through a chink in the embroidered silk curtains.

She was fully awake now and too excited to sleep. Today was the day. They were leaving for the railway station before midday. She might as well finish packing. Three stout leather-bound trunks stood against one wall. Two of them were packed with serviceable travelling clothes and the other with her most splendid evening gowns and accessories. Jonathan had commented that it was as well to include them. Native chieftains delighted in a show of ostentation.

Jonathan. It seemed impossible to stop thinking about him. Then I won't try, she thought. However angry she felt with him she had to admit that he was entirely different from anyone else she knew. So many men were affected, weak or suffering from the effects of over-indulgence. Some of the businessmen Edward socialised with hardly thought her worth speaking to. In turn she thought them ridiculous with their air of pompous respectability, their luxuriant side-whiskers, and their self-important gait.

Jonathan was at least honest and straightforward. She felt like more of a woman when he looked at her. It was clear now that he was powerfully attracted to her in a clean and thrilling way. Yet there was a threat inherent in his regard – a threat to her own ideals. Would he want her if he knew what dark and secret thoughts possessed her?

How odd it was, when she hadn't thought he'd noticed her on previous visits, that Jonathan could turn her world upside down; colour her senses with hot spicy hues; draw out the warmth from her chilly English nature.

Dare she allow it? It was terrifying to imagine herself out of control.

The artist in her reached out to him, to the forbidden delights he offered. She knew that she was deeply sensual by nature. Miss Templeton had despaired of her appetite for food and had insisted that she did not walk barefoot through the grass, as she loved to do. How could she help but respond to Jonathan? There was something untamed in him that called out to her. Perhaps aspects of his nature matched her own.

He had promised to show her – what? Everything. Yes, that was it. Oh, the promise contained in that one word.

When she was stronger and had experienced a little more of the world, she would feel able to meet Jonathan on his own terms. She so wanted to experience life, to go out and grasp all it had to offer. And it could not truly be a sin to embrace bodily pleasures, could it? Not if it felt as good as Hetty said it did.

Miss Templeton had been wrong. The governess had been a thin, spare woman, with cold hands and a hatchet face. Surely she'd never felt her blood stir at the sight of a handsome young man. But Gwendoline had the feeling that even Miss Templeton might have responded to Jonathan.

Well, for now she really must stop thinking about him. She made a mental effort to banish him from her thoughts. Africa herself beckoned. And the pull of the mysterious, dark continent was potent and irresistible.

Throwing a fine, woollen shawl around her shoulders, Gwendoline began sorting out underthings. She paused to ring the brass bell which stood on a side table next to her bed. Might as well wake Agnes and get her to help, besides she had a fancy for a cup of coffee.

There was a long pause before Agnes pushed open the connecting door and walked into the room rubbing her eyes. Her grey hair, secured into sausage-shaped ringlets hung down over her narrow shoulders. The white nightcap she wore was crumpled and askew.

'What's amiss?' Agnes said. 'It's the middle of the night. It's really too bad of you to disturb an old woman Mistress Gwenie.'

'Oh fiddle! It's almost morning Agnes. And I leave today. Had you forgotten? Come now. Fetch me some coffee and then help me finish packing.'

Agnes grumbled to herself as she went to do Gwendoline's bidding.

Gwendoline smiled. She was fond of Agnes, but the ageing woman had grown surly and bad-tempered of late. It was time she retired to her cottage where she could sit in the garden and let the sun soothe her stiff joints. Hetty would make a much more spirited lady's maid and companion. She found herself looking forward to the adventures they would share.

Hetty was going to need a firm hand to keep her in order, but Gwendoline was confident that she could manage her. And if not, there was always the crop . . .

She crossed the room, threw back the curtains, and opened the window.

Drawing in a deep breath of the tart, apple-scented air she let it out slowly. On the horizon the greys and greens of the hills and fields seemed fused with the sky. She imagined how different the view would look in Africa. Her artist's eye imagined the ochres and browns and the dull, hot glow of sunrise. There was so much to discover, so much to look forward to.

Her blood seemed to sing through her veins. At that precise moment she felt as if she could do anything.

'I want everything,' she said softly. 'I don't care

what anyone thinks of me. I want it all. And I shall have it Jonathan Kimberton. Just you see if I don't.'

Jonathan was walking through the shrubbery, taking one of his early morning walks. Unlike the Farnshawe household he seemed unable to stay in bed when the dawn presaged a clear summer morning.

He was aware of a strange sensation, as if something was calling to him. Stopping in his tracks he turned towards Halton Hall, seeing the wide sweep of the handsome stone frontage through a gap in the clipped yew hedge. His eyes were drawn upwards by a movement.

There was a figure at an upstairs window. With a little shock of recognition he saw that it was Gwendoline. She was smiling, a wide unaffected smile – like a child's. It was obvious that she had just risen from her bed. Her thick chestnut hair was loose around her shoulders. What a mass of it there was. He had never seen it undressed before. As he watched she lifted her arms and the loose frilled sleeves of her nightgown slipped back to reveal her bare arms.

Her forearms were slim and shapely. Her wrists delicate. He could almost encircle them both in one of his hands.

The little snag of wanting that hit him in the stomach was totally unexpected. He hadn't felt such a thing since he was a green lad, with more sap in him than a split pine tree. Even at this distance Gwendoline's natural sensuality reached out to him. Confound it, but she presented a challenge. She was more than a match for most men.

He could imagine some men being afraid of her. Edward was a little wary of her and with good reason. She'd outfoxed him and no mistake.

Jonathan grinned, showing strong, perfect teeth. For a moment he regretted the way he had treated Gwendoline down by the river. What had possessed him to tease her like that? She had been his for the taking, as hot and ready for him as any country lass. He regretted denting her pride, though she recovered it quickly enough.

Well it was done now. And maybe he didn't regret his actions after all. It did a body good to hold off sometimes.

Besides, he was certain Gwendoline Farnshawe would be well worth the wait.

The family and servants gathered on the front steps to see Gwendoline and Edward off.

Gwendoline kissed her father and stepmother, surprised to feel her throat close with unshed tears. The servants wished her well and Agnes shed a tear or two when she took her leave. The trunks and valises were loaded onto the back of the carriage. Edward folded down the step and helped Gwendoline and Hetty inside. He and Jonathan were to ride alongside the driver.

There were cries of 'Safe journey' and 'Good luck' as the doors were slammed. The harness trappings jingled as the horses pranced, impatient to be off.

Hetty, resplendent in a new bonnet and an old day dress of Gwendoline's, bounced up and down on the leather seat, overcome with excitement. Gwendoline felt like doing the same, but managed to maintain a dignified expression. As the carriage began to move, she waved from the window.

'Goodbye dear Papa. Dear Mama! Goodbye. I'll write to you.'

The wheels crunched on the gravelled drive and the figures of her mother and father grew smaller.

Hetty stared out of the window as the surrounding countryside sped past.

'I've never been out of the village before,' she said, ''cept on market days.' Her eyes were bright with excitement.

Gwendoline too watched the familiar sights pass by at speed. There was the hay field and the common, where pigs were grazing. She saw the carpenter's shop and the inn next to it and in the distance the corn mill with its pond, still and deep green. As a child she'd fished for eels in it with Edward.

She blinked hard. It would not do to feel regrets about leaving now. The whole world waited. Soon they would board a steam train and in a few hours they would be in London. She'd see the Thames, until now only a silver snake that twined its way across a picture book she'd once stolen from Edward's room.

Miss Templeton had discovered the book hidden in her sewing basket. She'd punished Gwendoline for the theft, but it had been worth it. Her step-mother, on discovering her interest in books, had declared that Gwendoline would learn her letters alongside Edward. And so she had.

Gwendoline and Hetty were buffered by the padded-leather seats from the worst of the ruts in the roads. Even so they were thrown from side to side as the coach lurched on its way, springs creaking and groaning under the weight of the luggage. Gwendoline was quite sore by the time they reached the station.

In the waiting room, Gwendoline sat with Hetty watching as the porters unloaded their luggage. She sipped a mug of porter and bit into a hot mutton pie.

Soon a distant rumble announced the imminent arrival of the Great Eastern.

Gwendoline found the ironclad monster exciting. It thundered into the station belching out huge clouds of steam. But Hetty was frightened by the throat-catching smell of the train and the clanging and hissing noise.

'Oh it's a huffin' and a puffin' fit to burst,' she said tremulously. 'I don't think it's safe.'

Edward took Hetty's arm in a firm grip and helped her to climb aboard. 'Come along m'dear. Faint heart and all that, eh?'

Hetty flashed him a grateful smile.

Jonathan offered Gwendoline his arm. 'Are you nervous also? It's understandable. The first time I saw a train I found it rather alarming.'

'Thank you, but I can manage. I am quite calm,' she said frostily, ignoring his outstretched arm.

Boarding quickly, she found her seat.

The journey passed quickly, but it was evening before the train steamed into Liverpool Street station. Gwendoline was fascinated by the hustle and bustle of London. There seemed so many people about. Edward took charge, calling for porters and hustling them into hansom cabs, so that there was little time to look around.

Soon they were passing under Liverpool Street's archway and out into the London streets. The horses' hooves clattered over cobblestones as the hansom cabs navigated Houndsditch on their way to the docks.

'See there. That's the Tower,' Edward said, pointing over the roofs of some buildings. 'And there's Tower Bridge.'

The area nearer the docks seemed lined with warehouses, and the narrow streets clotted with people and vendors. Sailors in striped jerseys walked the streets, or stood around in groups outside the many taverns, many of them the worse for drink.

'And there she is,' Edward said proudly. 'The *Persephone*. As sweet a clipper as ever sailed the seas.'

Gwendoline looked at the clipper berthed by the wharf, her sails and rigging making a fine sight silhouetted against the charcoal sky. The *Persephone* was dear to Edward's heart. He'd bought the ship from a previous owner who had used her to transport tea.

'She's low in the water,' Jonathan commented. 'What cargo is she carrying?'

'Besides us and all the equipment? Cloth. Good English wool. We're to trade it for goods when we put into the Gold Coast.'

Gwendoline noticed the look that passed between them and wondered at it. But she kept silent. Let Edward keep his secrets. It made him feel superior. Her eyes were all for the clipper. She was sleek and beautiful, built for speed and endurance. Gwendoline fell in love with her at first sight.

'I'll show you around her in the morning,' Edward said now to Gwendoline. His mouth thinned. 'Don't expect the luxury of a liner. She's a working vessel.'

Gwendoline smiled. 'She'll do admirably,' she said with such enthusiasm that even Edward smiled.

'Well then. Let's away to our rooms and get some rest. We sail on the morning tide.'

The room she was to share with Hetty was at the top of the Fish Inn and facing towards the river. The Thames looked wide and sullen, more imposing than she'd imagined. Masts from the many ships, large and small, were as numerous as the spines on a hedgehog.

A salt-scented breeze blew in through the open window along with the smell of fish and rotting food that clogged the narrow street. Hetty wrinkled her nose and dragged the window shut.

'Phew! If that's what towns smell like you can keep 'em,' she said. 'I'll take clean country air any day.'

Gwendoline had to agree. She unfastened her bonnet and put it on the bed she was to share with Hetty. The sheets looked clean although the mattress was a simple straw-filled palliasse. She supposed it would have to do. It was only one night after all and she was too tired to care.

She threw herself onto the bed and was half-asleep the moment her head hit the pillow. Dimly she was aware of Hetty moving around the room hanging up her coat and hat. She felt Hetty remove her shoes and pull a bed cover up around her shoulders.

'Thank you Hetty, dear . . .' she murmured, thinking how well the little parlour maid had taken to her new position.

In the night she heard whispering and opened one eye to see Hetty holding the door open. She heard Edward's deep voice and the sound of rustling garments.

'Come on, my dear. It won't take a moment. A man has his needs . . . Hetty. Here won't you just touch it . . .'

It seemed to Gwendoline that her brother's voice contained a note of irritation.

'No I will not,' Hetty said firmly. 'You can touch me but that's all.'

'But you're cruel. How can you expect me to control myself when I can feel your juicy little quim? Why it's all plump and wet and ready for me . . . Oh, what have I said. Come back here. Let me finger you the way you like me to . . .'

'Stop that now and go away. Things has changed. You has to realise that Edward. It won't hurt you none to go without. Perhaps when we're aboard ship. But I'm not promisin' nothin'.' She closed the door.

Gwendoline smiled. Hetty was indeed taking her new position seriously. And Edward had better get used to it. She heard him move off down the narrow passageway, muttering to himself. Hetty slipped into bed beside her and was soon asleep again.

Morning came noisily to Dockland.

Gwendoline and Hetty ate downstairs in the inn. The landlady found them a bench close to the large inglenook fireplace, where a fire burned in winter and summer alike. There they were left alone and not disturbed by the comings and goings of the dockers.

'I'll fetch you both a tankard of Bumpo. That'll be sure to put roses in your cheeks,' said the landlady chuckling.

Gwendoline sipped the drink, which was a mixture of rum, sugar, water and nutmeg, served hot. She suspected that Edward would not approve of her drinking strong spirits, so she decided she wouldn't tell him. The Bumpo was delicious and provided a robust breakfast with the rough bread and cheese.

Jonathan joined them in a while, bringing in the smells of tar and fish as he opened the inn door. Now and then came a whiff of unwashed bodies, but all pervading, blocking out everything else with its breath, was the muddy, sour smell of the Thames.

'Soon be making sail now. No last minute regrets?' Jonathan said to Gwendoline.

'None,' she said, looking him square in the face.

He looked in his element. His dark-brown hair was

loose and hanging in waves to his shoulders. He wore a leather waistcoat over an open-necked, white shirt and dark trousers.

'And you Hetty,' Jonathan said. 'Are you ready for Africa?'

'I don't know to be truthful, Sir,' she said blushing. 'But if Miss Gwendoline's goin'. Then I am too.'

'How loyal of you,' Jonathan said. 'Your mistress must be a special person to inspire such sentiment.'

Gwendoline looked at him sharply to see if he was being sarcastic, but he looked at ease, if a little serious. She decided that he meant nothing amiss. She looked out of the window to where Edward was supervising the loading of the last of the equipment and luggage.

And, sooner than Gwendoline had expected, it was time to leave.

She stood on the crowded deck of the *Persephone* hardly able to believe that the great moment was here. The dark waters of the Thames flowed swiftly past the clipper's hull. The captain bellowed out orders and the sailors ran to do his bidding.

Gwendoline and Hetty were left alone to look over the waist-high rail as London slipped by. A cool wind set Gwendoline's woollen shawl flapping and teased strands of Hetty's corn-gold hair from under her bonnet.

Ropes creaked as the sailors climbed the rigging, ready for when the sails would be unfurled.

As the clipper was towed out to meet the rising tide Gwendoline reached for Hetty's hand.

Hetty beamed at her. 'I'm not sorry I came. I'll be a good friend and companion. We'll have such a lot to tell our folks back home! Oh, Miss. It'll be a lark for sure.'

Gwendoline smiled warmly, catching sight of Jonathan's face and the light in his eyes. He's in Africa already, she thought. And felt an answering thrill echo within her soul.

She squeezed Hetty's hand.

'Oh yes,' she said, using Hetty's terminology. 'It'll be a lark.'

The adventure really had begun.

Chapter Four

*T*he waves were gunmetal grey, matching the sky. Soon all traces of the coastline had disappeared. By late morning a watery sun appeared, glinting on the troughs and hollows and turning the waves to aquamarine.

'In fair weather, with a strong head wind, the *Persephone* sails like a dream,' Edward said proudly.

Gwendoline had adapted to life on board ship with little trouble. She was fascinated by the way the small crew, some thirty men, managed to sail the big clipper and keep every inch of her spick-and-span. From the poop deck, where only the guests, the captain and first mate were allowed, she and Hetty observed the sailors working their four-hour watches.

'You are to keep to yourselves as much as possible,' Edward said. 'This is a working ship and I don't want passengers getting in the way of its smooth running.'

'I understand Edward,' Gwendoline said seriously. 'And I'll behave myself accordingly. I did not persuade you to take me along so that I could cause trouble.'

Edward grunted a reply, plainly not convinced.

But Gwendoline meant what she said. She had discovered that some of the men had doubled up with shipmates, so that she and Hetty could have a cabin each. It was more than she'd expected. She knew that seafaring men considered it bad luck to have women on board.

Neither Gwendoline nor Hetty suffered from sickness, prompting the Captain to remark, 'You've both found your sea legs and no mistake. It's mermaids y'are.'

Captain Michael Casey was a handsome Irishman in his mid-thirties. Old for a sea captain, and trusted and respected by the crew. He was courteous, if a little cool to Gwendoline, but she fancied that there was a sparkle in his eye.

The fine weather held and Gwendoline and Hetty spent long hours sitting on the poop deck behind a wind break; Gwendoline sketching and Hetty sewing. It did not escape Gwendoline's notice that one of the young officers, a brawny man who acted as purser, threw many glances Hetty's way. Hetty paid the man no heed and appeared to be concentrating fully on being a lady's maid.

Edward and Jonathan spent much time together, going over plans and studying maps. Jonathan was attempting to teach Edward something about the African continent. Gwendoline loved to listen as Jonathan spoke. Her quick brain was thirsty for knowledge and she found herself absorbing details and remembering facts with little effort.

Jonathan was a natural teacher, his love for his subject making him fascinating to listen to. For the first time Gwendoline gained a sense of Jonathan's formidable intellect. This was the man who spoke six languages, had travelled extensively and was the author of many books on native customs.

He seemed to have come into his own now that they were underway. Once, during one of these sessions, he looked up and caught her watching him. It was too late to look away. She saw the quick pleasure on his face before his expression changed. Under the scrutiny of his deep-set eyes she felt like an insect on a pin.

'Breathe in, Miss,' Hetty said, tightening the laces on the back of the corset. 'Just a bit more. You need to be laced tight to get into the apricot silk.'

The dinner gown was cut low across the neckline and showed off Gwendoline's shoulders to advantage. There was a suggestion of shadowed cleavage. Hetty brushed Gwendoline's hair until it shone, then wove apricot ribbon and dyed feathers through the pinned-up curls.

'How do you like being a lady's maid?' Gwendoline asked, her green eyes dancing in the reflection of the looking-glass.

'I likes it fine, Miss,' Hetty smiled. 'Your clothes are so pretty. And I have all my lovely new things to wear. I feel like a proper lady myself. There. All finished. You look a picture. Captain Casey won't be able to resist you.'

'Hetty!' Gwendoline said, then taking one look at the younger woman's face, she burst out laughing. 'I'm dining at the Captain's table not keeping an assignation!'

'Aren't you?' Hetty grinned. 'I've seen the way the Captain looks at you when he thinks you're not lookin'.'

'Nonsense,' Gwendoline said, then wondered if it was true.

Michael Casey seemed rather old to her. She had not considered that he thought her anymore than the owner's daughter. But now that she came to think of it he was often there when she looked around or standing some way off, looking in her direction.

'The purser's takin' me for a turn around the deck when he finishes his duties,' Hetty said.

'Ah, yes. The purser. I'm not sure I approve,' Gwendoline said. 'Perhaps you'd better come to my cabin later and tell me all about it.'

Hetty bobbed a curtsey. Her eyes sparkled. 'You mean I'm to tell you everything?'

Gwendoline nodded. 'Just as you have been doing.'

'Oh, Miss. I don't know as I should. It was different back in England . . .'

'I don't see how.' Gwendoline paused. 'Wouldn't Edward be annoyed if he found out that you are flirting with the sailors?'

Hetty grinned. 'He'd go wild. But you won't tell him will you?'

Gwendoline shook her head. 'Not if you co-operate. There's a lot I need to learn about the things men and women do together.'

Hetty had been her source of information back at Halton Hall and she was going to make sure that that particular relationship continued. The sooner Hetty realised that, the better.

Hetty's eyes swept down. Two bright spots of colour appeared on her cheeks.

'Very well,' she said softly. 'I'll tell you all about it later. If there's anything to tell . . .'

Gwendoline smiled. 'Oh I think there will be.'

As Gwendoline swept out of the cabin, Hetty picked up the clothes she had discarded. She bundled the chemise and petticoats into a ball, ready to put them with the other laundry. Then she stopped and began stroking the fine material, admiring the rows of tiny pin tucks, the broderie anglaise and the bows and rosebuds made of blue ribbon.

Her own underwear, though new and of good quality, was plain and serviceable. She would love to wear such beautiful garments as these.

Her full lips curved in a mischievous grin. Why not? Gwendoline would never know. Swiftly she undressed. Standing in front of the cheval glass, she turned up the oil lamp. Her skin looked creamy in the golden light. Her generous curves looked luscious and inviting. She ran her hands up over her big round breasts, tipped by dark-brown nipples, admiring the firmness of them. She lifted the generous underswell, holding them up and squeezing them together.

Her passions, always only just below the surface, simmered in readiness. As she looked at the soft mound of her belly, at the thick, glossy hair between her thighs, she felt herself growing moist. The purser was a big and muscular man. Just what she needed.

She pulled on Gwendoline's discarded chemise and petticoats, delighting in the feel of the soft fabric against her skin. Gwendoline still wanted to play her games, did she? That didn't come as a great surprise.

Well she'd have plenty to tell the young mistress later that night.

'Good evening Miss Farnshawe,' Captain Casey said, when Gwendoline entered the narrow map room, transformed for dining by the addition of white linen, oil lamps, and crockery.

He folded down the back of a bench so that she might seat herself.

Beside the Captain and other officers, Edward and Jonathan were spaced around the table. They all rose as she sat down. Next to her Jonathan took advantage of the small diversion to bend down and whisper in her ear.

'You look ravishing,' he said.

Gwendoline stared fixedly into her lap. Jonathan had bent so close that she felt his warm breath on her neck. It was a moment before she composed herself.

The meal of chicken stew and vegetables was plain, but tasty. Gwendoline smiled at the purser as he served the meal. Was he thinking about Hetty and their coming assignation, she wondered.

'Better enjoy this while you can,' Edward said. 'We'll be eating hard tack and salt beef once the fresh food is finished.'

Her brother seemed to be taking every opportunity to underline the fact that there would be privations to come and that she had been foolish to insist on travelling with them.

'I'm sure I can manage if you can,' she answered him sweetly.

The Captain smiled at her. 'You're a plucky young woman. I admire your spirit.' He picked up a serving dish. 'Will you be having some more chicken stew?'

Throughout the meal Edward talked about what they would do in Africa. Jonathan told how he wanted in particular to amass a large number of shields, ceremonial jewellery and masks, and wooden carvings.

'This exhibition at the museum will add greatly to your reputation in the locality, Edward,' he said.

Edward assumed a gratified expression. 'If all goes well I might be prepared to finance other trips. I've always had a hankering to go to India. Marvellous place, don't you know . . .'

Although Jonathan was an animated conversationalist, Gwendoline noticed that he also listened, concentrating fully on whoever was speaking at any given moment. He really is interested in other people, she thought, unlike her brother who loved the sound of his own voice. She was growing to like Jonathan more and more, though she had no intention of forgiving his cavalier treatment of her.

She remembered their exchange by the river with a little shiver of mingled anger and pleasure. I meant every word, she reminded herself. I'll make him want me so much that it hurts.

During the meal she was conscious of Jonathan's eyes flickering often over her bare shoulders, lingering on the front of her bodice where the thin silk was stretched across her breasts.

Captain Casey was attentive, taking every opportunity to engage her attention. He refilled her glass with wine and pressed more food on her. Once or twice his fingers brushed hers and she felt the pressure of his knee under the table. The signs were subtle, but Hetty had been right.

Gwendoline smiled inwardly, enjoying the feeling of being admired by two handsome and experienced men at the same time. She felt a new feeling of power. It was a heady sensation. When the Captain's hand next brushed against her bare forearm as if by accident, she leaned towards him and gave him her most brilliant smile.

How satisfying it was to feel his fingers tremble against her warm skin and to see the new light in his eyes. He looked so strong and dependable in his uniform; the polished brass of his buttons and trims gleaming in the lamplight. Yet she could cause him to react with the slightest touch.

'You must give me a tour of the ship,' she purred,

trying out her newfound skills. 'Such a man as you must have many interesting things to show a young woman.'

It was a good thing that Edward was engaged in conversation, she thought, as Captain Casey flushed deeply and almost choked on his wine. I've shocked him, she thought. He couldn't have expected such a forthright reaction. But any worries that she might have offended him were soon put aside.

Captain Casey lifted his glass. 'Might I propose a toast,' he said. 'To the success of your African trip.' And then to Edward. 'I hope you will be taking good care of your charming sister. I confess that I cannot bear the thought of any harm coming to her.'

It was Gwendoline's turn to blush. 'You are too kind Captain Casey,' she said, giving him another dazzling smile.

Though Jonathan gave no sign of it, she was sure he had perceived the undercurrent. She felt his amusement. He knows exactly what I'm doing, she thought. And felt a little guilty for flaunting her intentions.

She glanced swiftly at him when he wasn't looking. In the light of the oil lamps, Jonathan looked almost swarthy and more mysterious than ever.

Would he care if she allowed the Captain certain liberties? She lifted her chin as their eyes met across the table, and she saw that he did care. He looked coldly furious and quite surprised at being so.

A cruel little grin lifted her mouth. Oh good.

'I'm sorry . . . What did you say?' Gwendoline said. From Edward's expression she gathered that he had spoken to her and was awaiting an answer.

'I was telling the Captain about your painting,' Edward said irritably. He hated to have to repeat himself.

'I'm a patron of the arts myself, Miss Farnshawe,' said the Captain smoothly. 'All Irishmen have poets' souls. Would you be allowing me to view some of your work?'

Gwendoline inclined her head.

'I'd be pleased to show you some. But so far I've only completed some rough sketches.'

How strange that she sounded so calm, so assured. When inwardly her blood was racing with excitement. Captain Casey now had his knee firmly pressed against hers. When he leaned across to direct a comment at her she caught the smell of him; Macassar hair oil and shaving soap.

'Well no doubt you'll do more before long . . .' Edward said, losing interest.

Coffee was served at the end of the meal. Normally the men would withdraw for cigars and port. Gwendoline expected that they would all sit and converse for a while longer, but Edward seemed keen to get to 'men's talk'.

'I'm afraid there's no room to observe the niceties on board ship,' Edward said pointedly. '*Persephone* has no salon for you to retire to while we gentlemen smoke.'

'That isn't necessary for my comfort,' Gwendoline said. 'I expected to have to make adjustments while we're at sea. Besides I have a fancy for reading in my cabin – '

'Perhaps you would like – ' began the Captain, half rising from the table.

'But the evening is mild,' Jonathan cut in quickly. 'What a pity to waste it. Will you take a turn around the deck Gwendoline? I have a fancy for a breath of air myself.'

Gwendoline thought of refusing, but she realised that she could not keep up her frosty exterior with regard to Jonathan. They would be spending weeks at sea. Better to establish a truce of sorts.

She smiled at Jonathan. 'Thank you. I should like that.'

After thanking Captain Casey for his hospitality, she settled the fringed shawl of printed silk around her shoulders and allowed Jonathan to lead her onto the deck.

The sky was a great blue-black vault pricked with silver star points. She could smell the salt tang of the sea on the breeze that ruffled her hair and teased strands from the pins. The waves resembled ridged, grey glass in the moonlight.

'And how are you finding life on board ship?' Jonathan asked with a note of irony, when they paused and were leaning on the ship's rail.

Overhead the sails rippled in the light wind.

In the same tone she answered, 'There's much to be learnt for a young woman who can keep an open mind.'

He was silent for a moment, absorbing the double meaning of her words. She waited, expecting him to comment on the way she had flirted at dinner, but he seemed intent on letting that matter lie. If that's the way he wants to play it, then so be it, she thought. Both of us know perfectly well what's really going on.

'It cannot be easy for you, being so cramped for space and being rationed with fresh water like any common seaman,' Jonathan went on.

'Home comforts are few. But I shall manage,' she said stoutly.

He laughed. 'I'm sure that you will. You are a remarkably strong young woman – if a little way-ward, a little cruel. I can see that you learn fast. I do believe that you are meant for Africa. As I was.'

So he could not resist after all. She smiled

inwardly, pleased by the small victory. She chose to ignore the subtle reference to her behaviour in the dining room. But she too could not entirely resist rising to his challenge.

'Meant for Africa? How so?'

Jonathan leaned closer, a smile on his lips, his dark eyes bright with moonlight.

'I see it in your eyes. In your body which is imprisoned in the rigid clothing of our homeland. You were meant for the blistering red heat Gwendoline. For the smell of the dust and the fire and bloodstreaked dawn skies. Your hair should be loose, loops of beads and circles of polished metal around your neck – '

'That's enough,' Gwendoline said sharply. 'You are not to say these things to me. I forbid it.'

'Indeed?' He sounded vastly amused. 'And how are you going to stop me?'

'If you wish me to behave in a civil manner towards you – '

'Oh I do. And so much more . . . as you well know . . .'

She parried his interruption. 'Good. Then you must modify your behaviour or I shall take offence. And this clipper is too small for us to avoid each other. Let us try to get along. That ought to be possible. Can we not try to be friends?'

He inclined his head. 'That will be no hardship at all for me. Shall we walk on?'

She was pleased with the way she had handled things and, despite his nearness, was certain that he had no idea how her heart was racing. He quite took her breath away. Whenever he spoke of Africa the colourful images flooded her mind, drawing out a quite unexpected response.

Damn that keen mind of his. How was it that he

saw into the secret places inside her? No one else knew of her dreams, her longings. To her father and brother, she was of little account, beyond being a burden on the family resources. She had long rebelled against the image they had fashioned for her. Now it seemed that Jonathan had found her out.

How disquieting a thought that was. And how compelling.

They completed their walk in silence, except for Jonathan's comments on the beauty of the night. To outward appearances they might have been mere acquaintances exchanging pleasantries. At the hatch which led below, he paused and turned towards her.

She felt his hand on her arm, the heat of his fingers burning right through the silk of her sleeve.

'I knew I was right about you when I saw you in the summerhouse with Hetty,' he said with a strange reluctance, almost as if he could not contain his thoughts.

'You . . . saw . . .?'

She had hardly time to get over the shock of this disclosure before he went on.

He nodded, 'That doesn't matter. It just confirms what I think about you. You're different to other women. Stronger. You go after the things you want. Just as I do. Oh, Gwendoline. What times we shall have. I shall show you Africa. The real Africa. You will grow to love it, as I do. It will be an awakening for you. In every way possible – if you are brave enough to meet the challenge. Are you Gwendoline? Are you truly that brave?'

He had promised not to say such things. And here he was doing it again. Perversely she felt the urge to laugh, but suppressed it. Lord, but he was as wayward as she was. Did he ever do anything he didn't want to?

She lifted her chin and met his gaze squarely.

'Brave? I believe I am,' she said a trifle stiffly.

He gave a husky laugh.

'Oh, I don't doubt that you are possessed of a fine, high, moral courage. What daughter of an English gentleman would not be? But do you, I wonder, have the greatest courage of all? The courage to break out of constrainment, to put the restrictions of your breeding, the narrow ideas of what your place is in society, aside. In short – to find yourself?'

He did not wait for her answer.

'Good night, Gwendoline. I shall dream of you to-night,' he said. And then, with a wicked little smile, 'And I hope that you will speak to me in the morning.'

Gwendoline descended the stairs and hurried along to her cabin. Once inside she slammed the door and stood with her back pressed against the wood. She had thought that she could deal with Jonathan, but now she was not so sure.

He was infuriatingly unpredictable. What was worse was that she could not help but respond to that trait in him. Perhaps because he was such a reflection of herself.

Now she knew him to be manipulative too – just as she was. Things could hardly be worse. He had seen her in the summerhouse with Hetty, so had also known of her plan to walk in on Hetty and Edward. Lord, but the thought of it made her cheeks burn.

Oh, she had been so smug, thinking that she had controlled Edward, taken charge of her own destiny. She felt so angry and confused that she could weep. Jonathan had peeled her like a grape. He accused her of cruelty? He was cruel too – in a subtle way. She knew the reason why he had told her about the summerhouse.

He was paying her back for flirting with Captain Casey.

Well, she'd only just started. Just you watch me, Jonathan Kimberton, she vowed. I'll learn. I'll become as worldly as you are. Then you'll have *no* advantage over me.

Alone in her cabin Gwendoline felt restless and in need of company. She wished that Hetty was around.

The dinner gown was tight and uncomfortable. She would like to undress and put on a robe, but she needed Hetty to help her with the many hooks and loops. Opening the cabin door she crossed the narrow corridor and tapped on the door opposite.

'Hetty! Are you in there.'

There was no reply. Hetty was no doubt enjoying herself with the purser. They wouldn't have been together for long, the purser having to wait on table and bring cigars and brandy before he was free from his duties.

Gwendoline pushed open the cabin door and went inside. Sitting on Hetty's bunk, she decided to wait for her. She plumped up a pillow and settled back in the darkness.

'Oh, leave off do, Ned! I can't,' Hetty giggled and pushed the young officer away.

At her back a great hank of rope, twisted in a figure of eight, dug into her spine. A fine salt spray blew across the ship's rail, silvering her golden hair with tiny droplets.

She pressed her hands against Ned's slab-like chest. Under the fabric of his uniform she could feel the hardness of his muscles. His thighs held her pinned between them.

Lawks, but she loved a strong man. The purser was built like a tree, reminding her of the farm

71

workers back home. His face was nothing remarkable, square-jawed and plain, but he had the bluest eyes she'd ever seen. Eyes to drown in, her mother would have said.

Ned nuzzled her neck and thrust one of his large hands down her neckline.

'You cheeky thing you!' Hetty said, as Ned began squeezing her breasts.

She didn't want him to get the idea that she was a common wench who he could tumble and not give a 'thank you' to. After all, she was a lady's maid now and mindful that she commanded some respect.

Oh, but he was hot and eager and her body was responding even while she held herself back. When his busy fingers found a nipple and began rolling it into a hard peak, she found that her resistance was fast ebbing.

She sagged against him as he kissed her ear, nibbling at the lobe.

'Aw, come on, girl. I know you're hot for me. We can't go to my place. There's always someone asleep afore his watch. You've a snug cabin all of your own.'

'So what if I 'ave,' Hetty said pertly.

'Well, you take me there and I'll show you a thing or two.'

Hetty let him kiss her. His mouth was firm and the way he thrust his tongue into her mouth was exciting. It would be risky, taking him back. The other officers' cabins were just down the corridor from her own. Then she felt his hand slide up her thigh, the salt-hardened palm scraping against her flesh.

When his fingers slipped inside the open-legged drawers and brushed across her pubic mound, the lust fluttered in her belly. For a big man he was gentle and seemed desirous of pleasing her, not just himself.

'Come on then. But you be quiet mind. Else we'll both be in a mess of trouble.'

Muffling her giggles with her sleeve, Hetty hurried along to her cabin, Ned in close pursuit. No one was about. The corridor was dark and the cabin pitch-black.

'Never mind the lantern,' Ned whispered. 'I can feel my way.'

They almost fell into her cabin, Ned so eager to get his hands on her bare flesh that he fumbled in his haste. Hetty wriggled against him. Gentle he might be, but he didn't know his own strength.

There was a ripping sound.

'Now you've torn my dress. You great lummox!' Hetty scolded. 'Get off me a minute.'

Feeling her way across the cabin she located the brass lantern. A moment later the cabin was flooded with light. Hetty turned at Ned's inrush of breath and saw Gwendoline sitting up and rubbing at her eyes. Her mouth looked petulant and her dark eyebrows were drawn together in a frown.

'My Godfathers! What's she doing here?' Hetty said, the words bursting out before she could stop them.

Ned took a step back. Hetty regretted her outburst immediately, absorbing the fact that the young Mistress looked well and truly out of temper.

Gwendoline pushed herself upright.

'I was waiting for you, but I fell asleep,' she said stiffly. 'I did not expect you to be entertaining a guest.'

Hetty bit her lip. 'You'd better go, Ned. I'll see you later.'

Ned's cheeks flamed. He nodded curtly and turned to go, having to stoop to navigate the low doorway.

'Well?' Gwendoline said.,

'Sorry, Miss,' Hetty said looking shamefaced. 'I know I shouldn't have brought him back, but I . . . well I was hot for him. Ned's a fine, big, lusty man. Where's the harm?'

Gwendoline smiled thinly. 'And no doubt you wanted to impress this – Ned?'

Hetty frowned, not understanding. Gwendoline pointed to the torn neckline of Hetty's gown, where the embroidered frill of her chemise was showing. Realising what Gwendoline meant, Hetty's hand shot up to cover the offending garment.

'I'm sorry, Miss. I only meant to borrow your underthings. I wasn't goin' to steal them. Honest. It's just that . . . I haven't anything half so fine.'

Gwendoline sighed. 'I suppose I should be angry with you. But it's no matter. You can keep them.'

Hetty's chin came up. She smiled delightedly, then her eyes narrowed with understanding. She knew that look on the young mistress's face. She was after something.

'What – do you want me to do?' she said calculatingly.

Gwendoline paused before replying.

'I want to watch,' she said evenly.

'Watch what, Miss?'

'You know perfectly well Hetty. I want to watch you and Ned – together.'

Hetty's eyes grew round as saucers, then they began to sparkle wickedly.

'Oh, Miss,' she said softly with something like awe in her voice. 'You can't mean it.'

'Oh I do Hetty. I most certainly do.'

Chapter Five

*E*dward paced up and down the deck, unable to sleep.

It was late. The night watch had just come on duty. All around were the noises of the clipper as she cleaved through the dark waters. The deck timbers creaked and the wind whistled in the rigging.

He craved a cigar but all fire was forbidden on deck.

Leaning over the ship's rail he watched the moon glimmer on the sea as it rolled back from the bow. He fretted and frothed in an agony of lust and frustration. It was no good. In a few minutes he'd have to gather the shreds of his pride and try her door again.

Confound Hetty. What the deuce had got into her? He'd been good to her in England, given her presents, paid her compliments, and now here she was acting as if they were hardly acquainted. That was bad enough in itself, but he'd seen the way she smiled and flirted with the officers. They, of course, responded with relish to her fresh prettiness.

Edward didn't blame them. Men would be men. But what irked him the most was the way that great raw-boned Ned Woodley couldn't keep his eyes off her. He was always asking her if there was anything he could fetch her, or whether he could do anything for her.

Edward knew what Ned wanted to do. He wanted to do the same things to Hetty himself.

Jealousy was a new experience for Edward and he didn't like it; not one little bit. To his mind Hetty ought to be loyal to him. Surely she knew that he cared about her – as much as he was able to in his position. Back in England he'd considered setting her up in her own small cottage on the estate. Perhaps his mistake was in not telling her that.

Well he'd remedy that right away. When she realised his intentions she'd come to her senses and do his bidding, as she always used to. Hetty must be made to realise that it was best for her to rely on him. Everyone knew that a woman needed a man to take care of her and make all decisions for her.

He thought of her pleasure when he told her the news. How grateful she'd be. He thought also of her lush curves. His tumescence was actually painful. It seemed like an age since he'd smelt her skin, tasted her, and pushed himself into her tight, hot body.

Straightening his cravat and smoothing his side whiskers he prepared to go below.

It was time that he and Hetty set a few things straight.

Hetty sat upright in her narrow bunk and thought of Gwendoline's demands.

Gwendoline was a one and no mistake.

She didn't mind telling the young mistress about the things she did. But to let her watch. Hetty had never done such a thing. Something had upset the young mistress, she was sure of it. There was a look of new determination on that pretty, well-bred face.

Gwendoline was at her most perverse when challenged. The way things were going she would be trying things out for herself before long.

Hetty wondered if she ought to refuse to participate, but Gwendoline had a way of getting what she wanted. There had been the beating in the summerhouse. Strange how, since then, they had grown closer. Almost like real friends.

Hetty mulled things over and over, knowing that, in the end, she'd do anything Gwendoline asked. A breathy little giggle escaped her.

Whatever would Ned say!

Then she realised that Ned mustn't know. Not at first. Men were funny about things like that.

She wished Ned was here now. Her body was all ready for pleasuring. She'd been looking forward to his caresses but he'd scuttled off sharpish when he saw Gwendoline.

There was the sound of a soft footfall outside her door. Had Ned come back?

She knew it wasn't Ned when she heard a soft scratching noise on the door. Ned would have tapped it.

She smiled. It was Edward again. He'd come creeping along the narrow passageway, begging to be let in every night since they left London. So far she had refused him. He must be dying for it now.

She decided he was about ready for a lesson. Swiftly she got out of the bunk.

'Come inside, Edward,' she said opening the door so abruptly that he almost fell into the cabin.

Edward recovered quickly, reaching for her at once.

'Oh Hetty. You've let me in at last.'

His hands roved over her generous curves. Pulling her close he buried his head in the hollow of her throat. The quilted-silk smoking jacket was soft against her skin. He smelt of cigars and brandy.

'I'm hot and hard for you,' Edward murmured happily, forgetting everything he meant to say to her.

As he rubbed himself against her, Hetty felt his erect cock against her thigh. The feel of him made her feel weak. There was the familiar rush of warmth to her stomach. With a great effort she calmed herself.

'Stop that now,' she said.

If she gave in now, things would never change. She would always be the ignorant country girl who the young master used for his pleasure whenever the fancy took him.

Gradually Edward became aware that Hetty was standing with her arms pressed to her sides. He drew away a little and looked down at her in surprise. He grinned a little uncertainly.

'Hetty? Aren't you pleased to see me?'

She took a step back, putting him at arm's length. ''Course I am.'

'Well then . . .' He made a grab for her.

Hetty moved nimbly away and sat down on the bunk. She pointed to a chair that stood in a corner of the cabin.

'Sit down Edward,' she said. 'We has to talk.'

'What's to talk about?' Edward grinned, advancing on her. 'I know what you want. And I want it too.'

'You'll listen to me, or get out this very minute!' Hetty said sharply.

Edward's whiskers trembled. He looked suddenly unsure of himself.

'How dare you use that tone with me . . .' he began, sure that she'd respond to his tone.

His voice trailed off as he saw that she was serious. For a moment Hetty thought he was going to leave. But his lust won out. Face blank with shock Edward sank into the chair.

'I don't undrstand. This isn't like you.'

Hetty folded her hands in her lap. Her knees were pressed primly together. Edward's eyes ranged over her full breasts. She knew that the big brown nipples were visible through her new, thin cotton nightdress.

'It's exactly like me. The new me. Now Edward we has to get things straight.'

'That's what I've come here for – ' he began eagerly.

'Will you let me finish?'

'Oh, er yes of course.'

'I'm not a parlour maid now. I'm a lady's maid and I won't 'ave you creeping up to my room whenever you feels the need. You has to earn that right.'

Edward was fast recovering. His eyes gleamed with lust still and something else – a new respect. The bulge at his groin seemed to have got bigger.

'Earn my rights, eh?'

Hetty smiled inwardly. She sensed that there was a way to pull Edward's strings. And once he was trained she would be able to do anything with him.

'What . . . what must I do?'

'Well, now. Let me see,' Hetty said, enjoying herself.

'Do you want money?'

'No. It's not that.'

'Then what?'

'You must do as I tell you,' she said. 'And if you pleases me I shall reward you. Otherwise you won't

79

get no more pleasure. You'll have to pull on that big cock of yours all alone in your cabin.'

Edward licked his lips in alarm. His mouth trembled slightly.

'I . . . I don't understand.'

His broad cheeks were flushed. Throwing himself from the chair he knelt on the carpet and looked up at her. Hetty suppressed a smile. Even at such a time Edward was stilted and formal.

'Tell me you'll do as I say.'

'I'll do anything Hetty. Anything you want.'

That was better. He looked properly humble now. She patted his head, stroking the thick hair back from his damp forehead.

"Course you will. You'll be good won't you? And you'll show me the proper respect a man feels for his young lady?'

Edward nodded vigorously.

'I will darling Hetty. Oh, I will. I'll do whatever you like. If only you'll let me have you. It's been an eternity since we set sail. Lord but I'm dying for you. I'm about to spill over. Can I . . . can I just look at your lovely quim for a moment?'

Hetty assumed an expression of displeasure.

'There you go. Makin' demands. Just like you always does. Pretty words won't win me round. I don't think you understands. I think you need a lesson.'

Edward sat back on his haunches. He looked crestfallen.

'I'm sorry. What . . . what must I do?'

Hetty stroked her upper lip, appearing to consider before she replied.

'You has to show me that you mean to do as I tell you.'

'Oh, I will. How can I prove it to you?'

Hetty's eyes gleamed. 'Go and get my hairbrush from the dresser.'

Edward hurried to do as she told him. His broad shoulders were hunched with anticipation. She felt a unique thrill at the thought of making him do her will. Edward was gentry, good-looking in his way and wealthy. Usually men like him were in control of her life and surroundings. The tables were turned now and no mistake.

Edward looked at her expectantly and she was struck anew by his physical attractiveness. Although he wasn't as tall and imposing as Ned, Edward's body was well-formed and strong. His enthusiasm and vigour had always been part of his charm for her. Now she was experiencing another facet of him. A subservient Edward was a new challenge.

Edward handed her the brush. She took it from him and smiled sweetly.

'Now get down on all fours in front of me. I'm going to give you your first lesson.'

Edward was breathing fast. His chest rose and fell under his quilted smoking jacket. Without being asked to he began to disrobe. Wearing only his shirt and trousers he assumed the position she required. His full, muscular buttocks were outlined by the dark fabric stretched over them.

Hetty passed her tongue over her full lips.

'Now, you're not to make a single noise, or else I'll be very angry. Take your punishment like a good boy.'

Edward emitted a hastily suppressed groan as she began spanking him with the hairbrush. The sounds were crisp, though muffled somewhat by the thick trousers. Edward held himself steady as she applied the strokes with moderate force. Soon he began to work his hips back and forth, trying to avoid the blows.

'Keep still!' Hetty ordered. 'If you don't obey me, it'll be the worse for you!'

'I'm sorry, Hetty. But I can't help it.'

Hetty's lips thinned. She stood up and walked slowly over to him. Silently she walked around him. Edward looked up at her, his expression so wracked by desire and passion that she felt her knees go weak.

She hadn't expected to enjoy this so much, but the sight of Edward so willingly humble, so eager to please, went to her head like rough country cider at harvest-time.

'You're a bad boy, aren't you now,' she crooned. 'So naughty you've been, my young master.'

'Yes. Oh, yes,' he murmured.

'You're not my master now. Are you? Tell me what you are.'

In a strangled voice Edward said, 'I'm . . .bad. A bad boy.'

'Yes. You're bad. And what do we do with bad boys?'

'Beat them,' he said in a voice hardly above a whisper.

'I can't hear you.'

'Beat them,' he said his voice rising.

'That's right. Beat them,' she echoed. 'Until they begs for mercy.'

'Oh yes. Oh, God,' Edward groaned, as she lifted one leg and straddled his head.

Facing towards his abused backside she clasped his head firmly between her knees. Reaching down she unfastened his belt and dragged his trousers and drawers down. Then she pulled her nightgown up to her waist and secured it there.

Edward's reddened buttocks and hairy thighs looked vulnerable and exciting. She slapped him hard with the flat of her hand, delighting in the way the flesh vibrated and stung her palm.

Edward yelped, the sound muffled by the way his chin was tucked into his chest. She slipped a hand under his belly to assess the degree of pleasure he felt. Her mouth curved as her fingers closed over his cock. It was stoutly erect. The crested end, partly free of the cock-skin, was slick with salty dew. She rubbed the ball of her thumb around his cock-end, pushing the skin fully back.

Edward's buttocks contracted. A long tortured groan escaped him. She knew he was near to spending. Well he would have to wait. Before she let him reach his release she wanted to be sure that he knew what his new status was.

'Now to finish your punishment,' she said, her voice sounding breathless in her own ears. 'I want to see those buttocks of yours go nice an' red.'

Oh, what a game this was. She'd spend many happy hours devising new and more humiliating punishments for him. She wished she'd thought of it before. Edward was just the type to respond to such treatment.

She recalled the way the servants at Halton Hall had gossiped about his past relationship with that haughty governess. What was her name? Oh, yes, Miss Templeton. All of them knew about the boyish yelps and screams that came from behind the nursery door, but Edward was devoted to his governess.

There was a story there and no mistake. She'd get him to tell her all about it some time.

But right now she was enjoying herself too much to break the mood. She was wet and hot. The scent of her arousal was strong. She swayed her hips so that Edward, catching a waft of spiced musk, gave a sort of strangled cry.

'Please Hetty,' he whispered. 'Please finish me.'

He twisted his head around, trying to look up between her spread legs to her furred sex.

'No you don't, my lad.'

Lifting her hand, Hetty brought the back of the brush down on his naked buttocks. The sound was satisfyingly solid. The firm flesh trembled and grew redder. Edward seemed beside himself. He made little animal sounds while he bucked and thrust as if he had his cock buried inside her.

Hetty stood up. Edward remained on all fours. His head hung down. His arms and legs were trembling. He looked thoroughly chastened. Hetty decided he'd had enough for his first lesson. She took a few paces back.

'May I get up?' Edward said.

'Ask properly,' Hetty snapped.

'Please. May I?'

Hetty laughed. 'You can do better than that. Try harder now. Ask as nicely as you can. Remember to show me the proper respect.'

Edward was silent for a moment. Then he turned to meet her gaze. The naked admiration, the pleading expression in his eyes, sent a warm jolt of pleasure to her throbbing sex.

'Please – Mistress. May I be permitted to stand,' he said slowly and with relish.

'You may,' Hetty said. 'Keep your shirt raised and approach me.'

Edward stood up slowly, wincing at the soreness in his buttocks. Obediently he held the shirt high above his waist.

'Turn so that I can look at you,' Hetty said.

She cast cool eyes over his deep rose-red buttocks,

a startling contrast to the whiteness of the rest of him. He watched her face anxiously for signs of approval. She was careful to keep her face expressionless as she looked him over. His thighs were trembling slightly still. His erect cock stood up straight and proud. The purplish end bobbed against his navel.

He was trying hard not to look at her white belly and thighs, revealed by the tucked-up nightdress. Lowering one hand Hetty moved her fingers across her pubic curls. Edward's eyes followed the movement. She seemed about to speak, but thought better of it.

Hetty smiled widely. 'You've been quite a good boy. I'm going to let you spend.'

'Oh thank you – '

'But only if'n you do as I say,' she cut in. 'It's no good begging me to let you have me. That'll have to wait for another time. I want to see you pull on that big cock of yours.'

'You mean you . . . You want to watch . . . To watch . . .' he tailed off, unable to complete the sentence.

'To watch you spurt your seed,' Hetty finished for him.

Edward's eyes opened wide. She knew that he had never admitted to anyone that he abused himself. She laughed at his naivety. Did he think she didn't know that men, women too, did such things?

'Well?'

'I can't.'

She hardened her voice. 'Are you a good boy or not?'

'I am. But . . .' Edward's face was scarlet. He seemed to be wrestling with himself.

'D'you want to be sent straight back to your cabin?'

Edward swallowed audibly. Slowly he shook his head.

'I'm a good boy – Mistress,' he whispered. 'Please don't make me do . . . that.'

Hetty ignored him and began stroking the soft bristles of the hairbrush over his exposed belly. Edward drew in his breath sharply. She moved the brush down and brushed the hair that curled around his thick cock-stem. Then she brushed his sensitive inner thighs.

'Well, Edward. Take a hold,' she said.

His face crimson with shame, Edward brought his hand up slowly and curled his fingers around his cock-stem.

'That's it. Do it the way you always do.'

He began moving his hand up and down, slowly, haltingly at first. The glistening purple end moved slickly in and out of the tube shape of his fingers.

Hetty watched in fascination. The tip of her tongue poked out to moisten her lips. Edward saw it and groaned, working his fingers faster. Beads of sweat stood out on his forehead. Faster and faster he worked, his nostrils flaring slightly and his face bound by concentration.

His scrotum tightened as his climax approached.

Hetty moved the hairbrush around to his backside and began stroking lightly across the flushed and burning skin.

Edward's face screwed up as he grunted and tensed. Hetty watched avidly as a jet of milky sperm spurted from his cock, followed by another and another. Edward's knees trembled and the muscles of his abdomen twitched as the last drops emerged and ran down his still engorged penis.

Hetty's breath came fast. She needed her own release. It had taken great control to concentrate solely on Edward when she was longing for his touch on her heated flesh. She stood up and moved away, leaving Edward holding up his spattered shirt.

'Clean yourself up,' she said, making her voice sound cold.

'But Hetty . . .'

'You can go now. But first take your leave of me in the proper manner.'

Edward looked puzzled for a moment, then he dropped to his knees and crawled over to her. He planted kisses on her feet, murmuring, 'Thank you, Mistress. Oh, thank you.'

'And next time you want to come to my cabin, you be sure to beg permission during the day. And if I agrees I'll slip you my handkerchief. If I gives you my handkerchief, without you asking for it, it means I want you. Then you must come. No disobeying me.'

'I won't. I will come Hetty darling. I mean – Mistress . . .'

Edward stammered his thanks as he wiped himself on his shirt. Donning his smoking jacket he crossed the room. In the doorway he looked over his shoulder. The expression on his face bordered on adoration. In another moment he had gone.

Hetty threw herself across the bunk with a groan. Her sex pulsed and throbbed and felt like it was on fire. Never had she been more aroused. She was almost sorry that she'd sent Edward away but it had been the right thing to do.

He'd be desperate for more – and soon.

Before long he'd be ready to do anything she asked. She'd bind him to her so strongly that he wouldn't be able to do without her.

A well-bred male slave, all of her own. A heady thought indeed. Hetty the parlour maid would never have dared to be so bold, but Hetty the lady's maid was another matter.

She'd remember this day as the day she discovered ambition.

She found she could not forget the sight of Edward's large cock as he worked it with his own hand. It had been a singularly exciting sight. How she longed for the feel of hard male flesh inside her. Her eye fell on the hairbrush lying discarded on the bedcover.

She picked it up. The handle of polished wood was about four inches long and thicker at the base than where it flared out into the mirror. She slipped it between her thighs and nudged experimentally at her outer sex lips. The wooden handle felt warm and firm, perfect.

Rolling onto her back she slipped the handle deep inside herself and worked it in and out. With the other hand she smoothed her sticky wetness over the flesh-hood and aching bud. While her busy fingers described circles around her engorged nub she moaned aloud.

The scenes with Edward were imprinted on her mind's eye. His big muscular buttocks glowing poppy-red; the way he worked his hips. She recalled details, each one adding a note of spiciness to her pleasure.

Her gasps of pleasure spurred her on and soon the wrenching waves were spreading over her sex and throbbing inside her belly. Her climax was strong and deep, fading gradually to leave a feeling of warmth and wellbeing.

Soon she snuggled down into the bunk, too sated to dwell any longer on the events of the night. The brush was pushed beneath the pillow, just in case she might wake and have need of it before the morning.

'Oh, Edward,' she sighed on the brink of sleep, 'what times we shall have.'

Chapter Six

Gwendoline used the length of her pencil to measure an angle on her drawing of a section of the *Persephone*'s rail. She took care to get the curves just right, the play of light and shade on the wood. But even as she completed the shading she felt her enthusiasm waning.

Oh the drawing was well enough, it was no worse than the others in the folder at her feet, but it wasn't what she wanted. All her drawings of the ship, the detailed studies of ropes, sails, the ship's wheel and capstan, were technically perfect, but they lacked – life – spirit.

Yes, that was it. She was bored. She needed a subject that would inspire her anew.

She set aside her drawing tools and stared out at the great heaving mass of the sea. Twenty days now. They'd passed Nantes and Lisbon and the fair weather held. Captain Casey had told her that morning that they were sailing past the bay of Cadiz.

'Before the month is out we'll be reaching the Gold Coast,' he told her.

'So soon?'

'Aye, the winds had been fair. Didn't I tell you you'd brought us luck? We've made good headway.'

'Will you have time to look at my drawings?' she said pertly.

He gave her a sidelong smile. 'Oh, there'll be time enough, my dear. You won't find me lacking in appreciation. Don't you fret none.'

She knew exactly what he meant. There had been a silent conspiracy between them since the night she'd dined with him and the other officers. Sometime there would be a reckoning, but she was not ready for that yet. She still needed to gather her courage.

'In . . . in my own time,' she said, marvelling at her daring. By answering she had made it clear that she understood his inference.

'As you wish, my dear,' he said smiling with all the confidence of his years. 'I'm at your service.'

He was just what she needed, she decided. Relaxed and experienced. Nothing seemed to ruffle him. Captain Casey would soon do her the great favour of relieving her of the troublesome burden of her virginity.

As Captain Casey strode about the deck inspecting and giving orders, Gwendoline put some thoughts firmly aside for the present. Africa was drawing closer. She could almost feel the change in the wind. The waves were white-capped today. She fancied that she could see the galloping white horses of fairy tales.

It was perceptibly warmer though there was still a chill from the wind. Soon she would be able to change out of her stout twill suits and into the lighter muslin dresses in her trunk. She would get Hetty to sort them out. They would need hanging so that the creases fell out.

It had been almost a week since she surprised Hetty with Ned Woodley. She knew that Hetty and Ned had snatched odd minutes together, but they hadn't been able to sneak away to Hetty's cabin.

'Don't forget,' Gwendoline said to Hetty, knowing that she need say nothing more.

Hetty grinned knowingly. And Gwendoline felt a tight little knot of excitement in her stomach. Hetty would tell her when the time came and then she'd be able to watch. For the first time she'd actually *see* what men and women did together.

With that new knowledge, might she not be tempted to ask Captain Casey to enlighten her and soon? Her chin came up at the thought. You could have been the one, Jonathan, to show me what bodily pleasures are, had you not scorned my inexperience.

It surprised her still that each time she recalled the incident by the river she felt so angry and hurt.

Across the poop deck, partly screened from Gwendoline by the ship's wheel and the wooden casing that held the mechanism which controlled it, Jonathan looked up from the book he was reading.

Dammit but he couldn't concentrate when Gwendoline was nearby. He had seen how she threw down her pencils and thrust the drawing into the folder that rested against her knees.

What was she thinking as she stared out to sea? Was she picturing Africa, as he was? He wasn't surprised that she had lost patience with sketching parts of the clipper. She had talent, real skill – but she needed to stretch herself. He grinned, imagining her retort if he was to suggest such a thing.

He and Gwendoline had established a truce of

sorts, but their conversations were all on a superficial level. If he attempted the slightest familiarity she bristled at him like an alley cat. Yet he thought that she expected him to challenge her and even enjoyed their verbal sparring. She had a fine mind and was quick to reply with a cutting comment.

How charming she looked with her green eyes flashing. It was tempting to goad her, just a little, to observe her reactions.

Pushing himself upright he moved across the poop deck to where she sat with the windbreak at her back. The tails of his frock coat flapped against his trousers and the wind tore at his hair.

'Not inspired this morning,' he said casually. 'Do you mind if I share your shelter for a moment?'

She turned towards him as he hunkered down beside her. He saw her start slightly at his proximity and then collect herself. Ah, she might pretend that she was cool towards him, but underneath . . .

'Inspired? Oh, you mean my sketches.'

She smiled and put up a hand to brush away a strand of hair which was protruding from her bonnet.

'I'm quite out of temper with drawing. I can't seem to settle to any subject today.'

Jonathan grinned, showing his perfect white teeth. 'Perhaps the subject matter is what's wrong,' he said.

She looked at him steadily. 'You have something to say. I can see that.' Her mouth twisted into a wry little grin. 'I shall probably regret asking you, but what subject do you suggest I concentrate on?'

'You could try drawing from life. I can see that your studies of the ship are proficient. But don't you think that your style is too – lively? Too exuberant for seascapes and – '

'Thank you for your advice,' she interrupted stiffly.

'I did not know that you included art criticism amongst your many skills.'

He inclined his head. 'I do not. I am only a willing amateur. Everything about you fascinates me. So, for the present I have an opinion about art. But, even so, I recognise real talent when I see it.'

'Really?' Gwendoline said, pointedly ignoring his intimate tone. 'But you will allow me to decide on my own subject matter?'

He inclined his head. 'As you wish. But you did ask. Do not reject my comments out of hand. Look over there. Why not give that a try?'

Without waiting to see whether she took him seriously, he turned his back and began walking towards the ladder which led down to the main deck. He heard her little intake of breath as she looked in the direction he'd indicated and knew that she'd understood.

The sailor swabbing the deck, who was just coming into her line of view, wore only a tattered pair of trousers, cut off at the knee. His torso was spare and golden-brown, each muscle sharply defined. The young man was not yet twenty, but aged prematurely by the sea and the sun, as were all sailors.

Gwendoline had probably never considered drawing the human form, especially a partly-clothed male. It was a daring suggestion and would be considered outrageous by the women of her own class.

If Gwendoline noticed the sailor's undress she would normally have politely ignored it – or at least have pretended to. He could imagine the shock on her face. If she drew the half-naked man she would have to make a considerable mental shift. Even to acknowledge the sailor's presence would be considered the height of bad manners in polite company.

Gwendoline was a rebel amongst her own kind,

but Jonathan didn't know if she would be able to bring herself to shake off the shackles of outward respectability. He knew how she felt inside, but this would be a further leap into independence for her. To sketch the sailor she would have to stare at him, to study him minutely.

But if he knew her as well as he thought he did, she'd rise to the challenge.

Sneaking a look at her as he descended the ladder backwards he saw her pause. Slowly she picked up her pad and pencil and began squinting down the pencil's length, measuring and judging perspective. Her face was bound by concentration and something else. There was enthusiasm and passion in her eyes now.

She looked around quickly to see if anyone was watching, then he saw her bend over the drawing pad and set to with a flourish.

'That's it Gwendoline,' he said aloud. 'You only needed showing the way.'

With a satisfied smile on his lips he went below decks.

'Tonight Miss,' Hetty said with a nervous smile. 'If you still means what you said.'

'You know I meant it, Hetty. So, is Ned to be told?'

'Oh, no Miss! He'd never agree. You must hide somewhere. He mustn't know that we're being watched.'

Gwendoline was silent for a moment while she sought a solution.

'Ah I have it. You shall use my cabin. It's bigger than yours. Tell Ned that I'm to be keeping the Captain company. Now, help me empty this trunk and position it. This will do well for a hiding place.'

* * *

Gwendoline made herself comfortable on cushions inside the trunk. She wore only her chemise as there was no room for bulky garments. Besides she expected to be inside the trunk for some time and it would get hot.

Hetty propped the trunk lid open a little and stood back.

'Can you see, Miss?'

'Yes. Perfectly. How does it look?'

'Oh it's fine enough from here. No one would know that you're in there.'

Hetty began to giggle and Gwendoline, infected with the same sense of the ridiculous, joined in.

Her chuckles were muffled by the trunk lid. Hetty opened it up and looked down on Gwendoline who was curled up with laughter.

'Oh Hetty. This is the limit! I can hardly believe that we're doing this. I must have quite taken leave of my senses.'

Hetty spluttered with laughter.

'Oh it's a jolly jape and no mistake,' she said holding her sides. 'What would Edward say? I can just imagine his face!'

The question provoked more giggles. They laughed until the tears filled their eyes and their faces were red. Gradually they calmed.

'That's enough now,' Gwendoline said. 'Close the lid and fetch Ned. It's probably a good thing that we had our little outburst, but I'm quite composed now.'

Hetty took hold of the lid. She looked serious. 'Oh Miss, I don't know as I should . . .'

'Fiddlesticks! You always say that. And then you go and do whatever it is. Go on now.'

'But this time – I'm not sure . . .'

'Hetty . . .' Gwendoline said in a warning tone.

'All right. Don't get your dander up. I wasn't saying I was backin' out.'

'Good. Just forget I'm here and enjoy yourself.'

Hetty let out her breath with a sigh of indignation. 'Forget you're there? I'll try.'

Gwendoline heard the cabin door close softly as Hetty went out. She settled down to wait. It wouldn't be long. She heard the noises of the ship all around. There was the scuff of feet as the watch was changed. Somewhere a door slammed. And then the cabin door was opened.

Gwendoline held her breath, not daring to move a muscle lest she gave away her presence.

'Come on in. It's all right,' Hetty said, her voice soft and wheedling.

'What if we're discovered. Are you sure it's safe?' Ned's heavy tread made the floorboards creek. He sounded reticent but he closed the door quickly.

'Shhhh,' Hetty admonished him. 'Come over here to the bunk and sit down next to me. You'll make less noise that way.'

'Happy to oblige,' Ned grinned and reached for her.

Hetty snuggled into his embrace, responding eagerly to his kisses. Ned's big hands slid up her arms and cupped her breasts. Hetty pulled away smiling.

'Easy now. I've waited a while for this. Make it good for me Ned and you won't be sorry.'

Ned grinned. 'You know what you want all right. And Ned here's about to see that you get it.'

Hetty gave a little squeal of delight as he pushed her back on the bunk.

'Show me then Ned. Let me see what you've got inside that uniform of yorn to pleasure a country lass with.'

She sank back on the pillow and looked up at him.

Ned swore softly under his breath as his fingers reached for the buttons on the flap of his trousers. Hetty's eyes narrowed and the tip of her tongue snaked out to moisten her lips.

In her hiding place, Gwendoline's eyes opened wide. She knew what Hetty was doing. This was all for her benefit. Her breath came faster and she could not look away as, slowly, Ned took out his engorged cock.

'That do you?' he said to Hetty, a smile curving his full mouth.

'Oh, yes Ned,' Hetty breathed. 'I never saw one finer.'

Gwendoline stared transfixed by her first ever sight of a male organ. All Hetty's descriptive words had not prepared her for the actuality. It was so big, so thick around, marked with strong-looking veins and rather ugly. She hadn't expected it to be so . . . so florid. And the dark hair curling around the base of Ned's belly, the two stout balls . . . Why it looked rather dangerous.

Ned's fingers stroked lovingly up the stout shaft of his penis. The loose cock-skin covering the swollen tip slid back and forth as Ned stroked himself. Gently he pulled back the skin until the moist, purple glans was laid bare.

'Well, now you've seen it, why don't you take a closer look,' Ned said gruffly.

Hetty moved down the bunk until she was lying close to the kneeling Ned. Ned pulled down his trousers and Hetty laid a hand on each muscled thigh. As Hetty took the swollen cock-head into her mouth, Ned let out a sigh of pleasure.

Gwendoline slapped both hands over her mouth so that she could not cry out. What was Hetty doing? She was sucking on that great monstrous – thing.

She had never mentioned that women did such things. It seemed a dreadful thing to do, but Ned was obviously enjoying it. Hetty too. Ned's face was creased with pleasure and he uttered short little gasps as Hetty moved her head back and forth.

'Better stop now,' he said pulling back. 'Else I'll spend in your mouth.'

Hetty smiled and sat up. 'That would never do would it? Here's the place for that fine fellow.' And she lay back and raised her skirts above her knees.

With a groan Ned thrust his hands up the sides of her legs, squeezing her sturdy thighs, and pushing her skirts higher. Hetty wore loose cotton drawers, open at the crotch. She let her thighs fall open as Ned caressed her, his thick fingers stroking her pubic mound.

'Do you like it when I do this – and this,' Ned murmured, slipping one finger into her juicy little cleft and working it back and forth.

'Oh yes,' Hetty whispered. 'Spread me with two fingers and rub my little bud.'

Gwendoline could not believe her ears. Hetty was telling Ned exactly what to do and he was responding eagerly. She had thought that men *did* that thing to women and women let them. Mating was some animal thing of hurting and thrusting. Until Hetty told her otherwise she had thought that there was no pleasure to be had for women.

She was vastly intrigued. Hetty was moving her hips towards Ned's hand as he continue to tease and rub at her exposed sex. Gwendoline stared at the area between Hetty's thighs. She had never seen a woman's sex, not even her own. That was a state that must be remedied immediately.

Hetty had a lot of hair at the base of her belly. Ned seemed to like it. He tugged and twirled the dark-blonde curls playfully, while Hetty laughed huskily. When Hetty spread her legs more widely Gwendoline saw her parted sex. It looked shockingly red and wet. There were delicate folds and shadowed places. How complex it looked. And how fascinating. So that was the seat of a woman's pleasure.

Gwendoline was keen to know more. How did it feel when Ned used his fingers to stroke lightly across Hetty's secret flesh? She would ask her to describe the sensation in detail later. A throbbing had begun between her own thighs. She felt moist and there was a sort of aching heaviness. Did her sex look like Hetty's, she wondered, all plump and receptive?

Hetty moaned deep in her throat as Ned pushed one thick finger inside her. Her pubic curls were wet with her juices. Ned's knuckles grew damp as Hetty ground her hot sex down onto him. With the pad of his thumb he rubbed at a spot near where the flesh-lips joined Hetty's belly.

With a series of sharp little cries Hetty climaxed.

'Oh Ned, you know how to pleasure a girl. And right soundly,' Hetty murmured against his mouth.

'My turn now,' Ned said, positioning himself between Hetty's still spread thighs.

Gwendoline watched as Ned rubbed the plum-like cock-head up and down Hetty's wet slit. Then he pushed his thick cock all the way inside Hetty. Gwendoline wondered if it hurt. It seemed to be a tight fit. Hetty's red flesh collared Ned's shaft as if reluctant to let him go.

And by the way Hetty was moaning and wrapping her legs around Ned's broad back, Gwendoline decided that it must feel very nice indeed to have a man do that thing to you.

Ned's muscular buttocks pumped back and forth

and Gwendoline saw how the big cock slid in and out of Hetty. They both seemed engrossed in their own pleasure. Hetty's head tossed back and forth on the pillow and Ned's eyes were screwed tight shut.

Soon Hetty was making those high-pitched little noises again and Ned buried himself ever more deeply inside her eager flesh. With a great cry, muffled by the skirts rucked up round Hetty's waist, Ned climaxed.

Gwendoline was spellbound. Nothing, not even her secret talks with Hetty, had prepared her for the beauty and savagery of the act of love itself.

The artist in her rose to the fore. Suddenly she knew exactly what she would draw from now on. She was eager to get to her artist's tools. Already she was sketching the scene on the bunk in her mind. Oh what a picture she would make. And wouldn't Hetty be shocked and pleased.

She hoped Captain Casey hadn't changed his mind. Suddenly she was certain that she wanted to experience the pleasures of the body for herself.

The only question was – when?

'Look here Gwendoline,' Jonathan said the next morning, pointing across the expanse of sea to what looked like a line of mist in the distance.

Gwendoline strained to see. 'It can't be already. Can it? Is that . . . is it Africa?' she said.

'It is indeed. The African coast. We have a way to go yet before we reach our destination, but that's Africa for certain. I wanted to be the one who showed it to you. So, we've had our first sight of the Dark Continent together.'

She couldn't look at him. It was such a special moment of intimacy.

'But it isn't your first sighting. You've been here lots of times before,' she said, hiding the emotion she felt behind a light tone.

'True. But I never felt the way I do at this moment.'

Gwendoline swallowed. Her mouth had dried. He hadn't tried to hide how he felt. The emotion in his voice was naked, raw.

She felt that he had given her a special gift. Unwanted. Unasked for. Oh why must he always make her feel this way? She had tried to think of him as just a friend, but it was impossible. They were both passionate, artistic people. It was inevitable that they would strike sparks from each other.

She turned to him and laid a shaking hand on his breast. Under the leather waistcoat she felt the strong, heavy beat of his heart.

'Jonathan . . .' she began.

He enfolded her hand in his, holding it so tightly that she was a little afraid of the strength of him.

'Don't say anything else Gwenie. It would spoil the moment. There'll be time enough for everything later. I haven't forgotten that we have unfinished business.'

She was silent, listening intently with inheld breath while he continued.

'You and I were meant to come here. Just look at that faint line on the horizon. Can you imagine what lies waiting for us. Soon you'll see her more clearly. She's green and gold and scarlet. You'll never get the smell of her or her taste out of your head. Oh, Gwenie, once she's in your blood there's no denying her. She puts her mark on you, burning into your soul like a brand!'

Gwendoline trembled at the depth of passion in his voice. He sounded like he was speaking about a lover. For the first time he had used an endearment.

No one had ever called her 'Gwenie' like that. She liked the sound of it on his lips.

And Jonathan called Africa 'her'. Female, the way men referred to their ships. Jonathan loved the Dark Continent with all his heart and soul, that was plain to see.

Could he ever feel that way about a woman, however complex or talented? One day she was determined that she'd find out.

But for now, she savoured the moment. The faint, misty line of the far off coastline looked insubstantial; like a dream. But this was no dream. Soon they'd be there.

Another week or so Captain Casey said, before they sailed into the Gulf of Guinea and put into a port somewhere just beyond the Gold Coast. He'd told her the name of the place but the African word was difficult on her tongue.

And then, intruding into her thoughts, came the realisation that she had little time left to accomplish that other task. How could she even think of that at this moment? She felt a little ashamed even while a hot excitement at what she was about to do coursed through her.

A secret smile curved her lips. It was a good thing that Jonathan wasn't a mind reader, though at times he came close to it.

What a creature of disturbed passions she had become. Africa and Jonathan Kimberton might not be good for me, she thought. But it was far too late to worry about that.

There was no going back now, not in any sense whatever.

Chapter Seven

*H*aving made her decision to approach Captain Casey, Gwendoline was eager to arrange things. Perhaps an intimate dinner in her cabin would be a good beginning. She lay making plans, imagining what she'd say to the captain.

Her cheeks grew hot as she tried to picture his naked body. Would he be strong and muscular, like Ned? And would his cock be so impressive? She could hardly wait to find out. Tomorrow night, she decided. That's when I'll tell him that I've made my mind up. With that thought she drifted off to sleep.

She awoke in the middle of the night to find herself being tossed from side to side in her bunk as the clipper pitched and rolled. There was a noise like the screaming of wounded animals and a great creaking and groaning of the ship's timbers. The cabin door flew open and a distraught Hetty stumbled into the room.

'Oh Miss, I'm scared. It's a terrible wild night out there. We'll all be drowned.'

'Nonsense,' Gwendoline said stoutly, though her

own heart was hammering with alarm. 'It's just a storm. Captain Casey will see us through it.'

As there came the sound of a great wave crashing down onto the deck, Hetty whimpered. Gwendoline threw back the bedclothes.

'Climb in with me, Hetty. It'll be a squeeze but we'll manage.'

Gwendoline moved back to make room for Hetty, more glad than she cared to admit for the other woman's company. Hetty snuggled up close to Gwendoline and clung tightly to her.

'At least we're wedged in so tightly that we won't be thrown from the bunk,' Gwendoline said, trying to ease their fear with a trace of humour.

She might have sounded more convincing if her voice hadn't shaken so. The sounds from on deck were terrifying. Above the din of the wind and waves, they heard the faint sounds of raised voices as the Captain and officers shouted orders.

Hetty trembled. 'It sounds as if all the hounds of hell have been let loose,' she murmured. 'Oh, poor Ned. Poor Edward. I hope they're both safe.'

At that moment the ship gave a shudder and listed so sharply that Gwendoline had to cling on to the side of the bunk. The lantern crashed to the floor and went out. Hetty screamed and began to cry. Despite her brave words earlier Gwendoline went cold with terror. She put her arms around Hetty and held her tight.

'We can only wait and pray for the storm to end,' she said, hoping fervently that no life would be lost to the savagery of the angry sea.

Sometime during the long night Jonathan fought his way to Gwendoline's cabin. The flicker of his lantern pierced the inky blackness.

His face, framed by strands of wet hair, looked

white and strained. He wore oilskins and a thick seaman's sweater. Runnels of salt water streaked his clothing.

'Are you all right?' he said anxiously.

'No!' Hetty burst out. 'We're blasted terrified!'

'Me too,' Jonathan said with a narrow grin. 'And soaked right through. We all are. At least you're dry down here. Just hold on and stay put. The Captain thinks the storm will blow itself out in a few hours. This stretch of coastline is famous for its squalls.'

'A few more hours of this!' Hetty wailed. 'Oh Lord deliver us.'

'Thank you for coming to check on us,' Gwendoline said fervently. 'It helps to know that the end's in sight.'

Jonathan nodded. 'I've weathered worse than this. Rest assured. I must get back, I'm needed on deck.'

In another moment he had gone.

It was difficult in the darkness to gauge the passing of time, but there were signs that the storm was abating. Gwendoline judged it to be near dawn before the terrible screaming of the wind died down. The clipper still rolled from side to side, but there were no more of the alarming pitches that threatened to throw Gwendoline and Hetty to the cabin floor.

Gwendoline thought it safe to relight the lantern and both of them felt better when the fitful yellow light filled the cabin.

Hetty relaxed a little, though her face looked white and her lips were still pinched by fear.

'It's better now, but this could still go on for hours,' she complained. 'I wish I could sleep. It's borin' just lyin' here. I'd kill for a mug of grog.'

Gwendoline agreed. She could almost taste the mixture of rum and hot water. 'The storm's bound to have put the cooking range out. There'll be no food or drink for some time yet. Maybe if we tell each other stories it would pass the time.'

'I don't know no stories . . .' Hetty began.

'There must be something we can talk about.'

Hetty smiled wickedly, half-turning towards her and propping herself on one elbow.

'Maybe you'd like to ask me some more about pleasuring. I knows you already asked me all about how it felt when Ned futtered me, but you always has more questions.'

Gwendoline laughed. 'You know me too well, Hetty. And you're a good friend. Who else would tell me all the things I want to know?'

'Captain Casey?' Hetty said cheekily. 'He's hot for you and you know it. He'd be eager to talk to you. And to do a lot more besides.'

'Hetty!' Gwendoline said. 'How is it that you seem to know everything?'

'I know men, Miss. I've had a fair few since the ploughman showed me the way. In some ways they're all the same. You'll see that when you start on in with them.'

Gwendoline was silent for a moment. Hetty was so much wiser than she was in many ways. Certainly when it came to bodily pleasures, Hetty was an expert.

'Hetty, there is something . . .' she began.

'Thought so,' Hetty said with satisfaction. 'Fire away then Miss.'

'It's about . . . well, I'm not sure whether I'm normal.'

Hetty waited, her eyes wide with interest. Gwendoline swallowed hard and plunged in, speaking in a little rush before she lost her courage.

'When Ned was futtering you I saw your – quim, as you call it – for the first time. So after that I . . .

looked at myself there – with a hand mirror. The thing is my – quim doesn't look the same as yours. And I thought perhaps . . .' She tailed off unable to continue.

Hetty chuckled. 'You think you's malformed? Lord love ya' Miss. Quims is not all the same. It's the same as with faces. Same thing with cocks too. Some are big, some small. But whatever they're like they're all fine for pleasuring – even if it's only the solitary vice! But you surely know a bit about that.'

Gwendoline listened in an agony of embarrassment. She shook her head.

'No. I know absolutely nothing, beyond what you tell me.'

Hetty grinned. 'Go on with you. You don't have to keep no secrets from me.'

Gwendoline looked at her blankly.

'But I haven't.'

'You can't mean . . . Ain't you never pleasured yourself?'

'Of course not! I mean – even if I'd wanted to. I wouldn't know how.'

Hetty pursed her lips and expelled the air in a whistle.

'But everyone does that. It's natural like. I found out how to do it when I was ten years old. My cousin showed me in the barn one summer. We used to do it to each other. Oh, I know the gentry don't talk about such things, but they do them all the same.'

Gwendoline felt ignorant and foolish. Part of her education had been missed out. If everyone did it, as Hetty said, how cruel it had been of her old governess to mislead her.

'But I'm sure you're wrong Hetty. Miss Templeton said that our female parts were sinful and not for touching or even thinking about. She would certainly never have abused herself in that way.'

Hetty gave a shout of laughter. 'You don't know the half of it, Miss. She wasn't the dried up old spinster she seemed, that's for sure! You ask Edward.'

Gwendoline looked at her blankly. 'Oh. I . . . I don't know what to think now.'

Hetty sighed. 'I think it's time you learnt what every country girl knows.'

'How?'

'Well, if'n you want, I'll show you how to do it. To pleasure yourself.'

'Oh, Hetty. Would you? I hardly dared to ask.'

Hetty's generous mouth curved in a smile. 'It'll certainly help pass the time.'

There was hardly room for both of them to lie full length in the bunk, but they managed it with a squeeze. Hetty gathered her nightgown in two hands and pulled it up to lie in folds around her waist. Hesitantly at first Gwendoline did the same.

'Now put your hand on your quim and sort of press and roll your fingers,' Hetty said.

Gwendoline did so. It felt nice so she continued to do it.

'You has to find the way that's best for you,' Hetty said. 'Try rubbing your fingers up and down a bit now. Feels like a split plum there, don't it? If'n you slide your fingers inside the plum, you'll find a hard little bud near the top. It's got a tiny hood of flesh over it.'

'Oh, yes,' Gwendoline said delightedly. 'I've found it. It feels nice when I tickle it.'

Hetty laughed. 'And so it should. That little scrap is like a tiny cock. It swells up and gets all sensitive when you plays around with it. If a man's experienced he knows that a woman will reach her peak if he strokes or sucks her pleasure bud.'

'Sucks!' Gwendoline said, a shiver of mixed horror and awe flooding over her.

'You've so much to find out,' Hetty murmured, her breath beginning to quicken.

While Gwendoline stroked herself tentatively, lost in the subtle sensations, Hetty worked away at herself. Soon she was breathing fast and beginning to move her hips. Her arm brushed against Gwendoline as she pleasured her juicy little sex, bringing herself expertly to a peak.

Hetty groaned deep in her throat as she climaxed. The sound sent a dart straight to Gwendoline's stomach. Her own sex had grown soft and pliant and her fingers were wet with the juices seeping out of her. The erect little bud was more prominent now. She flicked it gently back and forth with her fingertips.

How intriguing was the sensation, like rolling a bead in oil. The tiny scrap seemed to pulse and itch with a life of its own.

Gradually the feelings intensified. She felt a gathering, a pooling of pleasure in her belly. She tensed the muscles in her belly and thighs, reaching for some unknown release. Surely she couldn't bear the build up of sensation.

Then, unexpectedly, a hot wave seemed to break over her. She felt deep internal pulsings, and tingles all over her body. So intense were the feelings that she cried out with the joy of them.

Triumph and happiness seemed merged inside her. She could do it. Everything worked. There was nothing wrong with her. She was no different from all the women Hetty had told her about.

'Hetty, I did it! I did it!'

'What? Oh, good,' Hetty said sleepily.

Gwendoline turned her head. Sated and relaxed Hetty was snoring softly. Gwendoline smiled and bent over to kiss her forehead.

'Thank you Hetty,' she breathed.

Then she slipped her hand between her legs again. Such a wonderful sensation must be experienced more than once. Besides, she needed the practice. Captain Casey would no doubt be relieved to find that she was not a complete novice.

The dying storm blew great gusts across the clipper's bow and sent spouts of water streaming from the poop deck. With a crack a spar detached itself and fell onto the deck, but neither Gwendoline nor Hetty noticed anything.

The crew were engaged in making repairs to the storm-damaged clipper over the next few days. The only injury had been to one young sailor who had been struck a glancing blow by the falling spar.

'Let's be having everything in order,' said Captain Casey. 'We're only days away from putting into port and I want the *Persephone* fairly gleaming.'

From her position on the poop deck Gwendoline watched the activity. Captain Casey kept a well-run vessel and everyone was engaged in some task. The Captain himself seemed to be the only man who had time on his hands.

Edward and Jonathan were together, poring over more maps and examining various artifacts from Jonathan's store of treasures. No doubt Jonathan was still schooling Edward in Swahili and Bantu amongst other languages. She could imagine Edward's wooden expression and wondered when Jonathan would give up Edward as a lost cause on that count.

Hetty was busy too, chatting to the sailmaker as he sewed a rope around the edge of a finished sail.

Gwendoline gathered her courage. There might never be another chance as good as this one. As Captain Casey walked towards her, preparing to go below, she caught his attention.

'Might I ask your advice?' she said.

He paused, his eyes lighting up with interest.

'Surely now. How can I help you?'

'You'll think me foolish, but I cannot decide what apparel would be appropriate for when we land. I thought with your experience . . .' she finished lamely.

It was a transparent enough excuse to get him to come to her cabin, but she could think of nothing else. Besides she knew that he would understand what she was really saying.

He smiled, a mature and knowing smile.

'Well then, my dear. Let's be going to your cabin and I'll be happy to give you all the benefit of my experience.'

Gwendoline felt nervously excited as she preceded him down the corridor. At the door to her cabin she stopped suddenly, almost overcome by the enormity of what was about to happen.

'Captain Casey,' she said, her voice sounding breathless and a little panicky. 'I must tell you that I'm as nervous as a kitten.'

'Please call me Michael,' he said smiling gently. In the narrow corridor they stood pressed closely together.

'My very dear girl,' he went on seriously. 'Let me reassure you. I swear, on my honour, that I will not say or do anything to harm you. Neither will I seek to hurt you or cause you distress. Do you believe me?'

112

Looking up at his handsome face, at the attractive grey streaks in his hair, she nodded. There was an air of dependability about him and a certain kindness in his blue eyes. She smelt the aromatic tobacco on his clothes. There was the scent of lemon oil too and the faint salty musk of his maleness.

His proximity made her feel weak. When she did not speak, he said, 'I'll go if you wish it. If you've changed your mind . . .'

'No,' Gwendoline said, a trifle huskily. 'Please, do come in, Captain . . . Michael.'

It seemed that he was happy to go along with the pretence of helping her choose some clothes. She was grateful that he let her take things at her own pace. Sitting on the bunk, he watched as she pulled a trunk into the centre of the cabin.

Her brief flare of courage had quite deserted her. But Michael Casey seemed completely at ease. He did not take her into his arms, as she half dreaded he would. Instead he threw himself full-length onto the bunk and lay back, watching her calmly. His arms were folded behind his head, his long legs stretched out, ankles crossed.

Gwendoline flashed him a nervous smile. She unbuckled the leather straps and opened the trunk lid.

'Well then, What shall I wear?'

'Hold the garments up for me,' he said smiling reassuringly. 'I've been told that I have impeccable taste in clothes!'

Gwendoline folded her lips on a grin.

'I won't ask who told you that.'

It was so easy, so companionable between them. Michael might have been a female friend, lying there.

The tension remained, but she was growing used to it. She began to relax.

'What do think of this one?' She held up a pale green muslin day dress.

'Hmmm. A possibility,' he said appearing to give the matter serious consideration.

Gwendoline felt the urge to laugh. One after the other she held up a number of light, summer-weight dresses. Soon the cabin was festooned with a froth of pale muslins and pastel-dyed silks.

She spread her hands. 'That is all.'

'Surely not.'

She coloured slightly. 'Well. Except for some – underthings.'

Michael smiled broadly. 'They are the best of all! Let me see them.'

He must have seen her hesitation, the briefest moment of embarrassment. They were approaching a dangerous intimacy.

'If you would rather not . . .' he began. 'Remember what I told you? I meant every word.'

Gwendoline didn't want to stop. She felt very excited. Michael's attractive, mature presence seemed to fill the small cabin. They were enclosed in their own small world. There was no one to see what they did.

With shaking fingers she held up a fine cambric chemise. It was low at the neckline and trimmed with lace.

'Beautiful,' Michael breathed. 'Hold it against your body. Like that. Yes.'

She held up the next garment and the next. Garments of fine openwork, frilled drawers, ribbon-trimmed, embroidered stockings, she held them all up. Michael just lay there, looking at her with a relaxed smile.

Gwendoline grew bolder. The camisole she held

up now, was of fine, peach-coloured silk, almost transparent. It had narrow straps and a deep wide neckline.

'Lovely,' said Michael appreciatively. 'The colour flatters your pale skin.

Smiling, she looked down. The peach silk was gathered in deep folds in her lap. The silence stretched between them. She held her breath. Unspoken words hung in the air. This is it, she thought, from here there's no going back.

'You know what I want, don't you now?' Michael said softly with meaning.

'Yes,' she whispered. 'I . . . I think so.'

'Let me hear you say it. I want to know that this is what you want too.'

She flushed deep scarlet, knowing that he would not force her past any self-imposed limit. Her next words seemed forced from her:

'Would . . . would you like me to put this chemise on?'

'Yes. Oh, yes,' he said.

She heard the naked desire in his voice and was glad that he was so much older than herself, so experienced. She found the way he was looking at her devastatingly attractive. She liked his languor; a younger man would have been too eager.

Standing facing him, she slowly unfastened her bodice. The loops were snug over the buttons and it took her some moments to undo them and to slip the tight sleeves down her arms.

Next she pulled her chemise over her head. Underneath she wore a sleeveless camisole and over that, her stays.

Her courage dimmed. She threw Michael a pleading glance. He looked at her steadily, a slight frown of concentration between his eyes.

'Your stays and that other garment now,' he said softly. 'Let me look at your skin, your breasts. I know they will be beautiful.'

She felt the leashed tension in him. His excitement communicated itself to her. He did not look so calm, so collected now.

Slowly Gwendoline unhooked her stays and laid the garment aside. Free from constriction her breasts fell forward, pressing against the only covering that was left to her. She crossed her arms protectively across her bosom.

Michael said nothing, only smiling gently and waiting. But his eyes were dark with passion. Gwendoline conquered the dawning shame, and before she lost her courage, gripped the final garment and pulled it over her head.

Now she was naked to the waist. For the first time in her adult life, her torso was open to the glance of another. Michael let out a sigh, that was almost a groan.

'I knew you'd look like that,' he whispered. 'Will you come a little closer?'

Gwendoline moved nearer to the bunk. She felt no shame now. Holding her shoulders back, so that her breasts were thrust out proudly, she let him fill his gaze.

'Your skin is like cream,' Michael said in a low hypnotic voice. 'And your nipples are like cherries. Ah, it's lovely you would look if your nipples were erect.'

Dare she? Gwendoline half-closed her eyes. Her hands moved upwards, seemingly of their own accord.

'Ah yes, my dear. Caress yourself. That's it. Like that.'

Gwendoline rubbed her hardening nipples

between fingers and thumbs, until they grew rigid. They tingled and throbbed. She rolled them, pinching them harder until the peaks were swollen, turgid. Looking down she watched the movements of her hands. The nipples, protruding from her fingertips were the colour of rosebuds.

She had never seen them look like that. Her hands described circles, moved downwards and stroked her ribcage. She spread her hands on her narrow waist, the fingers and thumbs almost meeting.

Delicious sensations swept her body. She revelled in the thought that Michael watched, enjoying her, as she enjoyed the budding of her new womanhood.

She was conscious of the texture of her skin. All of her seemed to have come to life. Between her thighs, moisture gathered – newly familiar since Hetty's tutoring. Lifting her arms she drew the pins from her hair. Red-brown tresses tumbled over her shoulders. The caress of hair on her overly sensitive skin, brought a gasp to her lips.

She wanted . . . something. Something more. Raising her eyes to the captain she smiled, knowing that her expression had softened, become languid.

'Yes. Oh, yes. Ask me, my dear girl,' he said, his voice sounding strained now as if he too could hold back no longer.

'Touch me, Michael. Please . . .' Gwendoline whispered. 'I think I shall die if you do not.'

With a groan Michael rolled off the bunk and knelt at her feet. He gathered Gwendoline to him, his arms encircling her waist as he pulled her close. Pressing his face to her full skirts, he slid his hands up her naked back, stroking, massaging the skin. Then his hands moved down to cover her buttocks.

Gwendoline bent over as his hair brushed the bare skin of her stomach. Michael pressed his mouth to her skin. Through her skirts and petticoats, he kneaded her flesh, rolling the firm globes of her buttocks between his strong fingers.

The moisture between her thighs increased. She felt engorged there, sweetly aching.

'Show me what to do,' she breathed.

Gently Michael led her over to the bunk. She remained standing while he sat down. She ran her fingers through his thick, grey-streaked hair, cradling his head in her arms. Then she almost cried out, as his hot questing mouth closed over one of her nipples.

'Oh, Michael,' she breathed, as he grasped both breasts, squeezing so that the engorged flesh stood out further and became an offering for his hungry mouth. His salt-roughened palms were rough on her flesh. He began suckling, firmly, taking each nipple in turn.

The pleasure was so intense, that Gwendoline felt faint. She swayed, her hips beginning to move in a rhythm as old as time itself. Michael took her weight, laying her on the bunk beside him. His mouth travelled up to her neck and then traced a burning path back to her breasts. His tongue and teeth teased her aching peaks until the pleasure became a kind of sweet agony.

'Oh, oh,' she gasped. 'I never felt anything so exquisite.'

Michael kissed her chin and nibbled at her mouth, nuzzling her bottom lip. The length of his long hard body was pressed close.

'This is the beginning only, my dear. There are so many delights in store for you. I envy your innocence.'

'Show me, quickly,' she pleaded.

He kissed each of her eyelids. 'That I shall. But not

118

everything at once. Pleasure is to be savoured. And you have time on your side. You will have many lovers in your life. Let this first time be special for us both.'

She moaned against his mouth as he teased her lips with his tongue.

'What would you have me do?' he said thickly.

Gwendoline raised her hips, excited beyond reason.

'Take off my skirt. Do everything. Do whatever you wish to me.'

Chapter Eight

Michael pulled off Gwendoline's skirt. He tossed it on the floor. Then he kissed her lips lightly and smiled in encouragement.

'Sit up my dear, and help me to take off these petticoats.'

Gwendoline did so and soon they joined the other garments on the floor. All she wore now was knee-length drawers, black stockings and high buttoned boots.

She reached for the ribbon at her waist, preparing to slip off her drawers, eager for Michael to resume his explorations, but he put his hand over hers.

'Leave them on. You look so beautiful, so wanton, as you are.'

Dipping his head he claimed her lips in a deep passionate kiss. Gwendoline felt a shock as his tongue met hers. The heat and wetness of his mouth was arousing. He tasted slightly of tobacco. Soon she gained the courage to explore Michael's mouth for herself, running the tip of her tongue around the inside of his lips.

It occurred to her only then, that Michael was still dressed in his captain's uniform. She felt the rough caress of the woollen jacket. The gilt buttons were cold and exciting against her skin. How strange it was to be undressed and vulnerable in the presence of this self-assured man. Strange and a little dangerous.

Then she forgot to think as Michael's hand slipped into the open crotch of her drawers.

The feeling was entirely different from when she stroked herself. As Michael trailed his fingers lightly over her shadowed mound, she gave a soft groan.

He smiled against her lips and asked her teasingly, 'Do you like that?'

'Oh, yes,' she breathed.

'And you want more? You're sure of it?'

'I want . . . I want you to do everything.'

Then she found herself beyond words as the stroking of his fingers over the soft pubic down changed to a light but firm pressure. Michael rubbed his fingers in a circular movement and all of her seemed to concentrate into a whirlpool of warm and languorous sensation.

She felt her centre turning to molten liquid. When he parted her sex-lips with his knowing fingers and began to lightly tease her hard little nub, she opened her thighs and pressed herself more closely to him. Her body seemed to open itself to him. The secret folds of her sex were eager to his expert touch.

He stroked upwards across the little flesh-hood, spreading her moisture over the emerging bud. The little scrap of flesh burned and tingled. She rubbed her pubis against his hand.

'Oh, Michael. Do not stop . . .'

'You have only to command me,' he whispered against her mouth.

Gwendoline felt how Michael trembled. His breath came in shallow gasps, seeming to match her own, but he held back from taking his own pleasure. She was again grateful for his maturity and patience.

As his knowing fingers continued to stroke and tease, her flesh-folds grew ever more slick and swollen. The sensations grew until she tossed her head from side to side on the coverlet. Nothing had prepared her for such pleasure. The thought that a man was touching her so intimately, committing a forbidden act on her unawakened body, added spice to the feelings coursing through her.

Her own moans rang in her ears. Oh the pleasure was wicked, so illicit, so intense.

'That's it, my dear. Reach for it. Give yourself up to it completely,' Michael urged her, his breath rasping in his throat.

There came that building, the coalescing of all the incredible pleasure until her flesh seemed to explode into rhythmic pulsings. Gwendoline was borne along on a high tide that threw her up and out and left her spent and gasping.

Michael kissed her tenderly. 'I love to watch a woman reach her peak,' he said. 'Your face looked so beautiful in the grip of passion.'

She smiled shakily, still bound by the afterglow of her climax.

'But . . . what about you? Did you not want to pleasure yourself?'

'I can wait,' he smiled. 'Though it's hard to resist you the way you look now, with your bold green eyes all drowsy and your lips swollen from my kisses.'

'Then do it to me – now. There's no need to wait.'

Michael's face was tender. There were lines around

his eyes and a slight slackness around his jaw, but he was still a startlingly handsome man.

'Is this truly what you want?' he said.

'Yes. I want it to be you,' she said, reaching up to stroke the slight stubble on his cheek.

'Once lost, your virginity cannot be regained. Will not your future husband wish to have the honour of claiming that prize?'

Gwendoline tossed her head.

'The "prize" is surely mine to give away or keep. Virginity is a burden to me. Take my innocence from me Michael. I truly wish you would.'

'In that case . . .' he grinned. 'How can I refuse?'

He kissed her again and she felt his gentle questing fingers move between her thighs and resume his ministrations. Her swollen sex was still sensitive and she leaned into him as he stroked and stimulated her afresh.

'There might be pain at first. I'll try to make it easier for you,' he said.

He inserted the tip of a finger inside her, working it back and forth, opening and readying her for the larger intrusion to come. When he pushed two fingers inside her, she made a little sound in her throat. Michael paused and looked down at her with concern.

'Have I hurt you?'

'No. It feels strange but somehow nice. Will you put – it, into me now?'

'To be sure I will. Part your thighs, my dear,' he said, adjusting his clothes.

She could not help recoiling slightly when she felt the length of his cock pressing against her skin. It felt hot and hard. Surely it would be too big. It would tear her as it entered her body. She wanted to look down at it, but she was too eager to have this moment done with.

Michael knelt between her thighs and raised her knees. The blunt head of his cock brushed against her sex, rubbing up and down her moist slit. He took time to let her get used to the new feeling, playing his cock-head across her bud, then down to nudge gently at the entrance to her body.

Gwendoline moved under him, stretching herself wide to accommodate him. Then Michael pressed forward and suddenly he was inside her. With a little cry she linked her legs around him.

There was pain, but less than she'd expected. And soon the feelings of pleasure built and banished the slight soreness. After Michael thrust a few times she found the rhythm. Moving her hips, she sheathed herself on the rigid shaft, meeting his passion with her own.

'Ah, you're a grand girl, so you are,' Michael murmured, cupping her buttocks in his rough hands and drawing her up towards him so that he could penetrate her more deeply.

Michael's face was intense and centred as he thrust strongly in and out. When he withdrew almost all the way and rimmed her entrance, Gwendoline felt her second climax approaching.

She closed her eyes, screwing up her whole face with concentration as Michael worked her up and down his thick cock. His heavy balls brushed against her upturned buttocks. She loved the silky caress of them. And she loved the way he held her, so lightly, but with such strength, pounding into her with his stout cock. She seemed to be filled with his flesh. The cock-head nudged against her womb on each inward thrust.

Suddenly he tensed and drew out of her. With a

loud groan Michael climaxed. Thick creamy fluid spurted onto her belly.

Gwendoline moaned with frustration. She had wanted him to keep on for longer. The feeling of his hardness inside her was so delightful. It had felt so good to be used and to use him in return. She was so near, too near to deny herself. Reaching down between their bodies she rubbed her sex in hard little circles.

Almost at once the wrenching waves of pleasure came over her. She clasped Michael tightly, rubbing her pelvis against him until the inner pulsings died away.

Michael pushed himself away and looked down at her. His face wore a grin from ear to ear.

'What a flower of passion y'are. You learn awful fast to take what you want from a man!'

Gwendoline smiled wickedly.

'I started late. Now I want to learn everything about the pursuit of pleasure.' Her voice softened with affection. 'I'm very grateful to you, Michael Casey, for your care and kindness. You've made me into a woman.'

He dropped a kiss on her nose. 'Nay. You needed no help there. You're more than enough woman for any man. 'Tis you I'm grateful to. You've made an old sea dog very happy.'

'Old? Surely not,' Gwendoline said. 'I'd hoped that we could repeat this exercise. But if you've no strength for it . . .'

Michael caught her to him and slapped her playfully on the buttocks.

'Maybe you're needing a lesson in manners, my dear! I'll show you what happens to young women who mock their elders!'

'Oh Michael . . .' Gwendoline murmured happily,

as he tossed her onto her stomach and yanked down her drawers.

'Must you go?' Gwendoline said sleepily much later.

Michael Casey kissed her lingeringly, then gently put her aside. Standing up, he began dressing in his uniform.

'You tempt me sorely. But I've stayed longer than I intended to already. I have duties to attend to. I'm captain of this clipper, remember? Besides you wouldn't be having Edward discover us together, would you? He'd keel-haul the both of us!'

'Oh I can handle my brother,' she said with a confident grin.

She smiled a secret smile. If Edward, Jonathan too, knew what she'd been doing for the past few hours they'd be profoundly shocked! It was all very well for Edward to futter Hetty whenever he felt like it, but absolutely forbidden for his sister to take her pleasure in a similar way.

She felt a wicked satisfaction at the thought of their joint outrage.

'It would just serve you right if I told you, Jonathan Kimberton,' she murmured, in a voice too low for Michael to hear. 'And wouldn't you feel jealous at the thought of Michael Casey's hands on me?'

Perhaps she would tell Jonathan one day, as payment for his eavesdropping of Hetty and herself in the summerhouse. How long ago that seemed now. Lord, but she was drowsy. Loving was such hard work. All she wanted to do now was sleep.

'Go then, and run your ship if you must,' she said, yawning and stretching voluptuously. 'I think I'll stay here. I'm not eager for my ration of salt pork and hard tack. Where shall we be when I awaken on the morrow?'

'We'll be set to drop anchor at Lagos. You'll have a short journey by steam-launch to the mainland before you reach your destination.'

'Oh good,' she said burrowing into the pillows. 'I can't wait to leave the ship. All these weeks at sea and now I shall actually see – her, as Jonathan calls Africa.'

'That you will. And I hope Africa is everything you hope it is.'

'Oh she will be. I'm certain of that.'

And Captain Casey, smiling a little sadly as he opened the cabin door, knew that she had forgotten him already. The young could be very cruel without realising the fact, he thought without rancour.

Gwendoline found that she wasn't as tired as she had first thought.

The growing heat made it difficult to get comfortable. And she kept thinking about what was waiting for her. They had travelled past the Gold Coast now and had entered what Jonathan told her was the Bight of Benin.

Visions of the glorious sunrises they'd been experiencing for the past few days impinged on her rest. How much more beautiful the skies would be when they formed a ceiling for the African landscape.

Tomorrow. Oh she could hardly wait for her first glimpse of the island of Lagos.

After resting for an hour or so, she gave up trying to sleep and rose from the bunk. She did not feel like dressing and joining the others. If Hetty had come in she would have confided in her, but Hetty was probably with Ned, making the most of her last hours aboard the clipper.

Poor Edward, Gwendoline mused, wondering if her brother had had his nose pushed out of joint.

Hetty told her that Edward pleaded for her favours now. It was hard to imagine her self-important brother asking for anything.

Lifting the heavy coils of hair away from her neck, Gwendoline looked at herself in the cheval glass. Would anyone guess that I've been changed forever, she thought. Do I look different?

Pulling on her drawers, she fastened them at the waist, but made no attempt to dress. Carefully, she studied her semi-nakedness in the mirror.

Her hair hung in a wild tangle of red-brown curls. Her face was flushed and her mouth looked like a bruised flower. The evidence was there for all to see. Oh how her body had awakened under Michael Casey's touch. She would always be grateful for his kindness.

Her breasts felt swollen and heavy. The nipples tingled as if they recalled Michael's fingers.

As she stared at herself with wonder and appreciation, she realised with a shock that she was becoming aroused by the sight of her own body. She forced herself to meet the eyes of her reflection and was pleased to see no trace of shame therein. Where was the harm in admiring her nakedness, after all? Michael had found her beautiful. And now she seemed to see herself through his eyes.

She felt a sense of wonder at her newfound sensuality. Sexual pleasure was a magic of sorts. It had left her spellbound. She felt that she had discovered a wonderful secret.

She wanted to experience more and right away. But she could hardly summon Michael Casey to her cabin. As pleasant as the interlude had been, they both knew that there would be no further contact between them.

Greatly daring, Gwendoline began to caress herself. Up until now she had stroked herself to a furtive climax under the bedcovers. How much more arousing to study her reactions, to watch herself as Michael Casey had watched her.

Her eyes flickered over her reflection in the mirror as she toyed with her nipples until they stood out, hard and erect. The little flares of sensation drew an answering response from her sex. She swept her hands down to her belly, dragging her fingertips over the slight ridges of her ribs.

Smiling she made herself wait, tantalising herself by stroking the soft bowl of her belly.

'It's so much better to be a little hungry. Isn't it, my dear,' she murmured to her reflection.

Gradually her fingers slipped lower and entered the gap in the crotch of the drawers. She stroked the silky brown hair on her mound. Shifting position, she opened her legs a little and slipped a finger inside the moist parted lips.

Gwendoline watched fascinated as her finger moved up and down. She could feel the hard little bud in its folds of tender flesh and glimpse a rim of pink flesh as the outer lips moved with the action of her fingers.

But although pleasant, the feelings were not as intense as earlier. She needed to be more relaxed, but she still wanted to watch herself.

Lying on her back on the bunk was better. If she propped her head on a pillow she could still see herself in the cheval glass.

Her shapely legs, clothed in long drawers, hung loosely over the side of the bunk. Her breasts were firm cones, falling a little to each side of her ribcage under their own weight. Lifting her legs, slowly and voluptuously, she splayed her knees. There, for the first time, her secret parts were displayed.

Now she could watch what her fingers did. Gwendoline spread her outer sex-lips with one hand and stared intently at the deep pink inner lips. They had a beauty of sorts, like the petals of a flower and there, hidden in the folds of delicious flesh, was the bud. That place which felt so wonderful when she stroked it.

She did it now.

Ah, the sensation as she stroked gently on the tip, then experimentally, she spread two fingers and rubber either side of the swollen bud. That was even better. Glancing in the mirror she saw her flushed face. Her eyes travelled down to her white thighs and open sex, surrounded by softly curling hair, framed in the the folds of her cambric drawers.

How much more – naked – she looked with her legs spread. Oh what a picture she'd make of this. It was a sight worthy of any artist's brush.

Oh, Jonathan, she thought, you would love to watch me do this. A surge of excitement flooded her anew at the thought. Her fingers became wet and slippery from the juices seeping out from inside herself. She exerted pressure on the outside sex-lips, stretching that deep-pink flower fully, so that all of her secret flesh was open to her avid gaze. Her bud stood proud of the surrounding flesh; a tiny hungry cock.

And there was the opening of her body, a little red still from the earlier activities.

Gwendoline pushed in a little way with one finger and met no obstruction. She was fully a woman now. Just wait until she told Hetty!

Using two fingers, she held her sex open and with the other fingers she stroked and rubbed herself. Her thighs quivered as the tension built. She rubbed faster, up and down her hot wet slit. Now and then she dipped two fingers into her body's opening, relishing the slight soreness.

With a breathy little sound, she plunged her fingers right inside her body, feeling the damp curling hair against her knuckles. Hot juices ran down her fingers. Her breath came in hoarse gasps as she moved her fingers in and out, simulating the thrust of a man's cock.

Oh, this was heaven. How wonderful that she could do this to herself as often as she wanted to.

Then she was there. Wave after wave of sensation flooded through her. It was too much. She clamped her thighs on her hand and rolled over, bucking and spasming, beyond all control.

Her buttocks clenched and relaxed, then finally grew still. Gwendoline's hand was trapped between her thighs, pressed firmly to her throbbing sex as gradually the pulsings died away.

'Oh, oh,' she groaned, loving to hear the sounds of her own pleasure. It seemed that the feelings grew stronger each time she accomplished that incredible rush of sensation.

She lay still, completely exhausted. It was some moments before she got her breath back. Then she smiled. A slow and lazy smile, full of a sense of self-achievement and with no small measure of pride.

She felt so clever and happy. Triumphant too. Her experience was unfolding in great leaps and bounds. Before long she'd be ready to challenge Jonathan. She had set out on a journey to Africa and the experience of that journey had widened immensely. And was to get wider still.

She hugged her knees to her chest. Jonathan set such great store by Africa and the effect that dark continent would have on her. She knew that he meant experience in the fullest possible sense. But had his plans for her included Michael Casey? She thought not.

How she had changed in a few short weeks on board this ship. She laughed and the sound was deep and husky.

Africa was almost upon them. She was like a glutton at a feast.

Sated for now, but eager for more.

The sound of the anchor chain playing out, rumbled through the ship, early next morning. A muffled cheer rose from the early watch.

Jonathan, a light sleeper, watched as the two-ton anchor dropped into the muddy waters of the coast off Lagos. Though the light was still thick and grainy, there were signs of activity on dry land. Lanterns made little tongues of flame, brilliant in the dawn haze.

The sound of huge breakers crashing onto the narrow strip of shore was loud and menacing. The *Persephone* could go no further inland. A steam launch would take them to the mainland and Dominic Rathbone would be waiting to meet them. Canoes would convey them upriver to the settlement.

Jonathan could imagine the excitement amongst the members of Rathbone's household and staff. There would be no one asleep this morn. Every man, woman and child would be awaiting the arrival of the clipper. A ship from England was a cause for celebration and they'd make the most of it.

Dominic Rathbone would have mustered his men early. A brief flicker of distaste crossed Jonathan's face as he recalled the dissolute persona that was Rathbone.

Dammit, he couldn't abide the man, though he

managed to be civil to him when he couldn't avoid a confrontation.

Dominic Rathbone was employed by the Farn-shawes to take care of the family's business interests in this part of the world. Jonathan found Dominic's methods and morals suspect, but Edward valued the man highly.

Well they wouldn't be staying long at Dominic's residence. Hopefully he could keep up the facade of friendliness until they set off into the tribal lands of the interior.

Jonathan shifted irritably. If there was a snake in Eden it was Rathbone. He glanced around the deck. Where the hell was Gwendoline? He had expected that she'd be standing beside him as eager to get her first sight of the port as he was.

Ah there she was. His bad humour dissolved. Smiling broadly, he watched her move across the deck towards him. God she looked beautiful in her dress of pale muslin and that wide-brimmed straw hat. What was different about her? He couldn't place it at first, then he realised.

It was the way she moved.

She had always been graceful, holding herself erect and walking with her chin lifted high in the manner of all well-bred ladies. Now she rolled her hips slightly as she walked, so that her long skirt swayed against the curves of her body.

As she drew nearer he saw that there were faint violet shadows under her green eyes. There was a new set to her mouth too.

Jonathan coloured. She looked downright provoc-ative. Didn't she realise the effect she was having?

He looked around but the sailors were absorbed in the happenings on shore. Edward was fussing over their cases and trunks, even now being hauled onto the deck, ready for transportation. Captain Casey rapped out orders, glancing only briefly at Gwendoline to smile and wish her 'good morning'.

Gwendoline paused and it seemed to Jonathan that a meaningful look passed between her and Michael Casey. Then she moved on, giving the captain a brilliant smile. The captain touched a hand to his cap and went about his duties.

Jonathan was left with the uncomfortable realisation that no one had noticed anything different about Gwendoline but himself. Did that mean that the supposed change was more to do with himself than with her?

She came to stand next to him at the rail.

'I could hardly sleep for excitement last night, then I couldn't seem to wake this morn!'

'And what had you been doing to need so much sleep?' Jonathan said smiling archly.

Her reaction to his comment was immediate. A red tide of colour spread upwards from her neck and stained her cheeks. She didn't reply to his question. Instead she fiddled with the froth of red-brown curls which had been arranged to fall low on her forehead under her sunhat.

'I . . . I knew we were here the moment I awoke,' she said on a note of excitement, which for all its naturalness, seemed to Jonathan to be a little forced. 'The *Persephone* was still. It was the strangest feeling after all the weeks of continuous movement.'

Jonathan knew the feeling. 'You'll feel strange on dry land for a while. Long-term sailors develop a sort of rolling gait which gives away their profession.'

She laughed. 'I don't think I've been long enough at sea for that!'

Jonathan waved his hand towards the shore. 'Does Africa meet with your approval?'

Gwendoline looked towards the great bank of tangled vegetation which formed a flowing green line in the near distance. Mist rose from the forest floor, trailing upwards like smoke. There was utter silence. It was as if the jungle held its breath, ready for when the brief African dusk brought forth its night life.

'It's a little frightening . . . but yes. A hundred times, yes,' she breathed. Her eyes rising to look at the great vault of the sky. 'It's so . . . so clear. And the colour of larkspurs,' she said. 'Oh, I'm sorry. I'm talking to myself. I mean the sky.'

'I know just what you mean,' Jonathan said. 'I felt that way too when I had my first sight of her. There are many wonders in store for you. The journey's only just beginning. Save some of that wonder in your eyes for later.'

She smiled up at him with real friendship and he felt his heart give a lurch.

'I'm so glad that you took my side about coming with you and Edward. Without your support I might never have seen all this. Thank you, Jonathan.'

'Come – the steam-launch is here,' he said briskly to hide his emotion. 'I'll help you aboard.'

'Wait for me!' Hetty called, running up to them.

She sparkled at Gwendoline. 'Had to say goodbye to Ned,' she explained.

Standing nearby Edward cleared his throat and came forward to take Hetty's arm.

'Come along m'dear,' he said brusquely, his broad face turning bright red. 'Take my arm.'

Hetty looked daggers at him. Edward seemed to wilt. His outstretched arm trembled. Then he bent close and said something in Hetty's ear. If Jonathan hadn't known him better he would have sworn that Edward said 'please'.

The next moment Hetty was all smiles again. She laid her hand on Edward's arm with a gentility she had surely copied from Gwendoline.

The journey to the landing stage by steam-launch was harrowing, but mercifully short. The muddy waters swirled around them and spray leapt up high against the rail. The pale mounds of sandbanks showed near the shore. In places the river and sea merged, spreading into wide, still lagoons encircled by jungle. Many small vessels passed to and fro, fighting the strong currents.

As their small craft steered into a wide channel, Gwendoline studied the mangrove swamps which stretched away in all directions. Aerial roots hung down from the upper branches of trees, some plunging into the water; the ends dividing into pale hand-like roots. Mud banks rose out of the water and the sweetish smell of decaying vegetation reached them on the breeze.

'Oh, what's that? Something moved in the water!' Hetty said.

Jonathan smiled. 'That's a crocodile. You'll see many more of those. See – there's one asleep on that sandbank.'

'He has his mouth open. What a terrible lot of teeth!' Hetty shuddered.

Gwendoline peered overboard, gazing at the narrow channels which disappeared amongst the mangroves. Strange shapes seemed to loom there, twisted shadows formed by the branches of trees.

Though she was perturbed at the strangeness of it all, her artist's eye was delighted by the quality of light. The air seemed pure and clear, allowing the colours of everything to glow with a unique purity. The sunrise turned the sea to scarlet and tipped the mud banks with flame.

Some way into the channel the passage grew narrower and it became plain that the steam-launch could go no further. There was a clearing in the tangle of vegetation. Gwendoline saw that there was a wooden platform and a group of huts. A number of people were waiting to greet the launch; among them was Dominic Rathbone, resplendent in a light linen suit and panama hat. Next to him stood a handsome young African.

'My dear fellow,' Edward said, alighting and pumping Rathbone's hand vigorously. 'So good to see you again. I trust that you're managing things with your usual efficiency?'

Rathbone smiled politely. 'Of course Mr Farnshawe.'

'You know Jonathan here already?' Edward continued.

Jonathan stepped forward and shook the man's hand, hiding his distaste at the feel of it. It was a hot, dry morning, but Rathbone's hand was cold and clammy.

'So. The adventurer returns,' Rathbone said, smiling narrowly. 'Do you intend to collect more native artifacts for the entertainment of the bored rich back in England?'

Jonathan's mouth lifted in a wry smile. 'That isn't the way I see things. You have a simplistic view of anthropology, Rathbone.'

Rathbone inclined his head. 'I bow to your superior intellect,' he said, his tone making it plain that he did no such thing.

'May I present my sister,' Edward said, stepping in hurriedly. 'And this is Hetty, her companion.'

Rathbone ignored Hetty. Gwendoline felt cold grey eyes rake her slim form. She saw a tall man, slightly stooped. Later she was to learn that Rathbone was in his mid-forties. He looked older, his face marked by downward lines. His eyes seemed too knowing, as if they had seen all there was to know of life, and found it wanting. As he spoke she caught the scent of rum on his breath.

'Charmed Miss Farnshawe,' he said, not troubling to hide his surprise. 'You are most welcome, even though Edward did not mention you in his letters. You must allow me to show you around the settlement. Do you ride? English ladies of breeding often have a good seat.'

Gwendoline stammered out a greeting, astounded by the man's familiarity. She hid her shock. Perhaps the way of life was more relaxed in the colonies. Rathbone was probably only being polite in his way. Surely he meant nothing. It was only his choice of words that was unfortunate.

'How do you do, Mr Rathbone,' she said stiffly.

He gave her a smile that did not reach his eyes. She knew then that he was aware of her discomfort and was amused by it. She smiled then, to show him that she wasn't as disconcerted as he'd hoped she would be.

'It would be most delightful to see the settlement – '

'Gwendoline will be coming with us when we go upriver,' Jonathan cut in. 'So she'll have little time for your brand of – entertainment.'

'Really?' Rathbone said, a new respect in his voice. 'I congratulate you on your choice of travelling companions.'

He grinned, showing his tobacco-stained teeth, and looked at Gwendoline with renewed curiosity. Uncomfortable under the scrutiny of his pouched grey eyes, Gwendoline took a step along the landing stage.

Rathbone recovered his manners.

'My staff are eager to welcome you,' he said. 'And I'll see to it personally that you are made comfortable Mistress Farnshawe. Come. Your carriage awaits.'

He's not without humour, Gwendoline thought, as she looked at the 'carriage' he indicated. It was a long dug-out canoe. A young African stood nearby, paddle in hand. Another was seated at the stern of the canoe. The handsome young man who seemed to be Rathbone's personal servant was organising the transportation of their luggage.

Hetty looked with horror at the narrow craft.

'We're to travel in that? It don't look at all safe . . .'

'Don't fuss Hetty,' Gwendoline said sharply, trying to conceal her own trepidation. 'I'm sure we'll have to get used to travelling in this fashion.'

Gathering her skirts around her, she stepped gingerly into the canoe. It swayed alarmingly and she clutched at Jonathan's hand to steady herself. Once seated she felt a little more secure. Jonathan climbed aboard and seated himself behind her.

Edward helped Hetty to her seat and took his place nearby. Rathbone seated himself at the prow and called to the strikingly handsome African.

'Finished with that luggage Iko? Then ride with us. What have you to say to our guests?'

The young man stepped into the canoe. Though he looked strong and wiry, his movements were graceful. Turning around, he greeted them.

'Welcome Bwana. Welcome Bebe Bwana,' he said to Edward and Gwendoline. 'And welcome Massa Jonathan and Missy.'

'Hello Iko. It's good to see you again,' Jonathan replied. 'Iko is a gardener and house servant at the settlement,' he explained to Gwendoline.

Gwendoline smiled at the young man. Iko beamed

at her, showing strong white teeth. He had a clear-cut profile and velvety black skin. A cap of close-cropped curls framed his well-shaped head. He wore a suit similar to Rathbone's. It fitted his strong young body well, the jacket stretching a fraction tightly across the expanse of his muscular shoulders.

'Pleased to make your acquaintance Iko,' she said. Then to Jonathan, 'What was that he called me just then?'

'Bebe Bwana? It's Swahili. It means lady boss.'

She smiled. 'I've never been called that before. I rather like it.'

The canoe set off, easing out into the channel and catching the current. Gwendoline stared all around, captivated by the handsome Africans and by the ease with which they manoeuvred the canoe. In her ignorance she had expected them to be dressed in skins and daubed with coloured pigments.

Rathbone's employees were as cultured and well-dressed as any servants in England. She felt ashamed of her preconceptions and decided that she must look at Africa and her people with a fresh eye, one unfettered by the constraints of her upbringing.

Jonathan caught her eye and smiled. She sensed that he knew what she was thinking. He leaned close and she thought he was going to speak. Instead he tapped her sharply on the back of the hand. She jumped and pulled her hand away.

'Mangrove fly,' he said. 'Have to watch out for those. They lay their eggs under your skin. The maggots hatch and work their way out.'

'Heavens!' Gwendoline said faintly, looking at the squashed creature. 'I'll be sure to take care.'

The canoe wove its way through the narrow channels, each of which looked exactly the same to Gwendoline. The mangroves seemed to stretch in all directions in a never-ending tangle of trunks and roots. In some places a thick mist shrouded the shore line.

After some time they entered a wider channel and then they were in a river. The canoe sped along now, free from twists and turns. The Africans began to chant in time with their oar strokes.

Raised on piles on the mud shore were white-painted buildings. Gwendoline asked Jonathan what they were.

'Factories and store houses for palm oil,' he told her. 'See the flag at half-mast? Someone is dead of the yellow fever.'

Gwendoline was silent for a while, watching the jungle which pressed into the river on either side. Vast trees with grey stems were visible a little way inland, some with curtains of hanging moss. Blooms of purple and white spotted the undergrowth. What a strange wild land this was. Jonathan's African 'lady' was not an easy mistress.

The sun was high overhead before they neared their destination. Gwendoline felt the heat prickling her skin. Sweat ran in a trickle down the valley of her breasts. She was longing for a drink, but no one had suggested stopping for refreshment. Indeed they had seen no place which was suitable for a landing.

As they rounded a great curve in the river Gwendoline caught sight of buildings through the trees. The jungle had been partly cleared and she glimpsed a dust road, thatched huts, and animal pens.

A high-pitched, jaunty wailing went up as the canoe turned in towards the shore. The bank sloped gently down to the river and clean shingle could be seen through the water. Some way back she saw the wooden roof and white-painted walls of a substantial house.

'Come on Gwenie. You must arrive in style,' Jonathan laughed, jumping over the side of the canoe into the shallow water.

His use of the endearment surprised her. She saw Edward dart Jonathan a pointed look.

'I say Kimberton, old chap . . .' he began.

Everyone ignored him. Hetty laughed delightedly as Jonathan scooped Gwendoline up in his arms and carried her ashore.

'Wouldn't do to get your skirts wet,' he grinned.

She put her arms around his neck and laughed up into his face. He could feel her slender waist and the swell of her hips and could not resist holding her more closely than he needed to.

'I have a feeling that getting wet could be the least of my troubles while I'm here,' she said dryly.

Jonathan threw back his head and laughed at the eagerness in her voice, which she didn't trouble to hide.

Gwendoline had changed. She was more self-assured. More confident of her bodily charms. Her perfume made him dizzy. He felt a stir of desire.

'You could well be right!' he said softly. 'Take care Gwendoline when you hold a tiger by its tail!'

Gwendoline stepped down and looked back at the canoe, waiting for Hetty before she made her way towards the house.

Dominic Rathbone was watching her, a frown on his ravaged face. He caught her eye and grinned sardonically.

Despite the heat she felt cold fingers crawl up her spine.

Chapter Nine

A double row of trees formed an avenue leading to the front of Dominic Rathbone's house.

Gwendoline was surprised by the neat borders and paths. She had not expected to find such a garden in the heart of the jungle. She said as much to Jonathan.

'That's Iko's work. He lives for the garden. By the look on his face I think he heard you. You're likely to find fresh flowers in your room every day from now on.'

'How delightful,' Gwendoline smiled at Iko, who smiled back hesitantly.

She was struck by the way his whole face lit up when he smiled. It was only then that she realised he looked a little sad in repose. Sad, or serious, or maybe something else. She could not quite decide which. She was intrigued. Later she'd ask Jonathan if her instincts were correct.

Striding up a path made of rounds of wood, set into the lawn, she breathed deeply of the garden scents. Fresh, green and with an underlying richness, like ripe fruit.

As they drew near she saw the house clearly. It was low and sprawling, built all on one storey. Large windows, wooden blinds drawn against the sun, looked out onto the slope of the gardens. A covered porch surrounded the house on three sides. Purple bougainvillaea sprawled up the walls, providing a froth of colour against the white-painted walls.

There was an area of cleared ground at the front of the house. It was weed-free and spotless. Not a stone marred the smoothness of the freshly brushed soil. Pots of bamboo, flowering shrubs and poinsettias were arranged in neat rows. It was all very beautiful, but Gwendoline had the uncomfortable feeling that the extreme neatness and attention to detail bordered on the obsessive.

She knew, without being told, that it was Rathbone who insisted on such order.

On the front porch they were met by the domestic staff. Rathbone made cursory introductions. Gwendoline knew that she would never remember all the names. Some of them were difficult to pronounce. She resolved to practise getting them right.

The men and woman greeted Gwendoline, all smiling brightly. She moved along the line shaking hands. A young woman, standing a little way apart from the others, caught her eye.

Nsami, the housemaid, was a girl of some eighteen years. Gwendoline was struck by her slender beauty. She had light brown skin, high cheekbones, almond-shaped eyes and delicate hands and wrists. Something about Nsami's looks reminded Gwendoline of Iko.

Rathbone saw her looking.

'Nsami is lovely, isn't she?' he said in a soft voice for her ears alone. 'She is talented too. She makes the long nights of the rainy season bearable – for all

144

of us. She and Iko come from the same tribe. The Samburu people are noted for their beauty.'

Gwendoline did not know how to reply. There seemed to be a double meaning in everything Rathbone said. What were these talents that Nsami had? She was not sure that she wanted Rathbone to enlighten her about them. She turned her back on the man. She might find Rathbone unpleasant but Nsami was perfectly charming.

She smiled at the African girl who flashed her a shy grin before lowering her eyes. Jonathan was engaged in conversation with a tall, broad-shouldered African who was evidently the cook.

Edward shifted impatiently.

'Come on Rathbone. Let's get inside out of the heat. I want a drink first and then a bath!' he said, stalking past Gwendoline and entering the house.

Plainly he did not approve of Gwendoline being too friendly with servants; the exception being Hetty. It was something her brother abhorred in England and it seemed that he was not going to change his habits in Africa.

Jonathan glared at Edward's retreating back, then flashed Gwendoline a look of exasperation.

'Your brother really is a stuffed shirt,' he said. 'Thank heaven you are of a more enlightened nature.'

The introductions over, the staff dispersed. Gwendoline and Hetty waited to be shown to their rooms. Jonathan and Edward went off in the opposite direction.

'Nsami will show you to your room,' Rathbone said. 'She speaks good English. I suggest you wash and change. Then rest before we eat.'

Nsami stepped forward.

'Please to follow me,' she said. Her voice was soft and husky and with an intriguing accent.

She was dressed in a simple blue shift dress. A piece of the same dress fabric was swathed around her head in a stylish turban. Metal discs adorned her ears and hung at her throat. Her black eyes were warm and friendly.

The rooms Nsami showed them to were spacious and cool. Gwendoline's room looked out onto the front porch. Hetty's room, reached by a connecting door, had a view from the side of the house.

'Oh, it is lovely. Quite, quite, beautiful!' Gwendoline said, turning around in a circle.

The floor was polished wood. Woven rush mats were dotted about the room. Slatted blinds hung at the French windows, which opened out onto the balcony.

The few pieces of furniture were of a light-coloured wood. A bowl of flowers stood on a small table. Someone had thoughtfully provided a cheval glass. In an alcove, formed by a woven grass screen, was an enormous bed. A mosquito net, secured to the ceiling, was draped to either side of the heap of white pillows. A huge bedspread made of fur covered the bed.

Nsami smiled, showing perfect, very white teeth.

'Missy like the room. That is good.' She moved to where the trunks stood ready, and began to unpack.

Hetty moved forward swiftly.

'I'll do that, thank you,' she said firmly, establishing her position.

'As Missy wishes,' Nsami said softly, standing to one side of the door, awaiting orders.

Gwendoline walked to the French windows and threw them open. She stepped out onto the balcony. Across the garden, Iko was watering the tubs and flower borders. He looked up and saw her. Rather shyly he grinned and waved. She waved back.

Nsami was smiling broadly when Gwendoline came back into the room.

'Iko like you,' she said.

Gwendoline smiled. 'I like him too, Nsami. Now, I would like water please. A bath? Is that possible?'

Nsami nodded. 'I fetch.'

She walked silently from the room. Hetty unpacked the trunks and hung Gwendoline's clothes in the large wardrobe. Gwendoline stretched out full-length on the bed, enjoying the luxury of light and space after so many cramped weeks aboard the *Persephone*.

She closed her eyes as Hetty bustled about, screwing up tissue paper and shaking the creases from silk skirts. The lavender scent of orris powder drifted across the room. In the bottom of one of the trunks Hetty found Gwendoline's drawing pad.

Idly she began leafing through the pages. Gwendoline heard the sound of turning pages and her mouth curved in a secret smile. She anticipated Hetty's indrawn breath.

'Mercy me!' Hetty cried. 'Why it's me . . . and Ned! And that's . . . Oh lawks. It's Captain Casey. Oh Miss. When did you go and draw these?'

'I began the first sketch the morning after I watched you and Ned together,' Gwendoline said calmly. 'Don't you like the drawings? I thought I had captured you both rather well.'

'It's not that I don't like them exactly. It's just that it's a shock to see myself . . . well, naked an' all. Look at my bottom all spread like that. And my breasts. They looks all wanton.'

Gwendoline sat up, propping herself against the pillows.

'Forget your surprise at seeing yourself on the

147

page. Look carefully at the drawings Hetty and give me your honest opinion.'

Hetty's pale brows drew together as she concentrated. After a pause, while she turned the page this way and that, she spoke again. An expression of delight spread across her pretty face. This time she smiled broadly.

'You've caught Ned right well. That's just the way his shoulders are, and his legs. Long and powerful. And his cock, with the big end and the bend in the shaft. Oh Miss you're truly wicked.'

Gwendoline sparkled at her.

'I might well be. I'm sure Edward and my parents would agree with you. But I intend to do as many drawings like these as I can.'

Hetty looked at her sideways. 'This one of Captain Casey. All laying back asleep and naked as a jay bird. When did you do that one?'

'I did it from memory, the morning after he shared my bed.'

'Ooooh, Miss,' Hetty said with relish. 'You're a caution. You never let on.'

Gwendoline grinned. 'I was going to tell you. There just never seemed to be the time. You were too busy saying your goodbyes to Ned.'

'Yes I was. Wasn't I?' Hetty grinned, seating herself on the end of the bed and stroking the soft fur coverlet appreciatively.

The trunks with their froth of petticoats and scarves spilling from them were forgotten. The drawing book lay open across Hetty's knees. Her eyes scanned the pages, drinking in the details of the skilfully executed drawings.

'Captain Casey has a good body for an older man. And he's a stout cock,' she said approvingly. 'Just the kind I like. Thick and not too long. Do tell. Was he a good lover?'

'I don't know as I should tell you that . . .' Gwendoline said, trying not to laugh as she mimicked Hetty's reticence in the past.

Hetty pouted. 'That's cruel. Haven't I always told you everything? Don't tease. You *will* tell me, won't you? Was your first time good?'

'Oh yes,' Gwendoline breathed, remembering. 'It was perfect. First he told me to try on my clothes for him. He made me put on the silk chemise.'

'The one that's so thin it shows your nipples?'

'Yes. And then he drew me close and began to caress my breasts. Oh, the feel of his hands on me made me go all hot and wet. He was very gentle and knowing. When he stroked my . . . my quim – well I couldn't help myself. I told him to do anything he liked to me.'

And while they waited for Nsami to reappear with hot water, Gwendoline told Hetty everything that had happened in the narrow bunk aboard the clipper.

Nsami paused outside the door and set down the pitcher of hot water. She could hear voices from inside the room. The two white ladies were laughing together, sharing some secret joke. Curious, she laid her ear to the door and listened.

Her full mouth curved as she heard what Gwendoline was saying. She was using strange words to describe parts of the body but Nsami understood everything she said.

It was a pleasant shock to hear such words from the mouth of a cultured English gentlewoman. The few female guests she'd known, wives or mothers of Dominic's business associates, had been stuffy, cold and prudish. All of them seemed like a race apart, not human at all.

Nsami had hated them. The way they looked down on her, treating her with condescension or ignoring her altogether. Their faces seemed frozen into expressions of permanent surprise, their lips thin and incapable of relaxing into a smile.

'You should pity them,' Iko told her. 'They do not know they are alive. But underneath, they are the same as you and I.'

Nsami was not so sure of that. Iko had another suggestion. She had laughed when he told her and followed his advice, picturing each of the ladies squatting to relieve themselves, holding their ridiculous clothes above their waists to expose their flabby bottoms.

That had helped. They didn't seem so superior when performing basic functions.

Nsami listened avidly to Gwendoline's soft voice and Hetty's rich, unaffected laughter. The last thing she had expected was to hear one of those haughty English ladies describing how a man had pleasured her. The revelations made Gwendoline seem like a real woman of flesh and blood. Someone who Nsami could relate to.

From their first meeting it had seemed that Gwendoline was a different sort of white lady. Now Nsami sensed that her instincts had been correct. Jonathan Kimberton liked Gwendoline too, that much was plain. That was something else in her favour.

Nsami respected Jonathan. He was a good man. He loved Africa and all her children. Not like her master.

Dominic Rathbone had a poor opinion of the human race, himself included. At least he was consistent, treating Africans and white folks with the same contempt. At least he would be on his best behaviour for a while. He drank less when they had house guests and Nsami understood that the Farnshawes were important people – they paid his wages.

Nsami tried to put thoughts of her master aside. He had summoned her to him the previous night. She had the marks to show for it, but he had more. She shivered, remembering how he had looked when she left him.

It was not likely that he'd call for her for a while. That meant that Iko too was safe.

Her fingers trembled as she reached for the pitcher of hot water. How she despised Rathbone, almost as much as she despised herself for wanting him. The worst thing about him was that he knew how much she enjoyed the things they did together.

Even that first time, she had been unable to hide her hunger from him.

It was bad enough that he used her. Worse was the fact that she would be driven to plead with him if he left her alone for too long. He'd trained her too well. Now her flesh cried out for the spiked pleasures he provided.

Tears pricked her long, black eyes. She and Iko were trapped by their own natures as much as by Rathbone's fleshly demands. Lying in each others arms they comforted each other. Sometimes, when their master's attentions had been a little too vehement, she wept and Iko kissed away the tears streaking her cheeks.

Perhaps she could have tolerated Rathbone if he was just a brute; excused his behaviour on the grounds of his lack of intelligence.

But he was clever, he saw too much, and he demanded everything. Even the self-respect of his lovers. That was what was unforgiveable. He left her and Iko with no dignity.

Dominic Rathbone was a predator. Far more dangerous than the things that moved in the velvet blackness of a jungle night.

Perhaps Nsami should warn Gwendoline about her master. The white woman had caught his eye already. Nsami saw how Rathbone's eyes followed Gwendoline. He was like a snake, watching and measuring its prey, waiting to strike.

She almost burst into the room and stammered out a warning but she held back. However much she was drawn to the white woman, Gwendoline was here for a short stay, then she'd move on. She was also one of *them*. The people with power and money. The people who decided the fate of those like Rathbone and subsequently – herself and Iko.

Rathbone was part of Africa. His life was here now. Whatever else he was, her master was deserving of her loyalty.

At least for the present.

Straightening her head cloth, Nsami took a deep breath and tapped on the door.

It was a luxury to strip off her travel-stained clothes and splash her body with warm water.

Gwendoline relaxed in the large wooden tub which Nsami had dragged from behind a screen. She sat upright in it, her knees bent up before her, in the manner of a hip bath.

In all the weeks aboard the clipper she'd had to wash with a cloth and small bowl of water. Her hair was gritty and lank and she unpinned it with relief. After washing the dust from her hair, she combed it out and left it to spill over her shoulders. The coolness of her damp scalp felt wonderful.

Slipping on a frilled cotton robe, she stretched out on the bed, intending to rest for only a few moments before dinner.

From the next room came splashing sounds as Hetty too took a bath. Gwendoline heard Nsami's soft footfall as she scooped up the soiled clothes and took them away. But by then she was already slipping away.

A sense of perfect happiness settled over her. Outside the French windows was the garden and beyond that the wild heart that was truly Africa.

Soon she fell into a deep sleep. And her dreams were filled with the cries of wild animals and a tangle of impenetrable greenery. Superimposed over the images were the pages of her drawing book, with the interlocked limbs, peachy flesh, and Hetty and Ned's faces slack with desire.

Nsami heard the soft moan that escaped Gwendoline's lips. She smiled, wondering what the woman dreamed about.

Unseen by them both, the shadow of a man passed across the blinds that covered the French windows.

Edward slipped silently around the corner of the house, moving along the porch until he came to the window of Hetty's room. Peering through the slats of the blinds he satisfied himself that the room was empty.

Good. That was perfect for what he planned.

He had bathed and taken pains to groom himself. Now he wore a light linen suit and fancied that he looked the perfect Englishman abroad. The clothes suited his square compact body. Hetty could not help but be impressed.

On board the clipper she had been quite unlike her normal self. A fact he had found exciting, it was true, but now that they were back on land, he expected them to revert back to their normal relationship.

He was looking forward to being once again the master, while she was the eager servant, hot-blooded and easy with her favours. He'd surprise her as he used to back at the house. She had loved him to catch her while she was working. Many times he'd thrown her skirts onto her back and slipped into her while she bent over the dining room table.

The sight of her broad rump moving back and forth while she dusted and polished never failed to excite him. Sometimes she'd let him unbutton her dress and kiss the rich overhang of her breasts where they were thrust up by the top of her stays. The threat of discovery had added an edge to their passion. He had loved Hetty's eagerness. Sometimes she couldn't open the buttons on his trousers, her fingers were trembling so with wanting.

Edward swelled with lust at the thought.

On the clipper he'd been obliged to solace himself most nights, while Hetty acted the indignant lady if he tried to get her alone. He couldn't understand it. She'd always been as eager for sex play as he was.

The only times she'd allowed him near her, she'd insisted that he perform all manner of indignities. His cheeks burned at the memories. Worst of all she told him that she meant to have the truth about his old governess – Miss Templeton. Inwardly he quaked at the thought of revealing those long-kept secrets.

Those days of his early manhood lived on inside him like live coals.

'One day,' Hetty promised. 'You'll tell me. When I orders it Edward, you'll do anything I say.'

He'd shivered at that note in Hetty's voice, so reminiscent of Miss Templeton.

'Yes Hetty,' he'd mumbled, too enraptured by her

lush beauty, too aroused by this new and darker side to her, to deny her anything.

But later, when he could think clearly again, Edward knew that he could never tell anyone about the things his governess had made him do, the indignities he had suffered hoping to please her with his complete obedience. Still less, could he admit to how much he had adored the thin, hatchet-faced woman.

That was all very well but he was a man now. A man who commanded respect and who was beginning to take on more responsibilities for the family business. It was time he reasserted his authority.

Carefully Edward eased open the window and moved the blinds aside. It was a simple matter to hook one leg over the sill and drop silently into the room.

Hetty's room was smaller than his own, but comfortable, and decorated in a similar style to the rest of the house. The enormous bed was covered with a tent of mosquito netting. A bath of water stood in one corner. Next to it was a bundle of clothing. A damp towel hung over a chair back.

He saw at once that he had been mistaken in assuming that the room was empty. Hetty lay on the bed, her corn-coloured hair spread out across the pillows. She lay on her side, the pure cameo of her profile pressing into the snowy pillowcase. A thin cotton sheet covered her body, outlining her rich curves with a series of hollows and folds.

Looking at her, at her sleeping face, quite took Edward's breath away. He felt something more than desire when he saw her lying there. She looked defenceless and utterly at peace. Only at that moment did he realise, with a pang of exquisite anguish, that he truly loved Hetty.

He took a step forward, intending to raise the corner of the mosquito netting and drop a kiss on her cheek, when she opened her eyes. For a horrible moment he saw fear pass across her face and he thought she was going to scream, then she recognised him.

'Edward!' she hissed. 'You frit' me half to death.'

She pushed herself into a sitting position and glared at him. The anger on her face excited him but he felt dismay too. Now she'd send him away. He couldn't bear that.

Dropping to his knees beside the bed he reached out for her.

'I'm sorry Hetty. I didn't mean to alarm you. I only wanted to be with you. I'm . . . I'm sick with longing for you.'

'A fine way you've got of showin' it! Creeping into my room like a thief. Didn't I tell you that I'd let you know when I wanted your company?'

'Well . . . yes. But I thought that was only on board the *Persephone*. I hardly got to see you alone on the clipper. Things can go back to normal now.' At the look she gave him he stammered, 'Can't they?'

'Now I wonders why you think that,' Hetty murmured. 'P'raps I'd better show you the way things are going to stay.'

Edward shifted uncomfortably, preparing to get to his feet. He felt so undignified kneeling there.

'Don't you dare move!' Hetty rapped.

She pushed the sheet and netting aside and stood up. Naked, she stood looking down at Edward. His head was level with her belly. The luxury of having her to himself, to be able to look at all her glorious creamy flesh, almost overwhelmed him.

Trembling, his hands moved towards her. If only she'd allow him to slide his hands up her thighs and cup her big bottom. Surely she'd awaken at his touch. He knew just what to do to inflame her.

'Don't,' she said again.

Edward dropped his hands to his sides, waiting miserably on his knees while Hetty brushed past him. He caught the scent of her freshly washed skin and the sweet musk between her thighs. Dizziness washed over him.

'Hetty,' he said pleadingly. 'Be nice to me.'

She laughed richly.

'Oh I will. I know exactly what you needs Edward.'

Twisting his head around he saw that she was bent over an open trunk, presenting him with the most delectable sight. Her flaring hips made a perfect heart shape and between her buttocks he glimpsed the little hanging purse of her sex. The dark-blonde hairs that grew around her sex and protruded moistly from her bottom crease, seemed to invite his touch.

She turned and saw him looking at her. A frown of displeasure marred her face.

'I told you not to move. Oh, you're a bad boy today. What are you?'

'A bad boy. A very bad boy . . .' Edward echoed, his mouth dry.

'That's right. And bad boys needs punishing.'

He saw that she held a bundle of silken cords. Edward was already excited. Now the tumescence at his groin became almost painful.

Hetty advanced slowly towards him. Her large breasts trembled as she moved. She threaded the cords through her fingers, laying them across her upturned palms. Edward watched mesmerised as the silky ropes dipped and swayed, like eager little snakes.

'Come here Edward,' Hetty ordered. 'Strip off your clothes and kneel on this chair.'

Edward pushed himself to his feet. His knees trembled as he crossed the room and began to disrobe.

'That's better,' Hetty said. 'Naughty boys knows they has to take their punishment. Ain't that so?'

Edward couldn't speak for the roughness in his throat. Hetty frowned again, her golden eyebrows drawing together fiercely.

'Tell me Edward, haven't you forgotten something?'

'I . . . I don't think so,' Edward stammered, hopping on one leg as he divested himself of his trousers.

'Oh you have, my lad. I want to hear you tell me that this is what you desire. Where'er your manners? Don't you remember the other times?'

'I . . . oh yes. I remember.' Edward took a deep shaky breath and dipped his chin. Staring at the wooden floorboards, he said, 'Please . . . Mistress. Will you punish me. I know I have offended you and I desire to suffer at your hands.'

And with a kind of sinking exultation Edward knew it was true. Hetty knew him better than he knew himself.

This was what he had wanted all along.

Chapter Ten

*H*etty saw Edward glance towards the door which connected her room with Gwendoline's.

'Someone might come in,' he said worriedly, looking down at his naked body and semi-erect cock.

'That's right,' she said. 'So we'd better do something about you at once. This,' she prodded his erection with a disdainful finger, 'certainly needs some attention.'

She pushed a sturdy cane chair towards him. It had a broad seat and a high, straight, ladder back.

'Kneel up now. And bend over the chair back.'

Silently Edward did as he was told. She felt the pleasure uncoil in her belly as the sense of power over him intensified.

'Like this, Mistress?' Edward said, leaning forward tentatively.

'Bend over more,' she said giving him a playful swipe with the bundle of silk cords.

He flinched, gasping as if he'd been burned, but he obeyed her. The high back of the chair rested on his ribs, just below his nipples, as he leaned over it.

'Put your hands behind your back.'

Edward did so. His cock, fully erect now and dark red in colour, jutted forward almost touching the bottom bar of the chair back.

Hetty tied his wrists together with one long cord. He could easily break the cord and escape if he wanted to. Indeed, he was much stronger than she and could overpower her and force her to pleasure him, but she knew that he would do no such thing.

Taking another long cord, she wrapped it around his waist.

'Hold your stomach in,' she ordered, and when he did so, she tied the cord tightly.

Edward waited in silence. She sensed his apprehension. Again the feeling of power swept over her. She could do anything she liked to him and he would allow it because this was what he wanted.

When she reached for his cock, he could not contain a little gasp. She curled her fingers around the thick shaft and eased back the cock-skin until the swollen tip was uncovered fully. The glans was purple and wet with a clear secretion. Smearing the moisture onto her fingers she thrust them into Edward's mouth, delighting in his little grimace of acceptance.

'How do naughty boys taste? Tell me.'

Edward licked his lips. His cheeks burned with shame.

'Please, don't . . .' he murmured.

'Tell me,' Hetty insisted.

'I don't know. A little salty . . . I never tasted myself before.'

Hetty laughed huskily. 'Well you have now! See. You can do anything I ask. You just has to want to.'

'Yes, Mistress,' Edward said softly, then he let out

a cry of dismay as she began winding a cord around his cock-shaft.

Beginning at the base of his belly, Hetty wound the cord tightly around Edward's cock. When just the glans was exposed she drew the cord upwards and secured it to the cord wound around his waist.

Tremors passed over Edward's arms and legs as she jerked on the cord which now imprisoned his throbbing cock inside a silken tube. His cock-head twitched, a single drop of clear fluid hung from the tiny mouth suspended on a silver thread.

As he shifted position the chair moved and threatened to tip over. Edward tensed his muscles, balancing precariously and the chair righted itself.

'Careful now,' Hetty said sweetly. 'That chair's sturdy. If you holds still you'll be safe enough.'

She came to stand in front of Edward and slowly and deliberately began placing knots in the lengths of cord she had left. Edward's eyes followed her movements. His tongue snaked out to moisten his dry lips.

When she had finished and the cords were decorated with a number of knots, she slapped them against her hand, testing the effect. Edward winced as if she had struck him. Smiling she walked around behind him.

She paused, letting Edward sweat. Slowly she ran her hand down his strong back and over the taut, rounded buttocks. Though he was broad and thickset there was no fat on his body. He was handsome, distinguished and could have any woman he wanted. Except that he was hers to command.

'Arch your back, Edward,' Hetty said, her voice vibrating with the pride of ownership. 'Present yourself for punishment.'

Slowly Edward did as she asked. His back hollowed and the broad cheeks of his bottom parted to reveal his hairy cleft, clean and damp after his bath. Hetty smiled at his willingness to abase himself.

She tapped him smartly on his buttocks. Edward needed no more urging. The tight brown mouth of his anus became visible as he struggled to adopt a more extreme position of penitence. His bulging scrotum hung between his parted legs looking potent and somehow vulnerable at the same time.

Such good behaviour should be rewarded, Hetty thought, as she dragged the cords across Edward's skin. He shivered with pleasure at the light caress. She let him enjoy it for a moment. Perhaps he thought that she'd do nothing more. Well, she'd soon let him know different.

Raising her hand she brought the bunch of knotted cords down smartly across the fullest part of Edward's buttocks.

He gave a little high-pitched yelp of surprise. On his white skin appeared a pattern of pink slashes. Before he could catch his breath Hetty struck him again, this time lower, across the parted cheeks. Edward flinched, but he did not pull away.

'Good boy,' she said approvingly. 'I'm goin' to give you three more strokes. You can count them for me.'

Edward tensed, waiting for the bite of the cords. He grunted when Hetty laid the next stroke lower, catching him on the underswell of his buttocks.

'One,' he said, with only a slight tremor in his voice.

The next stroke caught him across the backs of his thighs.

'Two,' Edward gasped.

Hetty knew that he was biting his lip, trying not to cry out as his skin burned and stung. His once white flesh glowed with red lines, the knots making deeper red marks. A faint sheen of sweat covered Edward's shoulders and ran down the indentation of his backbone.

'Last one now,' Hetty said jovially, feeling the joy rise up strongly inside her. She'd make this last one count and no mistake.

Raising the cords she brought them down with all her force across Edward's lower back and between his parted buttocks. A strangled scream burst from him as the cords bit into the cleft and lashed hotly across his exposed anus.

'Three!' he managed to grind out.

Hetty walked around to his head and lifted his chin with one finger. Edward blinked away tears of gratitude as she bent close and placed her lips against his. His mouth was hot and exciting. She plunged her tongue inside it, kissing him roughly.

'You've taken your punishment well,' she said, 'for a bad boy. You can relax now. It's almost over.'

At that 'almost' Edward's lips trembled against hers. When she moved away she saw how his tightly bound cock jerked and twitched.

'Please, Mistress,' he begged, looking down at his groin.

'Now, now,' Hetty said reprovingly. 'This bad boy can wait just a little longer for his release. Can't he?'

Edward hung his head.

'Yes, Mistress. If you wish me to,' he said.

'That's right. It's my wishes that count. You can get down off that chair and kneel on the floor now.'

Edward scrambled to obey. It was awkward with his bonds, but he managed to get to his feet. The sight of his cock almost at bursting point, tied so tightly to the cord at his waist, woke dark hungers in Hetty.

The cock-head was purple and angry looking. The

hair at his groin was matted with sweat. The smell of it, salty and acrid, aroused her even more. She reached for his taut scrotum, stroking the heavy balls which were pulled up tight by the constriction around his cock.

Edward closed his eyes and shivered.

He looked close to climaxing. The sight of his handsome face, streaked with tears and sweat was powerfully erotic. It was tempting to let him go over the edge, to watch the fragmenting of his composure as he spilt his seed onto the wooden floor.

But it was more tempting still, to make him wait. She removed her hand. He had one more ordeal to face before she let him reach his peak.

On her order Edward knelt on the floor and placed his stomach on the chair. She made him lean right over it, until his head almost brushed the floor and he was balancing on the tips of his toes.

'Part your thighs, Edward.'

Edward did so.

'Wider. Open yourself up for me.'

With a little moan of protest Edward shuffled his knees apart and tipped his bottom up. Hetty stood between his spread thighs looking down at the reddened cleft and the abused little anus. How pink and tender it looked, almost – virginal. A wicked thought popped into her head.

Why not? She wanted to see just how far Edward would allow this game to go on.

She gathered spittle in her mouth and let it trickle onto Edward's anus. As the warm fluid dripped down between his legs Edward struggled, trying to look over his shoulder to see what she was doing.

'Eyes front!'

She slapped one sore buttock, leaving a white hand print on the blushing flesh. Almost at once the colour rushed to fill the mark, adding a new shade of red to Edward's flaming bottom. The effect was so satisfying that she slapped him again on the other cheek.

Twice more she slapped him, each contact bringing a grunt of pain from him. She stopped when her palms began tingling, but there was to be no respite for Edward. Smearing the spittle onto the tight little anal orifice, she began working a finger inside him.

'Oh, please . . . no . . .' Edward almost whimpered and Hetty laughed aloud at her daring.

Poor Edward. She knew how much men hated to be penetrated in this way. It was something they longed for, yet hated, as if it was an affront to their very manhood. That was what made the act so appealing. And why many men resisted it so strongly.

But Edward had yet more to endure.

She wanted him broken-in completely. After this lesson there would be no more confusion about their roles. Never again would he come creeping to her room, seeking to dominate her. Edward was about to learn the meaning of complete submission.

Gently she began to work the tip of one of the knotted cords into his anus. The tension in him was almost tangible as she forced the knot past the closure of his flesh. Gradually, not hurrying the process, she fed more and more of the cord inside him.

Inside he felt hot and silky. Despite his professed reluctance to accept this new treatment she sensed his underlying eagerness. Was there anything he would disallow? The thought set her blood and her imagination racing.

Edward held his breath, bearing down against her hand, allowing the intrusion. Soon the whole cord, except for a few inches, was buried inside him.

Hetty stood up and ordered Edward to stand also.

'You're to keep that cord inside you, until I removes it.'

'But I can't . . .'

'You'll try. Tighten up now.'

Edward clenched his buttocks tight, the end of the cord trailing down behind him. She knew the effort it must be taking for him to hold the cord inside his body, when his natural reaction would be to use his muscles to expel it.

His face was crimson with shame. He could not help but be aware of the way he looked. The end of the cord brushed against one muscular thigh and swayed as he moved. The beating had not affected him as deeply as that last intimate act. Hetty smiled fondly at him.

'Your "tail" suits you,' she said. 'It's a fittin' decoration for such a naughty boy.'

'As . . . as you say, Mistress,' his voice shook and she saw that he was very near to tears.

When Edward raised his eyes, his expression was pleading. It was time she took pity on him. The lesson was almost over.

'Come here then,' she said gently.

She untied the cord at his waist and unwrapped his cock, leaving only the base of the shaft constricted. His cock jerked upwards. It was a deep purple-red, the skin taut and shiny, ready to explode. Edward's hands remained tied behind his back as she began stroking his cock-shaft. He leaned towards her, an expression of pained pleasure on his face.

Hetty worked him expertly and knew by the way his scrotum tightened that he was perilously near to climaxing. Reaching behind him for the 'tail' she pulled on it gently.

'Oh God. Oh God . . .' he moaned, his face screwed into an expression of the most exquisite anguish.

Edward convulsed as the knotted cord was drawn slowly out of his body. A great jet of sperm spattered the floor. Followed by another and another.

She thought that Edward might faint with the intensity of the pleasure, but although he swayed against her and bent his knees he remained upright. She withdrew the final few inches of cord and discarded it.

Edward was gasping and gulping in air, like a long distance runner. It was a few seconds before he recovered himself enough to speak.

'Thank you. Thank you, Mistress,' he managed to get out.

Hetty smiled sweetly.

'You can show me how grateful you are, Edward. Follow me.'

Walking across to the bed she lay down and parted her thighs.

'You must get used to being on your knees in my presence. Come here and pleasure me with your tongue.'

'Yes, Mistress. Gladly.'

And despite his utter weariness and the warm pain that radiated throughout the area from his waist to his knees, Edward crossed the room and buried his head between Hetty's sturdy white thighs.

Hetty groaned with pleasure as Edward lapped at her hungrily.

'I want you to come back here just before dinner,' she managed to say. 'I'll have something . . . ready for you . . . oh yes. Just like that. Good boy. Did you hear me?'

Edward lifted his head, his mouth shiny with her juices.

'Yes. Mistress.'

Cut glass oil lamps illuminated the dining room.

A huge table of polished wood dominated the room. Dominic Rathbone sat at one end of the table, Edward at the other. The others were seated along the sides of the table, which was adorned with fine china, silver cutlery and white napkins.

Dishes of hot and cold meats, salads and an enormous bowl of fresh fruit were served by Nsami and Iko, both dressed immaculately in uniforms of black and white.

Gwendoline chewed a mouthful of roast meat and took a sip of wine. Rathbone, who was in conversation with her brother, certainly saw to his comforts. The food was excellent and the wine was good, a full-bodied red.

She glanced around the room. Red velvet curtains hung at the windows, more for effect than for any practical reason – for surely the nights were never cold enough to draw them. Mirrors with ornate frames decorated the walls. The furniture was imported. She recognised a Chippendale cabinet and surely that chair was French.

Rathbone noticed her interest.

'May I flatter myself that you are admiring my taste, Miss Farnshawe?'

'On the contrary Mr Rathbone. I was wondering if my brother was not paying you too much.'

Rathbone grinned. 'Wit as well as beauty. What a charming combination.'

He raised his glass to her, inclining his head and giving her one of his uncomfortable smiles. She thought again how cold and flat his eyes looked, like a reptile. Realising that she was staring at him, she looked away. When she dared to look towards him again, he was speaking to Jonathan about the various native tribes in the area.

Later, Rathbone spoke about the excellent game-shooting there was to be had. Edward expressed great interest.

'There'll be time to bag a few before we set off, won't there Jonathan?'

Jonathan nodded. 'There's no real hurry. We'll wait for the rainy season to end before we set out. It'll be cooler then, more comfortable for travelling.'

Rathbone smiled and stood up.

'I hate to wait for anything. I'm a man of action myself. If you'll excuse me gentlemen I think I'll take a stroll around the garden. Iko will bring you port and cigars. Miss Farnshawe, would you like to accompany me?'

Gwendoline hesitated, unwilling to refuse out-right. The thought of being alone in his company was not pleasant. Rathbone noticed her hesitation and the way she glanced towards the windows. Between the slats of the blinds the African night looked as black as ink.

'Nsami will accompany us,' he said smoothly. 'And I'll have some of the servants carry flares. You'll be quite safe – from wild animals.'

He grinned, as if he knew exactly what she had been thinking, then, putting his hands on the back of Gwendoline's chair drew it back as she stood up.

'How very eccentric to explore the gardens by night!' she said trying for lightness.

But she found that her imagination truly was stirred by the thought of it. Such a thing would never happen in England. Rathbone went off to change, promising to meet Gwendoline on the front porch in ten minutes.

'Enjoy your walk,' Jonathan remarked to Rathbone drily. 'I'll away to my books.'

'Judging by the subjects you choose to translate, I hardly think the work will be dry or dull,' Gwendoline said archly, and had the satisfaction of seeing Jonathan's mouth curve in a slow smile.

'My dear Gwendoline,' he said softly. 'I did not know that you were acquainted with my work.'

She flushed. 'I'm not. I know it by reputation only.'

Jonathan lifted his glass and took a sip of port.

'We must remedy that sometime.'

'Is that wise?' Edward said. 'It's hardly fitting stuff for a young lady to read.'

'Don't be so stuffy, Edward,' Gwendoline said. 'You've a copy of one of Jonathan's works in your study at home. If you can read it, then so can I. Besides, I'm an artist and capable of a detachment of mind on certain matters.'

'Even so – ' Edward blustered, breaking off and wincing slightly as he leaned forward to help himself to a cigar.

'Are you quite well, Edward?' Gwendoline said.

Her brother had been shifting uncomfortably on his chair throughout the meal. She noticed that he was moving a little awkwardly. Perhaps he had need of a purgative.

'One's digestion can take a time to become accustomed to different food,' she said, choosing her words carefully. Such indelicate subjects were not spoken about in public.

She lowered her voice. 'You're not becoming ill I hope. I have some Carter's liver pills in my room if you need them.'

170

'Of course I don't need them!' Edward hissed, then he forced a smile. 'I'm perfectly well. Never better. Don't fuss, sister dear. Now run along with Rathbone and admire the gardens.'

There was something going on, Gwendoline was sure of it. For one thing Edward only called her 'sister' when he was displeased with her in some way or when he was trying to distract her. And for another, Hetty had been wearing an intriguing secret smile all evening.

Every time Edward caught her eye, he flushed and looked away. When he thought no one was watching, he looked at Hetty with the strangest expression on his face.

It was a mixture of fear and adoration.

Gwendoline would ask Hetty all about it later but for now she was looking forward to the promised tour. It would be an otherwise dull night anyway if Jonathan was going to shut himself away in the study with his books.

The wooden boards of the porch retained some of the day's heat. She could feel it through the thin soles of her shoes. The night air was warm and thick with the smells of vegetation and dust. Underlying everything was the richer, elusive smell that was purely Africa. Gwendoline knew that she would never forget that odour.

Four servants, each carrying a flaming torch, accompanied Rathbone as he emerged from the main door of the house. He had changed out of his evening clothes and wore a light-coloured jacket over jodhpurs and riding boots.

'Perhaps I should change my dress also?' she asked him.

'That's not necessary, unless you wish it. I confess

that I find evening clothes uncomfortable. I'm more used to these sort of clothes.'

Gwendoline had to admit they suited him better than the starched, wing-collared shirt and frock coat. The light jacket rested easily on his broad shoulders and the jodhpurs fitted his lean thighs like a second skin.

The flickering torchlight softened the lines of his tall, slightly-stooped form and was kind to his skin. The unhealthy pouched look to his face had disappeared to be replaced by an intriguing blend of shadows and highlights. Even the faded grey eyes had a luminescence they lacked by daylight.

With some amazement she realised that Dominic Rathbone had once been a startlingly handsome man. It was the marks of dissipation that had aged him prematurely.

She was glad that Nsami stepped out from behind Rathbone at that moment, distracting her from such thoughts.

It was disquieting to find anything positive at all about Rathbone. She preferred to dislike him on all counts.

Nsami came to stand next to Gwendoline. She still wore her black and white uniform but she had replaced her frilled white cap with a dark head cloth. Her neat head and long, graceful neck were showed to advantage by the closely wrapped fabric.

'Two of you lead the way. Two bring up the rear,' Rathbone said to the servants.

Surrounded by the flickering yellow light of the flares the small party moved across the lawn. Outside the pool of light the African night pressed in, as dense and rich as black velvet. The heady scent of flowering shrubs wafted around them.

Gwendoline was bewitched by the vista that

opened out to them. In the distance the river glimmered. Trees loomed above them, some of them having bark splashed with bright colours. Jagged shadows and brief flashes of tropical blooms added a magic dimension to the garden.

'There's so much noise,' Gwendoline said with wonder as the rustles and chirps of insects seemed to increase until it formed a chorus.

Rathbone laughed. 'Africa wakes after dark.'

For a moment they stood still and listened. Behind the rhythmic ticks and clicks close at hand, she heard the cries of birds and monkeys, then a coarse, barking cry that sent a shiver down her back.

'Hyena,' Rathbone said. 'Sounds like the pack have a fresh kill.'

'They rejoice because they taste blood,' Nsami said.

Rathbone nodded curtly. Soon after that they heard the rumble of a lion and Gwendoline shuddered.

'It's far away,' Rathbone said. 'Sounds travel a long way at night. No lion will come near a settlement.'

'Unless he is old or starving,' Nsami said in her softly-accented voice.

'It is as Nsami says,' Rathbone said, sounding none too pleased at the second interruption.

Nsami lowered her eyes but flashed Gwendoline a smile. She seemed aware of Rathbone's displeasure and amused by it.

The little group moved along the well-kept paths, emerging out from the shadows of tree-ferns and palms into secret glades. The garden was bigger than Gwendoline had realised. An ornamental pool shimmered with yellow light as they passed it.

A walkway, formed by the bent-over branches of some supple shrub, was festooned with a creeper. Sprays of white, lace-like flowers hung down from it.

Scents of musk and vanilla rose from the flowers as they brushed against them.

Once Gwendoline caught sight of a thatched roof through a gap in the trees.

'What's that?' she said, pointing. 'Can we go and see?'

'It's the summerhouse,' Nsami told her. 'It's a quiet and secluded place.' The tone of her voice told Gwendoline that there was something more to be said on the subject.

'It's a place best seen by day,' Rathbone said shortly, steering them in another direction. 'It is forbidden to the servants ordinarily. But Nsami goes there often, don't you?'

His voice had become clipped and cold but Nsami seemed not to notice.

'Beyond the summerhouse are the buildings where the field workers live. Stay away from there, Miss Farnshawe. It isn't safe to go there unescorted.'

Gwendoline started at the venom in his voice. Nsami did not speak but her long dark eyes glittered as she grinned.

She isn't afraid of him, Gwendoline realised, finding the fact odd. She sensed that most people were wary of Rathbone, herself included, and with good reason.

Why then was Nsami so bold? And why were there forbidden places in this garden and on the plantation beyond it?

The torches sputtered and their light grew fitful.

'Time to return,' Rathbone said. 'We sleep early and rise early.'

He strode on ahead as if losing interest in everything around him. It's as if he's shut us all out, Gwendoline thought. Despite her reservations about Rathbone, she had to admit that he intrigued her.

She felt a movement against her skirts, then Nsami's slim fingers closed over her own. It was so unexpected that Gwendoline almost pulled away. The delicate hand rested in her own and the squeeze Nsami gave her was open and friendly.

Yet, when Gwendoline looked round and smiled at her, she saw something else on the young woman's face. She was too shocked to react. It was something she had never expected to see on the face of another woman.

Her senses reeling with confusion, Gwendoline extricated her hand and hurried towards the house.

At that moment the beautiful black girl seemed to encapsulate Africa. Gwendoline was struck by the duality of everything around her. By day Africa was wild and beautiful, by night it was dark and mysterious. Nothing was as it seemed, including Rathbone and Nsami.

Chapter Eleven

Gwendoline awoke to the sound of the rain.

For days now it had been falling onto the roof in great drenching sheets, roaring down the guttering, splashing onto the ground in a torrent.

She walked to the French windows and peered out. She could see the porch, but the garden beyond was obscured by rods of water that poured from the sloping roof, forming a curtain of silver. She sighed. At first the heavy, tropical downpour had been fascinating but, after days of it, she was becoming tired of remaining indoors.

The relentless sound of it and the unreal half-light within the house was oppressive. Nsami had told her that the rains had been known to drive people mad. Gwendoline was beginning to believe it.

She judged it to be early morning, long before breakfast time, though the dimness within the room was misleading. She was wide-awake and restless. It was plain that she couldn't sleep for any longer.

Crossing the room she stopped by the table near the wall. Her drawing board and pencils were spread out. She lit an oil lamp, so that she could study the drawing she had begun the previous evening. The cheery yellow glow penetrated the gloom and lifted her spirits.

Picking up a soft pencil, she began shading down the edge of the woman's limbs, making them rounded and lifelike. The drawing was another one of Hetty. When in the mood, Hetty could be persuaded to pose. She sat in a rattan chair, naked to the waist, only a fold of fabric covering the luxuriant bush of her pubic hair. Hetty's expression was a mixture of innocence and worldliness.

Gwendoline warmed to the challenge of capturing Hetty's natural sensuality. For a while she was lost in her work, absorbed in laying on strokes of varying depth. With a finger tip she smudged some of the lines, blending the shadows into the creamy paleness of Hetty's flesh.

For a while she was unaware of the heavy rhythm of the rain, but the sound gradually insinuated itself back into her consciousness.

With it came a restless irritation. She slung down the pencil, unable to concentrate any longer. She knew from experience that she would ruin the drawing if she worked on it any longer in this mood.

It was no good, she had to do something active. She would have sought company but the house had that closed-in, shut feeling, that meant everyone was asleep – at least on the surface.

Her stomach rumbled. She stood up. Perhaps she'd find something left over from dinner in the kitchen. Going to fetch food would give her something to do.

It was too hot to put on a wrap. In England the rain cleared the air leaving a fresh smell and a delicious coolness. But the African rain seemed only to add to the general humidity.

She padded down the corridor in her bare feet, the hem of her cotton nightgown brushing the floor boards. Her hair stuck to her forehead and sweat dribbled between her breasts as she walked through the rooms of the silent house.

In the kitchen everything was neat and spotlessly clean. Cooking utensils and baskets hung on the walls. In a large pantry, on a slab of marble, she found dishes of the cooked grain, called couscous, and a jug containing a spicy bean and pepper sauce.

Her mouth watered at the savoury smells.

Opening cupboards and drawers, she collected a plate and cutlery. Piling the plate high with couscous she poured sauce over the top. The food looked so tempting that she dug a spoon into it at once and began to eat.

A soft footfall behind her startled her. Almost dropping the plate she whirled around.

'Oh, you frightened me!'

Dominic Rathbone stood in the doorway, a machete in his hand. He smiled slowly and put the machete down, leaning it against the kitchen wall.

'Forgive me. But I heard footsteps go past my room. I thought we had intruders.'

Gwendoline eyed the vicious-looking curved knife, as long as her forearm. She knew that a machete was used for chopping down vegetation to make a pathway through the jungle. It would also make an efficient weapon.

'Who . . . who were you expecting? Surely you would not have had cause to use that . . . that thing?'

'Probably not,' he said, 'but I do not believe in leaving things to chance. In fact,' and his voice was low and husky, 'it seems that I have found myself a thief. I would not have thought it of you Miss Farnshawe.'

She laughed uncomfortably. It was a bad joke. Surely he *was* joking, but there was no sign of that fact in his demeanour. His mouth was set in a straight line and the cold, pale-grey eyes were unblinking, reminding her again of a reptile.

She put the plate down on the table, a little alarmed at the way her hand shook.

'I hardly think this is thievery!' she said lightly. 'It is something far more simple . . . just hunger in fact.'

He took a step closer.

'Simple? I think not. Every act has its repercussions. It depends which culture one lives in. Did you know that the taking of food is punished by death in some tribes?'

'That's horrible. But I really can't think why you would mention such a thing. What has that to do with me?'

Rathbone wore an open-necked white shirt, hanging loose over his jodhpurs. His feet and ankles were bare. Obviously he had dressed hastily.

Raising one hand, he stroked the pad of his forefinger across his mouth in an amused speculative way. Leaning against the kitchen door, he arranged his long, slightly-stooped body, so that it filled the door frame.

Gwendoline's eyes opened wide. His movements did not seem threatening but he had blocked her exit.

She was aware that her heart had begun to beat fast. The taste of the spicy sauce filled her mouth, reminding her of the reason why she had come into the kitchen. The food was on the table but somehow she did not feel able to reach out and take it. In fact her appetite seemed to have gone.

Suddenly she was angry. What right had he to

comment on her actions, to make her feel like a child with its finger caught in a plum pie?

'I do not appreciate your sense of humour, Rathbone,' she said coldly.

He did not reply at first. His gaze flickered over her, lingering on the low neckline of her nightgown. A chill seemed to follow the path of his gaze. To her horror she found that her nipples were growing hard, thrusting against the thin cotton. Surely he could see them.

He could indeed, she realised, as a slow smile spread over his face.

'I do not make jokes, Miss Farnshawe,' he said. 'It seems perfectly plain to me that you are indebted to me, on two counts. But I will concede a point and call it – one.'

She was tempted to order him to stand aside and stop this nonsense. But she was intrigued by his audacity. What imagined crime must she pay recompense for?

'How so?' she said.

'Did you not sneak into my kitchen and take food without permission? If one of the servants had done such a thing they would expect to be punished. I'd strip them naked and give them a taste of the cane – '

'Mr Rathbone,' she said, her voice hard-edged. 'My family employs you. How dare you even think of speaking to me in this manner! Move aside at once. Let me pass. My brother shall hear of this.'

He did not move and he seemed unperturbed by her outburst.

'As you say Miss Farnshawe, we can forget the first point. I agree to that readily. But as to the second . . .'

He paused and moistened his mouth with the tip of his tongue, before continuing.

'You cannot deny that you woke me and caused me to believe that someone had broken into the house. Imagine my distress as I struggled to dress, my heart thumping, not knowing what I would find when I investigated. Why, I feared that we were under attack. It has been known to happen. Now I ask you, is this the action of a considerate guest?'

She could see that there was a flaw in his argument but he had a way of wording things so that they sounded plausible.

And she *had* woken him. There was no denying that. Oh, this was ridiculous. She couldn't believe that this conversation was happening. She yawned to show her boredom.

Rathbone's eyes flashed dangerously and she was once again fully alert. It seemed that she must pacify him. Very well. It was tedious but if that's what it took to make him step aside.

'I'm sorry,' she said reluctantly. 'I did not mean to wake you. Or to cause you any distress.'

'Ah, so you agree that you were at fault?'

She nodded shortly. 'I suppose I must. When you put it like that. But surely – '

There was no chance to finish her sentence. Rathbone moved swiftly.

She felt his hands on her arms, the strong thin fingers biting into her flesh as he propelled her out of the kitchen and into the dining room. The cry of surprise caught in her throat.

'Do not call out,' he said. 'I'm not going to harm you.'

Later, she was to wonder why she believed him. She kept silent, more astonished than frightened at his daring. His thin strong body pressed against hers.

She felt the coolness of his skin through her nightgown.

His smell was not unpleasant, sandalwood and hair oil, but it made her gorge rise.

Thrusting her towards the French windows, Rathbone half carried her across the room. She struggled again and would have ordered him to let her go, not caring if she raised the household with her angry cries. But his words silenced her.

'Would you have everyone see you like this?' he hissed close to her ear. 'A little undignified for a lady of your class, is it not?'

His breath was hot on her neck and sour with the smells of cigars and rum.

Opening the French windows he pulled her with him onto the porch. The scent of rain and wet vegetation filled her nostrils. It was infinitely preferable to Rathbone's body smells. The rain carried the scent of life and vigour. At some primaeval level, she sensed that Rathbone gave off the odour of corruption.

Twisting in his grip, she pushed hard against his chest. He laughed, letting her go so abruptly that she almost fell. Her arm connected with the corner of a wooden plant stand. The pain made her wince. Suddenly she found her voice.

'What the *hell* do you think you're doing?'

'Why Miss Farnshawe. I do believe that that's the first time you've ever used such language.'

The mockery in his voice stung her. The fact that he was right made it all the worse. His hard mouth wore a triumphant smile.

She faced him squarely, trembling violently with anger and frustration. Rathbone wasn't a heavily-built man, but he had dragged her out onto the porch with ease. To what purpose? Had his aim been simply to humiliate her? She had no idea what to expect from him next.

It occurred to her that he might force himself on her but she didn't think he'd go that far. He'd better not try anything of that sort. Her hands clenched into fists. If he took just one step nearer . . .

Rathbone stood looking at her calmly. His back was to the French windows, the darkness of the dining room behind him. The boards of the porch were warm and sodden under Gwendoline's feet. She felt the cool heaviness of the hem of her night-dress as it brushed wetly against her ankles.

'What do you want?' she said calmly. 'Why have you brought me out here?'

It was time that Rathbone laid out the rules of whatever game he was playing. For a game it was. He was watching her like a cat with a mouse.

He smiled then and his cold grey eyes lit up with interest.

'Ah, Miss Farnshawe you do not disappoint me. You perceive that it is a game we play. Well then, do not the English love their games? You will be familiar with croquet, lawn tennis. And charades? No doubt you play this game at Christmas in the drawing room where a log fire crackles merrily. Am I right?'

'Y . . .yes,' she stammered, unable to see the point he was making, but aware that he was mocking her and her way of life.

It was plain that Rathbone despised people of her class. Perhaps this baiting of her was some sort of twisted revenge for real or imagined slights.

'You wish to play a game of charades? Out here in the rain? Are you mad!'

Unexpectedly, he laughed.

'Some people think so but few would say it to my face. I do admire your spirit Miss Farnshawe. No, not charades, something similar. You know all about forfeits?'

In a flash she understood everything. For her transgressions – imagined or otherwise, it did not matter – Rathbone demanded that she pay his price.

He stood in the doorway of the dining room, his snake's smile not quite reaching his eyes. She might have been able to run away along the porch and escape. Just around the corner were the French windows that led into her own room. But Rathbone could move fast and he was strong, she had already seen the evidence of that.

Inwardly she trembled, but she would not let him see that.

'You could always beg me to let you go,' he said softly.

For a second she considered it but thrust the idea away. Rathbone would love to see her humbled but she knew that it wouldn't be enough. He wouldn't leave things there. He was too warped by his dislike and jealousy.

It would do no good to appeal to his honour either; Rathbone lived by his own code. Lifting her chin and staring him in the face, she said: 'Name your forfeit. Damn you!'

It was gratifying to see the slow flush which crept up from his open collar. His thin cheeks now bore two spots of red, one on each cheekbone. Those flat grey eyes of his were alive with some unhealthy emotion.

'Step backwards if you will, Miss Farnshawe. No! Don't turn around. I want to watch your face.'

Deliberately Gwendoline did as he asked. The roaring of the rain became louder as she moved outwards until she was under the porch roof. Rathbone watched her avidly.

She moved backwards towards the ribbons of water that poured in an almost solid wall from the edge of the porch roof. Her nightdress was soon soaked to her knees by the upsplash of the heavy drops on the floor boards.

'That's it. Keep your hands at your sides.'

His voice resonated with desire as he watched her hesitant steps.

She could see the growing tumescence at his groin and, suddenly, she was overwhelmed by a sense of her own power. It was time to pay him back. He might think that he was master of this game but he was about to learn otherwise.

A final step brought her under the full force of the downpour. The breath left her in a tiny groan as the warm, tropical rain gushed over her, enveloping her from head to foot in a single drenching flood.

Rathbone's thin lips parted as he watched her. She lifted her face, so that her hair was slicked back by the force of the water. Drops bounced off her face and poured in runnels over her shoulders and back, plastering the thin cotton nightdress to her body.

Lifting her hands she swept the water from her eyes and opened them. Peering sideways through the shifting silver curtain to where Rathbone was watching, she saw that he looked mesmerised. His arms were wrapped around himself and his dark eyebrows were drawn together in a frown of concentration.

Slowly she turned until she stood facing him squarely. Opening her mouth to smile, she stretched out her tongue so that the raindrops thudded onto it. She tasted the earthy sweetness of the water. Filling her mouth she swallowed greedily, at the same time cupping her chin in her hands and stroking the palms down her neck.

The sensation of the rain was wonderful. She felt like some pagan goddess, at one with the elements. As she turned, round and round, she could see the dark green background of the garden and the lightening of the sky above the trees, which meant that an African morning was breaking.

A flood of joy seemed to pour down with the rain. She let Rathbone see her enjoyment. What did it matter if the curves and hollows of her body were revealed by the sodden nightdress. Warm soft rainwater pounded her buttocks, trickling between her thighs and running into the cleft of her sex.

She laughed aloud with throaty abandon, the sound lost in the voice of the rain.

Forgetting Rathbone completely, she twisted and turned, scooping up the rain with cupped hands and trickling it over her shoulders and breasts. Throwing back her head she opened her mouth wide letting the torrent fill her, until it dribbled from the corners of her mouth and ran down her neck.

The force of the rain brought her nipples to hard peaks. They pressed almost painfully against the wet cotton. She lifted her breasts, holding them high like an offering to the potent forces of nature.

Rathbone made a sound partway between a groan and an entreaty. She ignored him.

Needles of pleasure radiated from her nipples as the rain cascaded onto her breasts. She had not been so aroused since Captain Casey showed her the way to full sexual awareness.

She put down one hand and cupped her sex, feeling the way the sodden material clung, outlining the bulge of her pubis. Arching her back she stretched like a cat, offering up her whole body to the downpour.

Her fingers began to work on her sex, rubbing in a

familiar circular motion. The warm sweetness of sexual pleasure filled her belly. Her fingers worked faster, stroking, teasing the little pouched sex upwards, so that the pressure was transferred onto the tiny erect bud.

Rathbone could never have expected this, she thought. You weren't meant to enjoy a forfeit so much. And, as if he had heard her, he gave a cry of rage.

'You damned hussy! Stop that. You've the instincts of an alley cat!'

She knew then that she'd triumphed over him.

Looking at him over one shoulder, she blew him a kiss.

'It's your fault. You made me do this. Wasn't I supposed to like it?'

His face twisted with rage. She saw that he'd lost his erection. She laughed again and raised her hands to the neckline of her nightgown. In one swift movement she pulled it down to her waist, exposing her breasts. The force of the rain swept the sodden material down her body where it bunched at her waist.

She gathered the fabric in one hand and ground it into her pubis. Her hips began to work back and forth as the muscles of her belly cramped. She could feel how swollen and slick her sex was.

Rathbone's eyes looked as if they might bulge from their sockets.

'Isn't this what you wanted?' Gwendoline taunted, thrusting her pelvis towards him. 'It's my gift to you. Come and take it – if you can.'

She almost wished that he'd take up her challenge. The way she felt right now, she'd welcome the thrust of hard male flesh into her body. She revelled in the feeling of power. Rathbone had tried to humiliate her. She laughed huskily. How the tables had turned. Given the chance, she'd milk him dry and leave him wanting!

'Rathbone – '

But he had gone. The doorway was dark and empty.

Her mood evaporated almost instantly. Instead of the desire there was only a sick emptiness and a belated surprise at her lack of inhibition.

As she stepped inside, out of the rain, she saw Rathbone hurrying from the dining room. She trembled with reaction, her elation draining even as she padded across the dining room floor. She sensed that Rathbone was a bad loser. He would not easily forgive the humiliation she had forced upon him.

It seemed that she and Rathbone had just become enemies. And she didn't need to be told that he would seek his revenge.

When Gwendoline reached her room, she found Hetty moving quietly around, laying out clean underwear and clothes for the day.

'Lawks Miss! Whatever's happened to you?' Hetty said, running to fetch towels.

Gwendoline told her, leaving out no detail. She stepped out of the sodden nightdress and into the robe which Hetty held out for her.

Hetty planted her hands on her hips and looked fierce.

'The blessed nerve of that man! Just who does he think he is?'

'He's someone who's had his own way for a long time. Too long,' Gwendoline said. 'Father and Edward have let the man have a loose rein. I think he bears watching closely.'

'Well, thank the Lord there's no real harm done,

this time,' Hetty said. 'You be careful of him, Miss. I've seen his sort before. He probably can't get it up unless he torments somebody. I reckon he could be dangerous.'

'Get it up', Gwendoline hadn't heard that expression before, but she suspected that Hetty was right about Rathbone. She had a way of speaking plainly that got right to the heart of matters.

'He seemed to lose interest when he saw that I was enjoying myself. Strange. I put on quite a show for him. I can't imagine Jonathan, or any other red-blooded man, turning me down if they'd seen me back there,' Gwendoline said.

Hetty looked at her shrewdly, but said nothing.

Wrapped in the robe and with a large towel covering her hair, Gwendoline felt safe and comfortable. Hetty's presence, practical and caring was soothing. All at once the whole episode seemed to take on an air of unreality.

As Hetty removed the towel from her head and began to rub the wet strands dry, Gwendoline began to laugh.

'And it all happened because I went to get myself some food – without asking permission! It's too ridiculous for words. Rathbone missed his vocation. What a governess he would have made!'

The next thing, she and Hetty were holding on to each other, helpless with mirth.

'He's worse'n that old tartar Miss Templeton! And I didn't think that was possible. Oh I wish I could've seen his face when you started stroking yourself!' Hetty chuckled. 'My, but you're getting bold. You're a caution Miss!'

Gwendoline giggled. 'I am aren't I? And do you know something, Hetty? I like the feeling. I like the person I'm becoming. I feel more alive in this place than I have in years.'

Hetty rubbed away at Gwendoline's damp hair, smoothing out the tangles in the long red-brown strands.

'I wonder what cook'll think when she finds a plate of food on her kitchen table!'

'And water all over the dining room floor!' Gwendoline added.

And they dissolved into laughter again.

Jonathan looked up as Gwendoline came into the room where he was working.

'Am I disturbing you?' she asked. 'I tapped on the door but you didn't answer.'

He laid down his pen and closed the journal he had been writing in.

'Come in. You are always welcome. Besides I've finished for the moment. Did you want me for something?'

She shook her head, smiling. 'I just wanted to see where you are hiding yourself away. You didn't appear for breakfast and no one has seen very much of you recently. The rains have let up but you still bury yourself away with your books.'

'I've had some work to do. I forget what time it is when I'm engrossed.'

He watched her as she walked across the room and sat down on the edge of a chaise longue which was covered in studded leather.

It pleased him that she had noticed his absence. He hadn't thought she would. There was so much to see, so much that was new to her. And he expected that Rathbone would be taking great pleasure in showing off his house, gardens and stables – the man was inordinately proud of his bloodstock.

'So, how do you like the room that Rathbone has given me for a study?' he asked dryly.

'It's . . . unusual,' Gwendoline said, searching for the right description. She cast her eye around the small room which seemed stuffed with all the oddments of furniture that were unsuitable for the rest of the house.

She wore a white blouse with full sleeves, tucked into a corded, cream skirt. A broad belt of brown leather defined her neat waist. There was a cameo brooch at her throat.

Jonathan thought how fresh and young she looked with her red-brown hair tied back in a simple bow. It was easy to imagine her picking flowers in an English country garden or sitting reading a novel under the shade of an oak tree.

For a moment he regretted giving his sanction to her desire to come to Africa. Might it not have been better to leave her to unfold slowly in surroundings familiar to her? There was so much to threaten her here, so many lessons to learn. She might need protection. Edward would be no use on that score. The onus would be on himself.

He felt the weight of that responsibility settle on him. Yet protecting Gwendoline was not an unattractive prospect. The pictures which came to his mind were very interesting, very interesting indeed.

'What are you thinking?' Gwendoline said.

'I'm sorry . . .?'

'You looked very far away there for a moment.'

'Did I? Oh it was nothing really. Just thinking out details, things to remember for when we leave here. What have you been doing while Edward and I have been poring over maps and talking with the local tribesmen?'

'Oh, you know . . . Finding my way around. Iko

has discovered that I have an interest in gardening. He's promised to show me the nursery beds and point out things which would grow in England. Nsami is friendly too. And Rathbone . . . I'm not sure how to take him. He makes me a little uneasy at times.'

He was about to ask her to elaborate but she stood up and walked towards him. The pleasure at her nearness and the faint scent of her, lilies and honey, washed all other thoughts from his mind.

Drawing close, she trailed her fingers along the polished top of his mahogany desk. He leaned back in his chair, a little smile of amusement playing about his hard mouth.

'You don't look like a scholar,' she said.

'Oh? And what does a scholar look like?'

'Well sort of dry and dusty. With perhaps a squint and mutton-chop whiskers. You're much more – vital looking. You look as if you're made to . . . to go out and do things.'

'If you mean, I know what I want from life, that's true.' He saw the slight tremor of her lips. His inference wasn't lost on her. Changing tack, he went on, 'And do I detect some impatience in you today?'

Gwendoline studied the books in a case on the wall above his desk. 'You've found me out. I'm eager to get going. How long will it be before we set off? Edward says we're going to Calabar in the French Congo.'

'That's right. In a week, maybe more. Not long now. You're surely not bored?'

'Oh, no. It's just that the rains have made me restless. I want to see more of Africa.'

He thought there was something she was keeping back but he did not press her. He studied her reactions as she examined a carving on his desk, a fertility goddess with long pointed breasts and a pronounced vulva. Next to it stood a male counterpart, the penis jutting straight out from the groin, a potent symbol of his virility.

Gwendoline's cheeks coloured slightly as she replaced the goddess next to the god, then began picking up books.

Jonathan watched her without speaking, tapping one finger on his bottom lip; a habit of his when thoughtful.

'May I?' she said, opening a handsome, leather-bound volume and flicking over pages.

He made an expansive gesture. 'Certainly. If my studies interest you.'

'They do. I would like to learn everything I can about the places we intend to visit.'

She turned to the title page of the book in her hand.

'Mungo Park,' she said. 'Who is he?'

'He's a man I admire greatly. A Scottish explorer. He was the first European to travel into the real heart of this continent.'

'He must have been very brave.'

'He was. But even more than his bravery, I admire his outlook. He did not set out to conquer or convert, like so many others have done. He wanted only to observe and to learn, to study the people and get to know them, their customs, their loves and hates.'

'Like you. He sounds like a man of great integrity.'

Jonathan looked up at the husky softness of her voice. The regard in her eyes warmed him – more than that, but he didn't like to dwell on the fact.

It was pleasant to have her company. Usually he worked alone, translating handwritten texts and making drawings of native artifacts – dry enough activities. He had never known another woman who

193

had expressed more than a passing interest in his work.

There was a moment of silence, while Gwendoline studied the open pages of the book. At first he had been attracted to her merely for her looks and spirits. The streak of perversity in her nature matched his own. But on board the clipper and again now, he glimpsed her bright intellect. They had far more in common than he had at first realised.

Over the past days, shut up in the house while the rains thundered down around them, he found himself becoming more drawn to her with every passing day. When the truth of his feelings was first borne in on him, he found himself as unnerved as if a python had just slithered out from under his chair.

He was uncomfortable with this fear. He considered himself to have courage, indeed he'd faced danger many times but this was a new and intangible fear – something he found very difficult to cope with. And that knowledge shamed him.

That was the real reason why he had buried himself away with his books and studies. If he set himself apart from Gwendoline, maybe he could exorcise these feelings. They were unasked for and unwanted.

Dammit, he had no room for a woman in his life.

'Shall we be covering any of the same ground as Mungo Park?' Gwendoline asked, breaking into his thoughts.

'Not on this trip,' he said, wondering at the fact that his voice was calm and even, when he felt the exact opposite. He smiled, trying to break his mood.

'We should fare better than he did.'

She looked quizzically at him.

'Park was captured by a group of Moors. Fatima, the wife of their king, wanted to see a white man.'

'What happened to him?'

'He was held prisoner, tormented and humiliated. By the time he got to meet the queen he was half-starved and racked by dysentery. Luckily she looked kindly on him but he only barely escaped with his life.'

'How dreadful. But it's intriguing too. I'd like to know more about him.'

'Take the book if you wish.'

'Oh I couldn't really. It must be valuable . . .'

'Please. I want you to. If I need it for my studies I will ask for its return.'

She held the book close to her breasts, her arms folded across the embossed leather cover as if it was the greatest gift anyone had ever given her.

'Well then. Hadn't you better be off?' he said curtly.

She looked at him blankly.

He indicated her clothes. 'You're dressed for riding, aren't you? It's the first day since we arrived that it hasn't rained. Aren't you keen to get into the saddle?'

'Oh yes,' she said. 'Edward and Rathbone are taking me to see the trading station. I'm keeping them waiting.'

Jonathan felt an unexpected surge of satisfaction.

Rathbone, in particular, hated to be kept waiting. He would be pacing back and forth in the stables, taking out his bad temper on whoever was the nearest.

A sardonic smile curved Jonathan's lips. It wouldn't hurt Rathbone or Edward to be inconvenienced. The former was too full of his own self-importance anyway. And Edward showed signs of becoming like him. Jonathan quite liked Edward but he was not blind to his faults.

'I'll take great care of your book,' Gwendoline said earnestly, half-turning away.

At the door she paused and flashed him a mischievous smile. 'I'll even sleep with it under my pillow.'

'For that alone I envy Park,' Jonathan said pointedly, watching with satisfaction the ready colour that stained her cheeks.

Gwendoline sat comfortably in the saddle as her horse followed Rathbone's mount. It felt good to be out riding, to feel the movement of the horse's muscles against her thighs.

If only she could forget about Rathbone's presence she would enjoy herself. Edward's stocky body moved in time with his horse. He smiled at her. His handsome, fleshy face wore a look of complacence. Edward was obviously at ease with himself and the rest of the world.

'You know Gwenie, I'm glad you came along. I had my reservations as you know but things seem to be working out well. I can see that the climate suits you.'

She smiled back at him indulgently. Edward hadn't the slightest idea how she felt about anything. He hadn't noticed the strained atmosphere between Rathbone and herself. Jonathan would have noticed it at once.

She wished she had asked Jonathan to come riding with them. She felt sure that he could have been persuaded away from his studies. Why hadn't she asked him? Perhaps because he had seemed to be in a strange mood. On the surface he was pleasant enough. But she had sensed his underlying wariness.

She did not know what had possessed her to borrow the book about Mungo Park. It had been an impulse to ask him. Perhaps the book would establish a tenuous link between them. She had begun to read it before the ride and was finding it fascinating.

She and Jonathan would have something to talk about when she returned his book. So often they seemed to be circling each other, uneasy as dogs from two separate packs.

Clouds of steam rose from the jungle which pressed in on all sides, some way back from the road. Fat drops, like crystals, dripped from the big tropical leaves.

Gwendoline had woken to the sound of silence that morning. After the constant noise of the last week, she had been disoriented, unable to understand the strangeness which was silence. Then she had thrown back the bedclothes and hurried to dress.

It was amazing that it could pour down for days, swelling the lakes and turning the rivers into torrents, yet the sodden ground had dried out in hours as soon as the sun broke through.

The sky was a clear, unblemished blue. The light seemed to show up all the colours around her with an almost merciless clarity. It was the quality of the daylight, she decided, that gave Africa its uniqueness.

The trading post, with its warehouse and landing stage, was behind them. They were making their way back to the house by a roundabout route. Rathbone, in front, urged his horse towards the fields.

'This is my own land,' he informed them proudly. 'Bought with the money I've earned. We grow food crops, cassava, mango, millet.'

Gwendoline recognised a track to one side as that leading back to the house and gardens. They seemed to have travelled quite a distance but they had come almost full circle. These were the buildings whose

197

lights she had glimpsed, from the farthest point of the garden, on the night they arrived.

They reached a group of thatched huts. Gwendoline waved at the villagers who came out to greet them. There were lots of happy brown-faced children. The adults looked rather thin by Western standards but she knew from Jonathan that many African people were naturally tall and slender.

'We'll take our ease for a while. I have some business to discuss,' Rathbone said, dismounting. 'This way Edward. I'll introduce you to the head man. If you want something doing you have to convince him first.'

He gestured to a young woman who brought a rug and a jug of drink for Gwendoline. Gwendoline thanked her and made herself comfortable in the shade of a baobab tree. The huge bulbous trunk provided enough shade for all the children who followed her.

The young woman smiled, showing strong white teeth with a gap in the centre. She wore only a woven skirt. Copper rings were clustered around her neck. More of them hung from her ear lobes, distended into long slits by the weight of the jewellery.

Gwendoline sipped the drink, which was a sort of fermented beer. The women and children clustered around her, chattering away in their own language. She smiled at them and allowed them to stroke her hair and pluck at her clothes.

Rathbone appeared at the door of one of the huts and shouted an order in an angry voice. At once the women and children dispersed.

'It's quite all right. I don't mind a bit . . .' Gwendoline said.

'They've work to do,' Rathbone said shortly. 'Doesn't do to encourage slacking.'

'But really, couldn't you make an exception? I was enjoying all the fuss.'

His face darkened and she knew she'd gone too far. This was his land and the villagers were his employees.

'You're not in England now Miss Farnshawe,' he said sourly. 'You'll not get your own way in everything out here. Perhaps you should get used to that.'

Rathbone turned his back on her. She found his habit of dismissing her, when he'd said his piece, infuriating.

Left alone, Gwendoline read a few pages of the book she'd borrowed from Jonathan, but she felt too hot and restless to settle for long. She decided to go for a walk. There was the faintest breeze coming from the direction of a nearby lake.

Pushing herself to her feet she unfurled a sunshade and began strolling around the village. There were pens containing goats and pigs. Yellow dogs ran about freely. Inside the open doorway of a large hut she could see Rathbone and Edward conversing with an elderly African.

The village consisted of one main street, with the largest hut set at one end. It didn't take long for Gwendoline to walk past the last hut and head for the glint of water in the near distance.

Flamingoes flew past overhead. White egrets leapt into the clear sky, disturbed by her approach. Near the lake, waterbuck and gazelle grazed. It all looked so peaceful and beautiful.

Gwendoline searched in her shoulder bag for pencils and paper and began sketching. There was a stand of trees to one side of the lake and a dusty track leading into them. She pencilled them in, concentrating on the shape of the shifting leaves.

Looking more closely she thought she saw the

shape of a building through the trees. It seemed an unlikely place for it, set apart from the village and the fields. Perhaps it was a place for storage. She reached for her box of paints and the little screw-topped bottle of water she always carried with her. Before long she had finished her sketch of the lake and trees and was laying-in streaks of ochre and sienna.

Engrossed in her work, she did not at first hear the voice. Then it came again, faintly.

'Help me. Please. Help me.'

Putting down her brushes, she listened. There was silence. Had she imagined the voice? She looked back towards the village but there was no one. Then she heard it again. It sounded as if it came from the trees, from the place where she thought she had glimpsed some kind of a building.

Packing up her paints and paper she started walking towards the track which led around the lake. She had gone a few yards when she felt a hand on her arm. With a cry of alarm she turned and found herself looking into Rathbone's face.

'We're ready to leave,' he said.

She shook off his hand, not bothering to hide her distaste. His face tightened and she saw the flash of anger in his eyes.

'I thought I heard someone call out. Over there.' She pointed towards the trees. 'There's a building of some kind there. I glimpsed it through the branches when the breeze moved them.'

'That's impossible. There's nothing over there but trees,' Rathbone said quickly. 'You must have heard me calling you. You were so engrossed in your painting that I couldn't attract your attention.'

It seemed a reasonable explanation. So why did she sense that he was lying?

'Possibly. But I'm sure that I heard someone else. Someone calling for help. They sounded afraid or desperate.'

'How did you know?' he said dryly, his cold eyes mocking her.

'Know what?'

'That they were calling for help.'

'I heard the words – quite clearly. "Help. Please. Help me,"' she said slowly as if speaking to a child. Did he think she was an idiot?

'This . . . person you imagined you heard. Did he speak in English?'

'Well . . . yes. Of course? What of it?'

'Then I'm afraid you must have been mistaken. There's only you, Edward, Jonathan and I who speak English. The villagers all speak Swahili. I'm sure it was my shouts you heard. Now, are you finished here? We're about to start back. Perhaps you've a touch of the sun Miss Farnshawe. That parasol seems a little flimsy for Africa. I suggest you take a nap when we reach the house.'

Without waiting for her answer, Rathbone started back towards the village. Gwendoline followed, fuming at his rudeness.

Could she have been mistaken? It was possible. As he said, she had been engrossed in her painting.

All the way back to the house she thought about the incident. Rathbone wore a closed-in look, his mouth set in a thin line. She knew that he considered the matter closed. It would be a waste of time to bring it up again.

It wasn't until they were nearing the house, that she realised what was still bothering her.

Suddenly she knew that Rathbone *had* lied. Otherwise how would he have known that it was a man's voice she had heard? She hadn't said it was a male voice, Rathbone had assumed it.

For some reason he wanted her to think that she had imagined the episode. She cast her mind back, bringing the image of the trees into her mental view. The way the breeze had shifted the leaves – there had been regular shaped patches in those shifting shadows. Windows. A door. The sunlight had glinted on white-painted walls – there *was* a building!

She was certain of it now. Rathbone had lied. She shivered. Not many people had the gall to look you in the eye and tell you a falsehood without flinching.

But Rathbone had. Not a flicker had passed across those flat, grey eyes. He must be a very practised liar. And if he had lied about the building, what more did he have to hide?

She must tell Jonathan about her suspicions. Then she remembered that he was out of the house for the rest of the day. Tomorrow then. If someone was in danger, the sooner she investigated the better.

Chapter Twelve

Gwendoline decided to spend the late part of the afternoon in the garden. She changed into a pale-green muslin dress and straw bonnet. The heat was less fierce than at midday, and it was pleasant in the shade of the trees.

Iko showed her around, urging her to pick a large bunch of flowers to decorate her room. She found the young man to be polite and charming. He seemed a little nervous of her at first but their shared interest in plants soon forged a bond between them.

She strolled down the grass paths, bending down to inhale the perfume of one exotic bloom after another and picking whatever took her fancy. She loved the huge canna lilies, with their beetroot-coloured stems and fiery orange blooms – the sprays of yellow mimosa too, with their honey-sweet scent.

Iko walked behind her, nodding approvingly at her choice as she filled her arms, burying her face in the cool petals. His tall, handsome frame was draped in white linen. Now and again he flashed her one of his remarkable smiles and she thought, as she had the first time she met him, how his whole face came alive when his expression softened.

He was like a larger version of Nsami. Though his frame was more powerful and his shoulders broad and strong, his features had the same pleasing symmetry and his dark eyes were as hypnotic and sensual as the housemaid's.

Gwendoline relaxed, trying not to think of Rathbone and the lies he had told her that morning. Brightly-coloured birds flickered in the branches overhead. The thickness of the vegetation and the humming of insects made the garden seem so – vital. There was the feeling of life teeming all around them. She saw ants clambering up the sides of a tree, little sawn-off pieces of leaves in their jaws.

Pausing near a clump of tree-ferns and palms, she trailed her fingers in the water of an ornamental pool, then, rounding a corner, she saw the woven cane walls of a summerhouse. She remembered glimpsing the little house when Rathbone had shown her the garden by torchlight.

Quickening her step, she made for the summerhouse. Iko was at her side in a trice, his long-fingered, brown hand on her sleeve.

'Missy wait, please,' he said, looking uneasy.

She stopped in surprise, looking down at his hand, then up at him for an explanation. Iko removed his hand and smiled apologetically.

'Forgive me, Missy.'

'Of course. You just startled me for a moment. What's the matter, Iko? I just want to have a look at the summerhouse.'

'Nothing the matter, Missy . . . it is . . .'

Before he finished the sentence, Nsami appeared round a bend in the path. She was wearing a red robe which fastened on one shoulder, leaving the other bare. At her waist was a belt of chased-metal links. It was twisted, as if she had just dressed hurriedly.

Gwendoline realised that Nsami was coming from the direction of the summerhouse. She must have heard their voices. By the look on Nsami's lovely face, she was none too pleased about being discovered there.

Nsami said a few words in her own language to Iko. Gwendoline heard the note of anger in her voice. Nsami bobbed her a shallow curtsey and hurried past. Gwendoline turned to watch Nsami walk back towards the main house and was in time to see her slant a look of venom at Iko.

Iko looked crestfallen.

'Why is Nsami so angry?' she asked him.

'She is not angry. Only – ' Iko stopped. He looked uncomfortable. 'I cannot say more. Nsami . . . I must go after her.'

'Yes, of course. I'll find my own way back.'

It seemed that wherever she went she stumbled upon mysteries and secrets. There was a conspiracy of silence in Rathbone's house. What were they all hiding? As soon as Iko was out of sight, Gwendoline continued down the path until she came to the summerhouse.

It was a tiny, two-storey building with woven bamboo walls and a thatched roof. Gwendoline was captivated by its doll's-house perfection. In an English garden it would have been called a folly. There was no one around. She took hold of the door handle and twisted it.

Nothing happened. The house was locked. Surprised, she tried again. This was ridiculous. Whoever heard of a summerhouse being locked? Shading her eyes with cupped hands she peered into the interior.

It was difficult to see inside. There was no glass but slatted, wooden blinds were fitted to the windows. Through a chink she could see bulky objects that must be furniture and a rack of some kind on the far wall. Riding crops and something like a bundle of thongs lay on a table just within the line of her vision.

She was puzzled. Whyever was there riding equipment in such a place? There was a stealthy rustling in the undergrowth to one side and she jumped. Had a large animal got into the garden? Her skin crawled at the thought that she could be in danger. She began backing away from the summerhouse, preparing to run for help.

A moment later a man stepped out of the bushes. Gwendoline's panic faded when she recognised Rathbone. He had a key in his hand and he was looking so intently towards the summerhouse that it was a moment before he saw her. At the expression on his face, Gwendoline almost recoiled. His eyes were wild and there was a look of desperation about him.

He saw her then and his face changed. The transformation was remarkable. His face became blank, while his mouth twisted with anger.

'Ah, Miss Farnshawe again,' he said dryly. 'Is it curiosity that brings you here? Or do you just have a genius for being in the wrong place at the wrong time?'

Oh he was insufferable. Never had she met with such arrogance.

'I don't know what you mean!' she said. 'Am I not allowed to walk in the garden? I didn't realise that I had to ask your permission for that as well as for taking extra food!'

At the reference to the incident in the kitchen, he

allowed himself a wry smile. The tension went out of him all at once.

'Perhaps I spoke hastily,' he said preparing to turn away.

Oh no you don't, not this time, she thought. I won't be dismissed like a servant.

'Wait! I want an answer. What *is* going on? I keep feeling like I'm intruding somehow. I know something's going on here. But it's just out of reach. It's like . . . like water slipping through my fingers. I don't understand.'

Rathbone smiled again, slowly and without warmth.

'Of course you don't, Miss Farnshawe. A woman like you wouldn't. It's best that you concentrate on those things that *do* concern you. And leave the rest of us to our secrets. Everyone needs them you know.'

Gwendoline watched him walk off. She was so angry she could taste it. Rathbone thought she was a fool. Well, she'd show him. Before she set out for the interior with Jonathan, she was going to get to the bottom of things. Rathbone was up to something.

Jonathan. He was the one man who would help her. She knew that he disliked Rathbone as much as she did. She'd speak to Jonathan. It was just a matter of picking the right moment.

With her arms full of canna lilies and fragrant, yellow mimosa, she stalked back to the house and went in search of a vase.

The next morning, Gwendoline woke to find golden sunlight flooding her room.

She looked towards the open windows and stretched luxuriously. Jonathan's book lay open on the side table. She was finding it a fascinating read, especially since she'd discovered the pages of text in his own handwriting, which had been hidden inside the book. How surprised he'd be when he found out that she'd been reading about fertility customs.

She smiled. Perhaps he wouldn't be surprised at all. He might have intended her to find the text.

The cotton sheets slid against her skin as she moved. For the first time in her life she had slept naked – it being too hot even for the thinnest of cotton nightgowns. The experience was so delightful that she intended to repeat it.

She remembered the previous night. The feel of the cool cotton brushing against her nipples, her thighs and buttocks, had awoken desire in her. Caressing herself with eager searching fingers, she had stroked herself to one climax after another.

The thought of the wicked pleasure brought a rush of blood to her cheeks. She had imagined a man watching her as she thrust her hips up off the bed and stood on shoulders and heels while her fingers were buried deeply inside her soaking sex.

It was Jonathan she saw. She had pictured his face as her pleasure built, imagining the harsh lines softening with desire, his mouth coming closer as he bent to kiss her. He would be flushed under his deep tan. The scar standing out on his neck . . .

And then, intruding on her fantasies, came the truth of their relationship. Jonathan might have become her friend – perhaps more than that – but it didn't change the fact that he had played with her; mocked her innocence when she had been ready to give herself to him. She had not forgiven him that. Nor would she, until he came to her and begged her for her favours.

So then she imagined that he watched her from a distance, wanting her, desiring her and suffering because she rejected his advances in favour of her own expert fingers. That image had excited her even more and she'd let her thighs fall open and gripped her engorged bud between finger and thumb, pulling on it gently until she could stand the rough pressure no more. Then she'd massaged her sex in firm circular motions. Her final climax had been a mixture of pleasure and soreness.

A wonderful lassitude had followed and she had fallen asleep, half-uncovered, on the pillow of her tangled hair.

Gwendoline yawned in the sun-bright morning. A warm, grass-scented breeze billowed the mosquito net, which covered the bed on all sides and softened her immediate view of the room. She could not remember pulling the net down so neatly. Nsami must have come in during the night and adjusted it.

There was a polite tap at the door and Nsami came into the room holding a breakfast tray. Gwendoline sat up and smiled a little warily.

'Good morning, Nsami. This is unexpected.'

Nsami looked striking in a pure white sleeveless tunic and spotless head cloth. A woven belt, sewn with brightly coloured beads, defined her slender waist. She gave Gwendoline a friendly grin as she rolled back the netting and hooked it out of the way. Whatever had been wrong with her yesterday in the garden seemed to have been resolved.

'You go on hunt soon this day. I hear Mr Jonathan talk with my master. I bring food to save time. Missy sleep well?'

'Very well, thank you,' Gwendoline said, reaching for the tray and settling it across her knees. 'It was good of you to pull down the net last night. I did not think to do it myself.'

'I cover you up. No get bites,' Nsami said in her

accented English. 'Missy have soft skin . . . very great beauty.'

Gwendoline was surprised and pleased at the unexpected compliment. She wondered what had prompted Nsami to such a declaration.

Then she understood. She had pulled the thin sheet to cover herself from her waist down only, enjoying the feel of the soft breeze on her damp skin. Nsami must have seen her lying there semi-naked. She was embarrassed to think of Nsami looking down on her unclothed body.

Once, Gwendoline thought she had seen a brief flare of desire on the African girl's face. She had dismissed the incident in her own mind, having convinced herself that she was imagining things, now she was not so sure. Nsami had the ghost of the same look on her face now. Gwendoline found it impossible to meet her eyes.

'Thank . . . thank you, Nsami,' she said. 'For the breakfast I mean.'

Nsami bobbed a shallow curtsey.

'I leave you to eat. I go fetch water for washing.'

Gwendoline realised that she was famished and fell to work at once on the dish of sliced mango and pineapple, all sprinkled with shredded coconut. It was delicious. There was also a pot of coffee. She drank two cups with cream and was just finishing when Nsami reappeared with two enormous jugs of hot water.

Gwendoline gave her the empty breakfast tray. Nsami placed it on a side table and pulled out the tub from behind the woven screen. Gwendoline waited for the young woman to leave before she got out of bed but Nsami showed no signs of doing so. Instead she laid out soap, a large sponge and a pile of clean towels, then she stood with her hands clasped loosely.

'I help wash now,' she said firmly.

'There is really no need . . .' Gwendoline began.

Nsami nodded emphatically. 'But yes. I like help. I wash you.'

Gwendoline was at a loss. Nsami seemed to have set her mind on helping. She stood perfectly still and composed, a slender figure dressed all in white. Her brown limbs looked smooth and shiny. Gwendoline had a sudden confusing thought. What would it be like to slide her hand down one slim brown arm? Or to touch the beautiful face with her fingertips?

Nsami smiled, her full mouth parting to display her perfect teeth.

'I wash. You like – very much,' she said.

Gwendoline felt a tightness in her chest. Nsami's voice was soft and full of promise. A pulse in her throat began to beat rapidly. The thought of those slim brown hands washing her was enticing. Why not? No one would know. She knew she should refuse – order Nsami to leave – call Hetty to help her dress.

Instead she found herself saying, 'Very well. Pass me my robe please.'

She slipped the robe on over her nakedness before she got out of bed. How foolish it seemed to preserve her modesty for a few more moments. But she couldn't help it. She felt shy and unsure of the situation.

Padding across the room to the dressing table, she opened a box of pins. Her fingers were trembling slightly as she swept the hair off her neck and pinned it up. Turning, she crossed the room to where Nsami waited next to the empty tub.

Gwendoline's every nerve seemed aware of the

presence of the other woman. The woven grass mats and bare boards were warm under her bare feet. She stopped next to the bath and paused before undressing.

With a graceful gesture Nsami lifted the light cotton robe from Gwendoline's shoulders and laid it aside. The air in the room was a few degrees warmer than her body heat and was perfumed with her own intangible feminine musk. It seemed to Gwendoline as if the air brushed against her skin, as if she walked through silk.

Her cheeks grew hot as she became conscious of Nsami's dark eyes looking her over. Only one other woman had ever seen her naked and that was Hetty.

But Hetty did not look at her with frank desire as Nsami did. Jonathan looked at her like that. It was exciting in a strange, forbidden sort of way. Gwendoline had heard of girls who had admired their teachers with a passion. Could this be the same? Nsami was exotic and beautiful and Gwendoline found pleasure in looking at her too. But she was shocked by the confusion of her own emotions.

Nsami gestured to the tub, indicating that Gwendoline should step into it. She did so, with some relief. The wooden tub resembled a hip bath, dipping low at the front and with a high raised back. It was just the right size for her to kneel comfortably and rest on her haunches.

Nsami picked up the sponge and soap. Gwendoline wondered why she did not tip the hot water into the tub. Then as Nsami dipped the sponge and soaped it, she realised that Nsami meant to give her a soapy bath.

The soapy water foamed across her shoulders as Nsami rubbed gently at her skin. Creamy runnels snaked over her breasts and ran down her belly, collecting in a pool in the indentation made by her closed thighs. She was soon covered with suds and expected Nsami to rinse off with clean water. Instead Nsami reached for what seemed to be a piece of some slightly abrasive plant material.

She began scrubbing Gwendoline's back and shoulders, working in meticulous circles down the small of her back and over her buttocks. Shifting her attention to the front of Gwendoline's body, she scrubbed more gently at her breasts, stomach and thighs.

The sensation was pleasant and invigorating – more than pleasant when the scratchy material brushed against her nipples. Gwendoline's skin felt warm and tingly. It slowly turned a deep rose-pink. The orchid scent of the soap rose around her in a cloud of fragrant steam.

As Nsami continued to scrub every inch of her body, Gwendoline relaxed into her expert touch, closing her eyes and resting her head against the high back of the tub. The warmth and the perfume, the rhythm of Nsami's scrubbing, all exerted a gentle lull on her senses. It would have been easy to fall into a doze.

Nsami tapped her gently on the shoulder, smiling, her long black eyes crinkling at Gwendoline's obvious pleasure.

'I told you you would like, no?'

She indicated that Gwendoline should change position. Gwendoline uncurled her legs and sat down, but there was not enough room to stretch out. Nsami showed her that she must loop her legs over the low sides of the tub if she was to be comfortable.

Gwendoline resisted the urge to clench her knees together. In her present position her thighs were parted and her sex was spread open. It was unthinkable that Nsami could see her pink inner lips, framed by the silky curls. She made a move to cover herself with one hand but Nsami stopped her. One slim brown hand covered Gwendoline's own, moving it and replacing it gently but firmly on the rim of the bath tub.

'Please. Let me see.'

Nsami did not trouble to hide her fascination. As she soaped Gwendoline, she glanced often between her legs, her eyes full of avid interest.

Gwendoline squirmed inwardly, not sure how to react. The many admiring glances were discomforting. She was experiencing most inappropriate sensations. Nsami was altogether too beautiful and her hands were too knowing, too dangerous.

As the young woman bent over the bath Gwendoline saw Nsami's profile in close-up. Her lashes were curling fans, lying like shadows on her dusky skin; her nose was neat and rounded at the tip; and her mouth – her mouth was full, the pigment of her lips so dark that they had a purplish tint. There was a darker line around the edge of Nsami's mouth, as if someone had traced its fullness with a black crayon.

Would Nsami's sex have the same coloration? Suddenly and shockingly, Gwendoline felt the urge to move closer, to press her lips to Nsami's mouth.

Gwendoline screwed her eyes shut. Enough was enough. She must put a stop to this. Why ever had she let it begin?

As she drew up her knees, preparing to resume her earlier, more modest pose, Nsami protested.

'No. Please no . . . Missy. A little longer only. I must wash there.'

And before she realised what Nsami meant to do, the African girl slid her soapy hands down over

214

Gwendoline's belly and began washing the silky hair on her mound.

Gwendoline was too surprised to push Nsami's hands away. Besides it felt far too good. The long fingers made tiny circles as Nsami moved over the plump outer lips of Gwendoline's sex and delved between her thighs, washing her thoroughly.

And now Nsami did not speak or look at Gwendoline but she knew that the beautiful African girl sensed her tension. To feel such pleasure at the hands of a woman was unnatural, wasn't it? She almost put her hand on Nsami's. Words rose to her lips. She lifted her arm . . .

And then Nsami's soapy fingers were moving inwards, moving over her intimate folds in a slow seductive rhythm and it felt wonderful. The feeling was lighter than the touch of Captain Casey's fingers, somehow still impersonal, but knowing nonetheless.

Now Gwendoline did not want to protest. The fact that the caress was forbidden, wicked, added an edge to her pleasure. There was a slippery heat, a diffused but intensely erotic pressure in Nsami's touch.

Using both hands, Nsami moved her fingers up the sides of Gwendoline's parted slit, exerting a slight pressure outwards, so that her sex was opened more widely. With each movement, each subtle stretching, Gwendoline's pleasure bud was forced to stand proud of the surrounding flesh. Before long Gwendoline was willing Nsami to touch her – there. If only she would brush against that tingling little spot, drag her fingertips against it by accident.

Nsami rubbed the pads of her thumbs over the delicate inner flesh, moving either side of the little pleasure bud, never quite touching it but stimulating it, as if she hardly realised what she was doing.

She took her time over stroking Gwendoline's eager flesh, spreading the scented lather over the whole of her sex. Sometimes she drew the outer sex-lips together and rubbed the enclosed little purse more firmly with her whole hand. Then she would spread the sex again, using her fingertips to smooth back the inner curves until, Gwendoline thought, her aroused sex must resemble a ripe fig.

The feeling of having her sex exposed, after being confined, added to Gwendoline's pleasure. She sensed Nsami's enjoyment in the act. Perhaps she had never seen a white woman spread so intimately before her.

And then, when Gwendoline thought she couldn't stand the teasing caresses any longer, Nsami moved one fingertip over the now rigid bud. Back and forth she moved, pressing firmly, smoothing the bud from its tiny hood of flesh.

Soon the little bud was even more swollen and throbbing rhythmically. Gwendoline was so aroused that she ached. The now familiar pleasure began radiating outwards. This was what she had done to herself in the night. But it was so much more tantalising to lay back and relax while someone else manipulated her. Nsami was obviously an expert.

Gwendoline wondered idly where Nsami had acquired her skill. Then she forgot everything and gave herself up to the exquisite thrill of having another woman pleasure her. She tensed the muscles of her thighs and buttocks, trying not to give in to the urge to work her hips back and forth. It was unthinkable that she press herself towards Nsami's hand, rub her hungry flesh against those slender brown fingers.

Gwendoline caught her breath as Nsami flicked her erect bud back and forth beneath her fingertips.

The rapid motion coaxed new sensations from her sex. A moan rose in her throat. She caged it behind her teeth.

Judging exactly the moment when Gwendoline would have lost control, Nsami paused and spread the creamy lather up over her breasts and belly, stroking and teasing, until Gwendoline's nipples too were hard and erect, standing up through the soapy bubbles, like rosebuds floating in milk.

Nsami looked Gwendoline full in the face and smiled.

'I am good, no?' she said softly, the tip of her pink tongue snaking out to moisten her full, shapely lips. 'Women know how to please other women.'

Gwendoline absorbed the truth of that statement as her breath came faster and faster.

'Yes, Nsami . . . Yes.'

She was past being able to stop Nsami, stroking, caressing – oh God, pinching her most tender flesh. The same delicious sensations she felt when she pleasured her own body had her in their grip now.

If Nsami continued, she would be swept up onto the high peaks of ecstasy and spend in great arching waves. She was overwhelmed by a raging lust. If only Nsami would plunge her fingers into her body or spread her sex-lips wider, wider and take the swollen bud between finger and thumb.

Her whole sex throbbed and throbbed so sweetly. She ached for every new touch, every intimate gesture, and she craved everything that Nsami was willing to give. If only the African girl would kiss her, grind that full mouth down over her own. Gwendoline wanted to thrust her tongue into the other woman's mouth, to taste her, to caress her sex too.

But it was too awful. The feelings were frightening.

Better that she did nothing but let Nsami have her way. Oh but she could not let Nsami see her reach a climax. It was too private . . .

'Missy like me, I think,' Nsami said. Then laughed throatily when, for a reply, Gwendoline moaned softly and let her head fall back under its own weight.

Whatever Gwendoline thought, her body had quite taken over. She could not utter a word. The pleasure grew, pooling and centring. Her bud had become so swollen that it stood out from its hood like a tiny cock. Her thighs shook with tension as she strained towards her release.

Almost. Almost there . . .

Then, abruptly, Nsami took her hands away.

Gwendoline opened her eyes wide, moaning with disappointment and frustration. She was on fire. What had gone wrong?

Nsami saw the look on her face and smiled. She patted Gwendoline's arm before moving away.

'Missy wait now.'

Gwendoline was stunned. Did Nsami intend to leave her like this? To continue with her toilette as if nothing unusual had happened? She felt that Nsami had toyed with her out of mischief. This must be her way of revenging herself for some imagined slight. She was annoyed and not a little confused.

Perhaps it was her own fault. She had encouraged Nsami by her passivity. She *knew* she should have stopped this earlier, when she had been in control of herself. She felt foolish and angry. But she had no one but herself to blame.

Pressing down on the sides of the bath, Gwendoline prepared to get up and dry herself. The thing to do was to pretend that nothing had happened. Her face burned with mortification.

'Missy wait. Please,' Nsami said, coming back to the bath and smiling down at her.

Gwendoline saw that there was nothing of malice in the young woman's smile. Nsami looked mischievous and totally in control. Game-playing seemed to be *de rigueur* in Rathbone's house. If Nsami wanted to pretend that this had been a normal bath, then so be it.

Silently Gwendoline sank back in the bath, waiting for Nsami to finish.

Picking up the second jug of warm water Nsami sluiced Gwendoline's body, washing off the soapy lather. When the jug was half full, she paused and positioned the stream between Gwendoline's parted thighs. Carefully she trickled a thin stream of water directly onto her aroused and sensitive folds.

It was so unexpected, so welcome, that a groan broke from Gwendoline.

A surge of intense pleasure washed right through her. She arched her back as Nsami poured the water, trickling it back and forth across her straining bud. Her crisis approached swiftly. She could not hold it back.

Her mouth opened on a little cry as she pushed her hips up towards the water. Then her climax broke over her, sweet and prolonged, seeming to spread inside and find an echo in her pulsing womb. Tremors passed over Gwendoline's belly as the internal flutters faded slowly.

She closed her eyes, allowing the weakness to spread through all her limbs. The pleasure had been so intense that she was utterly drained by it.

Nsami put the empty jug on the floor and picked up a large towel. Her face was impassive now.

But for the trembling in her thighs and the afterglow around her sex, Gwendoline might have imagined the whole episode. She stood up shakily and stepped out of the bath onto the grass mat. Nsami dried her, rubbing her limbs with a soft scented towel.

'Come. Relax now,' Nsami said, leading Gwendoline towards the bed.

She spread a clean white towel on top of the sheet. Gwendoline sank onto the bed and lay full-length. Nsami uncorked a bottle and a delicious fragrance of orchids and sweet spices filled the room.

'This give skin much beauty,' Nsami said, pouring a few drops of oil into her palms.

Using firm but gentle strokes, she massaged the aromatic oil into Gwendoline's shoulders and arms. It seemed that a special intimacy had grown between the two women.

Gwendoline felt totally at ease now and very relaxed. She did not mind that Nsami paid a great deal of attention to her breasts, commenting on their size and shape, nor did she mind when Nsami exclaimed at the narrowness of her waist.

Gwendoline explained that her small waist was due to the stays she had worn for most of her life. Nsami thought that most amusing. As Nsami chattered on in her accented English, Gwendoline waited for a break in the conversation.

While Nsami continued to massage every inch of her, she said casually: 'When you and Iko left me in the garden, I went to see the summerhouse. Rathbone was there. Was he waiting for you?'

Nsami nodded, her teeth gripping her lower lip.

'I thought so. He was going to punish you, wasn't he? Damn him to hell!'

She almost sprang up and grasped Nsami's robe. Certain that, if she was to pull it from her, she would find whip marks on her body.

Nsami pressed her back onto the bed, her hands gentle but firm. She seemed a little agitated, so Gwendoline fell silent.

'Missy turn over.'

Gwendoline did so and Nsami began massaging her back, buttocks, and legs.

After a while Gwendoline asked softly, 'Does Rathbone beat you often Nsami?'

Nsami paused in her movements, then went back to describing big oily circles on Gwendoline's skin.

'You not . . . understand,' she said.

'Then tell me. I want to understand. I know that something very odd is going on around here. And I want to know what it is.'

Nsami seemed to be weighing her words. Then she spoke in a little rush, her voice hushed as if she feared that someone beyond the room might hear.

'I beat. Rathbone, he like this. He . . . he get much pleasure from see me beat Iko too. Much pleasure. You understand?'

'But that's dreadful! Why don't you leave, go back to your village. I could help you – '

'No! Cannot go back. Rathbone . . . he need me. Iko too. I stay.'

Gwendoline was stunned. She hadn't expected this. She had deduced for herself that the summerhouse was used as a place of correction. But she had never dreamed of its true use.

It all made sense now. She knew why Nsami treated Rathbone with thinly disguised contempt and why he allowed it. No wonder Rathbone had been repelled by her own sexuality when she flaunted herself out on the porch. He was a man of twisted and dark desires, unable to respond to a woman like other men.

It seemed that Nsami and Iko colluded with their master, providing him with his singular pleasures. Guarding his secret vices. And enjoying them too?

She looked closely at Nsami, the question in her eyes. Nsami's long lashes swept down onto her cheeks. Her dusky skin did not show her blush but her mouth trembled and Gwendoline knew that she had her answer.

Nsami laid a hand on Gwendoline's arm. Gwendoline turned to look up at her. Nsami's long black eyes were bright with tears.

'You no tell anyone?'

In the face of the other woman's distress Gwendoline felt her shock and outrage drain away. If Iko and Nsami were willing to take part in Rathbone's sexual rituals, and find pleasure for themselves, then who was she to judge them?

'No, of course I won't tell anyone. But . . . there's something you can help me with.'

Nsami looked at her steadily. She had stopped her massaging now and was wiping her hands clean on a towel.

'You . . . my friend?'

Gwendoline stroked Nsami's arm. The skin was soft and smooth as silk. She knew what Nsami was really asking. It was more a matter of honour and trust. In that gesture was everything. She nodded and smiled. Nsami smiled back.

'Ask me then. I try help.'

'There's a building in the trees next to the lake. What is that?'

Nsami's eyes slid sideways. She shook her head. 'No building.'

'I know it's there Nsami. I saw it myself. I'm going to investigate whether you tell me about it or not.'

Nsami took a deep breath. 'It is place of pleasure.

That is all. Can tell no more. You no go there. Stay away.'

However much Gwendoline prompted, Nsami shook her head and began gathering up the towels and washing things. She edged towards the door.

'I go now. Have work.' She smiled and her lips curved voluptuously. 'I come give pleasure again?'

Gwendoline blushed hotly. 'Yes . . . I . . . Thank you for the . . . bath, Nsami.'

When Nsami had gone Gwendoline slipped on her robe and sat in front of the dressing table, brushing her hair with long smooth strokes. She was deep in thought. Her suspicions were confirmed.

There was definitely a building – a place of pleasure – whatever that meant when defined by Rathbone. And she was certain now that she'd heard a cry for help. An English voice. Somehow she had to get Jonathan to take her out to the lake.

Everyone was going on the hunt. Edward and Rathbone had been boasting about the number of antelope they were going to bag. The excitement over replenishing the supply of fresh meat should keep the whole of the household occupied for some hours.

There might be a way.

Chapter Thirteen

*T*he long grass, almost shoulder height, swayed in the breeze.

It hid the hunters from the herd of grazing antelope, their mouths moving delicately, nibbling at the sweet young grass in the clearing some way off.

In the distance the landscape was a mixture of reds and browns, broken every now and then by the gnarled shape of a thorn tree. The sun was a yellow wound in the sky.

'Just look at 'em, m'dear,' Edward hissed to Hetty, pointing at the antelope. 'I can almost taste the juicy steak we'll have for dinner tonight.'

Hetty smiled at him, infected by his excitement. She wore a fitted linen suit and a bush hat. Stout leather boots completed the outfit. She felt as fine as any titled lady in her new hunting clothes.

She knew that she would never have been allowed to accompany Edward on a hunt in England. The ladies and gentlemen went shooting grouse, while the servants readied the house for their return. Out here the rules were different. The distinctions of class were more relaxed, at least, when it suited Rathbone and those like him.

She knew that she was fast becoming indispensable to Edward. He did everything she asked him to and more. His capacity for adapting to each new task she set him amazed even her.

Only she knew that, under his plus-fours, he wore a pair of her open-crotch drawers.

He turned and slanted her a grin and she saw the bulge of his erection. She recognised that look in his eye and felt an answering flicker of lust. Quickly she glanced around. Everyone else was hidden, separated from Edward and herself by the shifting curtain of grass.

She nodded curtly, giving Edward the permission he craved. He edged closer, hefting his gun onto one bent arm, the loaded barrel hanging open for safety.

'Mistress?' he said, his voice hoarse with longing.

Hetty raised her skirts above her knees and lay back in the grass. Edward's breath came fast as he fell to his knees between her thighs.

'Oh God,' he whispered as he stretched out his free hand and buried it in Hetty's crotch.

Hetty closed her eyes as Edward's thick fingers stroked the bush at her groin.

'Push them into me,' she said, giving a small sigh as he obeyed her.

He worked two fingers in and out of her, gauging her reactions.

'Am I doing it right, Mistress?' he whispered.

'No,' she said. 'I'll have to see to you when we gets back.'

Edward shivered, drawing his fingers out and smearing her juice over his moustache.

'I want to smell you on me all the time,' he said. 'Darling Hetty . . . I mean Mistress. I worship you.'

Replacing his fingers he stroked and probed while Hetty's breath came faster. He had learnt his lessons well. She had only to order him and he would use fingers, tongue and cock for her pleasure. She never thought about his enjoyment, knowing that his most ardent wish was to serve her, to obtain fulfilment through the things she made him do.

'Oh, oh,' she moaned softly, her rich juices flowing over his fingers and her plump thighs falling wide open.

A shot rang out startling her. There was a flurry of movement in the grass in front as the hunters broke cover. Shouts and cries filled the air. More shots rang out. Edward looked at her pleadingly.

'The hunt . . .'

'Did I say you could go?' she said. 'You hasn't finished yet. You've been too slow. Be a good doggy for me and I'll let you go off on your old hunt.'

With a little cry he pushed his face into her groin. Lapping at her sex, moving his head from side to side, he brought her swiftly to a peak of pleasure. Hetty raised her hips and pushed against his face, while Edward made little grunts of encouragement. She grasped his head between her sturdy thighs and squeezed.

When she let him go Edward's face was florid, his forehead beaded with sweat. His cock must be bursting, she thought, but he wouldn't dare ask if she'd pleasure him.

Hetty sighed with contentment, sat up, and straightened her skirts.

'Off you go then. And make sure you bag a big 'un. I'll expect you to bring me that choice steak you spoke of.'

Edward ran forward, snapping the barrels of his rifle closed.

Hetty dusted herself off and stood up. She could see people running everywhere. Rathbone stood with his rifle to his shoulder, one eye squinting down the sights.

Two antelope lay dead already. The others ran back and forth in an effort to escape the hunters, their hooves stirring up clouds of yellow dust. The house servants chased the animals back towards the hunters, jabbing at any antelope that came near enough with long spears.

A flock of birds rose from the grass, shrieking as they flapped their black wings. The whole scene was vibrant and exciting. Hetty saw Edward run forward and shoot a wounded animal in the head. Blood pooled in the dust. He waved exultantly and she waved back, laughing.

Her eye was caught by a movement off to one side. She saw two figures making their way back to the horses. One of them was Jonathan, the other was Gwendoline. Jonathan had his arm around her and she seemed to be limping.

Something about the way Gwendoline was leaning on Jonathan, and looking up into his face, seemed odd to Hetty. Gwendoline wasn't given to such gestures. If she hurt herself she was more likely to insist on managing on her own. Gwendoline couldn't abide people fussing.

Hetty began to smile.

'You don't fool me with that act,' she said aloud. 'Just what are you up to now, Miss?'

Jonathan was enjoying the sensation of having Gwendoline in his arms. As she leaned into him, he could feel the bones of her corset and the way her hips swelled out from beneath it.

'Oh, drat this ankle,' she moaned, hopping along

as best she could, her long skirts dragging in the dust.

They reached the trees where the horses were tethered. Gwendoline hitched up her skirts, treating him to a glimpse of neat ankle and embroidered silk stocking.

He was surprised at the rush of heat to his groin.

Gwendoline swayed unsteadily.

'Oh dear. I don't think I can manage alone.'

'I'll help you up,' Jonathan said, taking a firm grip on her waist and lifting.

Gwendoline managed to get into the saddle. She winced as she adjusted her skirts and put one foot in the stirrup, then smiled down at him.

'I'm awfully sorry to spoil the hunt for you. You go back. I can manage alone now.'

'Who's going to help you dismount?' he said. 'Every man jack is out with the hunt. I'll come with you.'

'Oh no, really – '

Jonathan swung himself into his saddle. 'To tell you the truth I've no real stomach for killing. There're plenty of others who'll do that. I'll take my meat in the shape of a roast. It'll be no loss to me to take you back to the house.'

'Very well. Thank you. You're very kind.'

Jonathan felt warmed by her smile. There seemed a softness about her today. It was quite unlike her to give in so easily to an offer of help. She was brave too. Despite the discomfort of her damaged ankle, she was riding almost as well as usual.

As they neared the house Gwendoline's horse turned sharply towards the road which led to the village. Jonathan checked his mount.

'What's wrong!' he shouted, afraid that the horse had shied at a snake and bolted.

Gwendoline didn't answer. He saw her lean over the horse's back and urge it on. She turned her head and called over one shoulder.

'Jonathan. Follow me!'

He needed no second bidding, especially as he saw that she had both feet in the stirrups and was riding hell for leather. She was smiling widely, the pained expression completely gone. Sprained ankle be damned! She'd duped him. Just wait until he caught up with her.

Gwendoline didn't rein-in her horse until the village came in sight, then he saw her take the dirt track which led towards the lake. Jonathan slowed his horse down to a walk and came alongside Gwendoline.

'You have some reason for doing this I presume?' he said coldly.

She smiled. 'Don't glower so. I had to get your attention and persuade you to come here with me. It would have taken far too long to explain. And I couldn't be sure that you'd believe me.'

'Explain what?'

For answer she dismounted and tied the horse to a thorn bush. She pointed in the direction of a clump of trees which clothed a slope on the far side of the lake.

'There's a building over there, hidden by the trees. Rathbone lied when he told me that there's nothing over there. I heard someone shouting for help yesterday when I was sketching. I think Rathbone's holding someone prisoner over there. A European. He called out in English.'

Jonathan looked at her incredulously.

'Good God. Are you sure about this? Rathbone's no angel, God knows, but I don't think he'd do anything so foolhardy. He'd never get away with it.

229

And why are you so certain that there's a building over there? You say that Rathbone told you there's nothing in those trees?'

'Yes. But I saw something myself, the sunshine glinting on white walls and dark shapes like windows, when the trees swayed in the breeze. And something else – Nsami told me that Rathbone has a place of pleasure near the lake. She wouldn't say anymore on the subject.'

'Nsami said that? I'm amazed that the house servants would say anything about Rathbone. They're intensely loyal to him. Are you sure you can trust what she says?'

The deep flush which stained Gwendoline's cheeks surprised and intrigued him. He was tempted to ask more questions, sensing that she was keeping something back from him, but she answered him then and the moment for investigation passed.

'I believe her. And I'm going to see what's in those trees for myself. Are you coming or not?'

Turning back to her horse, Gwendoline prepared to mount. Jonathan put a hand on her arm.

'All right. I'll take a look. But we'll go on foot from here. Rathbone might have guards around the place. They'd hear us approach on horseback.'

She nodded. 'Won't they have seen us already? There's no cover here.'

Jonathan looked around, scanning the terrain with a practised eye.

'I don't think so. But to make sure we'll take the horses back along the track and secure them out of sight, then cut across country.'

They picked their way through the tangled scrub, Gwendoline wincing as sharp stones cut into her thin-soled riding boots. Jonathan used a stout knife to chop through vines and twisted roots. Gwendoline followed him doggedly, her head bent so that the wide brim of her hat kept the sun from her face. He had to admire her spirit. When she set her mind to something there really was no stopping her.

It was not far, but by the time they were nearing the wooded slope they were both soaked with sweat.

Gwendoline stepped into the shade of a tree and collapsed against the trunk, gasping for breath. Jonathan reached for the scarf he wore inside his safari shirt and untied it. He held it out to Gwendoline. She thanked him, mopping the sweat from her face and neck, then flapping the damp fabric to create a breeze.

'Better?' he asked after a few minutes. 'You could rest here if you'd like to. I'll go on alone and report back.'

'No you won't! I'm perfectly all right now. I'm coming with you,' she said stoutly, pushing herself away from the tree and setting off through the trees.

He smiled wickedly. He'd known she was going to say that but he couldn't resist commenting on her momentary weakness. Serve her right for tricking him.

The shade of the acacias was welcome after the trek out in the open. They waded through bracken, which grew almost waist high. Hart's-tongue fern poked from the roots of some trees and elkshorn spread like jutting brown shields from others.

They could see the building now. It was all one storey and painted white, as Gwendoline had said.

'There seem to be no guards about,' Jonathan said. 'Maybe Rathbone feels that this place is secluded enough not to merit them.'

'He's also arrogant enough to think that he can do as he wishes,' Gwendoline said bitterly.

'You really do dislike the man. Why? Has he done something to you personally?'

'I'll tell you about it one day,' she said.

And though vastly intrigued, he had to be satisfied with that.

Circling the building warily, they found a window and peered inside. The interior was dark and gloomy. They could see a large room divided up into stalls. A door led into the main part of the building. It stood ajar.

'It looks like a stable,' Gwendoline whispered.

'Yes, but I'd wager that Rathbone keeps something other than horses here.'

A strong suspicion was forming in Jonathan's mind. He didn't confide his thoughts to Gwendoline. He could be mistaken and it was best not to alarm her before he was certain of the facts.

'Come on. Let's find the entrance. This place looks deserted.'

They found the stout wooden door set between white-painted pillars. No one challenged them and there was not a sound from inside the building. Jonathan tried the door. It was locked. Slipping the blade of his hunting knife between the door and frame he exerted pressure until the wood splintered and the lock gave way.

Jonathan went inside first, one arm stretched out to stop Gwendoline pushing past him.

'It might be dangerous,' he hissed. 'It's too quiet. I don't like it.'

They looked around. The room they had stepped into was almost bare. There was a table and chairs set against one wall. A low platform, covered with a woven rug and brightly coloured cushions, took up the whole of the wall under the window. But it was the other two walls which captured their attention.

'What on earth are those for?' Gwendoline whispered.

Glancing at the sturdy wooden structures, the hooks which held manacles, leather harnesses and chains, Jonathan knew only too well what he was seeing.

'I think I should go through that door alone,' he said, indicating the open door – the one they'd glimpsed through the window.

'No, I'm coming too,' Gwendoline said, shaking off his hand. 'I'm not about to faint like some ninny!'

'I didn't think you were,' he said ruefully. 'Very well. But you'd better ready yourself. I don't think this will be pleasant . . .'

He pushed the door open wide, affording them both a clear view into the one other room. The row of stalls faced them. There were six in all. In each one of them was a pile of straw and a tin bucket. All but one of the stalls was empty, though it was plain that, until recently, they had all been occupied.

In the last stall, the one farthest away from the window and in partial darkness, was a young man so tightly restrained and gagged that he couldn't move a muscle.

'Oh my lord,' Gwendoline's moan of distress was loud in the silence. She clapped her hand to her mouth, her eyes wide with shock.

Jonathan's teeth were clenched so tight they hurt. He felt no pleasure in having his suspicions confirmed. Damn Rathbone. Damn him to hell!

The bastard was a slaver.

Gwendoline walked slowly towards the occupied stall. Was this place really what Nsami called 'a place of pleasure'? Perhaps it was – to Rathbone.

Her stomach churned as she imagined Rathbone

233

coming here. It was a hateful place, secluded and bare. Fear seemed to seep out of the very walls. How many people had passed through this building?

She looked down at the captive young man. He was much darker than Nsami or Iko. His skin was fine-grained and so dusky that it appeared to have purple lights to it. Above the leather gag his liquid brown eyes pleaded with her. Even from the small amount of his face visible above the gag, she could see that he was very handsome.

He had been forced to bend over a sort of wooden trestle and was chained in such a way that his bare buttocks were uppermost and his thighs were spread open. This was not simple restrainment, designed to keep him immobile, it was a perverse punishment.

She heard the sounds he made, partway between gasps and whimpers, all muffled by the gag. In that obscene position his muscles must have been screaming. Perhaps he was numb. She imagined the agony he would feel as the blood returned to his limbs and shuddered. How long had he been left like that?

The captive struggled and managed somehow to lift his head. It must have cost him a great effort. Gwendoline was suddenly impatient to set him free. Looking up she saw that Jonathan was hurrying into the other room. Metal rang on metal as he searched for keys.

'Don't worry. You'll be free in a moment,' she said, averting her eyes from the young man's nakedness.

She could see that he was powerfully built. The muscles of his biceps and chest bulged around the straps and chains that held him. There was not an inch of spare flesh on his body. Though she tried not to stare, she could not help but look between his spread legs where his scrotum and thick phallus hung, potent-looking and vibrant.

Jonathan appeared at her side. Bending down he fitted keys in the manacles and used his knife on the straps and leather gag.

'Soon have you out of this,' he grunted.

The chains fell away and the leather bonds parted. The young man spat the gag from his mouth, coughing and retching. He tried to move then, with a cry of pain, slipped sideways into the straw.

'Water,' he croaked.

Gwendoline dipped a tin cup into the bucket which was in the stall. Kneeling down she cradled the young man's head in her lap and held the cup to his lips.

'You speak English?' Jonathan said.

The young man gulped the water, then fell back on the straw. As he rubbed at his cramped muscles, he looked up at them warily, his eyes flickering over Gwendoline's concerned face. Addressing himself to her, he said, 'I am Kiva. Thank you for helping me.'

Gwendoline took his proffered hand, impressed by his composure and good manners. He was obviously still in a great deal of discomfort, yet he had hardly winced.

'Kiva?' Jonathan said. 'Is that your birth name?'

Kiva smiled, his lips parting to show strong white teeth.

'It is the name given to me by Madame Dudley. My birth name is difficult for white people to say.'

Jonathan nodded. 'I see. I have heard of Dudley. She's a missionary. Your people are the Fan, are they not?'

Kiva nodded, looking impressed.

'How did you know?'

'Studying people is my work. And you have the look of the Fan. Your height and build. How did you come to be here?'

Kiva's lip curled and he spat in the straw.

'It was that devil Rathbone. He pretended to be my friend and encouraged me to leave my people. He said that I spoke such good English that I could work for him and return to my village when I wished. My father agreed. He is headman. The whole village came to see me go. But Rathbone lied. He brought me here – to this place. And he tried to make me serve him, to . . . to pleasure him . . .'

Gwendoline stroked Kiva's arm. He flashed her a grateful look. For such a large, well-formed young man, he had an air of gentleness that was most attractive.

'There have been others. Sometimes one or two at once, women and men. Rathbone sold them to rich men like himself.'

'Men who could afford to buy a beautiful sex slave,' Jonathan stated. 'But he kept you.'

Kiva nodded. His eyes grew hard and flat-looking.

'He wanted me for himself. But I wouldn't do the things he wanted. That's why he tied me up and starved me. He thought I would give in and let him . . . let him . . .'

His chin came up and his deep-brown eyes flashed with anger. Gwendoline saw that behind the gentleness there was a powerful resolve.

'I will not act like a woman for any man!' Kiva burst out, his full mouth trembling despite his efforts at control. 'No matter what is done to me.'

'You won't have to,' Gwendoline said firmly, glancing up at Jonathan for his approval. 'We'll take you with us when we leave.'

Jonathan hesitated, then nodded. 'We'll be passing through Fan territory above the Ogowé River.'

Kiva's face cleared. 'But that is near to my father's village. I can go home? You will take me?'

Gwendoline smiled. 'Of course. And I shall inform the authorities about Rathbone's activities. Trading in slaves was outlawed many years ago. He won't be getting away with this.'

Kiva pressed his mouth to Gwendoline's hand, murmuring his thanks over and over again. She stroked his head, her heart going out to the young man whom Rathbone had abused so cruelly.

But as she stroked the soft wool of his hair and felt the warmth of his lips on her skin, she was aware of other, deeper and more subtle feelings rising in her breast. Despite her condemnation of Rathbone, she could almost understand his obsession with Kiva.

The young African was quite the most beautiful male she had ever seen.

Chapter Fourteen

*E*dward seemed shocked when Gwendoline told him about Kiva and the others whom Rathbone had sold. She saw by his face that he doubted her word but she had Jonathan to lend weight to her comments.

Presented with the evidence Edward had no choice but to take action.

'This is a serious matter,' he said at length. 'Leave it to me Gwendoline. I'll deal with it at once. Most unfortunate timing. If this got out it could seriously affect our business interests.'

'Is that all you care about?' she said coldly. 'Rathbone's a monster. What about all the suffering he's caused to those he captured? Not to mention their families.'

'Suffering? Ah, yes. Of course. The man'll have to be punished – the proper authorities and all that, eh? But let's not be too hasty. This needs careful handling. There'd be the devil to pay if father ever got wind of this.'

Gwendoline pressed her lips together. It was useless to reason with Edward. They spoke a different language. She strode away in disgust. Rathbone would probably be given a warning; little more than a slap on the wrist and told to behave from now on.

Well it wasn't enough. Edward might not want to upset a valued employee but she was going to see that Rathbone knew exactly what she thought of him. The only question was – how?

The next few days passed quickly with Gwendoline and Hetty packing for the trip into the interior.

'We're to go part of the way by sea,' Hetty said with a gleam in her eye. 'I wonder if the ship's captain will be as handsome as Captain Casey.'

Gwendoline laughed. 'I'm sure I don't care if he is. I'll be too busy admiring the coastline and anticipating our arrival at Gabon. From there we journey inland and pick up the Ogowé River. That's the Africa I came here to find. Not this . . . this colony, with its secrets and intrigues. I'm heartily sick of staying here. Even the thought of the narrow canoes we'll be travelling upriver in seems welcome.'

Hetty went quite pale.

'Oh yes. The canoes. I'd forgotten them,' she said in a small voice. Then she brightened. 'Is Kiva coming with us?'

'Of course. I promised that we'd take him back to his tribal lands. Besides I wouldn't leave him here to fall back into Rathbone's foul hands. Why do you ask Hetty?'

'I can't help noticing how Kiva looks at you. It's as if he worships you. There might be trouble if Jonathan notices. You know he's sweet on you under that harsh exterior.'

Gwendoline looked sharply at the other woman. 'Kiva is grateful to me for rescuing him – nothing more. And as for Jonathan . . . I don't care if he does notice. It's none of his business what I do,' she said with more bravado than she felt.

He had his chance to declare himself back in England, she thought, aware that she was beginning to feel slightly guilty for holding a grudge against him. It was true that he could be uncompromising, even cruel, but he'd proved himself to be a good friend. She sensed that he would be a trusted confidant.

One day, Jonathan and herself would have a reckoning. There was something enduring between them and she had to admit that he attracted her strongly. But the time wasn't right yet to explore her feelings about that.

Her heart lifted as she absorbed the truth of Hetty's other comment. So Hetty had noticed that Kiva looked at her in a certain way. She knew this of course. Hetty only confirmed the fact. The heat rose into her cheeks as she pictured Kiva – so tall, so strong – and with that devastating face.

Impossible to be blind to his beauty. No one had ever affected her in such a purely physical way before. One glance from those melting brown eyes and her skin began to tingle as if Kiva had reached out and stroked it with his long brown hands. The attraction he held for her was entirely different from that which she'd felt for Captain Casey.

She was aware that she had needed an older, more experienced man to teach her about the things men and women did together. Captain Casey had been the ideal lover for the woman she was. But she had changed. Having tasted the delights of the flesh, her senses had awoken. The woman she was now needed a new stimulus.

The mysteries of men's bodies, their responses,

were mysteries no more. She knew how to pleasure herself and took pride in her eager responses. Nsami had shown her new ways to arouse her senses. She was eager to expand her education.

For a number of reasons she still held back from approaching Jonathan in that respect. For one thing she was unwilling to complicate her relationship with him. Their friendship and new understanding was a tenuous thing.

If she was honest she was still a little afraid of him. The power of Jonathan's personality and intellect made her feel clumsy and lacking in culture. That was why she had borrowed his book. It brought her a little closer to him.

Ah, Jonathan was like the sun, incandescent in her mind. One day they might be lovers – but now, unexpectedly, there was Kiva; his persona streaking through her life like a comet.

Kiva woke new, confusing emotions in her. His was the freshness of youth. He was a healthy young animal, a child of nature, unfettered by the hypocrisy of her own culture. If she had been born in Africa she would have been Kiva's double.

She sought him out and, in her assumed guise of rescuer, questioned him. There was no reason for her to keep away, after all, she told herself, her interest was natural enough.

Kiva responded to her wholeheartedly, telling her all about his family and village and relating tales from his childhood.

'Festival times are the best,' he said. 'When we celebrate the earth mother's power. Then our blood awakes to the sound of the drums and we dance long into the night. We make pleasures then, to honour earth mother.'

He didn't expand on the subject but she imagined

him taking some dusky beauty by the hand and leading her away from the others. The image of Kiva's body covering a wriggling girl, his hips thrusting as he buried himself inside her hot flesh, was powerfully erotic.

Kiva also told her that he loved to carve wood.

'I will show you when we get to my village. I have made many masks. You shall have one, the very best, for yourself.' He beamed at her, showing his perfect white teeth.

How strange that Kiva should be an artist too. It was one of the many things she found them to have in common.

Sitting on the grass in Rathbone's garden, wearing only a woven cloth around his waist, Kiva told her many things. Gwendoline was impressed by his candour. She could not imagine anyone else of her acquaintance revealing so much of their inner selves to a virtual stranger.

It was charming and endearing. Gwendoline could not help but respond to Kiva. She saw through his eyes when he spoke of Africa; of the beauty and danger of his homeland. He told her how he loved to hunt and about the ceremony that followed his first kill.

His experience of life couldn't have been more different from her own. Kiva listened with wonder as she told him about England, laughing with her when she related some of the ridiculous rules that governed society.

The time they spent talking became precious to Gwendoline. Her dreams were invaded by images of beautiful men with ebony skins. She saw Kiva as he had been that first time, bent almost double in that obscene position.

How hateful it was to admit that she was aroused

by that image. The strong back, each muscle standing out in sharp relief; the taut buttocks, spread wide and the thick phallus and scrotum hanging between his powerful thighs.

After waking with her head full of such images, she couldn't look Kiva in the eye the next morning. He waved to her from the garden but she pretended not to see. She fled, actually ran from him, her heart hammering like a piston.

Confused by her rioting emotions and in a state of nervous tension, Gwendoline decided to let fate take a hand. She would do nothing about this fascination, obsession, or whatever it was.

Having set things straight in her own mind, she tried to put Kiva at a distance from herself. But it wasn't that simple.

She had insisted that the young man be treated as a house guest for the remainder of their stay, much to Rathbone's disgust.

'It's the very least you can do after the despicable way you've treated him!' she said to Rathbone, her eyes blazing with anger.

Rathbone shrugged and gave her one of his reptilian grins.

'Certainly he can have a room. What's one more house guest amongst so many,' he sneered. 'I really can't imagine why you care what happens to this native. What's he to you anyway? Or shouldn't I ask?'

Her fingers itched to slap his face but even the thought of touching him made her feel queasy. Under the dark stubble his face was greyish and his eyes were unfocused. The smell of brandy and cigars on his breath was especially pungent of late. Turning on her heel she marched into the house.

Rathbone kept out of her way after that brief

exchange and she was glad of the fact. They had nothing to say to each other. They met once a day at the dinner table and then the tension between them crackled.

Edward kept up an inane conversation while everyone ate, trying to dispel the frosty atmosphere.

'I say. This roast meat's very good Rathbone. You have quite a talent for employing good cooks – '

'Oh do shut up, Edward!' Gwendoline snapped.

Open-mouthed, Edward turned to Jonathan for support. Jonathan grinned and leaned close.

'I should do as she says old chap, if I were you,' he said with an ironic smile. 'Diplomacy isn't one of your strengths.'

Gwendoline flashed Jonathan a grateful look. He at least understood her feelings of anger and outrage towards Rathbone.

She knew that Rathbone expected her to explode and it was some kind of victory to keep him waiting for an outburst from her. He was master of the cutting comment and enjoyed sparring with words. Let him anticipate the fight that would never come.

Rathbone's cold grey eyes flickered around the room, alighting on Kiva who took his meals at the same table.

After Rathbone's treatment of him Gwendoline expected trouble from Kiva. But Jonathan had taken Kiva aside and talked the young man out of trying to kill Rathbone.

'Rathbone has lost face with his own people because of his actions. And what is a man without honour?' Jonathan said to Kiva, while Gwendoline clenched her hands together hard.

The look on Kiva's face had been murderous but he listened to Jonathan. When Jonathan had finished speaking Kiva turned to Gwendoline. 'And do you agree that Rathbone deserves to live?'

It had been an effort to nod. She thought that Rathbone deserved worse than being boiled in oil, but she agreed with Jonathan.

'Everyone knows what Rathbone did. He has to live with that stain on his honour,' she said evenly.

Kiva understood the concept of honour. He was content to let the matter rest. Now the young African treated Rathbone with utter contempt. His proud bearing and splendid young body only served to underline the dissipation of Rathbone's looks.

Many times Gwendoline caught Rathbone glancing at Kiva, his thin lips moist and speculative. Kiva stared through him as if he didn't exist. Even when Rathbone covered the elegant brown hand with his own, on the pretext of stressing a point in the conversation, Kiva ignored him. When Rathbone removed his hand, Kiva wiped it fastidiously on a table napkin.

And Rathbone looked so pained at that moment that Gwendoline almost felt sorry for him. He was obviously still besotted with Kiva. Once she saw the glint of tears in Rathbone's eyes. He could not help his nature, she conceded him that, but she could never forgive his cruelty.

Perhaps the best revenge after all, was letting Rathbone see what he had lost.

Kiva's room was down the corridor from hers. Hetty told her how Kiva shunned the bed, with its huge feather mattress and pillows, preferring to sleep curled up on a woven mat on the porch.

Gwendoline's heart hammered as she realised how close to her room Kiva was when asleep. She said with forced lightness, 'I expect it's what he's used to.

I don't suppose there are feather beds to sleep on in many African villages.'

'No I don't s'pose so,' Hetty replied. 'And I don't expect there's no furniture to speak of neither. That's why Kiva moves the way he does. Like a big cat pushing through long grass. Oh, he's beautiful isn't he? I bet you're just dying to paint him.'

Gwendoline had been thinking that very thing. She smiled.

'I've already primed a canvas. You know me far too well, Hetty.'

Hetty gave her a look from the tail of her eye. 'I certainly do,' she said. 'You just be careful.'

'Whatever do you mean?'

'Oh Miss, I think you knows,' she said in her most worldly tone. 'Still I suppose you'll go and do whatever you want. You usually do.' Then she laughed. 'We'll have to get used to sleeping on grass mats and furs. Might be interestin' at that! Edward won't like it though. He won't like it at all.'

It was early when they set out the next morning. Canoes waited at the landing stage at the bottom of Rathbone's garden, packed with luggage and provisions.

Gwendoline and Hetty were the last to take their places. Jonathan helped Gwendoline to her seat, his fingers warm and strong as he cupped her elbow.

'Thank you,' she said, smiling up at him.

Jonathan took his place at the head of the second canoe which was packed with equipment, leaving Edward in charge of Gwendoline and Hetty.

'Where've you been?' Edward said grumpily. 'We had to wait ages for you. First Kiva disappeared, then you and Hetty. I expect you were deciding what to wear. This isn't Ascot for heaven's sake!'

Gwendoline smiled at her brother.

'I'm quite aware of that Edward. I had some . . . business to attend to before we left. Kiva and Hetty lent me a hand.'

His eyebrows shot up. 'Oh?'

Despite her brother's look of curiosity Gwendoline didn't elaborate, instead she looked towards the wooden platform where everyone was gathered to see them off and beyond that to where a plume of black smoke rose into the sky.

A secret smile curved her lips as she waved. Nsami and Iko waved back, their dark faces looking sorrowful despite brave smiles. Gwendoline was sorry to be leaving them. The previous night she had asked them to come upriver with herself and the others. They'd refused. Whatever was between them and Rathbone was binding, Gwendoline had to accept that.

Kiva stood at the front of the canoe, straight and tall like a pillar of ebony. He turned and flashed her a brilliant smile. Along with the other natives, he dug a long wooden pole into the river and the canoe began to slide past the landing stage.

Rathbone leaned against the trunk of a tree. Gwendoline had known he would appear. A younger, more innocent self might have expected him to have been arrested. But she was wiser now and had accepted that Rathbone's life would carry on as normal, despite her protestations to Kiva.

She was furious with Edward but not surprised by his reactions. They were typical of businessmen of his class.

'Goodbye, my dear,' Rathbone called out, waving mockingly at her. 'Try not to get eaten by lions. They would find you very indigestible.'

'Really! That man's got a nerve!' Hetty said, sounding impressed despite her outrage.

'Hasn't he just. Well he's about to get a surprise,' Gwendoline said softly.

Rathbone put his fingers to his lips and blew Gwendoline an insolent kiss. It was obvious that he thought he'd had the last laugh.

When Gwendoline threw back her head and laughed, his face darkened. He looked confused and twisted his head around as Gwendoline pointed to the column of smoke, now thick and black.

'There's your place of pleasure, Rathbone. You'll keep no more slaves there!' she said triumphantly.

He blanched. 'You stupid woman! You did that? Don't you know how dangerous fire is in this climate?'

'Oh, I didn't burn the building,' she shouted back as the canoe slid out into mid-stream. 'Your native villagers did, after I told them about your little "business". The fire's under control. But you'd best go and talk to them. They were pretty angry when I left.'

Rathbone shook his fist, his mouth opening and closing. She could imagine the obscenities spewing out of him but the wind carried his voice away. As they reached a bend in the river he disappeared from sight.

She sat down in the canoe, a long sigh escaping her. Her hands were shaking with anger and reaction. She hoped never to set her eyes on Rathbone again for as long as she lived.

Kiva's soft brown eyes snagged hers and he smiled. A smile of approval and promise. A dart went straight to her stomach and she swallowed hard.

The canoe moved through the mangrove swamps and down to where the steamer waited to transport them. The natives sang as they dug the wooden poles into the river mud. From under the rim of her parasol Gwendoline watched Kiva's muscles work as he manoeuvred the oar with expert ease. His dark satin skin invited her touch. His mouth, full and well-shaped, invited her kisses. And the fact that she knew he desired her also was maddening.

She felt quite faint at all the possibilities that coursed through her mind. There was nothing for it, she must avoid being alone with Kiva at all costs.

The journey by steamer to Calabar and then on to Gabon took some days.

The small craft was not built for comfort and Gwendoline and Hetty were the only ones to be given any privacy. Everyone else slept on deck, stretched out on woven palm mats.

At the port the usual mangrove swamp greeted them. They were obliged to stay at Libreville overnight, where Jonathan and Edward visited the various French officials and obtained permits for their party.

'And now on to the Ogowé,' Jonathan said with a flourish as they boarded the gig which would take them up an inlet of the river.

Gwendoline watched the mud banks slide past the vessel. Slope after slope of ink-black slime bordered the river channel. She saw movements on the mud and strained her eyes to see what was causing it. Thousands of tiny crabs, blue, orange and green were clustered on mud, feeding or mating. She watched them with fascination.

Jonathan came up beside her.

'Sinister isn't it?'

'What?' she said, almost jumping out of her skin. He'd surprised her, walking softly up to her like that.

He seemed to be in a strange mood, pensive and brooding. She hadn't seen him like this before.

'That mud. It's so deep that you could sink right into it and never be seen again.'

'How horrible.' She gave a shudder. 'Will the terrain be better upriver?'

'Oh, yes. See there – beyond that belt of palms? You can just see the tips of red-wooded trees and those lighter smudges are acacias.'

'Yes. I can see them.'

'From there it's open country, with grassland and wooded valleys. It's Fan country too.'

'Fan? Aren't they Kiva's people?'

'Yes. But there are Fan villages all over this area. Kiva's village is much further upriver.'

'So he won't be leaving us just yet then?'

'No,' he said shortly, running his fingers through his thick dark hair to smooth it back. He put on his bush hat.

'How are you getting on with Mungo Park?'

'What? I'm sorry I don't . . .'

'The book I lent you.'

'Oh that. Yes . . . It's most enjoyable.' She sparkled at him. 'I suppose you know about the illustrated texts I found amongst the pages?'

'Of course. I thought you'd find them – stimulating.' His deep-set eyes were intense suddenly. 'Well didn't you?'

Did he have to be so direct? Jonathan always asked the questions that other people just hinted at. And for some reason she always felt moved to challenge his arrogance.

Her chin came up. 'I found the texts fascinating and the illustrations arousing.' With a touch of humorous pride she added, 'Though I think I could have made a better job of the drawings.'

He grinned and bent closer, resting his bent arms on the gig's rail and looking up at her from under the brim of his hat.

'I just bet you could at that. I don't know another woman who would admit to enjoying such an explicit piece of writing.' He sounded amused. 'You've changed Gwendoline. Grown up. Where should we go from here I wonder?'

There was a leashed strength about him which she found attractive and a little frightening. At Rathbone's house he had seemed almost scholarly at times but now he was wholly the adventurer. She had seen the way he took charge of every situation, the way the native guides and oarsmen looked to him for comment. Even Edward, pompous as he was, deferred to Jonathan in all decisions concerning the trip.

Jonathan's dark eyes were vivid in his tanned face and the old scar on his neck showed up as a silver white line. She sensed that they were bordering on a dangerous intimacy. To lighten the mood she attempted to flirt with him. Swaying towards him, she pressed close so that the frills on her blouse brushed against his safari shirt.

'I think that you're a scoundrel Jonathan Kimberton. And young women would do well to keep away from you.'

She could smell him now; clean hair; spicy cologne and his own warm maleness. When he closed one strong hand on her wrist she drew back a little, startled by the sudden movement.

'Don't play with me, Gwendoline. I know what you're doing. But you can't deny that there's something between us. I understand that that frightens you but don't pretend it isn't there.'

She stiffened.

'Let go of me,' she said coldly. 'You've no right to throw out challenges.'

He laughed softly. 'Oh I think I have. I told you once that I wanted you but you weren't ready then. Now I think you are.'

'Stop this at once!'

She did not want to hear declarations of passion from Jonathan. She wasn't ready for everything that would follow. Jonathan was an all or nothing type of man. He would want any woman to belong to him, to devote herself to him both emotionally as well as physically.

It was too much to ask. She was not done with discovering herself yet.

How had he come to make these declarations? It was so unexpected. But that was just like him. Then she felt her anger rising at his arrogance.

'You mean that you have decided that it's time for us to become – intimate?' she said sarcastically. 'Well how very generous of you. And do I have no say in this matter?'

She glared at him, her green eyes blazing. 'Surely you can't be telling me that you didn't mean the things you said to me at Halton Hall? Let me see whether I can recall them. Ah yes, you wanted me, but not as "a cool English virgin" isn't that what you called me? As I remember it you wanted to meet me "head on" when Africa had worked her magic on me. Is that an accurate account?'

Jonathan's fingers tightened, biting into her wrist. He looked surprised that she had remembered that conversation almost word for word.

'That was then. This is now,' he said softening a little, though his mouth was still set in a hard line. 'I don't retract anything I said. But things have changed. I thought we had become friends and I hoped that by now – '

'We have become friends Jonathan,' she interrupted, pulling away a little. 'But that doesn't give you the right to make assumptions. And I'm not entirely ready to forgive you for humiliating me.'

He released her wrist abruptly, a sardonic smile lifting the corners of his lips.

'I didn't realise how much I'd hurt you. I think I may have underestimated your strength of character. But I make a point of never regretting the past, it's a futile exercise.'

Before she realised what he was about to do, he'd gripped her shoulders and pulled her close. His mouth ground into hers for a moment, then he pulled back.

She brought her hands up between their bodies, pressing her palms against his chest but he held her tight. His breath was hot on her lips as he said in a low voice.

'I'm a patient man. That's one reason why I always get what I want. I can wait.'

'Damn your cheek! You'll wait until your hair turns grey then . . .' she began.

He kissed her again, more deeply. His tongue slipped between her lips, exploring her mouth. He held her tightly, his arms wound around her ribs. She could not fight him. He was too strong, his muscles as tough as whipcord.

He kept kissing her until he forced a response from her. When the tip of his tongue brushed against hers, little shock waves of sensation ran down her back. She swayed towards him, leaning into his kiss and was ashamed at the little sound that rose in her throat.

Jonathan pulled away a second time and looked

down at her. His hat had tipped back on his head and she felt a lock of his dark hair brush against her forehead. Despite all her brave words she felt almost ready to collapse against his broad chest.

She was trembling slightly and seemed aware of his very essence. In that moment he seemed something more than human; a potent force that drew her towards it like a magnet to metal. The feeling of arousal throbbed between her thighs and, from his expression, she thought that he knew it.

Was she holding back from him out of perversity alone?

She opened her mouth to speak but his next words fell on her like a shower of cold water.

'I understand what you're doing,' he said softly, raising one hand to toy with a strand of her red-brown hair. 'And I don't blame you. After all, I did tell you that I wasn't interested in deflowering virgins. It's true that I prefer sensual, experienced women and you are fast becoming both, my dear. But take care where you seek your pleasures. Kiva is no Captain Casey. He's from a culture with a different set of values to our own. Be very sure about what you want. You might just get it. It's a dangerous game you're playing.'

Letting her go abruptly, he stood back.

Before she could stop herself Gwendoline swung her hand back and slapped him hard across the face.

'Don't you dare to judge me! What about you and Nsami? I know that she came to your room night after night at Rathbone's house. And don't tell me that you were playing cards!'

Jonathan's eyes narrowed with fury. 'Don't ever hit me again,' he said in a voice that was dangerously quiet.

For a moment she thought he might hit her back.

It took a great effort not to cower away from him but she stood her ground. Jonathan grinned slowly.

'I said I wanted you and that I could wait. I didn't say that I'd live like a monk in the meantime. I'll take a woman when I need one. I know that you understand that concept.'

Laughing, he strode away down the deck.

Gwendoline pressed her fingertips to her lips. She could still taste his kiss. A little flutter of alarm had started up in her stomach.

He knew. Jonathan knew everything.

She imagined him charting her progress from untried girl to woman; watching her as she engineered that first liaison with Captain Casey aboard the *Persephone*. The vision of herself as some prized animal being fattened up for a sacrifice came to mind.

For a moment she actually hated Jonathan. He was so sure of himself, so complacent.

She suddenly felt very young and foolish. Was she so transparent, so easy to manipulate? No, she decided she was not. She was just a young woman who knew what she wanted and who set about getting it. Jonathan had no business interfering.

Now he was warning her about Kiva. She supposed that he was jealous of the younger man. Never mind that Jonathan took his pleasures, with whomever he wished, whenever he liked. Well she'd show Jonathan that she did as she pleased too. She was just as much a free spirit as he was. And out here in Africa the double-standards of English society counted for nothing.

But at the back of her mind was a nagging question. Did Jonathan knowing about her inner thoughts, her desires, make any difference to her feelings for Kiva?

It was undeniable that she and Jonathan were

involved in some inexplicable way. Perhaps the problem was that they were too alike; both headstrong, opinionated and stubborn. She was honest enough to recognise those same things in herself.

Should she set her obsession with Kiva aside? She didn't know if she could. In her position Jonathan wouldn't hesitate. He'd follow his instincts and desires.

Even as she formulated these thoughts she knew that none of it made any difference. She couldn't help herself. She wanted Kiva badly, desired him in fact with all her heart and soul.

At that moment Kiva walked onto the deck. He wore a strip of brightly-patterned fabric wound around his body and looped over one shoulder. Metal hoops were in his ears and a necklace of painted beads and dried seeds decorated his chest.

He was eating a slice of mango, the orange juice staining the fingers of one hand. In the other hand he held a slice of the same fruit.

She smiled as he walked towards her and held out the fruit.

'For you,' he said.

Looking into his velvet brown eyes she thanked him and took the fruit. His fingers brushed against her, lingering for a shade too long. She saw the tremor in his hand and the answering heat in his expression.

'New clothes?' she said.

'Yes. Rathbone took everything I had. Jonathan gave me them. These too,' he said, fingering the neckpiece and ear decorations. 'He has a collection of gifts given to him by my people. He said that I had more need of them than him. He is a generous man.'

'Yes. Yes he is.'

Raising the mango slice to her lips Gwendoline bit

into the flesh. Despite the sweet fruit juice running down her throat her mouth felt dry.

Damn you Jonathan Kimberton, she thought inwardly. Despite your generous spirit you don't play fair. Well you can wait until I'm ready to accept you. You set down your terms in England, now you can accept mine.

I have unfinished business before I can allow myself to take you on fully. Because she knew that there would be no half-measures if she gave herself to Jonathan it was a terrifying thought. Far easier to concentrate on the pleasures of the flesh alone.

How liberating it was to be utterly selfish.

She smiled up at the beautiful young man who topped her by a head. He had a small piece of fruit stuck to his lip. She reached up and smoothed it away with a fingertip, then slowly and deliberately sucked her finger clean.

She wanted Kiva and she was going to have him.

Chapter Fifteen

The Ogowé narrowed into a swift current and
curled itself into twists and turns. Walls of rock
stretched high overhead on either side of the river.
The sky was only a narrow strip, high above them.

The canoe carrying the supplies was out of sight.
It had swept past moments ago, carried by the strong
current. Gwendoline had glimpsed Jonathan at the
stern, his head down as he braced himself against
the force of the water.

Hetty clung grimly to the side of the second canoe
as the native oarsmen manhandled it around bend
after bend, the craft dipping and rising with the flow
of water.

Gwendoline reached for Hetty's hand and held it
tight. She knew that the other woman was terrified
that they'd all drown. Edward was pale and his
mouth had a pinched, bluish look to it. He looked as
if he was about to vomit.

Gwendoline was scared too but there was no time
to go to pieces. Someone had to remain calm, she
reasoned. Especially as she knew that there was

worse to come. She had overheard Jonathan telling Edward that there were rapids and rocks to battle with before their journey's end.

She shouted above the noise of the river. 'Just hold on Hetty. There's a Fan village ahead. Jonathan says we'll spend the night there.'

Hetty managed to nod. Her eyes were squeezed tight shut.

Soon the rock walls gave way to banks covered with willow-leaved shrubs. Gwendoline scanned the banks for signs of a village. She was exhausted, soaking wet and in need of a meal.

As the river straightened she caught a glimpse of Jonathan's canoe. She could see him peering into the gathering gloom, his hat tipped back on his head.

Kiva and the other natives were looking around too, while still concentrating on keeping control of the canoe. The satin skin moved over Kiva's muscles as he worked. He seemed inexhaustible, his fine-boned face set in an expression of concentration.

Suddenly he pointed towards the shore, then, cupping his hands, shouted. 'Over there Jonathan. See? Shall we beach the canoe?'

'I see it. Good man. We'll put in there. You pull over too,' Jonathan replied.

As they rounded a deep curve, Gwendoline saw that the river spread out to form a shallow lake. The far shore sloped down to a shallow depression filled with small stones. The natives dug their long wooden poles into the water and headed towards the natural landing stage.

Gwendoline became aware of the sound of drums above the rushing noise of the river. The drumbeats grew louder as the canoe neared the shore. Suddenly, with a lot of shouting and whooping, a number of children swooped into the river. They waved and called out a welcome, their dusky faces split by wide grins.

Gwendoline and Hetty waved back.

'Oh, Miss. I'm that glad to be settin' foot on dry land,' Hetty breathed. 'I was frit' to death in that canoe.'

They were made welcome by the Fan chief, a tall man draped in a leopard skin and wearing many ornaments. Jonathan stepped forward and spoke to him. Then, accompanied by the whole tribe, they were escorted to the village. A sprawl of huts made of sheets of bark surrounded the largest building which was the chief's house and meeting place.

The formalities and introductions over with, they were all invited to share a meal.

Gwendoline and Hetty changed into dry clothes in the guest hut allocated to them. The men were to share a separate hut. The Fan women peered into the hut giggling and pointing at the two white women.

With gestures and smiles Gwendoline made friends, allowing the women to stroke her hair and face while she admired their jewellery and hair styles. Many of the women were bare-breasted and some had babies tucked into a sort of fabric sling, so that they could suckle as their mothers worked.

When the food was ready, colourful rugs were spread on the floor for the guests to sit on. Gwendoline found Kiva sitting next to her. Jonathan sat opposite next to a beautiful young woman who gazed at him with sheep's eyes. The girl had high, pointed breasts and a narrow waist. A broad, beaded belt encircled her hips and she wore bracelets sewn with bells on her wrists and ankles. Apart from that she was naked.

'The chief's daughter has taken a fancy to Jonathan,' Kiva whispered to Gwendoline.

'It seems so,' she said coolly, remembering Jonathan's comment about his aversion to celibacy.

'Amongst my people it is an honour to share the bed of a guest,' Kiva said.

It seemed that Jonathan could look forward to an active night.

'I hope he's not too tired in the morning. I thought he wanted to make an early start,' Gwendoline said tartly.

'Is something wrong? You sound angry,' Kiva said.

'No, I'm fine,' she said. 'I'm just hungry.'

Jonathan offered the chief's daughter a choice piece of fruit and she opened her mouth so that he could place it inside. As he withdrew his fingers she pressed her lips to them, then raised her hand to cover his. Her sloe-like black eyes sparkled with promise.

Gwendoline felt Jonathan's eyes on her but did not look up. She determined not to give him the satisfaction of her acknowledgement. Let him do as he pleased. She didn't care.

The whole village blazed with light. Fires outlined the eating area and flame torches formed a circle around an area which had been stamped flat. Suddenly a number of young men and women jumped into the firelight. They were painted with vermilion and naked except for decorations of fringed leather and beads. Stamping and chanting, they moved to the sound of drumbeats.

Kiva showed Gwendoline how to scoop up cooked grain with her fingertips and roll the food into a ball before tossing it into her mouth. After a few tries she got the knack of it. There were no spoons, just knives. Cutting off a slice of roast meat she ate it, licking the fatty juices from her fingers. Then she bit into a baked yam. It was sweet and running with honey. She circled her lips with her tongue, searching out the sticky residue left there.

'Good?' Kiva said, smiling at her, his brown eyes luminous in the firelight.

'Very good,' she answered. 'I've never had a picnic like this before.'

'Pic-nic?'

'An outdoor meal. But in England it's usually a far less exciting affair.'

Kiva smiled. 'I have much to learn about your language.'

'You speak excellent English,' she said. 'But I can teach you more words if you like.'

Kiva nodded. 'I like. But now . . .'

He stood up and stretched out his hand.

'Will you dance with me?'

'Oh I couldn't. I don't know how.'

He gripped her fingers and pulled her gently towards him. 'I'll show you. Come.'

Gwendoline allowed him to lead her towards the dancers. Her cream twill skirts trailed in the dust. She felt foolish and overdressed at first but soon she began to relax. Everyone urged her to move to the drumbeat, their faces eager and friendly.

'Go on!' Hetty called out. 'You're doing well.'

Soon Gwendoline was standing with her feet apart and her knees bent. She rotated her hips as the other women were doing. Kiva stamped his feet and danced around her in circles. The drumbeat throbbed its way into Gwendoline's blood. She gave herself up to its influence, throwing back her head and closing her eyes as she moved.

The women cheered as she swayed, then began stamping her feet. Strands of her hair came free of its pins and whipped around her face. She laughed for sheer joy and Kiva laughed with her.

She looked towards where Jonathan was sitting, smiling with exultation and her forehead creased when she saw that he had gone. No doubt his African princess had claimed him. Or perhaps he couldn't bear to see her, Gwendoline, acting with such abandon.

He'd said that he didn't want an English lady. He wanted Africa to change her into something new and exciting, didn't he? Well, here she was reaching for her true self – and Jonathan had turned away.

Some of Gwendoline's enjoyment in her new-found freedom drained away.

But then she forgot everything as the drumbeat, the heat and the movement of the dancers began to exert an ever more potent pull on her senses. The smells of dust, roast meat, and heated bodies filled her nostrils.

Dimly she saw Hetty beckon to Edward. Edward's face was flushed. His normally stubborn mouth was open and moist looking. He looked at Hetty with excitement tinged with fear. Suddenly the two of them disappeared into the shadows.

Then there was nothing in the world but the drumbeat and the night air that felt like velvet on her face and neck. Runnels of sweat ran down the inside of her dress and soaked into her chemise. Her hair dripped with sweat and clung in damp strands to her face. The suffocating layers of petticoats and skirts pressed against her legs, hampering her movements.

Gwendoline couldn't breathe. She felt her limbs turn to water.

She raised her hands and tore at the neckline of her dress, pulling it open so that the tops of her breasts were revealed.

Kiva's eyes glistened. He moved close and ran his hands up her arms. His long hard body pressed against her briefly then he moved away, resuming his stamping and twirling.

Gwendoline raised her arms and swayed to the drums. Looking up she saw star points in the immense black sky. It seemed as if she had become part of the earth, the dust, the sky.

A new tension transmitted itself to her. Drumbeats thudded faster, ever faster. The dancing was becoming more frenzied and yet it seemed to have a focus.

Slender dark bodies crowded her vision. Here and there she caught a glimpse of oiled muscles, a carmine-tipped breast. The jangle of bells from wrist and armbands sounded loud and exciting.

She saw a young man thrusting his hips forward, a huge erection thrusting up through his belt of dangling leather thongs. A swollen purple glans topped the black cock-shaft. Firelight gleamed on oiled black buttocks and splayed legs, the muscles hard and sharply defined.

Looking round she saw that all of the men were visibly aroused now and the women teased them, darting forward as if to touch the erect organs, then darting away again out of arm's reach. The women were open-mouthed. They made a high-pitched noise, like a bird call. The strange penetrating sound touched a chord in Gwendoline.

She glanced at Kiva, her eyes glittering like jade in the shadow-printed light.

Kiva too was excited. He wore a printed cloth wrapped around his waist but she could see the outline of his phallus as it strained against the fabric. Heat centred in her belly as she responded to the sexual energy that roiled all around her.

Gradually the dancers formed couples and slipped away. Gwendoline turned to face Kiva fully – and found herself snagged by his gaze. Unable to look away she held eye contact with him, absorbing the longing, the sensuality he projected towards her.

When he raised his hand she swayed towards him, her feet moving in the steps of the dance. She felt as if she was watching herself from a great height. The English lady had disappeared. She no longer knew who she was. The breath of Africa had given her a new identity.

Her hand came up of its own volition and she felt Kiva's long fingers close over hers.

'Come with me,' he hissed close to her ear.

Unable to answer she followed, her heart in her throat. Kiva pushed through the undergrowth, making a path for her with his body. As leaves brushed against her face and neck Gwendoline shivered. Her senses seemed alight. Each slight contact tingled and burned her.

'Here,' Kiva said, stopping and turning into her.

His arms went around her, hard and unyielding and he lowered her gently to the ground. There was a leashed urgency about him. She smelt the spice of his sweat and the flatter, musky odour of his arousal.

He tore at her clothes and she laughed huskily at his little moan of frustration.

'Wait. I'll do it.'

Her fingers flew over the hooks and eyes, feeling their way surely in the flame-lightened dark. Quickly she drew off her dress and drawers. All she wore now was her chemise and over that, securely laced, was her corset. She lifted her hair and turned around.

'You'll have to unlace me.'

'What is this you're wearing?' Kiva said in a tone of amused wonderment. 'Is this thing meant to torture you?'

'I'll explain later. Only take it off.'

Now, she thought. Oh, do it now.

265

She could hardly wait for the touch of his hands on her bare flesh.

Kiva fumbled at the laces of her corset, then he made a sound of exasperation. She felt something hard press against her skin, then the laces parted and the corset loosened, fell away all at once.

He'd cut her corset off.

She almost laughed. It was at once absurd and the most arousing thing that had ever happened to her. Gripping the chemise by its hem she pulled it over her head.

She was naked except for her stockings. Suddenly shy she turned around, her arms crossed over her breasts. Would Kiva find her body beautiful? She was so pale and colourless beside the dusky beauty of the Fan women.

Kiva cursed softly in his own language and she relaxed. She let her arms fall to her sides and faced him with a smile of eagerness.

At once he fell on her with a soft groan. His erect phallus pressed against her thigh as he curled one leg around her. One long-fingered hand trailed across her breasts, cupping the swelling flesh and brushing against her nipples.

Then his mouth covered hers and she tasted him as his tongue entered her mouth. Gwendoline arched towards Kiva, her soft belly pressing into the ridged muscles of his torso. Her hands slipped down to stroke his buttocks, so taut and firm.

She wanted him urgently. Digging her fingers into his flanks she pulled him towards her, opening her thighs so that he lay between them. His mouth was hot as he kissed her and whispered encouragements. He tasted of the fermented drink they'd been served with their meal. She was lost in the smell and the feel of him.

Reaching down between their bodies she curled her fingers around his cock. He filled her hand and as she moved the loose shaft-skin back and forth, she felt the crisp wool of his pubic hair brushing against her hand.

His hair fascinated her; the way it curled so closely to his head and clustered in tiny whorls on his chest and around his cock.

Her palm grew moist from the fluid seeping from his cock-tip and the slippery warmth of it tipped her over.

'Now. Oh now,' she whispered against his mouth. 'I can't wait. Do it to me.'

For just a second he pulled away and looked down at her. He didn't speak but she knew that he was assessing her willingness. He wanted to be sure that she would have no regrets later. If she told him to stop, he would. But she couldn't bear even the thought of that.

She gripped the sides of his hips firmly and tipped her pelvis up to him.

'Please . . .'

Kiva gave a groan and pushed forward, nudging his swollen cock-head against her vulva. Gwendoline opened her legs wide as the full length of his cock slipped into her.

He was gentle at first, as if not wanting to alarm her, but she urged him on with hands and lips until he surged forward deeply with each thrust.

'Oh God,' she groaned, as he filled her with hot, hard flesh.

The head of his cock nudged against her womb with each inward thrust. She rose to meet him, matching him stroke for stroke. He murmured deep in his throat. She couldn't understand what he said –

something more in his own language – but it didn't matter.

Then he could wait no longer and with a great cry he climaxed. Biting her lip to hide her disappointment Gwendoline worked her hips in a frenzied rhythm, rubbing her pleasure bud against his body, trying to attain her own release.

'Gently now,' Kiva murmured.

Breathing heavily he supported his weight on his outstretched arms, pulled his cock free of her body, and moved it gently back and forth between the swollen lips of her sex.

He was still semi-hard and her sex quivered at the exquisite sensations as his shaft moved slickly over her bud of pleasure. Her fingers moved up and down his back in silent entreaty as his moist cock-head stroked gently but firmly up and down her sex, now and then pushing a little way into her.

When the pleasure built until she felt the pulsings start deep inside she opened her eyes and stared up at him. His mouth was curved in a smile and his deep-brown eyes looked full of pride and affection.

A woman could drown in those eyes, she thought.

Then she ceased to think as her climax washed over her, coursing through her from head to toe, leaving her weak and trembling.

Kiva gathered her into his arms and drew her crumpled dress to cover them. Turning onto his back he lay curled up beside her.

'Look,' he said. 'The sky-father sends his children to watch over us.'

Gwendoline looked up at the velvet-purple sky which shone with stars. The dust of Africa was pressing into her back and the forest was alive with the sounds of night animals. Fireflies danced amongst the trees.

She felt totally complete. And as much a part of the land as the spotted leopard which slunk out of the shadows just then and went off to hunt.

Mist was curling over the surface of the Ogowé next morning as the travellers set out for the canoes. The newborn sun touched everything with a diffuse orange glow.

Bird calls echoed in the silence. Gwendoline heard the screech of a baboon as it crashed through the trees on the far bank.

She moved slowly. Her head hurt and her mouth was sour. Her hand mirror had shown her a pale face and shadowed eyes. The fermented drink had been stronger than she realised. Hetty, Edward and Jonathan, all looked in a similar condition but Kiva and the other natives were bright and alert.

Kiva helped her to her seat. Unseen by the others he squeezed her hand. She smiled up at him, the memory of their joining so fresh in her mind that even the slightest contact between them brought a rush of blood to her face.

Jonathan was busy loading up his canoe with gifts of basketware and carvings. He couldn't have spent long with his African princess, Gwendoline thought, if he'd been trading goods with the chief. He seemed intent on his packing. She tried to catch his eye.

Kiva saw her looking towards Jonathan's canoe and evidently assumed that she was admiring the trade goods he'd acquired. Only Gwendoline knew of the confusion of emotions which thoughts of Jonathan brought her.

'The carvings are poor in this village,' Kiva said with contempt. 'I shall give you many better ones to take back to your homeland.'

There was no false pride in his words, only

complete confidence in his own artistry. Gwendoline had gathered that modesty was not something that was valued amongst the Fan.

Kiva meant to please her and she smiled to show that she acknowledged the gesture but inside she felt the first trace of sadness. His mention of England had underlined the fact that whatever was between them would be short-lived. Kiva had a family waiting for him at his village and she had her own life too, so far away that at this moment England seemed like the dream.

Would the passion of the previous night be repeated? She hoped so. Kiva was an eager and vigorous lover. And there were many miles to go by river and over land before they travelled to Kiva's village.

She wanted to pleasure Kiva as he'd pleasured her. The thought of taking his thick cock into her mouth and hearing his moans sent a tingle of excitement to her groin. He was so big and powerful. It aroused her strongly to think that she could make him weak with the actions of her mouth and hands.

Edward gave the word and the natives dug their wooden poles into the mud and pushed the canoes into shallow water. Jonathan lifted his hat and waved to the villagers who lined the bank. They grinned, shouting out good wishes, and continued to wave long after the two canoes had been pushed out into mid-stream and been taken up by the current.

Gwendoline pulled her hat forward to shade her eyes and dozed. Though the Ogowé was wide and flowed quickly it was free from rocks and rapids for some miles. The canoes sped past tree-lined banks where Spanish moss dripped from the branches to trail in the water.

After an hour or so they passed an island where

hippos grazed on the lush grass and sunned themselves on the surrounding sandbanks. Their greyish-brown skins, huge jaws and tiny pink-tinged ears fascinated Gwendoline. Kiva told her that they called the hippo a 'river pig' in his own tongue.

Around noon they stopped off at a village of the Ajumba, where Jonathan and Edward spent some hours talking with the headman and being shown around.

Having eaten and enjoyed the usual colourful welcome, Gwendoline and Hetty sat resting in the shade of some trees near the river. Stripping off their shoes and stockings they cooled their feet and ankles in the water.

Hetty waggled her toes and fanned herself with a bundle of large leaves.

'Oh, Miss. This is heavenly. I swear this heat'll be the death of me.'

Gwendoline laughed. 'You're tough as old boots, Hetty. Don't you pretend otherwise!'

They laughed. Hetty gave Gwendoline a sideways glance.

'You're hardy too, for a lady of your class. You've adjusted to life here very well. I wouldn't have believed it if I hadn't seen it myself.'

'What do you mean?'

'Well look at you. Your face is tanned and you've got freckles on your nose, yet you're not at all fussed. If I'm not mistaken you're not wearing your stays under that blouse and skirt. You'd never do that in England. It would cause a riot.'

Hetty's eyes sparkled with secret knowledge. She went on, 'There's other things I never thought I'd see you doing an' all. Like getting back to our hut at first light, wearing only a chemise and stockings and carrying the rest of your clothes! And as for that corset – well it's ruined ain't it? Looks like someone's been at it with a machete!'

Gwendoline grinned. 'I thought you were asleep, worn out after your – engagement with Edward.'

Hetty shrugged. 'Edward's easily pleased. I know just how to handle him. He had what he wanted, then went off to the men's hut. I was still wide awake and ready for more.'

Her curly blonde hair trembled as she started to giggle.

'I came back to the dance. It was those drums. They seemed to wake a devil in me. I saw you go off with Kiva and felt quite jealous. He's so beautiful, anyone would want him. I stood looking after you for a minute, wondering what to do. Then one of those strong young men pulled me into the dancing. He was almost as good-looking as Kiva. He had really big muscles. Oh, I came out in goosebumps. His name was M'fetta. I just couldn't resist him . . .'

'Hetty! You didn't!' Gwendoline said. She thought she knew Hetty well enough by now but the other woman could still surprise her. 'You did didn't you?'

Hetty's big brown eyes opened wide with mock innocence.

'Wouldn't that be tellin'. I remember how you'd make me tell you all my secrets back in England. P'raps if you tell me all about Kiva, I'll tell you what me and M'fetta did together.' Hetty paused and wetted her lips with her tongue. 'Was Kiva as good as he looks? I hope so, because Jonathan had a face like thunder when he saw you two dancing together. I reckon he couldn't stand to watch all those men admiring you.'

'He was too busy making-up to the chief's daughter to notice me,' Gwendoline said dryly.

'Sometimes you don't see what's under your nose,

Miss, if you'll pardon my saying so. Jonathan might have been futtering the chief's daughter but I'd wager she wore your face.'

Gwendoline grinned. 'That's rubbish Hetty. Jonathan does as he wants with no thoughts for anyone else.'

'Don't you be so sure of that,' Hetty said sagely. 'I'm right about him. You just wait and see if I'm not.'

Gwendoline chuckled. She put her arm around Hetty and gave her a squeeze.

'Oh Hetty you're absolutely incorrigible. What would I do without you! As for what Kiva and I did together . . .'

For the next two nights they camped by the side of the river. Gwendoline was glad of the mosquito nets as the biting insects rose in great clouds from the water's surface at dusk.

Jonathan gave her a bottle of evil-smelling oil to rub on any exposed skin. Though she wrinkled her nose at the smell of it, she had to admit that it worked.

'Shall I rub some on your back?' Jonathan asked, a wicked gleam in his eye.

'No thank you,' she said stiffly. 'I can manage well enough.'

Now that she had left off her stays and some of her petticoats she was more comfortable while travelling. But the damp, stifling heat of the forest still brought the perspiration bursting from her pores. Her blouse and walking-skirt were constantly plastered to her skin and her hair hung around her face in limp strands.

Each night Gwendoline and Hetty shared one low tent and Jonathan and Edward shared the other. Kiva and the other natives curled up in the beached canoes, content to sleep under the stars. The insects didn't seem to bother them.

Gwendoline tried to read for a while each night, but the light from the lamp attracted such a variety of giant insects that she shuddered with horror at the sight of them.

Her lips pressed tightly together, she swatted the worst of them away with a handkerchief. I won't scream, she told herself, knowing how Jonathan would enjoy having to rescue her. How he'd laugh at this evidence of feminine weakness, especially as she was so strident about being independent.

Hetty had no such inhibitions.

'Oh Miss, look at that monster!' she squealed, as an enormous centipede ran across the foot of her camp bed. 'Help! Oh, help. It'll bite me! I'm sure it's poisonous.'

To reassure Hetty, Gwendoline rummaged about under their beds with a forked stick, then, flapping the blankets and stamping about she pronounced the tent cleared of insects. After that she gave up any ideas about reading. It was time that she returned Jonathan's book and illustrated text anyway. But they weren't on the best of terms at the moment. She didn't want to make things worse between them, so had been avoiding him as far as was possible.

'I'll be glad when we spend the night in the next native hut,' Hetty said grumpily, settling down and pulling the blankets to cover her head.

She had a horror of insects crawling into her ears while she slept. Gwendoline was beginning to share her sentiments. The night seemed long and she slept little, disturbed by the sounds of the African night.

Once she heard a thin scream as some animal died in pitiless jaws. Bloodcurdling roars echoed across the vast plains in the clear air. And near dawn there was a loud snuffling around the tent. She reached for the rifle which Jonathan insisted she keep under the bed but whatever animal was foraging about lost interest and hurried away.

By morning, she was irritable and hollow-eyed from lack of sleep. She was beginning to see both sides of Africa. It was magnificent and awe-inspiring, delighting her artist's eye. But danger was ever present. Under the surface there was cruelty and death; unfeeling and emotionless. Like Rathbone, and to some extent Jonathan too, Africa was a continent with velvet claws.

She was also beginning to realise that it was those qualities that resonated to the dark side of her own nature. It was a discovery at once frightening and compelling.

Jonathan dug the oar into the swirling water, feeling the muscles of his arms bunching at each powerful stroke. Jagged rocks protruded out of the water, looking close to the canoe on both sides.

He concentrated on keeping the walls of the craft clear of obstructions. Spray rose up in a wall and crashed down onto the canvas-covered supplies. He was drenched. Water dripped off the brim of his hat and ran inside his open-necked shirt.

The canoe carrying the women was in front of him, Kiva expertly steering it through the rapids. Jonathan thanked God that the young man was such an accomplished oarsman, that was why he felt secure leaving Edward and the women in Kiva's safe hands.

He was less happy about the young African's effect on Gwendoline. The two of them were lovers now. His mouth twisted in a wry grin. Even without her wanton display at the dance at the Fan village he would have known. As a student of human nature and customs he ought to recognise the subtle signals; the eye contacts; the way that the touch of a hand would be extended for a little longer than was usual.

For the first time Jonathan regretted his expertise. He didn't want to know that Gwendoline was obsessed by the beautiful young man. He didn't want to feel the hot pain of anger and jealousy.

The canoe dipped suddenly, burying its nose under a gush of water. Jonathan shook his head to clear his eyes after a deluge almost washed him overboard. He must concentrate, leave thoughts of Gwendoline until later.

Besides, the present situation was of his own making. He knew that but was too proud to admit the fact. Damn Gwendoline's stubborness – it matched his own. He'd never had so much trouble with a woman before.

The river turned into a boiling mass of water, churned-up mud and rocks. Far ahead he could see calm waters. If only they could hold on for a little longer.

It was all he could do to keep control of the canoe. He saw the other craft thrown up by the current. For a moment it seemed to hover on the surface of the water, then it crashed into a trough and disappeared under a white foam of water and mud.

Jonathan's heart missed a beat, then the canoe reappeared downriver. He saw Kiva and the others struggling to gain control. Gwendoline and Hetty were clinging to the sides, water streaming from their hair and clothes. Edward was paddling for all he was worth.

Jonathan sagged with relief. They were all there. The calm water was getting closer now. Just a few minutes more and they'd be past the worst of the rapids. Suddenly the first canoe swerved around a rock, shuddering as the full force of the water hit it head-on.

Jonathan saw Gwendoline jolted forward. She tried to right herself and was thrown out of the canoe.

Hetty screamed as Gwendoline disappeared under the water.

In the near distance, big brownish shapes slithered into the water and began swimming rapidly towards them, a 'v' shaped wake fanning out from their protruding snouts.

Crocodiles.

Jonathan didn't think. He acted on reflex alone.

'Take over,' he shouted to the nearest native, as he dived headfirst into the river.

Using a powerful overarm stroke he knifed through the churning water. Gwendoline had surfaced. He saw her struggling to swim, hampered by her long skirts. The current carried her rapidly downriver, towards the oncoming crocodiles.

She saw them and her eyes opened wide with terror. She tried to scream but coughed instead, spitting out water. Her arms thrashed in the water and she disappeared for a second time.

'Hold on. I'm coming!' Jonathan shouted above the noise of the river.

In her panic Gwendoline was in danger of drowning. He put on a spurt. He had to get her quickly. Gaining on her, Jonathan reached forward. By kicking out strongly he managed to get a grip on her trailing sleeve.

Frantically Gwendoline grabbed at him, clawing for a grip on anything. Her green eyes were blank with terror. The rapids coursed around them, bearing them towards the wide, calmer waters where dark shapes broke the surface.

'It's all right now, I'm here. Let me do all the work,' Jonathan said, trying to reason with her.

If only he could get her to trust him. They'd ride the rapids, then he'd be able to tow her ashore. But he was unable to make her understand. She was blind and deaf to anything but the rushing water and the rapidly approaching crocodiles.

Shots rang out and Jonathan knew that Edward was firing at the crocodiles. Good man, he thought. Edward had his faults but he responded to a crisis.

He saw the nearest reptile turn belly-up, a cloud of blood ballooning into the river. Thank God Edward was a crack shot. More shots and another crocodile rolled over and over in a welter of brown and crimson.

Suddenly huge jaws loomed up to one side of them, crashing down just inches from Gwendoline's flailing arms. The scaly head brushed against her, grazing her skin. Too terrified to realise that the huge beast was sinking in its death throes, Gwendoline gave a strangled scream and renewed her struggles.

'It's dead! Gwendoline. It's all right!' Jonathan shouted.

But she was hysterical, her head shaking and her lips trembling uncontrollably. Hitting out she began slapping at his face and hands. For a moment he lost his grip and began to sink. Determinedly he lunged for her.

The weight of her skirts pulled them both under water. It was all Jonathan could do to keep a hold on her. At this rate they'd both drown. He felt the anger of desperation. Surfacing he coughed and spat, tossing his long hair back out of his eyes.

Gwendoline struggled in his grip but more weakly now. His arms were aching with the effort of holding on to her and fending off her blows. If they were to sink again he didn't think he could save her. Gritting his teeth, he punched her on the point of her jaw. Her eyes rolled back in her head and she sagged against him.

Getting a firm grip on the neckline of her dress he held her head above water and began to swim slowly towards the shore. There was a narrow projection of rock ahead. It was clear of crocodiles. He headed straight for it.

Slowly he made headway. Gwendoline was a dead weight, her long hair trailing round them both like red-brown weed. She moaned faintly. Her skin was very white and her lips looked colourless. He hoped he hadn't really hurt her but he'd had no choice. Her struggles had endangered both their lives.

Somehow he reached the rock and heaved himself partway out of the water. Gasping for breath and with the last of his strength he hauled Gwendoline up beside him, making sure that her torso was clear of the water before grasping her sodden skirts and pulling her legs onto the rock. With relief he saw that her stockinged limbs were unmarked. He shivered with horror at the thought of them being torn by merciless teeth.

Turning Gwendoline on her stomach he pressed and released her ribcage with expertise. She vomited water, gasped and coughed, then began to breathe normally.

'Thank God,' he said, expelling his breath on a long sigh.

He lay full-length, his heart racing. His arms and legs felt like lead.

Behind them in the river, he saw the log shapes of numerous crocodiles as they congregated in the area he'd escaped from seconds before. The water thrashed and boiled as they sank their jaws into the carcasses of their dead companions. Scaly tails beat the air as they took a grip and then turned over and over, tearing chunks of flesh free.

Gwendoline lay as he'd left her. He felt renewed alarm. Bending over her, he loosened her neckline and felt for the pulse in her neck. It was regular and strong. As he sat back she opened her eyes. He saw the look of terror, then she seemed to realise that she was out of the water. She tried to sit up and he helped her.

It took only a moment for her to recover her composure. He was impressed. Most women would have gone into a fit of the vapours. She looked around, then gave a great sigh of relief.

'We're safe here,' he said gently. 'Edward and Kiva are making their way towards us in the canoes. We'll be picked up soon.'

She looked towards the crocodiles and shivered.

'Edward's done for three of the brutes. The others were drawn away from us, attracted by the smell of fresh blood,' he told her.

She was silent for a moment, while she absorbed the fact that they'd escaped almost certain death. Then she looked up at him and said, 'Thank you for saving me, Jonathan. I wouldn't be here now but for you. I've never been so terrified in my entire life.'

He shot her a narrow grin. 'The thought of being drowned, eaten alive or both's enough to terrify anybody.'

'Don't joke about it. It's just like you to play yourself down. You risked your own life to save me. I won't forget that. Ever.'

Reaching up her hand she stroked his cheek. Her green eyes were glowing with sincerity. Taking hold of her wrist he turned her hand over and pressed his lips to her palm. She looked young and very desirable with her wet hair streaming over her shoulders.

For a moment she lay against him, her cheek pressed to his chest. He gathered her in his arms, feeling the curves and hollows of her body. She wasn't wearing stays, he realised, as his hand roved over her neat waist and discovered the softness of her breasts.

He didn't mean to caress her, only to comfort her but somehow his palm was cupping her breast, feeling the nipple as it hardened. His reaction was immediate, the weight at his groin throbbing in readiness.

He knew that she noticed his erection. She could hardly fail to see it, outlined by his sopping wet trousers. Her hand strayed downwards. She ran her fingers lightly along the length of his cock and squeezed the swollen glans playfully.

He drew in his breath, wishing they were anywhere but on a barren rock in the middle of the Ogowé. And now here were the canoes about to pick them both up.

As if Gwendoline knew what he was thinking, he felt her smile, then she winced.

'There *is* one thing,' she said.

'What?' he said softly, putting her at arm's length so that he could see her face.

'Did you have to hit me quite so hard?'

Sparkling at him, she cupped her bruised jaw, rubbing at it ruefully.

Jonathan threw back his head and laughed.

'Oh, Gwendoline. You really are unique! Come on. I'll help you aboard. You seem quite recovered. But Hetty and Edward look as pale as death!'

Chapter Sixteen

'Oh Miss. You're not really going to wear those?'
Hetty said in an awestruck voice.

'I most certainly am,' Gwendoline said, pulling on
the loose khaki trousers and belting them around her
waist.

'There's a similar pair for you and a shirt to go with
them. Jonathan suggested we wear them. And I
agreed. If you'd almost drowned because your dress
and petticoats dragged you underwater, you
wouldn't think twice about wearing men's clothes.'

Hetty held up the shirt, her mouth twitching with
distaste. She wore only a pair of light wool combinations, the same as those Gwendoline wore under
her new outfit.

'Well,' she said doubtfully. 'If you're wearing
them . . .'

Edward's eyes almost popped out of his head
when Gwendoline and Hetty came out of their tent.
Gwendoline's shirt and trousers fitted loosely but
Hetty's large breasts and hips pushed against the
khaki fabric and the buttons of her shirt seemed fit to

burst. The bottoms of her trousers were tucked into her usual high-buttoned boots, giving her ankles and feet a neat tapering look in contrast to the men's wear.

'Hetty!'

'Don't you dare say anythin',' she warned Edward.

Jonathan smiled appreciatively, while Kiva and the other natives shook their heads, marvelling at the strange dress habits of the white travellers.

Gwendoline ignored the interested stares and set about packing up. They were to start the trek through the forest today, having come as far upriver as Jonathan intended them to. The branch of the Ogowé they were following flowed into Lake Ncovi before continuing on towards the sea.

The canoes had been pulled up high above the waterline and secured safely by the lake for their return.

Their camp on the shores of Ncovi overlooked a vast expanse of water studded with many tiny islands. Thick forest stretched away from the shore in all directions. It looked impenetrable but Jonathan assured them that he'd been this way before.

It was blisteringly hot, even in the gloom of the great forest. Gwendoline's long hair was pinned up under a bush hat but her face and neck prickled with the heat. The front of her shirt was soon darkened with perspiration as she struggled on for mile after mile over fallen trees and rocks.

Hetty and herself were the only ones not carrying anything. Kiva and the natives were loaded with backpacks containing the tents and provisions. Kiva insisted on carrying Gwendoline's bag which held her artist's equipment. Jonathan and Edward carried guns. Each of them wore a thick belt studded with ammunition.

At midday they stopped for a meal then began descending into a ravine. In the bottom, rolling in the mud, was a herd of elephants; the first Gwendoline had seen. She eyed them with suspicion, awed by their size and the way they swung their trunks about spraying mud and water over their creased hides. A huge old bull, with one broken tusk, trumpeted at them as they approached.

She froze with alarm. Jonathan flashed her his narrow grin.

'Don't worry. He's just exercising his lungs. We're downwind of them. They'll take no notice of us if we move past quietly.'

This proved to be the case but Gwendoline's heart-beat didn't return to normal for some time. They had reached the far side of the ravine and were clamber-ing up the steep sides, when Gwendoline gave a cry of pain and slipped. Somehow she held on.

Jonathan was at her side in a trice.

'What's wrong? Have you twisted your ankle?'

'No,' she gasped. 'There's something hurting my arm. Oh it's pricking and burning dreadfully.'

'Let me see.'

Forgetting all modesty in her haste, Gwendoline unbuttoned her shirt and slipped it off one shoulder. Three shapes, like big bluish-red beads were stuck to her forearm.

'Oh, they're horrible! What on earth are they?'

'Elephant ticks,' Jonathan said calmly. 'Harmless. But very painful. Keep still. I'll remove them.'

Gwendoline bit her lip as Jonathan used the sharp blade of his hunting knife to scrape the ticks free. Her gorge rose when he squashed them with the point of his knife and dark blood oozed from them; her blood.

'Ugh. The filthy things!' she said, examining each

small wound on her arm. They ached and burned like fire, the pain out of all proportion to their size.

Kiva had seen Jonathan remove the ticks.

'I'll find something to help with the pain,' he said, searching around the rock face.

Finding what he sought he picked a small plant and stripped the fleshy leaves from it. After chewing the leaves for a second or two he packed the green pulp around the wounds.

Jonathan tore a square of lint from a bundle in the first-aid kit in his backpack, then used his neck scarf to bind the poultice in place.

'Thank you. Both of you.' Gwendoline said, grateful that the awful pain was subsiding. 'I'm sure I'll be all right now.'

For the first time she realised that the fine wool combinations were visible beneath her open shirt. The shape of her breasts was clearly visible through the fabric, the dark aureole of her nipples prominently displayed. Hurriedly she slipped her shirt back on but not before she saw the flash of appreciation on Jonathan's face.

They put up the tents for the night under a canopy of ebony and climbing palm. A nearby stream provided water for drinking and washing. Hetty and Gwendoline soaked handkerchiefs in the water and mopped their faces and necks.

'Careful Miss,' Hetty said. 'We're to watch out for snakes.'

'I'm so tired, I don't care about them,' Gwendoline said.

After a hastily prepared meal of meat and fufu – dumplings made from pounded cassava, Gwendoline collapsed onto her camp bed. She heard the men talking and smelt the tobacco from the natives' pipes but was too exhausted to join them around the camp fire.

285

Despite her swollen arm, she slept soundly until morning.

The next day, the going was much the same. Her arm was much better and the slight soreness was bearable.

Thin, grey-white trees pressed in on all sides, some of them festooned with rubber vines looking like frayed ropes. Bright, wax-like flowers covered the vines and spotted the forest floor, each bloom large enough to cover Gwendoline's spread hand.

Hetty gathered up some blooms and inhaled their perfume, then dropped them with a squeal when she saw the vicious red ants climbing all over them.

After the usual halt for food at midday, they pressed on. Gwendoline became aware of a dull roaring sound as they approached a stretch of hills, which reared up through a space in the trees.

'What's that noise?' she asked Jonathan.

'That's the falls,' he said. 'We have to cross them to get to Fan country.'

'How?' she said, imagining climbing down the sides of another ravine and not relishing the fact.

He smiled. 'Don't worry we're not about to ford another crocodile-infested river on a makeshift raft.'

'I'm very glad to hear it – ' she said.

'There's a rope bridge,' he broke in, grinning wickedly.

Gwendoline grinned back.

'That's all right then,' she said stoutly, although her knees felt weak at the thought of crossing a huge chasm on such a flimsy structure.

One after the other they edged their way over the rope bridge, which swung alarmingly in the up-draught of breeze and spray from the falls.

Hetty squeezed her eyes tight shut and inched forward, gripping the supporting ropes. She trembled with fear and Gwendoline forgot her own terror in the face of Hetty's obvious distress.

'Lord save us! I'm never going across that big hole!'

'Here. I'll hold onto the belt at your waist,' Gwendoline said to her. 'We'll cross together.'

The two women moved gingerly across the bridge, trying not to look down at the rocks and foaming water hundreds of feet below. Hetty's face was drained of all colour. She muttered under her breath.

Gwendoline thought Hetty was praying, until she made out the words. Hetty's curses would have put a navvy to shame.

On the far side of the falls Hetty collapsed gratefully onto the grass. Then she remembered her horror of insects and sprang upright again.

The next two days they trekked through narrow shaded swamps. All of them were spattered with the black batter-like ooze. Gwendoline felt the gritty residue working its way inside her clothes and boots. The smelly mud seemed to sink into her pores. It was impossible to remove, even at night. Soon, she forgot how it felt to be clean. At least the mud streaking her skin gave some relief from the ever present mosquitos and sand flies.

The swamps were beautiful in their own way. Golden sunlight poured down through dark-green leaves and dappled the pools of water with gold coins, but snakes and leeches abounded.

Gwendoline's feet were sore and her muscles ached from the unaccustomed endeavour. She didn't complain – determined to give a good account of herself – but even packing her boots with grass didn't cushion her feet against injury.

Though she said nothing to him about her blisters, Jonathan produced a bottle of surgical spirits.

'Rub this on your feet,' he said. 'It'll toughen them up.'

The surgical spirit did help, even though her boots were sodden by day and hard in the morning after being dried out around the camp fire. She remembered to check them for snakes before putting them back on.

As time wore on she began to long for the day when they'd reach a native village and she could spend the night in a clean, dry hut. The thought of a bath and cool cotton against her skin seemed the ultimate in luxury.

Steaming hot water, scented with perfumed oils haunted her dreams. But she and Hetty had to make do with a wipe-over in muddy water.

One night Gwendoline was returning to camp after relieving her bladder outside the circle of light, when Kiva approached her. She almost jumped out of her skin when he materialised out of the blackness of the jungle night.

Without a word he clasped her to him and began kissing her soundly. As his mouth moved on hers Gwendoline sank into him. She lifted her hands to cup his face.

Their joining back at the Fan village had been much on her mind. She loved to recall the feel of Kiva's hard body and the way he thrust so strongly into her. Memories of that pleasure excited her still, prompting her to stroke herself to orgasm before she slept each night.

But Gwendoline had decided that it was prudent after all to keep her distance from Kiva. As time passed and the young African did not approach her again, she let things lie between them. She was still confused about her emotions. In truth, she wasn't sure now if it *was* just purely physical attraction between Kiva and herself.

Perhaps she had been trying to make Jonathan take notice of her, albeit unwittingly.

But with Kiva's hands carressing her, opening the buttons on her shirt, it was another matter entirely. In the faint light from the fire she saw the fine planes of his face, the straight nose and wonderful mouth. His beauty and maleness called out to her. The heat and softness of his lips moved down her neck, nuzzling against the low neckline of her combinations.

Her mind might reason against repeating their passion but her body had a will of its own. Where was the harm in enjoying him once more? Her palms pressed against the warm muscles of his naked torso but there was no strength in them to push him away.

'Do you want me?' he whispered.

And she could only murmur, 'Yes. Oh, yes.'

'That's all I wanted to know.'

In the darkness she saw the flash of his white teeth, then he had loosened her belt and pulled her trousers down. The combinations had a buttoned flap. She felt the night air on her bare buttocks as Kiva freed them.

He urged her to lie stomach down over a fallen tree. She did so gladly. Leaning over her, his hands squeezed her breasts, teasing and rolling the nipples through the cloth of her shirt. Gasping she pressed back against him. She could smell the pungent feminine musk rising from her sex and the dried perspiration from her clothes.

In England she would have been horrified by her body's strong smell. But here in the heat and the rotten-leaf smell of the forest, it seemed right. Kiva too was smeared with swamp-mud. His skin was gritty and salty, smelling of oil and sweat. It was a sharp exciting scent.

Bending down he pressed his mouth to the crease of her buttocks and ran his tongue up into the fleshy groove. She shivered as he held the full globes apart, seeking out her flesh-lips and flicking the tip of his tongue over her pleasure bud.

Slipping his hands between her parted thighs from behind, he cupped her sex, squeezing and stroking gently. She felt herself growing wetter as her bud began throbbing and pressed her bottom towards him again. Kiva laughed deep in his throat at her wantonness. He smeared her juices around her entrance and whispered in her ear.

'You're almost ready for me.'

She strained to open her legs more widely but the trousers around her ankles prevented it. The combinations hugged her skin leaving only the parted buttocks exposed. The constriction of movement and the thought of what Kiva could see of her, added to the pleasure.

When Kiva pressed the tip of his erect cock against her sex and eased inside her, it felt deliciously tight. The ridged muscles of his stomach pounded against her buttocks as he surged into her. She bit the sides of her hands to muffle her moans of pleasure.

Drawing away a little to watch as his cock slipped in and out of her, she felt Kiva drag her buttocks apart almost roughly. She was too far gone to worry that he could see the whole of her sex as it surrounded his thrusting organ. Creamy juices trickled down her flesh-valley and smeared her inner thighs.

Suddenly she jerked in shock as he trailed his fingertips across the tight little mouth of her anus. His fingernail added a subtle scratchy pleasure that was intensely exciting.

When he inserted the tip of one finger, she moaned and arched her back. He laid a steadying hand in the small of her back, partly withdrew his cock and rimmed her vagina thoroughly, all the time tickling and penetrating her anus with one slippery finger.

Gwendoline climaxed helplessly, her head tossing from side to side. The deep internal pulsings, prompted Kiva's release. Pulling out of her he ejaculated onto her buttocks. She felt his shudders and heard the gasp he made, quickly caged behind his teeth.

For a moment he stroked his hands over her whole body, as if committing it to memory.

'You are beautiful my white princess,' he whispered, bending forward to drop a kiss on the top of her head. 'I thank you for the gift we shared. But I must leave you now.'

Swiftly rebuttoning the flap of her combinations and pulling up her trousers, he left her, melting silently into the trees. Still trembling slightly, Gwendoline adjusted her clothes. The whole thing had been so quick, yet so intense. It could have been a dream.

But it was a dream she would cherish and recall at will.

She smiled. Kiva understood her, and himself, perfectly. The fleeting pleasure of their joining was all they could hope to share, their cultures were so different. There was no place in her life for him. And, as the son of a chief, he would be required to fill the place that was his by birth. But here, in the forest, they were simply a man and woman, performing the ritual that was as old as time itself.

She was glad that he found her beautiful. He was the most stunningly handsome male she had ever seen. She doubted whether she'd ever meet anyone like him again.

At least she had the partly completed drawing of Kiva. She'd finish it as soon as possible. All that beauty and vigour ought to be captured for posterity.

That night she slept heavily. In the morning they would reach the plantain patches and sorghum fields on the outskirts of Kiva's village. The few moments of exquisite pleasure had been his way of saying a private goodbye.

Hornbills and vultures were perched in the trees that thinned out as they progressed through Fan territory the next day.

Gwendoline looked towards an outcrop of rock, where a large group of mandrill monkeys searched for food, scratching around in the sandy soil for grubs. Their colourful faces of crimson, blue and white with orange beards, fascinated her. The mandrill's harsh chorus kept pace with them for some miles.

The jungle is never quiet, never still, she observed.

As if to echo her thoughts a drumbeat began; the solid heavy sound having a penetrating quality. She had heard them sometimes during their travels but never so sustained nor so insistent sounding.

Jonathan explained that the drums were the means of transmitting information over large distances throughout Africa. Talking drums, he called them.

'They're the reason we've travelled in safety so far. The Fans are a fierce, vivacious people but they know that we have Kiva with us. They're telling of our imminent arrival at the village. The celebration to welcome the chief's son home will be well under way by now.'

The hypnotic rhythm of the drumbeat called out to

Gwendoline, prompting memories of shiny black bodies, twisting and swirling in the movements of the dance. She detected a pattern in the beats, very different from the throbbing primaeval music that found an echo in her soul.

They heard the sound of singing and chanting, before the roofs of the first houses came into view.

A great crowd of people came forward to welcome them. As always the children came first, grinning and shouting in shrill voices. They were dressed in all their finery and wore colourful headdresses of feathers. The women and men followed the children. In the midst of them was a tall, imposing man, decked with a great amount of jewellery. Ropes of painted seeds hung around his neck; suspended from one of them was an ivory breastplate. Ivory discs hung from the lobes of his ears.

'Father!' Kiva called out and ran forward into the tall man's embrace.

'My son! You are restored to us. Thank the gods.'

After embracing Kiva and exchanging words in his own language, Kiva's father addressed Jonathan and the others. Beaming with pleasure and showing strong white teeth with a wide gap in the centre, he said, 'I Makaja, welcome you. You have returned my favoured son safely to me. All I have is yours. Ask anything and it will be granted to you. But I see that you are travel-worn. Rest and bathe. Then let us all feast and celebrate.'

Makaja called out orders and a number of women ran forward to do his bidding.

'His wives,' Jonathan whispered to Gwendoline.

'All of them?'

She was shocked. There seemed a great number of wives, ranging from middle-aged women to mere girls.

Jonathan nodded. 'The chief's a wealthy man. Having so many wives adds to his status.'

Makaja's benevolence, his outstretched arms, encompassed them all. Nodding and smiling he greeted each of them in turn. Hetty, Edward and Jonathan passed the chief, each receiving a handshake and a warm embrace. They continued walking on towards the main street of the village, accompanied by the chief's wives and the chanting children.

Gwendoline walked more slowly towards the chief. She was looking down and smiling at two children who had slipped their hands into hers. The native children always captivated her. They were so open and friendly. There was no trace of artifice in their expressions.

When she glanced up she caught Makaja's eye. Her smile wavered and she was nonplussed for a moment.

Makaja said nothing for what seemed like a long time. He made no move to shake her hand or embrace her.

Gwendoline's face grew hot as she realised that he was staring at her with undisguised absorption. There was no mistaking his expression.

Kiva's father found her desirable. And he didn't care who knew it.

Hetty splashed water playfully at Gwendoline.

'Oh, I've thought about this for days,' she said. 'I didn't think I'd ever feel really clean again.'

They were bathing in a stream some way from the village. Upstream they could hear the laughter and shouts as the men, including Edward and Jonathan, washed themselves.

Gwendoline scooped up handfuls of sand and

rubbed it into her scalp as the Fan women were doing. Two of them attended Hetty, exclaiming at the wheat-gold colour of her hair.

Hetty was enjoying all the attention. She giggled when they pointed to the thick bush of dark-blonde hair between her legs. Gwendoline received the same attention. The Fan women were fascinated by Gwendoline and Hetty's pubic hair.

The Fans had hardly any body hair. What they did have was sparse and tightly curled. Gwendoline remembered stroking Kiva's chest, delighting in the springy wool that trailed downwards to cluster at his groin.

A wrinkled old woman tugged at Gwendoline's pubis, then jumped back as if bitten. Everyone laughed.

'If they weren't so charming I might be embarrassed!' Gwendoline joined in the laughter.

She lay back in the shallow water, while slim brown fingers scrubbed her skin with more sand. After a time one of the young women, with long limbs and high, conical-shaped breasts, nudged her and made hand movements. Gwendoline realised that she was expected to return the compliment. All around the women were taking it in turns to wash each other.

Scooping up more sand Gwendoline began applying it to the sleek brown skin of a young woman, who looked at her with shy, almond-shaped black eyes.

She'd noticed this woman watching her covertly and was intrigued by her grace and beauty. When the woman continued to study her, Gwendoline decided to investigate. Using Jonathan as her interpreter, she learned that the young woman was expected to marry Kiva. Her name was Benka.

The custom was, that a man would 'buy' his bride, making money from trading rubber and ivory and exchanging it for the Fan's chosen currency; tiny iron axe-heads. Kiva's being captured, meant that he'd had no chance to accrue the necessary bride price, but Benka had waited for him anyway. The whole village knew that this marriage would be a love match.

Gwendoline felt glad that Kiva would be happy with the woman of his choice. It made her sad to think that she'd never see him again after they left the village. But she had always known that the pleasure they'd shared was for a limited time only.

She still had some work to do on the drawing. It was coming on well. There were just details to add. She had an idea. If Benka was willing, she'd draw her too. The portraits would make a stunning pair and they'd remind her of Africa during the cold wet winters of England.

Gwendoline smiled at the Fan girl. Benka did not return the smile. She looked at Gwendoline so closely, that Gwendoline wondered if Kiva had spoken about her. The Fans had a very direct way of staring sometimes. It did not seem to be considered an insult, as it would have been in her own culture.

Perhaps she had mistaken the way Makaja studied her. Kiva's father was probably only curious. He could not have seen many white women. Few ventured this far into the jungle.

Yes. That must be it. How foolish she was to feel nervous of the chief.

Makaja was imposing and handsome but without his son's stunning beauty – that was inherited from Kiva's mother, along with her gentleness, according to Jonathan. Gwendoline had felt no real threat from the chief. She decided that she must have been imagining the intensity of his gaze.

Rinsing the sand from her hair, Gwendoline twisted it into a thick rope and let it trail down her back. She dressed in the large square of woven fabric which had been a gift from one of the chief's wives, then made her way back to the hut which had been assigned to her for the duration of the visit.

For the celebration feast, Gwendoline and Hetty dressed in brilliantly-coloured silk gowns, packed especially for just such an occasion.

'You look wonderful Miss,' Hetty said as she secured the emerald green gown. 'That neckline's daring though. Good thing your father can't see you wearing it.'

Gwendoline smiled. After all she'd experienced in Africa, she doubted whether she'd give a fig for her father's narrow ideas of propriety on her return home.

Hetty brushed out Gwendoline's waist-length hair and swept it up into curls, pinned high onto her head. There was a matching headdress of dyed ostrich feathers. Hetty fastened it with an emerald and gold brooch.

The gowns seemed incongruous against the vivid costumes and body paint of the Fan people but the appreciative glances and cheers told Gwendoline that she'd made the right choice. She must look as exotic and flamboyant to them, as the Fans appeared to her.

Makaja insisted that Gwendoline sit next to him. He ate with gusto, passing her many choice foods and urging her to eat heartily.

'A good appetite is prized in a woman,' Jonathan said, bending close. 'The chief is honouring you with his attentions.'

Makaja said something and Jonathan grinned.

'He says you are too thin. But he admires you greatly. If you were a wife of his, he would insist that you be fattened up!'

Gwendoline laughed, unable to decipher the wicked gleam in Makaja's eyes. For some reason the chief still made her nervous.

The celebrations went on long into the night. The men put on a display. One man, who she recognised as Kiva, was draped in a lion skin and the others stalked him, threatening him with spears. The women danced too, their naked breasts and buttocks bobbing to the beat of drums and insistent hiss of seed-filled gourds.

The dawn glow was pricking the sky before the Fans drifted off to their huts. Gwendoline and Hetty left Jonathan talking with Makaja, who seemed as fresh as when the celebrations began. Makaja called out as Gwendoline passed by.

'He says to sleep well and he hopes you will look favourably on all the presents,' Jonathan translated.

Gwendoline nodded, mystified by that last remark. What presents?

On reaching the hut, she saw what Makaja meant.

'Look at all this,' Hetty said crossly, pushing past the fine basketwork and earthenware pottery which was piled high just inside the hut.

'There's hardly room for a body to stretch out and sleep!'

'I expect Makaja's grateful to us. That's all,' Gwendoline said. 'He's plainly delighted to have his son back. Also, according to Jonathan, chiefs like to show off their generosity to guests.'

'Hmph!' Hetty said bluntly. 'He can show off all he likes, so long as we're not expected to cart this lot back through the jungle!'

She walked around examining the piles of gifts, fingering beaded belts and opening containers of carved and inlaid wood.

'There's ivory jewellery in this box and some lovely printed cloth. Ooh and some funny balls of black stuff in this basket. I wonder what they are.'

Picking one of the balls up, Hetty squeezed it, then she smelt one.

'It's like liquorice but more bitter,' she said.

'They're made of India rubber,' Gwendoline said distractedly. There seemed an excess of goods, even for a grateful father.

'And look at these – what are they meant for?'

Gwendoline looked at the huge basket which stood in a shadowy corner of the hut. She hadn't noticed it at first. It was filled to the brim with little bundles of iron, imitation axe-heads. She picked a clump up, a suspicion beginning to form in her mind. There were ten axe-heads to each bundle. Jonathan had explained that each bundle was called a *ntet*.

She realised that the number of *ntet* she saw before her represented a great deal of wealth in Fan terms.

'What's wrong? You've gone a funny colour,' Hetty said peering over Gwendoline's shoulder.

'I may be wrong but I think Makaja has honoured me a little more than I would have wished.'

Hetty looked puzzled.

'These,' Gwendoline said, holding out her hand to show Hetty what lay in the palm, 'are special currency. They're only used for one thing here.'

'What's that?'

'For buying a wife,' Gwendoline said, her mouth drying even as she formed the words. 'I think Makaja has sent me a sort of dowry.'

Hetty's mouth dropped open.

'Oh, my gawd,' she whispered. 'That's set the fox amongst the chickens!'

Jonathan confirmed Gwendoline's worst fears.

'That's a bride price you've got there and no mistake.'

He looked worried. 'This is something I hadn't foreseen. It isn't all that unusual for the different tribes to intermarry but for Makaja to offer for you so openly is rare. This goes against all the conventions.'

'But what are we to do about it? Can you reason with him?'

'I hope so,' Jonathan said and she felt a frisson of fear as she realised that he sounded none too sure.

'We'll have to sit through more entertainment and feasting I'm afraid. Only when the feasting is done is it proper to discuss business. One can't hurry these things.'

The day seemed to drag until the sun set in a glory of gold and crimson, then night was upon them. Gwendoline could never become accustomed to the lack of twilight in Africa. One minute it was day, then full dark came without warning.

Fires and torchlight lit up the village. This time they sat on animal skins, spread on the ground in front of low carved wooden tables. Throughout the meal Gwendoline was tense and edgy. She nibbled at a piece of roast meat but couldn't manage anything else.

Jonathan conversed with Makaja, smiling and admiring the gifts of carved wood which were brought before him. Gwendoline sensed Jonathan's underlying uneasiness and it frightened her.

Jonathan had always seemed so capable, so in command of everything. If he was disconcerted by

Makaja's behaviour, then something must be seriously wrong.

A smiling Kiva brought Gwendoline a parcel wrapped in a zebra skin. Glad of the distraction, she unwrapped the gift. Inside the skin was a beautifully executed statue of a fertility goddess. Her features were strong and her body powerful, with jutting breasts and wide hips.

'I told you I was an excellent craftsman,' Kiva said proudly. 'The black wood comes from the heart of the mpingo tree. It is a difficult wood to work but I saw the shape inside this tree and I gave it life.'

'Thank you,' she said warmly, thinking how lucky Benka was to be marrying such a beautiful and accomplished young man. She bent closer to whisper. 'I'll treasure your gift always. And I'll never forget the moments we shared.'

Kiva smiled, his dark eyes soft. 'I too shall remember my white princess, my saviour. Keep my gift near you. It will protect you on your homeward journey.'

So Kiva did not know of his father's plans to keep her in the wives' lodge. Gwendoline wondered what Kiva's reaction would be when he found out.

She sipped a cup of fermented beverage. It was sweet and fruity. On her almost empty stomach it went straight to her head. She drank deeply, finding comfort in the softening and blurring of her perceptions. She began to relax. Jonathan will think of something, she thought, her cheeks glowing from the effects of the beverage.

When she thought Makaja wasn't looking, she glanced his way. Each time, without fail, she found his eyes on her; assessing, measuring. His handsome face was intense as he studied her.

Then Makaja spoke and Jonathan translated.

'The chief asks if you are enjoying the feast. You are not eating. He is worried about your health.'

Somehow Gwendoline managed to smile politely. Through Jonathan, she thanked the chief for the delicious feast and the entertainment, then she wished him and his wives good health and long life; it was a traditional way of expressing thanks.

The chief looked pleased.

'The white lady has good manners as well as great beauty,' Jonathan translated.

Makaja bowed his head and said something in an aside to his nearest wife. The other wives giggled prettily, holding their hands up to cover their mouths.

Jonathan stiffened but was silent. Gwendoline threw him a questioning look but he shook his head.

After the food there was more music and dancing. The drums beat a rapid tempo. The dancers swayed in unison, stamping their feet and shaking their hips in time to the rhythm. They were naked except for woven grass belts and strings of beads. Many wore face and body paint of ochre and vermilion. Some wore headbands of beads and feathers, trailing with ribbons of dyed grasses.

As the women danced their breasts jiggled invitingly. They rotated their hips, making gestures of encouragement to the men. The scene was a reflection of that other time when she had gone into the forest with Kiva. The remembered pleasure of that encounter affected Gwendoline strongly.

But this time it was Jonathan she wanted. How had they resisted each other for so long? It was time to remedy that. She would tell him that she wanted him inside her, wanted his cock to thrust urgently into her until she ached with the potent pleasure of it.

She tried to move but found that she was dizzy. The drumbeat seemed to be inside her head. It found an echo in the pulse beating heavily in her neck.

The fermented drink had imparted a definite fuzzy edge to her vision. She could no longer be sure how many dancers there were. The leashed sexual tension in the dance seemed to be weaving an ever more erotic spell. She was aware that the chief was watching her closely and suddenly she was angry.

I'm not an insect on a pin, she thought. How dare Makaja look at her as if she was a prize heifer!

But her anger got lost somehow. The drums demanded all emotion, all thought. A wave of heat swept up her body, centring in the region around her groin. The smells of roast meat and hot bodies made her queasy. And underlying everything was the rattle of seed filled gourds and the powerful pulse note of the drums.

A wave of nausea flooded Gwendoline. She turned to speak to Hetty, to ask her for help, and locked eyes instead with Makaja.

The chief's eyes glistened, holding hers like a snake. The tip of his pointed tongue moistened his full lips. He leaned forward, fixing Gwendoline with a scorching glance.

There was no mistaking his meaning this time.

Gwendoline was shaken. She looked away in confusion. Dimly she was aware that Jonathan had been watching her for some time. He leaned over now and covered her hand with his own.

'Don't look so scared. I'll sort this mess out somehow.'

She was touched by his comforting words and his possessive gesture. She squeezed his hand and felt the answering pressure of his strong fingers.

It was going to be all right. Jonathan had promised.

Makaja looked displeased. His black eyes were hard as jet. He frowned and looked away. Standing up, Makaja clapped his hands. The music and dancing ceased abruptly.

Jonathan bent close and spoke softly to Gwendoline.

'I did not want to alarm you earlier, but you and I are invited to the chief's lodge. We have no choice but to go. There will be some spirited bargaining. This could be tricky. You must trust me. Be guided by me in this. Our lives may depend on what happens during the next few hours.'

Gwendoline was aghast. His words were like a draught of cold water. She felt sober suddenly.

'Then we're in real danger?'

He nodded. 'But all's not lost. Be brave, like I know you are. All right?'

Despite the heat she felt cold. When Jonathan stood up, she followed him mutely.

Inside the chief's spacious lodge the walls were covered with richly decorated artifacts. There were shields, masks, weapons, bowls and many painted statues. They were shown to a raised wooden dais, covered with fine pelts and made comfortable. More of the fermented drink was passed around. Gwendoline sipped it sparingly. She'd need all her wits about her.

For a while Jonathan and Makaja conversed. The atmosphere in the lodge grew gradually more tense. Jonathan's voice hardened and Makaja replied to him in a clipped tone.

Gwendoline listened, wishing that she understood more of the language. It was plain that all was not well. Jonathan began to look angry. He shook his head.

'No. It is impossible,' he said finally, in English.

Makaja looked stunned, then he began shouting. Jonathan faced him down. Suddenly Makaja stood up and made a curt gesture of dismissal.

'What's happening Jonathan?' Gwendoline said, her heart hammering in her throat. 'I thought this man was your friend. Why won't he listen to you?'

Jonathan's lips thinned. 'Yes, Makaja's my friend. But he's trying to use that fact to his own advantage. As his friend, he demands that I consent to his wishes. If I do not he'll keep his gifts, confiscate all the artifacts I've collected on this trip and keep us all prisoner.'

'Oh no,' she breathed. 'It's because of me, isn't it? That's what he's saying. He still wants to marry me doesn't he?'

Jonathan nodded grimly.

'And is there no way we can bargain with him? Nothing we can say?'

Jonathan looked doubtful. 'I've tried. You can see the result. What do you suggest? He's a man who is used to having his every wish granted. But, by God, he shall not have you – '

Gwendoline laid a hand on Jonathan's arm as he half rose, a murderous look on his face.

'Please! Don't do anything hasty!'

She was suddenly terribly afraid for him, for all of them. Her fingers were trembling. She clasped her hands together tightly and looked steadily at the chief, trying not to show her fear.

Makaja smiled back at Gwendoline, a triumphant smile on his face. His large dark eyes were moist and lustful.

'There might just be a way . . .' Jonathan began. 'If you are agreeable. You do trust me? You know that I'll never let any harm come to you.'

'I trust you,' Gwendoline said without hesitation.

'Promise Makaja what you will. I would do anything to save all of our lives.'

Jonathan spoke again to the chief. Gwendoline held her breath, trying to read that impassive darkly-handsome face. Makaja seemed to be considering Jonathan's proposal. He stroked his chin and turned to whisper to his favourite wife.

The woman giggled behind her hand, her eyelids sweeping down to cover her sloe-like eyes; then she nodded.

When Makaja smiled slowly and nodded, a huge sense of relief washed over Gwendoline. Some sort of a bargain had been struck.

'What's happened? Tell me Jonathan.'

'We're free to go on our way on the morrow,' Jonathan said evenly. 'If you'll . . . But I can't agree to his terms. Edward won't have it either.'

His face was grim. He did not seem to share Gwendoline's relief.

'What did Makaja want?' she asked, her voice shaky. 'Tell me Jonathan. And don't dress it up in pretty language.'

He shook his head. 'He asks that you spend one night with him . . . and his wives. You'd have to . . . I refused of course – '

'Tell him that I agree,' Gwendoline broke in. 'Do it Jonathan!'

'You can't. I won't allow it. I'll kill the bastard first!'

Thoroughly alarmed, Gwendoline pushed Jonathan aside. His stubborness and sense of honour was about to ruin everything. She ran towards Makaja and fell to her knees.

'Yes,' she cried. 'Yes. I'll do it.'

Seizing hold of the neck of her gown, she ripped it open to the waist exposing the tops of her breasts.

Makaja might not understand her words but there was no mistaking the gesture.

Makaja's eyes narrowed with respect. He nodded slowly and his mouth curved in a cat-like smile of satisfaction.

'No! Gwendoline don't . . .'

Jonathan made a rush for Makaja, his hand going to the hunting knife at his waist.

Makaja made a gesture and two young men grabbed Jonathan's arms and restrained him. Then Makaja threw back his head and gave a shout of laughter. He pointed at Jonathan and said something in his own language.

Jonathan paled.

'What? What did he say?' Gwendoline asked, her skin crawling with fear. 'For God's sake Jonathan tell me! If he's threatened to harm you, I'll go back on my word.'

'I'm not to be harmed. But . . .' Jonathan's mouth twisted. He had difficulty spitting out the words. 'Makaja . . . he said that I'm to watch while you pleasure him and his wives. I'm to be restrained, so that . . . so that anyone who wishes can use my body.'

Gwendoline gasped. She had expected Makaja to punish Jonathan for his outburst but she had never imagined such a subtle and cruel torture.

'Let him go damn you! I'll do anything you want – '

She was cut off in mid-sentence as hands were laid on her. Though she struggled, she knew that it was pointless to protest. Makaja would give no more ground. Finally she went limp and allowed herself to be hustled from the hut.

As she was led away by three of the chief's wives to be readied for the night to come, she had time to compose herself. At the back of her mind was a profound sense of relief, even a pride of sorts. By giving herself to Makaja she could save them all.

It was simply a practical arrangement, that was how she must view this 'bargain' if she was to get through what was to come.

But as she stepped inside the women's lodge and smelt the mixture of perfumed oils and dust, she was aware of deeper and darker tides moving within her. She found it difficult to admit, even to herself, but in a strange way she was excited. Her nipples were erect, pushing against the thin fabric of her chemise as if in anticipation of being touched.

The area between her thighs felt hot and moist. It seemed that the effects of the potent fermented drink, the atmosphere of danger and the unknown events to come, had sharpened her senses in a most surprising and provocative way.

And the image that seemed carved into her mind, so that she could not put it from her, was that of Jonathan. Jonathan stripped and restrained while Makaja's women pressed their oily bodies to him, sinking down to bury his erect cock inside their heated vaginas and teasing his unwilling flesh with their slender fingers.

As the three wives began to unfasten her gown, she shivered. She had wanted to pleasure Jonathan and in a strange, almost incomprehensible way she was going to get her wish.

Chapter Seventeen

*O*utside the peeled-bark walls of the lodge, the chanting and the drums throbbed to a sensuous rhythm. Gwendoline could feel the drums in her blood, her heart seeming to mirror the beat.

The real world seemed far away. There was only the shadow filled lodge and the yellow flares of the flame torches.

She knew that Hetty and Edward would be waiting tensely for this night to be over. Gwendoline had reassured Hetty about her safety, having managed to snatch a brief word with her before the wives brought her away from the stream.

'Just be ready to leave at first light. And don't worry. No harm will come to me, though I doubt I'll ever worry about modesty again after this!'

'Oh, Miss. How can you joke about it? What if that lusty old chief decided to keep you here anyways?'

'I think Kiva will step in and speak up for me if Makaja has ideas on that score. Now Hetty you're not to worry. Truly.'

They exchanged a brief embrace before Gwendoline

was led away. And although she looked unconvinced, Hetty had to be satisfied with that.

Scrubbed clean now and naked, Gwendoline sat on a fur covered dais in the chief's lodge, while three of Makaja's young wives rubbed perfumed oil into her skin and made her beautiful according to the Fan people's perceptions of the word.

Her long dark-red hair was divided into strands, oiled and threaded with beads, dried grass and feathers. Then flower petals were pressed all over her oiled skin, adhering to the sticky surface to form a tactile layer. Her pubic hair was given special attention. This too was combed and decorated. Slim fingers worked the perfumed oil between Gwendoline's legs, smearing it onto her vulva.

She pulled away when she felt fingers probing into her, anointing the inside of her vagina and anus with the same pungent liquid. But two wives held her still, pulling her knees apart while the third poured a thin trickle directly onto her parted flesh-lips. A hot flush of shame rose to her cheeks. She saw Makaja lean forward and gaze avidly at her exposed sex.

The wives took a long time stroking and smoothing the oil around her pubis, anointing every tender crease and circling the little bud hidden away in its hood of flesh. Gwendoline squirmed in their grip, hating the way they turned her so that Makaja could see everything. One of the wives spread her sex, pressing the outer lips open so that the little pleasure bud jutted into prominence and the mouth of her vagina spread invitingly.

Gwendoline bit her lip, trying not to grimace or make a sound, but she was acutely aware that her most secret flesh was beginning to swell and grow slick with her body's own juices. A tingling sort of burn was present inside her. Both orifices felt moist and receptive. Would Makaja want to sample them both?

Across the room, three other wives performed a similar service for Jonathan.

Gwendoline averted her eyes from Jonathan's face. He wore an expression of pained pleasure as he was oiled and manipulated. He was as unable as she was to hide the physical evidence of his arousal. His huge erection jutted up in front of him, the angry looking glans half protruding from his cock-skin.

His body was strong and well-formed, with broad shoulders and narrow hips. She saw that he had more scars on his torso, evidence of encounters with other, fiercer tribes than the Fans.

Jonathan's long dark hair streamed over his naked shoulders. Gwendoline had rarely seen his hair loose. He usually wore it tied back and pushed under a wide-brimmed hat. The way it fell forward to frame his face made him look younger and very desirable.

Makaja had ordered Jonathan onto his knees. Squatting on his haunches with his hands behind him and secured to one of the lodge's supporting poles, Jonathan must suffer the torment of having two young women make free with his body. The novelty of the situation prompted them to playfulness.

Jonathan cursed softly as one of the wives, an older more experienced woman, pinched his nipples, nipping each one with her long nails before painting them with yellow ochre. Another of the wives laughed softly as she reached between Jonathan's legs and took a firm hold of his scrotum. Winding a leather thong around the loose skin of the sac, close to his body, she secured it tightly. Then she wrapped the same thong around the root of his straining cock.

Smiling still, she sat back to survey her handiwork.

The skin of Jonathan's cock-shaft was full and shiny and now the glans was fully free of the skin it resembled a moist purple plum.

'You feel pleasure. Long time now,' the wife said in broken English. 'No break until we all pleasured.'

Makaja sipped his fermented drink and watched the proceedings calmly. His eyes gleamed as he feasted on Gwendoline's nakedness. She saw the approval on his face as one of the wives painted her nipples vermilion and then drew a circular design on her belly.

Then the chief spoke. Jonathan translated for Gwendoline, his voice surprisingly calm and even.

'Makaja gives his word that you and I shall come to no harm. He wishes only to observe how we enjoy the delights of the body. He is curious to see if you, in particular, are equipped in the same way as his wives. He is interested in your responses. The chief is a man of honour. I advise you to relax and try to enjoy yourself.'

Gwendoline flashed Jonathan a grateful look and nodded. Her nerves were beginning to disappear and although she was still trying to come to terms with her public nakedness, she assured herself practically that worse things might have happened.

Makaja was a man like any other. What had she to fear from him?

Then she was once again thrown into a confusion of emotion as the nearest wife gestured that she should lie on her back. She did so, reluctantly.

Oh God. Makaja would take her now. She turned her face away and tried not to look unwilling.

The chief waved his three wives back and approached Gwendoline. He knelt next to her and placed his hands on her breasts. Gwendoline held her breath while Makaja ran light fingers over her skin, murmuring to himself. He weighed her breasts in his hands, cupping the full underswell and slapping them gently so that they trembled.

He seemed fascinated by the fullness of her breasts and by the small pert nipples. Gwendoline had noticed that most young Fan women had small, high breasts and the older ones had long pendulous dugs. Her own breasts were firm and round, more apple than pear and Makaja obviously admired them greatly.

She suffered the chief's attentions in silence as he bent over her and began sniffing her skin. His tongue snaked out as he tasted her, licking at the tip of each breast in turn, then drawing one erect nipple into his mouth.

She tensed as his tongue circled the little cone of flesh, expecting at any moment to feel his teeth. But he removed his mouth and took the little nub between thumb and forefinger, pinching hard until it turned dark-rose in colour.

When she winced, Makaja grinned. Then he gestured to Gwendoline. She did not understand what he required her to do, so she shook her head. She could have asked Jonathan to translate but she could not bear to look at him at that moment.

Makaja spoke and two of his wives moved forward. They each took one of Gwendoline's ankles and bent her knees gently in to her chest.

The hectic colour flooded her face and Gwendoline could not suppress a little cry of alarm. Her white thighs looked so naked and vulnerable against the gleaming black flesh of Makaja's wives. The strong hands on her ankles made certain that her position was maintained.

Gwendoline's sex was upturned and splayed open to the chief's view. Makaja bent over her, examining her at his leisure. The curly brown hair, covering her mound, seemed to please him greatly. He laughed with delight, tugging gently at it, mouthing the springy curls. Then he pulled open her folds and examined her vagina. She felt the hard strong fingers push into her and curve slightly as he moved them in and out.

With his thumb he rubbed at her pleasure bud, rolling the mixture of oil and juices around it. Gwendoline felt him smooth the skin back from her bud until it swelled and hardened under his fingers.

She tried to hide her reactions but was unable to. Her sex was getting wetter. The fingers he slipped in and out were slick with her creamy moisture. Despite the situation she was becoming more aroused with each moment that passed.

The wives watching her, the knowledge that Jonathan was a witness to everything that was happening, added a forbidden spice to her pleasure.

Outside the lodge, the African night vibrated to the sound of the drums. Their infernal rhythm matched the tides of her heated flesh. It seemed that, deep inside, in the moist cave of her womb, a new and throbbing pulse began.

Suddenly she was pushing up to meet Makaja's hand, willing him to thrust more deeply into her. She expected him to mount her at any second and the prospect did not seem coloured with dread. She needed to feel hard male flesh inside her. Her hungry vagina demanded it.

Turning her head, she saw that one of the youngest wives was straddling Jonathan, kneeling over him and sinking herself on his rampant cock. She held onto his shoulders and rode him hard. Her muscular buttocks clenched and released and she groaned with pleasure, her head thrown back and the slim length of her neck exposed.

Jonathan could not contain his grunts of pleasure. He looked towards Gwendoline, watching her expression and the way she worked her hips back and forth on Makaja's fingers. For one moment they looked directly into each other's eyes.

Gwendoline saw that Jonathan was enjoying watching her, that his pleasure hinged on her own.

The intensity of his dark eyes, ensnared her. She felt a dart stab her deep inside. It was Jonathan she wanted. It was his swollen member she wanted inside her, filling her, the blunt head of it nudging against her ripe womb. But, if she could not have him, she would take Makaja.

She moved her arms forward in a gesture of acceptance but Makaja was already moving away. At the chief's curt command, one of his wives knelt before him, her rounded posterior lifted high in a provocative gesture.

Gwendoline watched in confusion as Makaja lifted the woman's scanty loincloth and took a grip on her buttocks. Makaja gestured to the two wives who still had a grip on Gwendoline's ankles. One of them rose to her feet and crossed to a carved trunk. The other remained next to Gwendoline.

When the wife returned she was holding something wrapped in snakeskin. Slowly she uncovered the object and gestured to the third wife to let Gwendoline sit up. Gwendoline stared open-mouthed at the object which was held out towards her.

It was an ivory phallus, beautifully carved and perfect in every detail.

The wife placed the phallus in Gwendoline's hands and with gestures indicated plainly what she was expected to do with it. It seemed that Makaja would not mate with her after all. He wanted Gwendoline to pleasure herself with the obscene object that lay across her palm.

Makaja grinned encouragingly as he slipped his hand into his groin under his loincloth and began to rub himself.

Gwendoline looked towards Jonathan for guidance. She'd never used any object to pleasure herself with before. It was a strange concept and she wasn't sure whether she was repelled or excited at the thought of pushing the ivory phallus into her body. For one thing, it looked far too big for comfort.

Jonathan spoke softly as she caught his eye, his voice strained and breathless.

'Do it to yourself, Gwenie. Do it for me. Think of the pleasure I shall gain from watching you.'

He'd only called her by that pet name once before. The urgency of the request made a deep impression on her. She realised how near to climax Jonathan was but he was holding back somehow – as if waiting for her.

Another of Makaja's wives was stretched out beside Jonathan, mouthing the length of his cock. Her full lips moved up and down his cock-shaft, then closed over the moist plum of his glans. With her tongue she scooped up the clear fluid that trembled in a single drop from the tiny mouth of Jonathan's cock.

In the midst of it all, Gwendoline felt some perverse desire to push Jonathan further. She wanted to test him. How far would he go in his passion and lust for her? Before she could think better of it, she whispered huskily, 'If you want to see me do that to myself, Jonathan, you must ask me nicely.'

She saw the shock on his face, then the slow grin.

He understood what she wanted. The words she'd spoken on the bank of the river in England, half a lifetime away, echoed silently between them.

I'll make you beg and go down on your knees before I let you make love to me, she'd promised him.

"Do it, Gwenie. I . . . I beg you.'

Her heart turned over at his words. It was a strange way for them to settle their differences but she knew that the chasm between them had been bridged in some way – at least for the present. She smiled slowly and made herself comfortable with the wooden back rest, placed where the chief could see her.

Makaja had been stroking and working his cock during the exchange between Gwendoline and Jonathan. There was a pronounced bulge now under his loincloth. The wives saw it and set up an excited muttering.

Gwendoline relaxed against the back rest and parted her thighs. The lion skin that covered the dirt floor was soft against her skin. All eyes in the lodge were on her. But she was conscious only of Jonathan, of the intensity of his expression, the near anguish as he tried to hold back his climax.

At Makaja's order, two of his wives came and sat, one on either side of Gwendoline. They began stroking her body, kissing her breasts, easing her thighs more widely apart. Their fingers stroked lightly over her mound and her wet engorged sex.

They made soft noises of encouragement and appreciation. One of them placed her mouth on Gwendoline's. Too aroused to feel shocked, Gwendoline responded when she felt a tongue probing her mouth. Then she moaned loudly, when a new and most exquisite sensation began.

The other wife was licking Gwendoline's sex, with long lazy strokes, moving from her pleasure bud all the way to the cleft between her buttocks. She tongued Gwendoline's tight anus, pressing inside it with the point of her tongue.

Jonathan gave a convulsive groan and shuddered as the wife who was pleasuring him, sank down onto him. Emitting a series of sharp little cries she climaxed.

Gwendoline hovered on the brink of her own release. The two tongues, working away at the sensitive flesh of her mouth and sex, were maddening.

Then the wife who'd been poised between her thighs moved away. She directed Gwendoline to move the hand holding the phallus in towards her soaking wet vagina. Gwendoline needed no more urging. She wanted penetration now, her ready sex demanded it.

Slowly she eased the huge phallus inside her. The tip needed lubricating thoroughly before it would enter her. She worked the head in her oily juices, twisting it until it was ready. She felt the walls of her vagina stretching to accommodate the cock-shaft. For Makaja's benefit she teased the tip around her entrance, sliding it back and forth, so that the rim of pink flesh collared the glistening phallus.

Makaja gave a great cry and threw off his single garment, displaying his fully erect member. His cock was long and thin with a pronounced bulbous end.

Positioning himself between the buttocks of one of the kneeling women he hesitated, then, as Gwendoline pushed the length of the phallus fully inside herself, he drove into his wife.

Gwendoline pushed the huge phallus in and out, raising her hips to meet her hand. Jonathan watched avidly as the pad of flesh between her vagina and anus was pushed out by the pressure of the phallus. The tight anal orifice, shiny from oil and the moisture of her arousal, pouted lewdly as she worked herself to the peak of ultimate pleasure.

If not for the thong which bound the base of his scrotum and cock-shaft Jonathan would have spurted his seed into the air. But the tight thong prolonged his pleasure, keeping him on the brink of orgasm for longer than he would ever have believed possible.

'Oh God, Gwendoline,' he groaned.

The chief watched Gwendoline's movements, thrust for thrust. Two of his wives lined up next to the one he was servicing, presenting their buttocks to him, forgetting Jonathan in their fervour.

The two wives attending Gwendoline began their ministrations again. All sensation merged as their fingers and mouths were everywhere. She felt an oiled finger slip into her anus and another began stroking her bud. Long nails flicked across her nipples.

Her whole body seemed to throb with pleasure. The universe closed in to become a red haze of sensation. She knew she could not bear much more. Her climax hovered but the pleasure was almost too intense. The phallus moved slickly, in and out. One of the wives licked Gwendoline's mouth, gaping wide now as she gasped for air. Her moans were loud and abandoned.

Jonathan strained towards her, unable to release himself from his bonds. His cock wept a salty fluid. The whole of it was flushed a deep purplish-red.

'God, but you're wonderful Gwenie,' he breathed hoarsely. 'I love your shameless delight in your own body. How I'd love to plunge my cock into you right now.'

At Makaja's nod, one of the wives crossed the

lodge with a knife in her hand. She cut the thongs that bound Jonathan's hands to the post. At once he lunged forward and took the phallus from Gwendoline's hands.

She looked startled, her eyes unfocused and dazed with passion.

Then she smiled and held out her arms.

'Ah, Jonathan. Come to me,' she said.

With a groan Jonathan buried his throbbing cock inside her. Oh God she was like hot silk inside.

Makaja began thrusting into the first of his wives in short rapid jerks. He watched Jonathan ramming into Gwendoline, her fingers curved into claws as she urged him on. The muscles of Jonathan's body were rigid with sexual tension.

Gwendoline could hold back no longer. As her climax flooded her body, a scream lodged in her throat. She lifted her hips up off the lion skin and rubbed herself shamelessly against the soaking root of Jonathan's cock.

She was unaware of anything around her. Her vision went dark for a moment as the intensity of her climax suffused her whole body. The spasms went on and on, dying away only gradually. She collapsed, exhausted, aware only faintly that Jonathan had collapsed against her his pleasure complete.

One of the wives picked up the discarded phallus and hurried over to the chief with it.

Makaja was thrusting away strongly, beads of sweat rolling down his forehead and running down his bare chest. The wife he was servicing climaxed with shrill cries and he withdrew from her and pushed his cock into the next one.

The wife holding the phallus pressed it close to Makaja's lips. His face twisted with pleasure-pain as he thrust ever more strongly into the woman beneath him but it seemed that he was unable to reach orgasm.

As Makaja's face tensed and his mouth twisted with anguish, he opened his mouth groping for the phallus. The wife slipped the object between his lips. Makaja sucked it eagerly, moaning, relishing the taste and smell of Gwendoline's musky juices.

The woman beneath him groaned and climaxed. Makaja bucked against her a final time and spent with a great cry of triumph.

For a long time it was quiet in the lodge. Jonathan cradled Gwendoline in his arms and pulled the lion skin to cover them. Despite the presence of the chief and his six wives, they seemed shut into their own private world.

Makaja lay as he'd fallen and his wives sat around him, each of them sated and completely drained. After a time Jonathan stirred himself and sat up. He helped Gwendoline to stand and dropped a brief kiss on her lips.

As they recovered somewhat the wives brought refreshments and warm cloths. Everyone cleansed themselves and lay relaxing. The wives served Gwendoline and Jonathan eagerly, treating them with great respect, and with something that bordered on adulation.

After a while, when Makaja had been washed and dressed, he began conversing with Jonathan. Gwendoline was struck by how the chief's manner had changed. He was totally charming and in high good humour.

Jonathan signalled that he would explain everything to Gwendoline later, so she steeled herself to be patient.

She found that she was ravenous and ate a great

many of the little balls of couscous, which were studded with dried fruit and rolled in nuts.

Much later, after many fine gifts had been pressed on them, Gwendoline and Jonathan were allowed to seek their own lodges and beds. Exhausted now that the ordeal was over, Gwendoline had only the strength to kiss Jonathan good night and go into the hut she shared with Hetty.

'Sleep tight,' Jonathan smiled. 'We'll talk in the morning. There's nothing that won't keep. We'll be leaving early, so try to get a few hours rest.'

Hetty fell on Gwendoline the moment she entered the hut, hugging her tightly.

'Oh, I've been so worried. Thank God you're unharmed.'

Gwendoline hugged Hetty back, touched by her show of emotion. The familiar, clean-smelling warmth and lushness of Hetty's soft body was comforting. She realised suddenly that Hetty really cared about her and she in turn was very fond of her lady's maid.

Theirs was not a relationship of mistress and servant anymore. It was a true friendship. Something she valued highly. She'd never found such loyalty amongst the women of her own class.

'When we get back to England, Hetty, things are going to be different. You and I shall be companions. We'll travel everywhere together and I'll engage a young woman to act as maid to both of us. What do you say to that?'

'Oh, Miss, I never thought to hear you say a thing like that. D'you really mean it?' Hetty sniffed and dabbed at her eyes with her lace cuff.

'From now on you must call me Gwendoline. Do you understand?'

'All right Miss . . . I mean – Gwendoline.'

Hetty wiped away a tear, a slow smile beginning at the corners of her mouth. She gulped a few times, then seemed to gain control of her emotions.

'Well?' she said. 'Aren't you going to tell me what you got up to in that chief's hut? Jonathan had a smile on his face as big as the Cheddar Gorge. He didn't get that for nothin' I'll be bound!'

Gwendoline threw back her head and laughed.

'Dearest Hetty! That's more like the woman I know. Sit down then and I'll tell you everything . . .'

Chapter Eighteen

*A*s they tramped through the undergrowth, next morning, Jonathan told Gwendoline that one of Makaja's wives had confided in him.

'It seemed that the chief had been suffering from impotence for some time. He thought that taking you as a wife would restore his lost ardour.' He grinned. 'Makaja may have been right. You did work something of a miracle on him. Anyway he seems to have overcome his problem. After we left the lodge he serviced all his wives again, in turn. They're delighted as you can imagine.'

Gwendoline understood everything now, the wives' joy at Makaja's prowess and the way they'd feted Jonathan and herself.

'The elder wife told me that they hope that some children will be the result of our unusual night of pleasure. A light-skinned baby would be just as welcome as any other.'

Gwendoline smiled. She hoped that the wives would find Makaja a potent lover from now on. Somehow she knew that they would.

The natives walked ahead in a thin line. Huge bundles of gifts and artifacts were balanced on their heads. Edward was ecstatic at the quality and amount of goods. He wore a self-satisfied smile, no doubt anticipating the heartfelt thanks of the trustees of the Natural History Museum and the envy of his business associates.

Hetty walked with a straight back and dignified stride beside Edward. Gwendoline hid a secret smile. Poor Edward. He still thought that he'd be setting Hetty up in a little cottage somewhere out of the way on the Farnshawe estate in England.

He'd be shocked when he found out that Hetty had altogether grander plans for herself. Nothing less than marriage would do and Gwendoline approved wholeheartedly. She would support Hetty every step of the way, speaking up for her when, first Edward, and then her father resisted the idea of Edward marrying out of his class. Indeed, she looked forward to welcoming Hetty to the family and to the furore *that* would cause in their circle of society friends.

She could hear Edward talking now. He seemed completely oblivious to the fact that they were all subdued at the thought of leaving – except him.

'I've been longing to get back to England. You'll be glad to be back to civilisation too, eh Hetty? Away from all this blessed heat and dust. And the interminable insects.'

Gwendoline's heart was heavy. The thought of England's grey skies and the bleached colourless fields of winter time depressed her. She could not bear to think of going back to her life as it had been.

But she did not voice any of this. She had yet to order her churning thoughts. She and Jonathan had shared a unique experience but there was so much left unsaid between them. The packing and leave-taking had been hurried, just in case Makaja decided to change his mind about letting them leave. Jonathan and herself had had no time alone together.

Gwendoline pushed her worries to the back of her mind, smiling and nodding as Edward rambled on, letting her brother believe that all was well with her.

'You'll have to do something about the way you look Gwendoline,' Edward said, with a laugh. 'Father would have apoplexy if he saw you in those clothes. Jodhpurs and khaki shirt indeed! And your skin is all tanned and freckled. Looks like you've gone native. It won't do in polite company you know. You'll be a laughing stock. Perhaps Hetty can make you a lemon facewash or somesuch . . .'

Although Gwendoline had decided against commenting on Edward's high-flown views, his pomposity began to grate on her.

'Now Edward, ' she said firmly, 'I have taken to these clothes as they are most practical for this climate. And I am perfectly happy with my appearance. I like my freckles and golden skin. I shall do nothing about my appearance. I might even take to wearing men's clothes in England. They're a deal more comfortable than all the furbelows I'm used to wearing!'

Edward looked horrified.

'But . . . but. You wouldn't. It's outrageous, dear girl! What would the servants think? How can you be so . . . so shameless?' His voice hardened. 'This trip hasn't been a good influence on you. You ought to listen to the advice of your elders and betters. You'd better mend your manners before you speak to father!'

'I shall do no such thing,' Gwendoline said evenly. 'You will all have to accept that I have changed. You and Father especially. I will not be ordered about, d'you hear? I am a grown woman, with a mind of my own, and I will have you respect that fact!'

Jonathan gave a shout of laughter and clapped his hands.

'Bravo! Well said!'

'I say Jonathan, you could give a fellow some support. It's deuced bad of you to take Gwendoline's side.'

'Oh Edward, do shut up!' Hetty said without malice.

Edward's mouth opened and closed. He looked like a landed trout. Realising himself outnumbered, he sank into a huffy silence.

Gwendoline quickened her stride and walked ahead of her brother, leaving him to Hetty's charge and hoping that he'd ponder her words.

She knew that, for her, nothing would ever be the same again. Her perceptions of what she was and the place she occupied in the world, had broadened, expanded. Part of her would live forever in Africa. The smells of heat and dust would never fade from her memory.

She only hoped that she could find some way to be happy in England.

In spare moments, to take her mind from thoughts of leaving, Gwendoline worked on her paintings and sketches.

The drawings of Kiva and Benka had turned out really well. There were others of the Fan bearers and the early erotic drawings of Hetty, Ned and Captain Casey. All she needed to complete her collection was a sketch of Jonathan.

She recalled how he had looked in Makaja's lodge with the young wife kneeling beside him, pleasuring him with her mouth. Every detail of his splendid physique, his face bound with anguished pleasure, was imprinted on her artist's memory.

She began drawing, filling the paper with bold strokes of a black pencil and leaving the white background to show through for highlights. She was so engrossed, that she did not notice Jonathan approaching until he stood by her shoulder. He peered at the page, not speaking for a full minute while she continued to work on the drawing. Then he said, tonelessly, 'How many more of these have you done?'

She jumped. 'Oh quite a few . . .' She couldn't tell whether he was pleased or angry.

'Hmmm,' he said, moving away and half-closing his eyes to get a better impression of her work. 'Are they all like this?'

'Erotic you mean? Do you mind my using you as a subject?'

'No, I'm rather flattered. What else have you done?'

'There are quite a few of the Fan people and some of the bearers, besides impressions of Rathbone's house and gardens.'

'Have you thought about offering them to a museum? And as for your – erotic studies, a private collector would pay handsomely for such a collection.'

He moved away, preparing to leave her to complete her drawing. Looking over his shoulder with a wry smile, he said as a parting shot, 'If you need to check any fine details, I'm available for a sitting.'

She laughed with relief. He really didn't mind.

'I'll let you know.'

Gwendoline thought about what Jonathan had said and an idea took root in her mind. There might be a way for her to make a life for herself back in England.

Why not? Others had made a career out of their talents.

She remembered Edward speaking derisively about some of the artists surrounding a new art movement. It was beginning to be called *art nouveau*. Her brother had known Aubrey Beardsley personally and there were others who'd followed in the dead artist's footsteps.

She'd persuade her brother to introduce her to some of that scandalous circle. In them she was certain that she would find kindred spirits.

As the journey homeward progressed, the tension between Jonathan and Gwendoline increased.

Both of them avoided mentioning what had happened in the chief's lodge. It was if they were afraid to admit it had been important.

They talked on all other subjects and were happy to sit together around the evening camp fires but they took care not to be alone together.

Jonathan wondered if Gwendoline regretted giving in to her lust for him, after all she'd sworn that she'd have him on her own terms.

And Gwendoline was afraid to repeat the experience. It was bad enough that they must part. Why prolong the agony by forging a deeper bond between them at this late stage?

She was edgy and fretful by day and she didn't sleep well at night. Thoughts of Jonathan invaded her dreams. It seemed unbearable that they'd go their separate ways before long.

Navigating the canoes down the Ogowé left her exhausted but active in mind. She grew pale under her tan and there were dark shadows under her eyes.

With every day that passed, Gwendoline's depression grew. Soon they'd be back at Gabon and the steamer would take them on to Lagos. From there they would pick up the clipper and head for England.

Hetty noticed that Gwendoline was brooding and expressed her concern. 'All this moonin' about ain't good for a body, you know. Why don't you just go to him? I know that you wants to. And he wants it too. But he's fighting it. A man like him don't like the thought of being made weak by his feelings for a woman.'

'Are we so transparent?' Gwendoline sighed. 'Am I?'

'Course not. It's just that I knows you so well. And I've a pretty good grasp of Jonathan's character too. You can't spend all these weeks in a man's company and not get to know him some. Jonathan's the man for you all right, Gwendoline. But you has to go and take him.'

Gwendoline admitted reluctantly that Hetty was right.

She'd have to do something. Hadn't she told Edward that she'd changed; become more independent and in control of her own life? They were just empty words if she didn't follow them through with actions.

It was time to show Jonathan that she knew what she wanted.

The next day they were forced to a halt by a massive fallen tree that lay across their path. It would take many hours to circle around the obstacle, the jungle being particularly dense in that area.

'It's getting late in the day. May as well set up camp over there,' Jonathan said, pointing to a small clearing. 'We'll make a fresh start in the morning, when it's cool.'

The lush undergrowth pressed in on all sides.

Huge banana trees, coconut palms, sisal, and many other exotic plants towered overhead.

Gwendoline went for a short walk and discovered a waterfall that poured into a pool upstream. Huge rocks surrounded a shallow basin, forming a safe bathing area. She was captivated by the shower of drops that sparkled with rainbow colours in the westering sun.

Back at the camp, the tents had been set up and the natives were preparing a meal. The tobacco smoke from their pipes spiralled into the air. Hetty and Edward were nowhere in sight. Gwendoline walked up to Jonathan and took him by the hand.

'Come with me. I want to show you something.'

At his look of surprise she almost laughed. He followed her without speaking.

Reaching the waterfall she let go of his hand and began to unbutton her shirt.

'It's so beautiful here. We can bathe in private. We haven't been alone together since . . . I thought . . .' But she couldn't go on.

Her fingers were clumsy as they fumbled with the belt that held up her trousers. Jonathan watched her for a moment without moving. At the look on his face her cheeks grew hot. She felt shy and virginal again. It seemed ridiculous that they were so wary of each other after the intimacy at the Fan village.

In another moment she'd lose her nerve and run from him. Why was he looking at her like that, as if trying to read her mind?

'The water looks inviting,' Jonathan said at last, without intonation.

He disrobed quickly, pulling off his knee-length leather boots and throwing aside his shirt and trousers, all the time keeping his eyes on her face.

The way he looked at her disturbed her. There

seemed a sort of violence about him, an uncompromising glint in his dark eyes. His mouth curved slightly, as if he'd come to a decision. He was fully erect and did not try to disguise the fact, his sturdy cock jutting up from the nest of dark hair at his groin. His erection was so big that the loose skin hardly covered the moist tip.

Gwendoline felt herself grow weak as she looked at his nakedness. She imagined his cock thrusting inside her, coaxing the wet heat within her into a whirlpool of sensation.

Jonathan stood on a flat-topped rock, his legs apart, hands on his hips. He looked challengingly at her. His hard-muscled body looked burnished by the sun, which was sinking fast in a glory of red and orange.

The pool looked like molten bronze. A trickle of sweat rolled down Jonathan's chest. Gwendoline watched it as if mesmerised.

Everything about Jonathan took her breath away. It was impossible to imagine a life without him. She felt an actual pain when she thought of parting from him for good.

Suddenly she knew why she had been afraid. She saw the reflection of her own emotion in his eyes. She could have shouted for joy. Jonathan needed her, like she needed him. They'd never spoken of love but sometimes you knew things without voicing them.

When he reached for her she almost fell into his arms.

'I thought you'd never speak up,' he murmured against her mouth. 'Do you know how the sight of your round bottom in those jodhpurs and your full breasts jiggling up and down in that shirt have almost driven me mad these past days? But I know how proud you are. If I'd approached you you'd have given me the sharp edge of your tongue.'

'Proud – me?' she laughed. 'I thought the same about you. Oh, what fools we've been.'

When he moved she caught the sharpness of their mingled sweat. The smell intoxicated her. As Jonathan's mouth possessed hers, a shiver passed right through her body.

'I don't know how I restrained myself,' Jonathan groaned. 'I wanted to spread your lovely buttocks and bury my cock inside you. Bury it deep, until I felt the neck of your hungry womb. I've been saving myself for this moment.'

He pressed her down. The stored heat of the rock scorched Gwendoline's skin but she revelled in the slight discomfort. She was ready for him at once. The long days of recalling their shared pleasure in vivid detail, of holding herself back from a self-induced orgasm, had prompted her to a furnace heat of arousal.

Sensing her readiness, Jonathan looped her legs over his shoulders and drove straight into her. Gwendoline groaned and cried out as he withdrew almost completely, then slammed back into her.

'I'm sorry my darling, I can't wait. Forgive me,' Jonathan whispered hoarsely, plunging strongly into her.

Too soon he withdrew and spilled his seed onto her stomach. Gwendoline made a small sound of disappointment and Jonathan laughed and kissed her breasts.

'What a little wanton you've become. Do not worry. In just a short while I'll pleasure you for as long as you wish. For the rest of our lives, if you'll have me. You'll have to beg me to stop. But first . . .'

Gwendoline had no time to reply. But she knew

that he needed no answer. The future stretched before them, uncharted yet sparkling with endless possibilities.

Jonathan stood up and pulled Gwendoline to her feet. Before she realised what he was about to do, he grasped her hand and leapt from the rock with a cry of triumph.

She hit the water a split second after him. The shock of the tepid water against her heated skin wrought a cry from her. Her wet hair tumbled down from its pins, spreading out behind her in the water.

'My beautiful water nymph,' Jonathan said, splashing her playfully. 'What a life we shall have together.'

The sky grew darker as the sun slipped halfway below the horizon. A huge glowing sphere, it hung suspended, gilding every leaf and petal with a final brief grandeur.

Gwendoline knew that she'd never forget this experience. This place was where everything came together. Africa and Jonathan were her destiny.

The conversation between Edward and Jonathan, overheard in the conservatory on the night of her birthday celebrations, seemed so long ago. That's where it had all begun. Had she sensed something of what was to happen that night?

After a time Jonathan gathered her to him again. They lay in the warm shallows and Gwendoline's breath quickened as Jonathan dipped his head between her parted thighs and ran his hot tongue over her sex.

The warm water stranded through her loose hair. The night breeze was warm on her parted thighs, blowing it's green freshness over her breasts and hardening nipples. Gwendoline opened her eyes and fixed them on the glorious purple sky, already studded with the first stars. Her pleasure built as Jonathan's tongue drew sweet sensations from her body.

A loud roar tore the air.

'What was that?' she said, alarmed, half-sitting up.

Jonathan pushed her back down gently. 'Nothing to worry about. Just a lioness crying out as her mate services her, darling. In the velvet darkness, the fight for life and renewal goes on.'

As it does here, she thought as she relaxed into him. In his own way Jonathan was as wild and dangerous as the continent he loved. He would always be unpredictable, capable of going after the things he wanted with little thought for anyone else's needs.

But she understood him perfectly, was prepared to meet him halfway. For her Jonathan would always have velvet claws.

Her juices flowed freely, soaking Jonathan's mouth and chin. She writhed against his mouth, tipping her hips up to him and tossing her head from side to side.

'Your cock. Now,' she said. 'Oh now Jonathan. Please.'

She felt him grin. He surfaced briefly, looking up at her from between her thighs.

'I'll fill you soon, darling. First I want you to climax against my mouth. Let me feel those delightful spasms with my tongue buried inside you.'

Gwendoline clutched at his head, drawing him closer, working herself up and down on his mouth. She felt his tongue flicking in and out of her hungry vagina. He used it on her like a cock, then swept it along the length of her slick folds.

She rubbed her pleasure bud against his lips, feeling the firm little scrap flicking back and forth. Jonathan's whole mouth engulfed her, covering her musky flesh and sucking at it in a sort of erotic kiss. With her head thrown back, and the lioness's roars harsh in her ears, Gwendoline climaxed.

As the sun disappeared in a last flash of brightest blood-red, her soul rushed to meet the soul of Africa.

The wonderful black continent.

Her enslaver and her saviour.

NO LADY
Saskia Hope

30 year-old Kate dumps her boyfriend, walks out of her job and sets off in search of sexual adventure. Set against the rugged terrain of the Pyrenees, the love-making is as rough as the landscape. Only a sense of danger can satisfy her longing for erotic encounters beyond the boundaries of ordinary experience.

ISBN 0 352 32857 6

WEB OF DESIRE
Sophie Danson

High-flying executive Marcie is gradually drawn away from the normality of her married life. Strange messages begin to appear on her computer, summoning her to sinister and fetishistic sexual liaisons with strangers whose identity remains secret. She's given glimpses of the world of The Omega Network, where her every desire is known and fulfilled.

ISBN 0 352 32856 8

BLUE HOTEL
Cherri Pickford

Hotelier Ramon can't understand why best-selling author Floy Pennington has come to stay at his quiet hotel in the rural idyll of the English countryside. Her exhibitionist tendencies are driving him crazy, as are her increasingly wanton encounters with the hotel's other guests.

ISBN 0 352 32858 4

CASSANDRA'S CONFLICT
Fredrica Alleyn

Behind the respectable facade of a house in present-day Hampstead lies a world of decadent indulgence and darkly bizarre eroticism. The sternly attractive Baron and his beautiful but cruel wife are playing games with the young Cassandra, employed as a nanny in their sumptuous household. Games where only the Baron knows the rules, and where there can only be one winner.

ISBN 0 352 32859 2

THE CAPTIVE FLESH
Cleo Cordell

Marietta and Claudine, French aristocrats saved from pirates, learn their invitation to stay at the opulent Algerian mansion of their rescuer, Kasim, requires something in return; their complete surrender to the ecstasy of pleasure in pain. Kasim's decadent orgies also require the services of the handsome blonde slave, Gabriel – perfect in his male beauty. Together in their slavery, they savour delights at the depths of shame.

ISBN 0 352 32872 X

PLEASURE HUNT
Sophie Danson

Sexual adventurer Olympia Deschamps is determined to become a member of the Legion D'Amour – the most exclusive society of French libertines who pride themselves on their capacity for limitless erotic pleasure. Set in Paris – Europe's most romantic city – Olympia's sense of unbridled hedonism finds release in an extraordinary variety of libidinous challenges.

ISBN 0 352 32880 0

ODALISQUE
Fleur Reynolds

A tale of family intrigue and depravity set against the glittering backdrop of the designer set. Auralie and Jeanine are cousins, both young, glamorous and wealthy. Catering to the business classes with their design consultancy and exclusive hotel, this facade of respectability conceals a reality of bitter rivalry and unnatural love.

ISBN 0 352 32887 8

OUTLAW LOVER
Saskia Hope

Fee Cambridge lives in an upper level deluxe pleasuredome of technologically advanced comfort. The pirates live in the harsh outer reaches of the decaying 21st century city where lawlessness abounds in a sexual underworld. Bored with her predictable husband and pampered lifestyle, Fee ventures into the wild side of town, finding an urban outlaw who becomes her lover. Leading a double life of piracy and privilege, will her taste for adventure get her too deep into danger?

ISBN 0 352 32909 2

AVALON NIGHTS
Sophie Danson

On a stormy night in Camelot, a shape-shifting sorceress weaves a potent spell. Enthralled by her magical powers, each knight of the Round Table – King Arthur included – must tell the tale of his most lustful conquest. Virtuous knights, brave and true, recount before the gathering ribald deeds more befitting licentious knaves. Before the evening is done, the sorceress must complete a mystic quest for the grail of ultimate pleasure.

ISBN 0 352 32910 6

THE SENSES BEJEWELLED
Cleo Cordell

Willing captives Marietta and Claudine are settling into an opulent life at Kasim's harem. But 18th century Algeria can be a hostile place. When the women are kidnapped by Kasim's sworn enemy, they face indignities that will test the boundaries of erotic experience. Marietta is reunited with her slave lover Gabriel, whose heart she previously broke. Will Kasim win back his cherished concubines? This is the sequel to *The Captive Flesh*.

ISBN 0 352 32904 1

GEMINI HEAT
Portia Da Costa

As the metropolis sizzles in freak early summer temperatures, twin sisters Deana and Delia find themselves cooking up a heatwave of their own. Jackson de Guile, master of power dynamics and wealthy connoisseur of fine things, draws them both into a web of luxuriously decadent debauchery. Sooner or later, one of them has to make a life-changing decision.

ISBN 0 352 32912 2

VIRTUOSO
Katrina Vincenzi

Mika and Serena, darlings of classical music's jet-set, inhabit a world of secluded passion. The reason? Since Mika's tragic accident which put a stop to his meteoric rise to fame as a solo violinist, he cannot face the world, and together they lead a decadent, reclusive existence. But Serena is determined to change things. The potent force of her ravenous sensuality cannot be ignored, as she rekindles Mika's zest for love and life through unexpected means. But together they share a dark secret.

ISBN 0 352 32912 2

MOON OF DESIRE
Sophie Danson

When Soraya Chilton is posted to the ancient and mysterious city of Ragzburg on a mission for the Foreign Office, strange things begin to happen to her. Wild, sexual urges overwhelm her at the coming of each full moon. Will her boyfriend, Anton, be her saviour – or her victim? What price will she have to pay to lift the curse of unquenchable lust that courses through her veins?

ISBN 0 352 32911 4

FIONA'S FATE
Fredrica Alleyn

When Fiona Sheldon is kidnapped by the infamous Trimarchi brothers, along with her friend Bethany, she finds herself acting in ways her husband Duncan would be shocked by. For it is he who owes the brothers money and is more concerned to free his voluptuous mistress than his shy and quiet wife. Alesandro Trimarchi makes full use of this opportunity to discover the true extent of Fiona's suppressed, but powerful, sexuality.

ISBN 0 352 32913 0

HANDMAIDEN OF PALMYRA
Fleur Reynolds

3rd century Palmyra: a lush oasis in the Syrian desert. The beautiful and fiercely independent Samoya takes her place in the temple of Antioch as an apprentice priestess. Decadent bachelor Prince Alif has other plans for her and sends his scheming sister to bring her to his Bacchanalian wedding feast. Embarking on a journey across the desert, Samoya encounters Marcus, the battle-hardened centurion who will unearth the core of her desires and change the course of her destiny.

ISBN 0 352 32919 X   *May '94*

OUTLAW FANTASY
Saskia Hope

For Fee Cambridge, playing with fire had become a full time job. Helping her pirate lover to escape his lawless lifestyle had its rewards as well as its drawbacks. On the outer reaches of the 21st century metropolis the Amazenes are on the prowl; fierce warrior women who have some unfinished business with Fee's lover. Will she be able to stop him straying back to the wrong side of the tracks? This is the sequel to *Outlaw Lover*.

ISBN 0 352 32920 3   *May '94*

Three special, longer length Black Lace summer sizzlers to be published in June 1994.

THE SILKEN CAGE
Sophie Danson

When University lecturer, Maria Treharne, inherits her aunt's mansion in Cornwall, she finds herself the subject of strange and unexpected attention. Her new dwelling resides on much-prized land; sacred, some would say. Anthony Pendorran has waited a long time for the mistress to arrive at Brackwater Tor. Now she's here, his lust can be quenched as their longing for each other has a hunger beyond the realm of the physical. Using the craft of goddess worship and sexual magnetism, Maria finds allies and foes in this savage and beautiful landscape.

ISBN 0 352 32928 9

RIVER OF SECRETS
Saskia Hope & Georgia Angelis

When intrepid female reporter Sydney Johnson takes over someone else's assignment up the Amazon river, the planned exploration seems straightforward enough. But the crew's photographer seems to be keeping some very shady company and the handsome botanist is proving to be a distraction with a difference. Sydney soon realises this mission to find a lost Inca city has a hidden agenda. Everyone is behaving so strangely, so sexually, and the tropical humidity is reaching fever pitch as if a mysterious force is working its magic over the expedition. Echoing with primeval sounds, the jungle holds both dangers and delights for Sydney in this Indiana Jones-esque story of lust and adventure.

ISBN 0 352 32925 4

VELVET CLAWS
Cleo Cordell

It's the 19th century; a time of exploration and discovery and young, spirited Gwendoline Farnshawe is determined not to be left behind in the parlour when the handsome and celebrated anthropologist, Jonathan Kimberton, is planning his latest expedition to Africa. Rebelling against Victorian society's expectation of a young woman and lured by the mystery and exotic climate of this exciting continent, Gwendoline sets sail with her entourage bound for a land of unknown pleasures.

ISBN 0 352 32926 2

WE NEED YOUR HELP . . .
to plan the future of women's erotic fiction –

– and no stamp required!

Yours are the only opinions that matter.
Black Lace is the first series of books devoted to erotic fiction by women for women.

We intend to keep providing the best-written, sexiest books you can buy. And we'd appreciate your help and valued opinion of the books so far. Tell us what you want to read.

THE BLACK LACE QUESTIONNAIRE

SECTION ONE: ABOUT YOU

1.1 Sex (*we presume you are female, but so as not to discriminate*)
Are you?
Male ☐
Female ☐

1.2 Age
under 21 ☐   21–30 ☐
31–40 ☐   41–50 ☐
51–60 ☐   over 60 ☐

1.3 At what age did you leave full-time education?
still in education ☐   16 or younger ☐
17–19 ☐   20 or older ☐

1.4 Occupation _____

1.5 Annual household income
    under £10,000   ☐   £10–£20,000   ☐
    £20–£30,000   ☐   £30–£40,000   ☐
    over £40,000   ☐

1.6 We are perfectly happy for you to remain anonymous; but if you would like to receive information on other publications available, please insert your name and address

_____

_____

_____

_____

SECTION TWO: ABOUT BUYING BLACK LACE BOOKS

2.1 How did you acquire this copy of *Velvet Claws*?
    I bought it myself   ☐   My partner bought it   ☐
    I borrowed/found it   ☐

2.2 How did you find out about Black Lace books?
    I saw them in a shop   ☐
    I saw them advertised in a magazine   ☐
    I saw the London Underground posters   ☐
    I read about them in _____
    Other _____

2.3 Please tick the following statements you agree with:
    I would be less embarrassed about buying Black
    Lace books if the cover pictures were less explicit   ☐
    I think that in general the pictures on Black
    Lace books are about right   ☐
    I think Black Lace cover pictures should be as
    explicit as possible   ☐

2.4 Would you read a Black Lace book in a public place – on a train for instance?
    Yes   ☐   No   ☐

SECTION THREE: ABOUT THIS BLACK LACE BOOK

3.1 Do you think the sex content in this book is:
     Too much ☐ About right ☐
     Not enough ☐

3.2 Do you think the writing style in this book is:
     Too unreal/escapist ☐ About right ☐
     Too down to earth ☐

3.3 Do you think the story in this book is:
     Too complicated ☐ About right ☐
     Too boring/simple ☐

3.4 Do you think the cover of this book is:
     Too explicit ☐ About right ☐
     Not explicit enough ☐

Here's a space for any other comments:

SECTION FOUR: ABOUT OTHER BLACK LACE BOOKS

4.1 How many Black Lace books have you read? ☐

4.2 If more than one, which one did you prefer?

4.3 Why?

SECTION FIVE: ABOUT YOUR IDEAL EROTIC NOVEL

We want to publish the books you want to read – so this is your chance to tell us exactly what your ideal erotic novel would be like.

5.1   Using a scale of 1 to 5 (1 = no interest at all, 5 = your ideal), please rate the following possible settings for an erotic novel:

Medieval/barbarian/sword 'n' sorcery ☐
Renaissance/Elizabethan/Restoration ☐
Victorian/Edwardian ☐
1920s & 1930s – the Jazz Age ☐
Present day ☐
Future/Science Fiction ☐

5.2   Using the same scale of 1 to 5, please rate the following themes you may find in an erotic novel:

Submissive male/dominant female ☐
Submissive female/dominant male ☐
Lesbianism ☐
Bondage/fetishism ☐
Romantic love ☐
Experimental sex e.g. anal/watersports/sex toys ☐
Gay male sex ☐
Group sex ☐

Using the same scale of 1 to 5, please rate the following styles in which an erotic novel could be written:

Realistic, down to earth, set in real life ☐
Escapist fantasy, but just about believable ☐
Completely unreal, impressionistic, dreamlike ☐

5.3   Would you prefer your ideal erotic novel to be written from the viewpoint of the main male characters or the main female characters?

Male ☐   Female ☐
Both ☐

5.4 What would your ideal Black Lace heroine be like? Tick as many as you like:

Dominant	☐	Glamorous	☐
Extroverted	☐	Contemporary	☐
Independent	☐	Bisexual	☐
Adventurous	☐	Naive	☐
Intellectual	☐	Introverted	☐
Professional	☐	Kinky	☐
Submissive	☐	Anything else?	☐
Ordinary	☐	_____	

5.5 What would your ideal male lead character be like? Again, tick as many as you like:

Rugged	☐		
Athletic	☐	Caring	☐
Sophisticated	☐	Cruel	☐
Retiring	☐	Debonair	☐
Outdoor-type	☐	Naive	☐
Executive-type	☐	Intellectual	☐
Ordinary	☐	Professional	☐
Kinky	☐	Romantic	☐
Hunky	☐		
Sexually dominant	☐	Anything else?	☐
Sexually submissive	☐	_____	

5.6 Is there one particular setting or subject matter that your ideal erotic novel would contain?

_____

SECTION SIX: LAST WORDS

6.1 What do you like best about Black Lace books?

_____

6.2 What do you most dislike about Black Lace books?

_____

6.3 In what way, if any, would you like to change Black Lace covers?

_____

6.4   Here's a space for any other comments:

_____
_____
_____
_____

Thank you for completing this questionnaire. Now tear it out of the book – carefully! – put it in an envelope and send it to:

Black Lace
FREEPOST
London
W10 5BR

No stamp is required if you are resident in the U.K.